Crystal Shadows

An Ellora's Cave Romantica Publication

www.ellorascave.com

Crystal Shadows

ISBN #1419952048

Edited by: Briana St. James
Cover art by: Syneca

Electronic book Publication: November, 2004
Trade paperback Publication: May, 2005

Warning:

The following material contains graphic sexual content meant for mature readers. *Crystal Shadows* has been rated *S-ensuous* by a minimum of three independent reviewers.

Ellora's Cave Publishing offers three levels of Romantica™ reading entertainment: S (S-ensuous), E (E-rotic), and X (X-treme).

S-*ensuous* love scenes are explicit and leave nothing to the imagination.

E-*rotic* love scenes are explicit, leave nothing to the imagination, and are high in volume per the overall word count. In addition, some E-rated titles might contain fantasy material that some readers find objectionable, such as bondage, submission, same sex encounters, forced seductions, etc. E-rated titles are the most graphic titles we carry; it is common, for instance, for an author to use words such as "fucking", "cock", "pussy", etc., within their work of literature.

X-*treme* titles differ from E-rated titles only in plot premise and storyline execution. Unlike E-rated titles, stories designated with the letter X tend to contain controversial subject matter not for the faint of heart.

Crystal Shadows

Chapter One

"Gina, it's perfect."

Gina Petrillo eyed the transparent gown Mikala had unearthed from a murky corner of Crystal Shadows, a funky New Age boutique not far from the Princeton University campus.

"Right," she said. "Perfect. If I want to star in a porn remake of *The Addams Family*." The dress was a see-through cousin of the one Morticia Addams had worn in the old television series.

"Oh, come on." Mikala held the black and silver creation against Gina's chest. "It's not that bad. With all that dark hair cascading down your back, you'll be an incredibly sexy sorceress."

Gina just looked at her.

Mikala shoved the dress back on the rack. "You've got to find something. The Wizards' Ball is tomorrow night."

"I never said I would go. Hanging out with a bunch of role-playing geeks isn't exactly my idea of a good time."

"I know, but do it for me, okay? I told my students I'd be there and I really don't want to go alone." Mikala renewed her safari through the costume rack. "Besides, you've been divorced for six months and the only place you go after dark is the crystals lab. That's not healthy."

Gina feigned interest in an aromatherapy display. "Did you transfer to the Psych Department when I wasn't looking?"

Mikala moved too close and touched Gina's arm. "You know, I'm here if you want to talk about it."

"What's to talk about? My husband couldn't keep his pants zipped. I was lucky I found out before we had kids."

"He took Heather Clark to the Math Department picnic, you know."

"Yeah, I know." Gina moved farther down the aisle.

Mikala followed. "You're hiding, Gina, when you should be out showing the world you're glad you dumped that loser. Put on something outrageous and go to the Wizards' Ball. Who knows? You could meet someone new."

"Like a tall, dark, computer wizard?"

"That's very funny, but you can't win if you don't play. Ooh, look—" Mikala ran a manicured fingernail over the trim on a purple velvet gown. "Crystals—right up your alley."

Gina squinted at the rows of stones. "They're glass. Not crystalline at all."

"Even this one?"

A faceted pink gem the size of a silver dollar accented the costume's plunging neckline. "Rose quartz. Very common."

"I hear it's great for opening your heart chakra."

Gina snorted. "You know, before I met you, I never realized a Math professor could be so whacked."

"Hey, it's not until you study higher mathematics that you appreciate how bizarre things really are. For example, did you know it's possible any number of universes occupy the same space as ours?"

"You've been watching way too much late night sci-fi TV."

Mikala shrugged. "Maybe." She held the purple dress higher and tapped the rose quartz crystal. "But Gina, you spend all day—and most nights—surrounded by crystals. How can you not feel the auras radiating from your lab specimens?"

"They're just minerals, Mikala. Rocks. It's not like there's anything magic about them. Look, I'm sorry about the Ball, but finals were yesterday. I have a ton of papers to grade."

"That's the lamest excuse—"

"Blessings, daughters." An old, hunched woman wrapped in ruffles and scarves slipped into the space between Gina and a rubber mask of Yoda. "You see something that pleases, no?"

"Yes," said Mikala, holding out the velvet gown. "My friend wants to try this on."

"No, she doesn't." Gina extracted the costume from Mikala's fingers and shoved it back on the rack. "We're just looking."

"Ah." The crone nodded. "Searching. Just so." A blue-veined claw clutched Gina's arm. "Come." She nodded toward an alcove obscured by strings of beads.

"Wait a min—"

"Look, Gina," Mikala said, pointing at a crude, hand-lettered sign. "Crystal readings by Madam Rose. You should get one."

The old woman smiled, showing a row of crooked, yellow teeth. "Yes. I do for you."

"That is such bull and you know it," Gina said to Mikala under her breath.

"Oh, lighten up. It'll be fun. My treat." Mikala gave Gina a little push toward the alcove.

Madam Rose's beady eyes gleamed.

"I'm getting you back for this," Gina muttered. She ducked through the swinging beads into a tiny room lit by flickering candles and obscured by perfumed smoke. A low table and two stools were wedged between a haphazard assortment of cupboards and shelves. Every available surface was piled with crystals.

Whoa. Madam Rose had some incredible specimens. Gina trailed a finger over a hunk of azurite the size of a softball. You certainly didn't see that every day.

"You've got a fantastic collection," she told the woman.

"You like? Good." Madam Rose bobbed her chin. "Pick."

"What?"

"Pick stone. For reading."

Gina's gaze traveled over the shelves and halted on a clear, flat prism with a surface like wet ice. Selenite. Crystallized gypsum. Her chest tightened. No two natural crystals were exactly alike, but this particular specimen bore an uncanny resemblance to the one her father had given her on her eighth birthday, after Gina had announced her intention to become a geologist. It had the same glassy face, the same jagged imperfection along one edge.

Of course, it couldn't be the same stone. Gina had placed that crystal inside her father's coffin almost two years ago. Still…

She picked up the selenite and cradled it in her palm.

"Ice stone," Madam Rose said. "Good choice. Open eye of future. See what comes." She stretched a bony finger toward one of the stools. "Sit."

An odd tingle crept up Gina's spine. She sat, clutching the selenite specimen like some kind of talisman. The old woman took the opposite stool and leaned forward, her silver hoop earrings striking the sides of her wrinkled neck. Her gnarled hands covered Gina's. The stone warmed, as if it had come alive.

Damn. Mikala's New Age psychobabble was dribbling into Gina's brain.

Madam Rose's breathing ran shallow. Her eyes lost their focus. "You have known deception, my daughter. Death."

Gina gave a nervous laugh. "Who hasn't?"

The old woman lifted Gina's hands and peered at the crystal. "I see dark stranger." She frowned. "Your enemy. He is hidden."

Gina heard Mikala out in the shop, humming as she rummaged through the merchandise. This was beyond ridiculous. The only hidden enemies Gina had were computer viruses.

Madam Rose closed her eyes. "Danger." She uttered a word in an incomprehensible language. "A journey. Far from home. Few choices."

A shiver chased down Gina's spine.

Madam Rose's voice deepened to a throaty whisper. "Dark man is strong. He comes for you. Will you defeat him?" Her withered arms trembled.

Gina held her breath.

The old woman bowed her head. "The outcome is uncertain," she whispered. She withdrew her hands, leaving Gina's resting on the table.

Gina let the selenite slide through her fingers as she expelled the air from her lungs in one long stream. *The outcome was uncertain?* What a crock.

And some people really believed this garbage. Now *that* was truly frightening.

She pushed her way through the beaded curtains into the shop. Mikala appeared from behind a display of goddess statues.

"Well, how was it? Tall, dark and handsome in sight?"

"The outcome is uncertain," Gina told her.

"Isn't it always?" Mikala sighed. "Madam Rose, what do I owe you for the reading and the dress?" She nodded toward the cash register.

The purple velvet gown lay in elegant disarray on the scarred wood counter. "Oh, no, you don't—" Gina said.

"Humor me," Mikala interrupted. "Be a sorceress for the Ball. I swear the next time you need a roommate for a rip-roaring crystallography convention, I'll be there."

"Oh, all right. But if one of your students hits on me, I'm turning him into a frog."

*****

The damn dress itched like hell.

Gina shoved past three wizards and a Hobbit in an effort to get closer to the door. Mikala hadn't been kidding when she'd said the place would be packed. Gina had to admit she was impressed. The Victorian mansion rented by The Wizards, Princeton's underground fantasy society really set the atmosphere.

Fake cobwebs dangled from the gaslight chandeliers in the ballroom, casting creepy shadows over the crowd. Costumes ranged from horrific to banal. A rotting zombie stood near the fireplace, an evil queen danced with a tarnished knight and a particularly unrealistic werewolf leaned against the bar, scarfing down a lite beer.

The alternative band The Undead was setting a new record for volume. Gina scanned the room, but Mikala—the traitor—had snared a sexy vampire about an hour ago and was nowhere in sight.

The party had started at midnight. It was now almost dawn. She should have brought her own car. At this rate, she'd be lucky to get home before noon.

She reached the doorway at last, gulping air as she freed herself from the worst of the crush. The early morning breeze raised goose bumps on the exposed portion of her breasts, which—due to her plunging décolletage—was far too much territory. She tugged at the velvet neckline, trying to coax the rose quartz crystal to a more modest position.

The slate-tiled veranda was nearly as crowded as the ballroom, so Gina elbowed her way into the garden. Thick woods crowded the edges, lending an aura of seclusion. A tall hedge of antique roses edged a cut grass path, and a few early blossoms were even open. She moved down the winding trail. Here in the garden, Princeton and the rest of New Jersey seemed far away, as if the plot existed in some other time or space.

The calm reached out to her, teasing memories of spring days spent digging in the dirt with her father. He'd been a doctor, but had loved working the earth with his hands. Mikala was right about one thing. Gina spent entirely too much time in the lab.

She ducked into a deserted gazebo at the edge of the garden and sat down on the circular bench ringing the center column. Her brief marriage to Michael had been the one aberration in her otherwise perfectly ordered existence. Now that she was free of him, she should be getting on with her life.

Trouble was she just couldn't summon up enough enthusiasm to do it.

Footsteps intruded on her musings. A woman giggled, drawing a husky male laugh. Gina sat up, heart suddenly pounding. She knew that throaty chuckle only too well.

Michael. With Heather, his lay-of-the-month.

The voices drew closer. "Ooh, look—a gazebo! Let's do it there, Michael."

"Anything you want, baby."

Damn.

Thick woods crowded the rear of the gazebo—was there a back way out? Yes. A panel of gingerbread trellis had come loose. She slipped through, yanking her velvet skirt after her an instant before her ex stepped into the gazebo. The splintered edge of the wood scraped her bare arm.

She watched through the trellis slats as Michael sank onto the bench in the exact spot Gina had vacated. He was dressed as a pirate in a striped shirt and snug breeches, a ridiculous patch obscuring one eye. Heather, her double-D breasts spilling from a tavern wench costume, dropped to her knees and got right down to business. Her fingers made short work of the tie on Michael's breeches. His long, thin cock sprung into her hands.

Heather dipped her head. A loud slurp followed. Michael let out a muffled groan. Gina inched away, brambles grabbing at her hair. A thorn snagged her skirt. She pulled the velvet free, trying not to make a sound, cursing under her breath when she heard it rip.

Geez, Petrillo, where is your spine? She should have headed back to the ballroom by way of the garden path, breezing past Michael and Heather without a glance. Instead, she was skulking away, as if she had been the one caught groping in the dark like a horny teenager.

Stop the insanity. She should turn around right now and retrace her steps through the gazebo.

Another slurp reached her ears.

On the other hand, she had no desire to watch Heather Clark suck off Michael's pencil-dick.

Michael's rough voice drifted on a breeze. "Oh, yeah, that's sweet. Take it deeper, baby."

"I can't, Michael." Heather voice was a combination of breathless and whiny. "That's as far as I can go."

"I like it deeper, babe."

A gagging sound told Gina that Heather was trying her best to give Michael a deep throat blowjob. Too bad it wouldn't be enough. With Michael, it never was. Mikala was right about another thing—Gina should be glad she finally got free of him. And she would be, if only she could figure out how to shake the feeling of utter failure her ruined marriage had brought.

Turning her back on Michael's increasingly lusty groans, Gina plunged deeper into the forest, stumbling a little on a sudden downhill slope. Which way was the mansion? She was trying to get her bearings when a flash of light burst from the stone at the center of her costume's neckline.

Frowning, she peered down at it. How odd. The rose quartz crystal had taken on a faint glow.

She touched it. *Warm.* How could that be? She craned her neck, trying to get a better view.

The stone's inner light strengthened. Flashed. Ringing stirred the air, obscuring the faraway music from the Ball. A thousand bells sounded, chiming softly at first, then growing strident.

Fierce nausea assaulted her. Oh, God. That's what she got for drinking hard liquor on an empty stomach. Her vision was weirding out, too. A shining strand of light hung before her eyes, floating like a golden spider trail. The thread split, became two, then four, then countless glittering filaments, turning and twisting, close enough to touch, yet at the same time a universe away.

The forest shimmered. The ground dissolved. A gust of wind passed through the trees and sent the world spinning.

Gina hit the earth with a jolt that knocked the air from her lungs. Leaning forward, she concentrated on sucking in a series of painful breaths as the nausea washed over her, then slowly faded.

Struggling to her feet, she stood on shaking legs. What the hell had happened? She squinted down at the rose quartz crystal. The light was gone.

She touched it. *Cold.*

She must have imagined the changes in the stone. There was no other logical explanation.

The air was still and silent. The faint strains of music from the Ball had faded. The band must have called it a night.

"I greet you, Mistress."

Gina spun around. A gangly undergraduate wearing a tunic, breeches, and a black cloak swept her a bow. Where the hell had he come from? There was something strange about his speech. An accent or something. He was probably a foreign student.

"Are you one of The Wizards?" she asked.

"Yes."

"I got a little lost," Gina told him. "Which way back to the Ball?"

He lifted his hand, pointing to one side. "This way, Mistress."

The kid turned and started up a faint trail. Gina followed. The mansion had to be at the top of the hill.

Early morning sunlight slanted through the trees, illuminating a forest that seemed half-dead. Mottled leaves littered the ground and clustered in the hollows between moss-covered roots. Brittle branches creaked overhead. Funny. Gina hadn't noticed the condition of the woods last night, but then again, it had been dark when she and Mikala arrived at the Ball.

After a short hike, she waded through a tangle of brush and blinked into the rising sun. No Victorian mansion greeted her. No garden or parking lot. Only a bucolic, mist-shrouded valley.

A knot formed in her gut.

Across the fog, a steep hill climbed lazily into the sky, carrying a city of gray stone. An enormous monolith in the shape of a shining black pyramid capped the peak. What the—?

A ray of light glinted off the fantastic structure, sending a flash of light across the valley. The knot in Gina's stomach tightened.

She locked her knees to keep from falling, panic clawing at her lungs. To her left, rolling hills and thick forests stretched to a distant horizon. No highways, no housing developments, no shopping malls. A wide expanse of ocean lay to the right, but Gina knew she wasn't at the Jersey shore.

She had to be dreaming. Or hallucinating.

Or dead.

Because the scene before her didn't—couldn't—exist.

* * * * *

A woman?

Derrin frowned. A woman was not at all what he had expected to emerge from the brilliant strands of light.

True, the web binding the edges of the world held unimaginable power, but Derrin had never considered the possibility another world—other beings—existed beyond it. He shook his head. This woman's appearance boded ill, of that he was certain.

He touched the shadow crystal hanging from a chain about his neck, sinking his mind into the gem as he did so. The crystal, the most powerful one he'd ever created, nestled in a cage of pure silver. He'd called forth the stone's power before following High Wizard Balek's apprentice from the city, but that had been in the hour before dawn, when the forest had been dark. Now, with a single thought, Derrin deepened the protection, wrapping his crystal's shadow around his body like a cloak. Confident he would not be detected, he stepped into the light of the rising sun.

He circled Maator, all the while keeping his eyes trained on the woman from beyond the web. She was staring across the valley at Katrinth, Galena's proud capital city, her dark eyes wide with disbelief.

Her face paled, accentuating her fine, high cheekbones. A long tangle of dark hair hung down her back. Her aspect seemed unremarkable enough, though her dress was scandalous by Galenan standards. Her breasts were all but spilling from her gown.

Her fingers fisted into her torn skirt. Tiny bits of glass edged the dark fabric. Those were unremarkable, but a magnificent pink crystal nestled in her cleavage. Derrin's breath hissed through his teeth. He had never seen a crystal the color of the pale sea roses. Was she a sorceress? Had Balek summoned her because of it?

Maator spoke to the woman, but Derrin was not near enough to make out his words. The sorceress tore her gaze from the city to stare at the apprentice. She appeared dazed, and more than a little unsteady. Her mouth opened, as if to reply to Maator's remark, but no answer emerged. Instead, her eyes fluttered closed and her knees buckled.

Maator sprung forward and caught her before she hit the ground. Straightening, he shifted his burden in his arms and extracted a silver prism from the pouch at his belt. A shadow crystal, not unlike Derrin's own. The stone flared and the two figures faded. Shadowed, but not completely.

Derrin would be a poor wizard indeed if he could be thwarted by an apprentice's defenses.

He allowed his vision to blur. Within seconds, he detected the slight disturbance in the air currents that indicated his quarry had started the descent to the city. He closed in swiftly. The path led into the scattering fog along the river road.

He passed a scattering of half-timbered cottages and entered the city through the market gate. The broad, unpaved plaza beyond was alive with shouts and good-natured haggling. At the far end of the square, fishermen were already unloading the morning catch onto the docks.

Maator avoided the bulk of the activity, skirting the vendors' stalls and slipping into the fetid warren of crude dwellings that marked the Lower City. Derrin ducked into a gloomy alley after him, sidestepping a pile of excrement where a derelict lay wheezing. Open pustules covered the man's skin. His matted beard crawled with insects.

Another victim of the Madness.

The guards stationed at the gates to the Upper City did not stir as Derrin trailed Maator through the wide archway. Here, the paved streets were wide and straight, the graystone mansions large and well-appointed. As always, their sedate façades seem to frown on Derrin's passing.

Maator's footsteps didn't slow. He carried the limp body of the sorceress through the steep streets, climbing ever higher. Entering the High Plaza in the shadow of the Lords' Citadel, he skirted the elaborate façade of the Temple of Lotark and the sweeping main stairway of the Wizards' Stronghold. He entered the Stronghold through a seldom-used entrance on a side wall of the pyramid.

Derrin waited a few moments before following Maator into the home of the Wizards' Hierarchy. He turned the corner leading to Balek's chambers as a door thudded shut.

He approached it and listened. Maator and his mentor were speaking, their voices muted by the thick wooden barrier. Derrin slid a clear stone disc from the pouch at his belt and set it aglow with a silent command.

"Is she the one, Master?" Maator asked.

Derrin peered into his scrying stone and watched as the apprentice lowered the unconscious woman onto a bench. Her torn dress fell open, exposing one shapely thigh. Balek advanced, the sash of the Upper House of Wizards blood-red against the black of his tunic. A faceted crystal, tinged with gold, nestled in the high wizard's upturned palm. Power shimmered around it.

Revulsion tightened Derrin's gut. He'd touched the unholy gem Balek called the webstone only once. He wasn't eager to repeat the experience.

Balek brushed the crystal against the woman's forehead and whispered a single word. Her spine arched.

The high wizard leaned forward. "Yes," he whispered. "She is the one." He passed his hand over the woman's face, causing her to gasp.

Derrin swore under his breath. Balek had linked the woman's mind to the webstone.

It was not a union her psyche would survive.

He withdrew and waited, shadowed in an alcove by the stairs, all the while watching the scene in Balek's chamber in the scrying stone. He saw Maator carry the woman to a rear chamber, then returned to the workroom. After what seemed an interminable time, Balek left to join the High Wizards' Council.

Derrin eased from his hiding place. Wrapped in the dark cloak of his shadow crystal, he entered Balek's suite through a rear portal. Within moments, he had transferred the woman to his own chamber. She rolled to her side on his bed and curled into a ball, moaning. Already, the webstone's power seeped through her mind. Could the link be broken?

Derrin knew of only one person—other than Balek—who could tell him, but the journey to her door was long.

The woman groaned and tore at the bedcovers. Derrin knelt at her side, frowning, his gaze fixed on the crystal between her breasts. Was she a sorceress? If so, Balek risked much to summon her. A woman's magic was as potent as it was unpredictable. The Hierarchy had banned females from the practice of wizardry for just that reason. Yet Balek had sought this woman since before the winter snows.

A sorceress from a world beyond the web would be a deadly weapon in the high wizard's hands. There was no telling what ill forces she could unleash on Galena.

He should kill her. Now.

His hands stole to her throat. His fingers touched her skin, felt the pulse beating just below the surface. Warm. Alive. His gaze dropped to her breasts, round and firm and all but bare.

He hesitated. By all appearances, the sorceress wasn't in league with Balek by choice. If Derrin could question her, the answers she provided might shed some light on the high wizard's motives. Yet as long as her mind remained ensnared, she could tell him nothing.

He snatched his hands from her throat, his decision made. Swiftly, he gathered the few supplies he would need for a journey into the northern wilderness. Zahta would surely know how to free the woman's mind.

Derrin only hoped after all these years, his grandmother would not turn him away.

*****

Gina's head felt like it had been cracked open from the inside. A dirty yellow haze scattered her thoughts and about a million little hammers pounded on her temple. But it wasn't until she opened her eyes that she realized she had much bigger problems than a morning-after headache.

Like, where the hell was she?

She was propped upright against a rough wall, sharp stone biting into her spine. Tight cords chafed her ankles, sending shocks of pain up her legs. The scents of smoke and earth mingled with the musk of her own sweat. She twisted her arms, but her wrists were bound in front of her and the knot held fast.

The skirt of her gown was in shreds, the quartz crystal that had decorated the neckline gone. The bodice was torn, exposing her simple white bra. It was the skimpiest one she had, thanks to the low-cut of the costume, but at least it was something. Thank God she had ignored Mikala's advice and worn it.

She fought a fierce urge to vomit. She'd been kidnapped. By whom? The memory of a black pyramid floated at the edges of her mind. The last thing she remembered was looking across a valley at a city that couldn't possibly have been real. Someone had been there—a harmless-looking blond kid. After that, her memories disintegrated into sensation.

A yellow haze choking her brain. Movement. Struggle. A jarring ride, as if she'd been thrown on the back of a horse. She thought she'd screamed, fought, but she couldn't be quite certain, as if she'd been...

Drugged. Someone must have slipped something into her drink at the Wizards' Ball.

She peered into the dim light at her prison, a small room enclosed by a ring of primitive masonry. A ceiling of wooden ribs arched overhead. An animal skin draped the single doorway. Faint illumination dropped from a hole in the center of the roof onto a heap of smoldering ashes. The scene wavered, bringing a fresh rush of nausea. Whatever she had ingested, it hadn't completely worn off.

Whoever had given it to her was sure to show up soon. She twisted sideways and eyed a sharp protrusion on the stone wall. Ignoring her lurching stomach, she hooked the rope binding her wrists over it and began to saw.

Movement outside the doorway. Muffled voices. "No," a man said. His tone held a note of anger.

A woman answered. "My son, you alone have the power. There is no one else." Her voice faded. Gina renewed her assault on the rope, but all too soon the drape at the door lifted.

Her time had run out.

She turned to see a figure silhouetted against a rectangle of light. Not the blond kid from the forest. A man.

He was costumed in black—tunic, breeches and boots. He approached with quick strides, his dark hair grazing his shoulders as he walked.

"Who are you?" she blurted out. "Why did you bring me here?"

In lieu of an answer, the man dropped to one knee and touched Gina's face. Heat flashed across her skin.

An open gash slanted across his right cheekbone. If not for that imperfection, and the rigid cast of his features, Gina might have thought him handsome. As it was, the cold, gray mist of his eyes sent her heart pounding for an entirely different reason.

She fought another surge of vertigo. "Do you want money? Take me home and I'll get it."

"Are you a sorceress?"

"What?" The words were unfamiliar, as if he spoke in a foreign language, yet his meaning was clear. No doubt another effect of whatever drug she'd been given.

His hand came forward. She shrank back, against the stone, but he merely flicked a strand of hair from her eyes and drew back, watching her.

"Are you a sorceress?" he asked again.

"I was a sorceress at the Ball, yes. Are you one of The Wizards? Is this some kind of role-playing game?"

Disbelief flitted across his face. "Game? I assure you, Mistress. This is no game."

The room lurched again. "I don't remember seeing you at the Ball. When did you give me the drug?"

"Drug?"

"Cut the bull and tell me what the hell is going on," Gina snapped. The yellow haze in her mind blazed hotly and a blinding surge of anger eclipsed her fear. She swung at him, her bound fists glancing off his shoulder. He caught her forearm. She twisted out of his grasp and fell on her side. The room spun faster than before.

The man rose over her. She bucked, trying to jam her knees into his groin. He dodged her awkward attack and leaned close, trapping her gaze in his, then sprang up with the grace of a cat to crouch at her side.

Gina tried to move. Her body refused to obey, though her captor was not restraining her in any way. The hazy yellow cloud in her mind dulled and thickened. Her breath heaved as he leaned forward, filling her vision.

His mind touched hers. A gentle probe at first, then a more persistent, intimate stroke.

No. This couldn't be happening.

Open.

The command, heard in the deepest recesses of her brain, was not a distinct syllable. Had it truly come from the man's mind? Impossible. It was an illusion, an effect of the drug.

Yet it felt so real. He called again, more urgently this time, and for a fleeting moment Gina wanted nothing so much as to let him in.

"Please," the man said aloud, his voice tight. "I don't want to hurt you."

Open.

In the space of a heartbeat, she obeyed.

Chapter Two

The dark stranger surged into Gina's mind. He tore through her psyche like a plundering thief, searching, touching every private place. The yellow fog scattered in his wake, leaving Gina acutely aware of each stroke of his invasion. Time lost its meaning. Did a moment pass, or an hour? Impossible to tell. She knew only his raw strength as he drove into her center.

Impossible. She clung to the thought. *Not real.*

No one could enter another person's mind.

But the probe continued, like a sharp, intimate knife. The intruder sliced through each hidden emotion and cast away the shredded remnants. He thrust deeper, and deeper still, until he touched the innermost essence of her being.

Gina lay still, struggling for breath. The man wasn't touching her physically, but somehow—*somehow*—he was in her mind, and the violation was more profound than anything he could have done to her body. She was spread open, completely vulnerable to his will.

And despite her terror, she was responding to him.

A wave of pure erotic flame shot through her, leaving her gasping. She writhed, trying to flee the sensation, but with each sure pulse she felt the unwanted pleasure grow, racing through her veins, pooling in her nipples and her groin. It expanded to the edges of her brain, driving her toward a fate she craved as desperately as she struggled to escape it.

Finally, she snapped. The white heat blazed and exploded, sending a vivid orgasm tearing through her mind and body. Her hips arched and she cried out.

The sound reached her ears as if it had come from very far away. The pulsing force receded, leaving Gina gasping. Dear God, the pleasure had been so intense she'd almost blacked out.

As the aftershocks of the shattering climax rippled through her, Gina's gaze darted to her kidnapper. He'd not touched her at all during the wild ride, yet he seemed almost as affected by their strange union as she had been. His face had gone pale and his hands were shaking. He bowed his head and pressed his fingers to his forehead, his breath coming in sharp, uneven bursts.

She inched away from him, hindered by the ropes on her wrists and ankles. He stopped her with one hand. A thin-bladed knife appeared in the other. Sheer panic slammed into Gina with suffocating force, but her captor merely sliced her bonds and returned his blade to its sheath.

She sucked a dizzying breath and scrambled away. This time, he let her go.

He pushed to his feet and captured her gaze for one brief instant. His gray eyes flickered with some dark emotion. Shame? Regret? She couldn't tell.

He turned and ducked under the lintel.

Gina pressed the heel of her hand against her throbbing temple, only too aware of the humiliating moisture that had collected between her thighs. How could she have found pleasure in whatever it was her captor had done to her?

The last remnant of the dirty yellow fog in her mind evaporated. She tried to stand. A wave of vertigo sent her back to the ground, where she lay still for what seemed like an eternity. When she looked up a second time, the room had stopped spinning. Maybe the drug was wearing off at last.

Her heart was still beating double-time, though. She eased into a sitting position and hugged her knees to her chest. She wasn't yet ready to stand, but this much, at least, she could manage.

Shame heated her cheeks as the memory of the kidnapper's mental invasion played through her mind. The drug he'd given her must have contained some kind of aphrodisiac as well as a sedative. It had given her a stunning orgasm without any physical stimulation. What kind of man would have given her such a drug?

Terror clogged her lungs and squeezed her chest like a vise. The dark-haired man hadn't been acting alone—there had been the kid in the forest and a woman beyond the door. Were there more of them—some kind of sex cult? Would a physical assault follow the mental one she'd endured? Would they ensure her body's response with more drugs?

Gina shoved the thought from her mind. If she followed the path her imagination was taking, she would become paralyzed with fear just when she needed to stay calm. She had to plot her escape. There was no alternative. She drew a deep breath and focused her energy on taking stock of her prison.

The tiny hut showed no trace of modern civilization. Herbs and baskets hung from the ceiling, wooden bowls and crude utensils occupied one high shelf. A straw mat covered with furs lay against the wall. If this was some fantasy role-playing scene, the players hadn't skimped on authenticity. Were her kidnappers offshoot members of The Wizards? If so, they had taken their role-playing games to a whole new level.

At that moment, the animal skin at the doorway lifted, admitting an old woman. Creases etched her face, yet she seemed curiously young, as if she had existed since the beginning of the world, unchanged. Narrow braids lay in precise dark rows across her scalp. The ends hung free, secured by tiny wooden beads. She wore a plain animal skin dress and a headband ornamented by a carved stone disk. Simple lines marked the milky-white stone—two rings, linked, with a spear thrust through the place of their joining.

The crude symbol eclipsed Gina's attention. It seemed familiar. Where had she seen it before? She rose to her feet, steadying herself with one hand on the stone wall when her knees threatened to give way.

The crone took a wooden cup from the shelf and filled it from a larger vessel on the floor. "Water, my child."

Gina regarded her warily. It hardly seemed likely The Wizards recruited their members from nursing homes. "Who are you?"

"I am Zahta." The woman's free hand traced a graceful arch, her fingers eloquent. "You are in my home, among my clan. We are the *Baha'Na*, the People of the Goddess."

The cadence of the old woman's speech flowed in soft waves, a very different sound from the speech of the dark-haired man. But again, though the individual words were unfamiliar, the meaning was clear. Was the illusion a residual effect of the drug? The pain behind Gina's forehead intensified.

"Water," the old woman repeated. She took a sip, as if to show there was nothing to fear.

Reluctantly, Gina accepted the cup. She couldn't remember her last drink, and her throat was sore and parched. She gave the clear liquid in the crude vessel a cautious sniff. It seemed pure. She drank, praying it was.

The old woman was watching her closely. "You are fearful, Gina," she said. "But there is no danger for you here."

"You know my name. What else do you know?"

"My daughter's son brought you to me. He hoped I could save you."

"The man who abducted me is your grandson?" Gina's fingers slipped on the cup. It fell to the ground, the water splashing dark on the dirt floor.

"Do not fear, my child." Zahta's fingers brushed Gina's arm.

The sharp throb in Gina's head abruptly vanished. Gina snatched her arm away. Had the old woman's touch caused the pain to disappear? What kind of drug had they given her, anyway? She drew a breath, trying to stave off the panic. "What do you want from me?" she asked.

Zahta retrieved the fallen cup and set it aside before answering. "Derrin brought you to me after another wizard attempted to snare your spirit, but I could do nothing to aid you. Only one path to your soul remained. Among my people there is a joining of spirits called the *Na'tahar*, an intimate bond of a man and woman. Derrin used this bond to enter your mind. Once inside, he used his wizard's power to destroy the other wizard's control."

Grandma was either crazy or on drugs herself. "If your grandson takes me back right now," Gina said in a terse voice, "I won't press charges,"

"He cannot. He does not possess the power to open the web."

"The web?"

"The golden net that binds the edges of the world."

The shining threads Gina had seen in the woods behind the mansion resembled a net. "What do you mean?"

"You have crossed the web. You are no longer in the world you call home."

"Is that so? What world am I in, then?"

"My home," Zahta said simply. "You are welcome here." She inclined her head. "Yet you have suffered much, and are in need of healing. Come. Permit me to help you."

The old woman moved to the door. After a brief hesitation, Gina followed.

She ducked under the stone lintel and emerged into the bright midday sun, raising her hand against the sudden glare. Her heartbeat accelerated as she took in the scene before her.

The room in which she'd been imprisoned was a simple stone and thatch hut. It stood near the bank of a stream within a cluster of similar dwellings. Beyond the sparkling water, the land swept into a forested valley, then rose as a sheer cliff. Lofty, white-capped mountains crowded the horizon.

Gina swallowed hard. Where the hell was she?

You are no longer in the world you call home.

Impossible. She must have been unconscious for days, long enough to be transported out west, or to Canada.

But who would set up such an elaborate abduction? And why?

The village—if that's what it was—appeared to be deserted, with the exception of a teenage girl and a man sitting a short distance away. The man, Gina realized with a start, was her kidnapper, and he was watching her intently. When her gaze locked with his, he nodded and shifted to a crouch. With his palms spread on his thighs, he rose to his feet with slow, masculine grace.

Suddenly, it seemed very hard to breathe.

His face was set in rigid lines, accentuated by the gash on his cheek. Dark hair flowed free, touching his shoulders. The fabric of his black tunic and breeches clung to a tall frame, hard with lean muscle. He regarded her in silence, arms at his sides, his weight balanced on the balls of his feet, as if preparing for sudden movement.

His intimate scrutiny touched Gina's skin, sent sparks down her spine. His eyes were cool, knowing, veiled in gray mist.

He'd been inside her mind.

Gina took a step back, her heart pounding into her throat.

Zahta steadied her with one hand. "Tasa," she called.

The teenager sprang to her feet. She pressed her palm to her forehead and bowed her head. "Yes, Grandmother?"

"Guide Gina to the Wellspring."

Gina tore her gaze from her kidnapper. "The Wellspring? What's that?"

Tasa smiled. "It is not far."

Some answer. Gina looked back at the dark-haired man. His attention had not wavered, but he made no move toward her. When the girl motioned, Gina followed. Any distance she could put between herself and her captor was at that moment very appealing.

Tasa took a path behind the village, skipping easily up the steep slope. Gina followed more slowly, grasping at saplings and watching for rocks on the trail. She'd lost her shoes somewhere. The smooth dirt felt cool on her feet.

The trail curved into a spray of warm mist. A waterfall, tinged with red, roared over a rocky crescent and spilled into a pool far below. Tasa climbed to the top of the cascade and followed the red river to its source, a fissure in the face of the cliff.

Rough lines chiseled into the rock near the cave's entrance matched the mark on Zahta's headdress—two rings, linked, with a spear thrust through the place of their joining. Gina stared at the symbol, then traced the rough lines with her finger. She knew this mark. She was sure of it.

"The Wellspring is the first of the Signs." Tasa's voice rippled, blending with the flow of the water.

"Signs?"

"There are seven clans of the Baha'Na, and seven Signs. A talisman, a stone of great power, belongs to each. With it, a wise woman, our *Na'lara*, reveals the face of the Goddess to her clan."

"Zahta is your Na'lara, then?"

"Yes. We are the Water Clan. The Wellspring is our Sign. As Zahta's granddaughter, I will bear the talisman when she passes beyond the veil."

"The man who brought me here—is he your brother?"

"Derrin is my cousin, but I do not know him. He left the clan many winters past, when I was a small girl. He wishes to speak with you."

"Oh, he does, does he? What does he want to talk about?"

"I do not know." The girl gestured toward the cave. "Come inside. I will prepare food and drink for you."

Gina gazed into the dark, narrow passage. It smelled faintly of moss. God only knew what—or who—was waiting for her in there.

There was no freaking way she wanted to find out. She waited, breath shallow, until Tasa turned her back to enter the cavern.

Then she gathered her shredded skirt and ran.

She tore through the forest as fast as she dared. She stumbled as she plunged downhill, then righted herself just as quickly, ignoring the scrape of rocks and roots on her bare soles. When the path forked, she veered onto the trail she thought led away from the village. A wide stream glittered through the trees, flowing swiftly. Water always led to civilization. If she followed the bank she'd come to a town, a ranger station, or even a campsite, where surely someone would have a cell phone.

A stitch in her side brought her up short. Steadying herself with one hand on an enormous tree trunk, Gina caught her breath and willed herself not to panic. As far as she could tell, the girl hadn't followed her. She peered to the rear. Nothing. Good.

She turned back to the trail and walked straight into her kidnapper.

His fingers closed on her wrist. "Are you going somewhere, Mistress?" The hard gray glint in his eyes prompted a dose of pure adrenaline to surge through Gina's veins. She jerked her arms, trying to free herself, but his grip might as well have been an iron manacle.

She used his arm for leverage and slammed her knee straight into his groin. He convulsed, bending double with a strangled curse lodged in his throat.

Gina twisted from his grasp and plunged down the trail.

She'd not gone far before she heard him behind her. She pushed herself harder, trying to ignore the slicing pain in her side and the thin stream of blood oozing from a nasty scratch on her arm. Her long skirt snagged on a branch. Her pursuer's footsteps pounded on the trail. She tugged at the velvet and heard it rip.

Angry arms closed about her from behind, wrapping around her torso, pinning her arms to her side. She kicked, but to no avail. Her kidnapper hoisted her and slung her face-down over his shoulder with as much ceremony as he might have given a sack of dog food.

Gina pounded his back with her fists. "Let me go!"

"I think not." He strengthened his grip on her legs and strode back up the trail.

"Who the hell are you? What do you want from me?"

He didn't bother to answer. Gina renewed her struggle. His palm shifted, covering one buttock, stroking upward with blatant familiarity. Gina went deadly still at that, reluctant to provoke him further.

His long legs made short work of her escape route. He climbed the trail beside the waterfall, hefting her weight as if she were a child. He halted at the entrance to the cave.

Tasa stood watching, her dark eyes wide with shock.

Gina's captor set her on her feet and stepped back. "Do not try that again."

She glared at him but made no reply.

Tasa stepped forward, her touch on Gina's arm hesitant. "We mean you no harm."

"Like hell you don't," Gina muttered. She had little choice but to enter the cave under the watchful eye of her captor. He didn't follow.

A path of stones bordered the red stream, leading to a roughly circular cavern. To Gina's great relief, no horde of sex-crazed cultists waited for her. The space appeared deserted. A wide pool filled the center of the grotto, its surface shining red through the blanket of mist on its surface.

"The blood of the Goddess," Tasa said.

Blood? Gina drew in a sharp breath, then let it out in a long stream. Not blood—a mineral spring with a high iron content. Most likely the glow was caused by reflected sunlight passing through the bottom of the pool.

"It is quite warm," Tasa said. "And you are welcome to bathe. I will fetch food and clothing while you wash."

Gina looked down at her ruined dress. The cuts on her feet and arms were starting to sting. "I'd like to, but…" She glanced toward the cave's entrance.

"Derrin will not enter."

God, she hoped not. The thought made her stomach clench with fear and another sensation she was loath to define. She walked to the edge of the pool and dipped her fingers into the water. Warm, but not too hot. She pulled off the remnants of the dress and eased into the water.

She bathed as quickly as she could. When she emerged a few minutes later, Tasa was waiting with a simple sheath dress. It was fashioned from a soft animal pelt—the skin of a mountain doe, the girl told her. Strips of hide laced the neckline.

Gina's own clothes were gone.

"Where's my underwear?" she asked.

Tasa merely smiled and offered the dress again. Gina sighed and took it. Her bra had been filthy and her panties torn, in any case. She slipped the new garment over her head. The doeskin was cool, but surprisingly light and soft on her bare skin.

A basket contained dried berries and something that looked like old leather and tasted like beef jerky minus the salt. While Gina ate, Tasa produced a wooden comb and began the task of untangling Gina's hair. She braided it into dozens of thin strands, like her own, and secured each end with a wooden bead. She had just finished when footsteps sounded in the passageway.

Gina tensed. "I thought you said he wouldn't come."

Tasa cocked her head. "It is not Derrin. My grandmother approaches."

Gina rose as Zahta emerged from the cave's entrance. The crone halted before Gina, placed her palms together and touched her fingers to her forehead.

A warm light wrapped around Gina's mind. Had the sensation come from the old woman? She took a step back. *Impossible.*

"Let the Goddess take your fear, my child," Zahta said.

"I'm not afraid of you."

The crone smiled. "There are storms in your past. The death of one you held close to your heart. And..." Her eyes widened, then shut.

Gina shifted her weight onto one foot, staring at the old woman with a mixture of fascination and dread. A mind reader? No way. A kook. But even so, something wasn't quite right about this place. For one thing, the strange illusion that her captors spoke a different language persisted, despite the fact the drug Gina had ingested surely had worn off by now.

A journey. Far from home. Few choices. The old fortuneteller's words had been eerily prescient. Could Gina have passed into one of the alternate dimensions Mikala had insisted were mathematically possible? No. That was just too far beyond imagining.

"Where is the man who brought me here?"

"Derrin sits by my fire," Zahta said.

"He has to take me back to New Jersey. Now."

"He has not that power."

"I don't believe you."

Zahta nodded. "I see that you do not."

Gina let out a long breath. "All right, then. How long are you planning to keep me here? And why?"

The old woman tilted her head, her bright eyes darting like a bird's. "Trust in the Goddess, child. She will not allow you to wander astray. Already you have bathed in her blood. You have touched she who is not the water, nor the rock, yet is found in the rush of the stream and the cascade of the falls."

"Cut the New Age crap. Do you want money? How much?"

"There are seven Signs," the old woman continued, as if Gina hadn't spoken. "The Goddess dwells also in Rock and Fire, Wind, Tree and Skyeagle." She bent and drew a ring in the dust. "And in the Seventh Sign, which has no name. Journey to each and you will find the place you belong."

The crude circle seemed to glow softly before fading to a mere scratch in the dirt. Gina stared at it, resisting a fierce urge to kneel and trace it with her finger. An emotion stirred in the recesses of her mind, but when she reached for it, it flitted away like the remnant of a dream.

"You are no longer in the world you called home, Gina," Zahta said softly. "Can you not feel it?"

"Where are these Signs?" The question slipped out almost before Gina realized she'd spoken.

"Hidden deep in the wilderness. You must seek them."

"How?"

"The path is clear to those who know the Goddess, but you have never dwelt here." Zahta gave Gina a searching glance. "Derrin has. He will guide you."

The statement had the air of a challenge. Gina's gaze narrowed, but she could detect no malice in the crone's serene expression. Quizzing her was clearly a waste of time. Questioning her grandson might prove more fruitful.

Not to mention more dangerous. But if he'd wanted to kill her, he could have done it already. If she could get clear of the village, there was a chance she could escape him and find help.

She met Zahta's gaze. "All right. I'll go to your Signs. Tell your grandson."

* * * * *

Derrin stood on an outcropping of rock near a mountain stream and skimmed a flat rock across the water. Seven skips, his mind registered automatically. Curious, how skills gained in childhood never seem to be forgotten. He squinted at the sun, gauging its descent toward the horizon.

He should have questioned the sorceress and been gone by now. Yet here he stood, pitching rocks into the stream. All because Zahta wanted him to remain until the woman consented to see him. His unexplained absence from the Wizards' Stronghold had surely been noted. Ariek could make Derrin's excuses for a few days, but after that…

He threw another stone. He could bring the sorceress back to Galena. She would need to stay hidden while he searched for the path to her home, but he had no idea if she would be willing do so. Until she was gone and the web sealed behind her, he could not rest. Balek's experiments with the web had already sparked plagues of Madness and Blight. Would the sicknesses worsen now that a sorceress had passed through the barrier? And what of Balek's reasons for summoning the woman? What further ill did the high wizard plan? Derrin could not risk surrendering the woman to Balek. If Derrin was unable to send the woman back to her own world, it was better that he kill her.

That might not be an easy task, he thought, wincing as he touched the gash on his cheekbone. The sorceress was strong and clever, even when her mind had been clouded by the webstone. She'd gashed him with his own knife during the journey from Katrinth. He'd been forced to bind her hands to prevent a second assault.

Once he'd reached the edge of the Northern Wilderness, the horse Ariek had stolen from his father's stables had been unable to negotiate the steep trail. Derrin had set the beast free and tied the woman's ankles. He'd hauled her, wild-eyed and struggling, the last miserable steps to his grandmother's village.

The memory of the journey swirled on the surface of his mind's eddy. Below it, submerged, floated dark eyes. Eyes like a mountain doe's, flooded with terror. He had brought the sorceress to Zahta, hoping his grandmother could save the woman's mind from destruction.

Zahta had given that task back to him.

Derrin flung a good-sized rock across the stream. It landed in the trees with a crack, loosing a swarm of sparkling *ghilla* bugs. He'd compelled an unwilling woman to the Na'tahar, the sacred joining of lovers. He'd felt her terror at his violation, and her shame that they had shared an erotic mental release. Guilt choked him, though he knew he'd had little choice. If he had realized the intimate Baha'Na bond could save the woman's mind, he would have used it at once, while still in the Stronghold.

The last stone weighed heavily in his hand. Milky white, with veins of amber. Broken, sharp along one edge. Zahta had refused Derrin's second request as well—to open her link to the Circle and call the web. She did not understand the twin threats of Madness and Blight, or, if she did, she chose not to acknowledge them. It fell to Derrin to return the woman to her home. He had an idea as to how he might find a path through the glittering strands without his grandmother's assistance, but he couldn't pursue it here in the wilderness.

A soft voice hailed him. Zahta. Of course, she would know where to find him. This place had been his boyhood sanctuary. He dropped the final stone into the stream and watched the ripples disappear into the flow of the water.

"What are you thinking, my son?"

Derrin guessed his grandmother already knew his thoughts. He met her gaze. "The Circle—"

"The Circle is empty. The web cannot be opened."

He couldn't stop himself from asking one more time. "If you would but try..."

"It is not our way. The Goddess has her own time."

An old anger rose. He knew only too well how capricious the Goddess' favor could be. He started to reply, then thought better of it. He nodded instead. "I'll proceed without your help, then. At the sun's rising, I leave for Galena. I dare not take the sorceress with me. Keep her safe here. I'll leave a crystal for her protection."

He hesitated, then asked the question foremost in his mind. "Have you told the woman why I drew her to the Na'tahar?"

"Yes, my son, but Gina did not believe me."

A knot in Derrin's stomach twisted. Guilt rose in a smothering wave. *Gina.* Hearing the woman's name spoken aloud made her more real. More vulnerable.

"Derrin, you must not return to the Outside."

He frowned, looking past his grandmother to the forest. "I can wait no longer. I must stop Balek's folly before it's too late. The Blight worsens daily. I fear it will spread even here, to the wilderness."

"You will not conquer your fears by fighting on the Outside. I have need of you here. You must guide Gina to the Signs of the Goddess."

His gaze snapped to hers. "The Signs? What are they to a woman from another world?"

She moved closer and placed a wrinkled hand on his arm. "The power of the Goddess knows not limits of this world. Gina must seek the Signs."

"The Seventh as well?"

"Yes," she replied. "Especially the Seventh."

Derrin eyed his grandmother, his broodings forgotten in his amazement at this extraordinary request. He could think of a thousand reasons to ignore her petition and only one reason to grant it. Because she had asked.

Derrin may have lived among the Galenans for years, but not long enough to forget what it meant to be of the Baha'Na. The request of a Na'lara could not be denied. But why did Zahta think it necessary for an alien sorceress to seek the Signs? He could see no sense in it.

He shook off her arm. "Do not ask such a thing of me. I am no longer of the Baha'Na."

"You were born a son of the Goddess, Derrin. So you remain, no matter where your choices have led."

"Choices?" He spat out the word with a short, mirthless laugh. "When have I ever had a choice?" His rage flared, but it met only the deep calm of his grandmother's eyes.

After a long moment, he looked away.

"In the visions of the night," Zahta said, "I saw you and Gina journeying together, your fates entwined. You must guide her."

Derrin muttered a curse. The dreams of a Na'lara were considered to be the will of the Goddess. Still, he had good reason to refuse. He began to explain again why such an undertaking would be impossible, then paused and reconsidered. Zahta had refused to open the web, but Zahta was not the only wise woman of the Baha'Na. Each clan honored its own Na'lara. There was a chance he might persuade one of the others to call the golden strands. If Derrin pursued his current plan—calling the web himself, with Balek's webstone—his use of the unnatural crystal might well serve to amplify the plagues ravaging Galena.

"As you wish," he said. "I will go." After a moment's pause, he added, "but the woman will not want to come with me."

"Gina asks for you."

The sorceress was asking for him, after the obscene union he'd forced on her? Either she was very brave, or very powerful. Derrin was glad she no longer had a crystal in her possession. The unusual pink stone from her gown nestled in a leather pouch with his own gems.

"Come," Zahta said. Turning, she made her way up the narrow trail without a backward glance.

Derrin followed, the shadow of the boy he'd once been covering him like a shroud. In Galena, he could pass an entire season without a thought of the Baha'Na or the years before his manhood. Now he stood in the familiar landscape of his childhood, immersed in a world of aching beauty.

How had he ever found the strength to leave it?

He traced the flow of the sacred red river to its source. Gina sat near the entrance to the Wellspring cave, head tilted against the rock, eyes closed. Sunlight played on her face and on the cascade of her braids. Her firm breasts, molded by the doeskin of her dress, rose and fell in an even rhythm, merging with the song of a hidden bird. Her legs and feet were bare.

Derrin drew in a sharp breath as a jolt of raw desire shot straight to his cock. The sorceress from beyond the web no longer seemed so alien. He could all too easily imagine doing to her body what he had done to her mind.

Her eyes opened and he was falling, drowning. He'd been inside those eyes and beyond them. Dark eyes, nearly black. They had burned with shame as she'd shuddered with the pleasure of the Na'tahar.

The memory struck him like a kick in the gut and landed an even greater blow to his confidence. Gina scrambled to her feet. Derrin stared, unable to think of anything to say.

Zahta spoke. "Derrin has consented to be your guide, Gina. Will you seek the Signs with him?"

Derrin sensed turmoil coiling around Gina like a serpent. He felt her apprehension as a touch on his own mind. The sensation took him by surprise, though in truth he should have expected it. His spirit had been tuned to hers during the long heartbeats of the Na'tahar. Willing or not, she shared that bond with him now. A joining closer than any purely physical union. It was a tie that could not be easily broken.

Yes, he scented Gina's fear as surely as the buck scented the doe, but when she lifted her chin he saw no sign of it on her face. She'd schooled her features into a cool mask, one Derrin recognized as courage.

"Yes," she answered, speaking not to Zahta, but to him. "I'll go with you."

*****

By the morning of her departure, Gina was doubting the wisdom of her vague escape plans. The thought of spending any amount of time with her abductor made her heart take on an uneven rhythm. He'd said little when she'd met with him, but his gray gaze had pierced her façade of false confidence far too easily. She had the most sickening suspicion he could read her thoughts and emotions with appalling accuracy.

He'd been inside her mind.

Rationally, she knew it was impossible. Despite that fact, a sense of violation clung to her like a nightmare, try as she might to shake it off. And then there was another oddity to ponder—the lingering illusion that her kidnappers spoke a language other than English. A musical, lilting language she was sure she'd never heard before, but was able to understand nonetheless. She'd thought at first it was an effect of the drug, but it had been at least three days since the Wizards' Ball. Nothing lasted that long.

Could the glittering web of light really have transported her to some other dimension? Her mind balked at the thought. No. This mountaintop clearly wasn't New Jersey, but that didn't mean it inhabited an alternate reality.

She drew a deep breath and picked up the small knife Tasa had given her earlier that morning. To use in the forest, the girl had said. It was only a bone handle fitted to a stone blade—obsidian, she thought—but its weight felt reassuring in her grip. Odd that her captors would give her a weapon, though—even a crude one. Gina ran her finger along the edge of the blade, then jerked her hand away and sucked the drop of blood oozing from her fingertip. With new respect for the primitive tool, she slid the knife into the rawhide sheath strapped to her thigh.

She tugged the hem of her doeskin dress back into place. She'd grown accustomed to the unusual fabric, but the lack of underwear left her feeling more than half naked. Kneeling, she tugged on her soft leather boots and tied the laces. At least Zahta's salve had soothed the cuts on the soles of her feet. Incredibly, after only a day, they were fully healed.

She left the cavern. Outside, Derrin stood at Zahta's side, half turned away, arms crossed and legs spread wide. Gina halted. In the glare of the morning sun, her kidnapper appeared even more disturbing than she remembered.

His head swung in her direction, causing the sunlight to dance on the glossy black fall of his hair. He'd exchanged his black tunic for a shirt made of deerskin. The golden fabric rippled across the muscles of his chest. A kilt of the same sinuous material pulled tight across his hips. His long thighs were bare, his feet and calves encased in high boots.

The costume did little to disguise the power of his body. His build wasn't bulky, but Gina remembered the ease with which he'd aborted her escape attempt. She sensed his strength now as a force he kept under tight control, coiled like a spring and ready to be set loose.

A dark stranger. Your enemy. Had Madam Rose seen the future in the selenite crystal?

Derrin came to a halt an arm's length in front of her. She gave him a cool look and lifted her brows. His jaw clenched and his gray eyes took on an inscrutable expression.

She turned to Zahta, unwilling to let her captor see her fear. "How far is it to the next Sign?"

"A journey of two days," the old woman replied.

Gina eyed Derrin's empty hands. "Two days? Won't we need supplies? Food...water...something to sleep on?"

A flash of what could have been amusement lit his eyes. "You speak like an Outsider," he said. "In Galena, a journey requires adequate provision. Here in the wilderness, the Baha'Na go empty-handed. We will travel as they do."

Zahta raised her hand in a gesture of farewell. "The face of the Goddess shines on our parting, Gina."

Without further comment, Derrin turned and started down the trail. Gina stared after him, battling an urge to run in the opposite direction.

A journey. Far from home. Few choices.

So far, Madam Rose was batting a thousand.

Chapter Three

Danat opened her eyes and stretched, cat-like, rolling over the blankets she'd spread on the floor of her attic room the night before. She stroked one finger along the jaw of the man beside her. With his face unmasked by sleep, Ariek resembled a small boy. She watched him for a time, savoring the deep, even rhythm of his breath.

Then the boy woke and the man pulled her into his arms.

"I love you," he said, cupping her bare breast and toying with its hardened peak. He brushed a kiss over her lips. Danat's hand closed on his cock, semi-hard from his slumber and growing more erect with each passing second. Ariek groaned and deepened his kiss, drinking deep, his hot tongue questing in her mouth. She opened more fully and drew him in.

His hands stroked down her torso and settled on her buttocks. With a swift, sure movement born of familiarity, he lifted her and set her astride his thighs. She ran a finger over the tip of his cock, spreading the moisture over his wide head before guiding him in to her slick cleft.

She sank down on him, letting him fill her completely, enjoying the sensation of his flesh deep inside her as he moved. Their joining never failed to take her breath away. It was as if they had been made to be one.

She arched her back, thrusting her breasts toward Ariek, and was rewarded by the flare of satisfaction in his eyes. He was so beautiful with his face shadowed in pleasure and the sculpted planes of his chest rising and falling beneath her. He caressed her breasts, circling his palms on her nipples until she thought she would go mad.

"Please," she whispered.

He grasped her hips and moved her body in time with his thrusts, rocking her like a boat on the sea. Gradually, he increased the depth and tempo of the rhythm, expanding her bliss with each stroke. Danat's climax broke in a long, exhilarating swell. Exquisite ripples pulsed through her body. She savored each one, willing it to last.

But in the end the final lap faded, leaving her bereft. She sagged against Ariek's body and nestled her cheek in his chest. She breathed deeply of his scent and listened to the beat of his heart. She would remember these things always.

For he would soon be gone.

As if he sensed her desolation, his arms tightened around her. "I want to take you away from this place," he said.

Danat gently disentangled herself from his embrace until she'd gained enough distance to meet his gaze. "Oh, Ariek. You know such a thing is not possible. I am the property of the temple."

"Of the temple priests, you mean. That bastard Solk and his simpering acolytes."

She pressed her lips to his, hoping he wouldn't pursue the topic.

He responded briefly, then gripped her shoulders and pulled back, looking into her eyes. "I'm serious. I can't stand to think of you here any longer. We'll leave at night. I'll take you to Sirth, or the Eastern Plains."

A small spark of hope flickered, then died. She shook her head. "Ariek. I am the Bride of Lotark. No matter where I go, people will know me—if not by sight, then by the brand on my forehead."

She held up one hand to stop his protest. "Wizards are required to live in Katrinth. What would you do if you left? Become a farmer, or a shepherd? I won't ask it of you. After a time you would resent me for taking you from your life's work."

Ariek fell silent, and Danat knew her words hit upon a truth he didn't want to admit. She sighed. Her lover was an idealist, the pampered youngest son of a rich aristocrat. He'd seen so little of the darker side of humanity. She'd seen so much of it.

"Let it go. Tell me more of Derrin."

Ariek scowled. "Five nights have passed since he kidnapped the woman he claims is a sorceress. He said he would be back in three."

"Have you no notion of where he has gone?"

His frown deepened. "No one can find Derrin when he doesn't wish to be found. He wears a shadow crystal of incredible power." He stood abruptly and began to pace the bare floor, his blond head almost brushing the rafters. "Danat, I've known Derrin for ten years. He's not easily shaken, but he went wild when Maator brought that woman into the Stronghold. Within the hour he had me at my father's stables, stealing a horse."

"Where did she come from?"

Ariek ran one hand over his cropped hair as he walked the length of the narrow room. "I doubt you'll believe me when I tell you my esteemed partner's theory. It all started last Harvest. We were submerged in our research of the Blight. Derrin became convinced the sickness of the land was connected to Balek, and to the Madness."

Danat nodded. The Madness was now rare in Katrinth's wealthier quadrants, but the disease still plagued the commoners who lived in the hovels of the Lower City. They had no hope of obtaining the antidote crystal Balek had created to treat the illness.

"Derrin began to spy on Balek. I told him he courted disaster, meddling with the affairs of a High Wizard." Ariek drew up short at the far end of the attic room, where a fine netting hung behind the temple's pediment. He peered through the intricate carving in the grillwork to the High Plaza below.

"I suggested his obsession was personal. Five years ago, Balek tried to bar Derrin's acceptance to the Hierarchy. He'd been incensed when Master Niirtor accepted Derrin—who had no money or family name—as an apprentice."

He shook his head and he resumed his trek across the chamber. "Derrin ignored my concerns. He continued to watch Balek, but said little. Then, a month ago, he told me what he'd seen. I still can't believe it."

"What did he say?"

"That Balek had created a crystal he calls the webstone—a five-sided crystal, with each face a perfect pentagram. Danat, such an object couldn't exist! Yet Derrin insists Balek uses the stone to create common crystals of the highest purity. What's more, he claims the webstone enables Balek to open a golden web at the edge of the world, a source of unimaginable power."

He halted. "Derrin's convinced Balek's tampering with this web is the cause of the Madness and the Blight. He's been saying since Year's Beginning that Balek was searching for something within the web. But a sorceress from another world? It's ludicrous! Yet it's true the woman is not of Katrinth, or even Galena."

"Do you believe she is truly from another world?"

Ariek spread his arms wide, palms up. "I don't know what to believe. I saw her myself. Her clothing was obscene, and she wore a large crystal between her breasts. She could well be a sorceress. But if Balek wants her, he hides his desires well. He goes about his business as usual even though Derrin—"

A bell sounded, interrupting Ariek's tirade. Danat jumped. "It's Solk! You've stayed too long—he mustn't find you!" She scooped Ariek's tunic off the floor and threw it at him.

He caught it in one hand. With the other he grabbed her wrist and pulled her close, his kiss lingering on her protesting lips. "You know I could pass within a hand's breadth of Solk's pointed nose without him feeling so much as a breeze."

He released her and pulled on his clothes, then picked up a silk scarf embroidered with a blue circle, the Mark of Lotark. "A piece of you to take away with me." His lips brushed her hair. "When can I see you again?"

"Come tonight, unless the lamp is dark."

Ariek kissed her one more time, then was gone.

Danat sighed and moved to the wardrobe set against the wall. She chose a robe of cold white silk, embroidered with gold and silver thread. A sash of spun silver mesh cinched her waist. Chains of gold and silver, studded with gems, dragged at her wrists and ankles.

She brushed out her hair and set a circlet of gold and diamonds atop the curls. The bell sounded a second time. She opened her narrow door and made her way down the wooden staircase, her face set in a careful mask.

A profusion of gilded images burst upon her as she stepped into the Outer Sanctuary, sacred scenes from the time when Lotark had walked among his people as a man. Danat despised the long hours she spent within these walls, assisting Solk in the tedious ceremony of the Holy Rite. Wide windows and doors looked out on an open courtyard, into which jutted the curved form of the Inner Sanctuary.

She hurried under the gilded archway to the most holy sanctum of the One God. Here the walls formed a perfect circle, symbolizing the eternity of Lotark's rule. Scenes of the world's creation danced around the perimeter. A mosaic floor lay gilded and intricate at her feet.

The ceiling deepened into blue, with silver specks dispersed throughout, recalling the night sky. A raised circular platform served as an altar. Above it hung a canopy of white satin with strands of silver fringe at its edges.

The high priest stood to one side of the altar, his tall, gaunt form robed in white. Although he was not much older than Ariek, Solk's features were immeasurably harder, illuminated by righteousness. Four Lesser Servants, wearing vestments of blue and silver, flanked him. Danat knelt, eyes downcast and arms outstretched. Her heart turned numb, but she kept her expression carefully serene.

"This evening, a True Believer will come to Lotark's Sanctuary. You will please him well. He has offered much to assume the Visage of the One God."

"Yes, Your Grace." Danat choked back her disappointment. Tonight! She'd hoped to be in Ariek's arms, but now…

"Rise."

Danat obeyed, her gaze lowered, as was required. She saw Solk's hand reach out, felt his icy fingers pass between the folds of her robe to pinch her nipple. She couldn't suppress a gasp. *Not this, not now, so soon after loving Ariek.*

The Heir of Lotark acknowledged her loss of composure with a tight, cruel smile. He untied the sash at her waist.

Two of the acolytes stepped forward and accepted her robe. Solk stood silent for a time, his gaze traveling the length of her body. Danat's stomach turned. She resisted a fierce urge to cover herself with her hands.

The last acolyte stepped forward, the Book of Law cradled in his arms. Solk opened the tome and bent over the appropriate chapter and verse. He closed his eyes briefly, his face illuminated with fervor. Then, in a deep, musical voice, he intoned the sacred words.

"—and Lotark chose a Woman from among his people to be his Bride, a woman more beautiful than the stars, purer than the moon. She had no desires, save one. To serve her Master with her mind, her body, and her soul." His hard gaze raked over Danat's naked body before returning to the Book of Law.

"Lotark rewarded his Woman well. He allowed her to ascend with him to Paradise."

Solk straightened, then lifted the Visage of Lotark from its niche near the altar and placed it over his face. The God held out one hand to his Bride. Danat took it and allowed herself to be led to the altar.

Her spirit hardened and her mind emptied.

The high priest parted his vestments and revealed the tool of his authority. When he entered her, she was far away, locked inside a place no man could touch.

Chapter Four

"Watch out!" Derrin steadied the sorceress with one hand.

She snatched her arm away.

He scowled and ducked through the limbs of a fallen tree, leaving the stubborn woman to negotiate the steep slope on her own. Sunlight dropped through the gap in the forest's canopy, scattering patches of light on the mosaic of last summer's fallen leaves.

He closed his eyes and inhaled. Anger faded as the forest seeped into his senses. *Life.* So different from Katrinth. An intense wave of longing broke over him, followed by a flood of dark melancholy. He pushed both away.

Brooding was a Galenan habit.

"So let me get this straight," Gina said. "You're telling me I went through a web of light and entered another world."

Derrin slid her a glance. So far, she'd given him precious little information. Her tone was hard, her eyes dark with mistrust. He was very glad she had no crystals. But why had she not asked for the one sewn on her dress? It had looked to be a powerful stone, but he'd never seen its like. He hadn't been able to discern its specialty.

"Do you not remember your crossing?" he asked carefully.

She frowned. "I saw a light in the woods outside the Ball, but that was an effect of the drug."

"Drug?"

"The one you gave me at the party."

He shook his head. "I know nothing of a celebration. High Wizard Balek has created a crystal that opens the edges of the world. He used it to summon you across the web. His apprentice awaited your arrival in the forest outside Katrinth."

She gave him an odd look. "You're saying a wizard brought me to this place with a crystal?"

"Yes." He watched her closely. The woman most likely had a vast knowledge of crystals. What game was she playing?

"That's impossible," she said.

He fell in with her pretense of innocence. "On the contrary, it's quite possible."

"You expect me to believe that?"

"Believe what you wish."

"Maybe I'm in a coma or something," she continued, her tone faltering. "Maybe I hit my head and scrambled my brain. That might explain why it seems like you're talking in a foreign language."

"I find your speech strange, as well," Derrin told her. He searched her eyes and found uncertainty. Could she be telling the truth? Could she have no idea what powers crystals held? It didn't seem likely. He extended his mind, drawing close enough to feel the shadow of her emotions, but not close enough to cause her alarm. Fear was the easiest emotion to sense. Deception was more subtle. He stilled his mind and probed as closely as he dared. He felt no dishonesty flowing from her.

Of course, that might just prove that she was an exceptional liar.

"This could be a dream," she said. It sounded as though she was trying to convince herself and failing miserably.

"Do you feel as though you are dreaming?"

She turned away and started back up the trail, leaving his question unanswered. He examined the rigid cast of her shoulders, then, despite his best intentions, his gaze dropped lower, taking in the sway of her hips and the outline of her buttocks molded by the soft doeskin. His cock stiffened. He muttered a curse. Despite the danger her powers represented, and his doubts as to her integrity, the sorceress aroused him.

That thought brought another. There was a sure way to determine whether the sorceress was feigning innocence. When he'd entered Gina's mind in Zahta's hut, he'd been bent on destroying the webstone's influence, not probing her emotions. But if they became Na'tahar a second time, he could use their mental bond to discover her true intentions toward him. It was within his power to do it. She'd yielded to him once. He did not need her consent to join with her a second time.

Derrin swore softly under his breath. What kind of man he was becoming, to even ponder such a thing? It was as if his union with Gina had awakened a ravenous monster inside him. He badly wanted to plunge into her again, with his body as well as his mind. Unfortunately, she didn't appear to share his craving.

Scowling, he trudged the trail at a quick pace, making sure he didn't step within an arm's reach of Gina. Some time later, he stopped to drink from a spring.

"Are you hungry?" he asked.

"No."

He bent and separated the canes of a short, bushy plant. Red berries and white flowers clung to the stem beneath shiny green leaves. He picked a handful of the fruits.

"These are *tonadi,*" he said, making an effort to keep his tone light. "The berries ripen as the new leaves begin to cover the trees. They continue to form until the…"

He frowned. Gina had moved out of earshot. She stood half turned, her spine stiff, her gazed fixed at a point across the stream. Though she tried to hide her emotions, he could sense them churning like the ocean before a storm.

She was afraid. *Of him.*

Guilt washed over him. Sorceress or not, she hadn't deserved to have her mind violated. Didn't deserve to have him wanting her again.

He approached her slowly, as he would a forest creature. "You needn't worry that I'll harm you," he said. "I want only to help you return to your world."

She looked away. Derrin suppressed a sigh and continued down the slope into the valley. He stopped only to forage for food or to drink from a spring. When the sun dropped below the crest of the mountain, he chose a campsite on a patch of level ground some distance above the streambed.

"We'll stay here for the night," he said, trying to ignore the way his cock jumped at the thought.

Gina sank onto a boulder. Her shoulders slumped with fatigue, causing Derrin another pang of guilt. He'd pushed her too far today. It was clear she wasn't used to such physical exertion.

He had an insane urge to put his hands on her shoulders and work the strain from her muscles with hard, deep strokes. Then, when she was relaxed and soft, he could slip into her mind before she knew what had happened. He'd pleasure her psyche, then turn his attention to her body…

No.

With a wrenching effort, Derrin turned his back on the source of his obsession and began the task of building shelter for the night. A branch set at waist height between two trees served as a ridgepole. Branches covered with moss formed a sloping roof. Soft pine needles provided a bed. He took a sharp stick and dug a shallow firepit near the open side of the shelter. By the time he'd stacked a night's supply of firewood, the sun had left the valley entirely. An icy whisper called on the breeze, unusual for the season.

Derrin pushed the implications of that fact to the back of his mind and swung his gaze toward Gina.

Her expression only reinforced the chill. How he wanted to kindle a spark of passion in the depths of her eyes. His breath caught as the memory of the Na'tahar sprang to full life. His mind had burned with a fire he'd barely managed to contain. He'd felt her shattering release blend with his own. The mental orgasm had been more intense than any he'd ever experienced in the flesh. Even so, he'd been acutely aware that there could have been more.

Derrin had never in his life taken advantage of a woman, but during the endless heartbeats of the Na'tahar, the desire to claim the sorceress' body had nearly squeezed the breath from his lungs. It would have been so easy to do—she hardly could have stopped him. Only the knowledge of her fear had held him back.

Now, as he held Gina's gaze a moment too long, he wondered how it would feel to be welcomed into the sanctuary he had longed to take by force.

A fresh surge of lust accompanied the thought. Stifling a groan, Derrin tore his gaze from Gina's wide doe's eyes and snatched his knife from its sheath. Gripping the bone handle with considerably more force than was necessary, he set himself to the task of carving the tools of firemaking.

A short stick with tapered ends. A notched chunk of wood to steady the spindle. A flat board with a shallow socket would provide a nest for the infant fire. He strung a crude bow with a twisted length of vine and shredded dry bark for tinder. Kneeling, he laid the fireboard over the tinder and looped the bowstring around the spindle. He fitted the shaft between the fireboard and handhold. The bow stroked. The spindle turned.

He increased his speed and dark powder spilled from the fireboard. Woodsmoke touched his nostrils. Derrin lifted the spindle and blew away the dust. A tiny coal, the promise of a fire, glowed in the socket. He scraped it into the tinder and bent close to the ground, blowing in long, gentle streams.

The birth of fire became more important than breath. Red lines danced along wisps of bark. Derrin cradled the tinder in his palms and blew again. Black smoke poured from between his fingers and the bundle burst into flames. Quickly, he transferred it to a nest of twigs in the firepit, then built up the infant fire with kindling and larger pieces of deadwood.

"I cast my breath into the flames. The fire is born. It fills my heart."

The words came easily, though it had been eleven winters since they'd passed his lips. As the prayer faded, Derrin became aware of Gina standing behind him. He looked up, surprised.

"If you're supposed to be a wizard, why not start a fire with magic instead of this survival stuff?"

He ignored her tone. "Wizards don't use fire. They use crystals that generate heat without a flame." He pushed to his feet. "I left my crystals with Zahta."

She frowned. "And the crystal on my dress?"

Ah, so she was asking for it at last. "With the others."

"Why?"

"Zahta said the Goddess had no need of them."

Skepticism showed in her eyes. "Do you believe in this Goddess?"

Did he? Derrin chose his words carefully. "I believe in her as I believe in the mountains and the sky."

Gina's dark gaze dropped to his chest. "But there's one crystal you didn't leave to your grandmother."

"Yes." Derrin's hand closed on the silver cage dangling from a chain around his neck. Its delicate bars shielded his shadow crystal.

"May I see it?"

"No." He shoved the stone into his shirt with a silent curse. A Galenan curse, since the Baha'Na language had no foul imprecations.

He'd been a fool to let the sorceress catch a glimpse of the most powerful gem he'd ever created. No telling how she might use it against him. Unnerved, Derrin strode to a cluster of saplings. He cut the straightest and fashioned a sharp point at one end.

"Tend the fire," he said. "I'm going to fish."

The shadows of late afternoon fell across the shallow stream. After eleven winters without practice, Derrin hoped his hand would be steady on the spear. He missed twice before pinning a good-sized fish to the streambed. He slid it up the shaft and flipped it onto the bank.

A pair of birds skimmed the water, calling madly. Their song surged into Derrin, displacing a portion of the darkness he'd come to believe was his soul. He caught three more fish and was almost smiling when he returned to the camp.

Until he saw the pile of charred sticks.

"Lotark's cock!" Derrin flung his catch on the ground. He'd thought keeping a fire alive would be a simple enough task for the sorceress. Even the smallest Baha'Na child treated such a responsibility with care.

But Gina was gone.

He tracked her to a trail that paralleled the stream, not bothering to keep his footsteps light. She spun about when she heard him approach.

"Where do you imagine you're going?" he said tersely.

Gina stood very still. "Let's get one thing clear. I don't take orders from you."

Several long breaths passed before Derrin trusted himself to speak again. "Then you won't survive for long."

"Is that a threat?" She whipped her knife from its sheath and pointed the blade in his direction.

She meant to fight him? Derrin's anger abruptly transformed into bone-deep weariness. "No," he said. "It's not a threat. It's the law of the Goddess. In the wilderness, all are bound by her rules."

He relieved Gina of her weapon and hauled her back to camp. She glared at him while he cooked his catch, but took her portion when he offered it to her. They ate in silence as the night wind rose. After they had finished, Derrin threw a log on the fire and settled into one end of the lean-to.

"Don't try to leave," he warned. "You won't last long alone in the dark. And I'll find you, in any case."

Gina wedged herself into the opposite corner of the shelter, knees drawn to her chest. He met her gaze. Her expression hardened, but not before he saw a flicker of dread in her eyes.

He knew what she feared.

Much to his shame, he knew how fiercely he wanted it.

His cock stiffened. He rolled over and shut his eyes, trying to ignore his arousal, though there was precious little hope he'd be successful. It was going to be a long, miserable trip. He'd been insane to agree to it. The Blight in Galena would spread while he dragged this unwilling woman through the wilderness, wanting her more and more with every step.

Even worse, there was no guarantee he would convince any of the Na'lara to call the web and send Gina home.

Once again, he was trapped. But it would do no good to fight it, just as it had done no good to question the path he'd been forced to take eleven winters earlier, when all he had held close to his heart had been ripped away.

He pressed his fingers to his forehead. He had vowed never to return to the Baha'Na. Yet here he was, in the wilderness, speaking the language and offering the prayers of the life he had left behind. An old wound bled, one Derrin had thought long healed.

He felt the pain as if it were new.

*****

Gina waited until Derrin's breathing slowed, then deepened. When she was sure he was asleep, she eased out of the lean-to. If her kidnapper thought he'd scared her into abandoning her escape plans, he was sorely mistaken.

Night was falling fast, but it was not yet too dark to navigate in the forest. If she wanted to cover a good chunk of distance before morning, she'd better make use of every available scrap of twilight. She pulled a branch from the fire and brandished its glowing tip. It would have to serve as flashlight *and* weapon.

She found the path by the stream and set out in the direction of the water's flow. She hoped the nearest town wasn't too far.

If there was one.

You are no longer in your world.

Gina tried to squelch the thought, but found it just wouldn't die. Her footsteps slowed. Things were a little too weird. Derrin's speech, for one. If he talked some unknown foreign language, why could she understand it? She'd thought it was the drug, but now…

The trees were another problem.

Oh, they had looked normal enough at first glance, but after a whole day of hiking, she'd begun to notice the color of the foliage looked a bit off. The leaves were a little too blue, and their shape was odd. Too square.

The sky, on the other hand, seemed a little too purple, and the sun a little too white.

And let's not forget the bugs.

Derrin had called them *ghilla*. The tiny fireflies rose in a glittering, multi-colored cloud whenever their resting place was disturbed. Enchanting, really, if Gina had been in the mood for enchantment. They were like no insects she had ever seen.

She had a nasty feeling that wasn't a good thing.

Had she traveled to another dimension? Was the city with the pyramid a real place?

No. It was too preposterous a theory. And yet…

"Just where is it you imagine you're going this time?"

Gina spun about, heart pounding. Derrin loomed over her, only about three feet away, yet she hadn't heard even a whisper of his approach.

How the hell did he *do* that?

He stalked closer. "Answer me, Gina. Where do you think you're escaping to?"

"A town. Help."

His answering laugh was harsh. "If you found such a place, who would you ask for help?"

"The police, for starters. I bet you have a record a mile long."

"Police?" She could hear genuine puzzlement in his voice. "Record? I know not what these words signify in your world, but I assure you, they don't exist in mine."

Gina's stomach churned. "You don't really expect me to believe I'm in another world."

"Yes," he said. "I do." He shifted again, drawing even closer.

"Stop there," Gina said. She lifted her stick. The glowing tip had faded to ash.

"Listen to me, Gina. You were brought to this world by a high wizard named Balek. He's a very powerful man, but for all his power, he is ever seeking more. He sought to use your mind in that quest.

"I took you from him. No doubt he's now searching for both of us. If you are so sure of your own powers, then by all means, seek him out. Though I'm unsure how you can hope to battle Balek without your crystal."

"My crystal? Do you mean the rose quartz from my costume?"

Derrin didn't answer. Gina would have pressed him further, but at that moment a bloodcurdling shriek pierced the stygian gloom. Gina froze. Not a human call. An animal. And it was much, much too close.

Suddenly, escaping Derrin didn't seem like such a great idea.

"What was that?" she whispered, instinctively drawing closer to him.

"A *tarma* hunts nearby." Before Gina could protest, Derrin grasped her icy hand with his own large, warm one. "Come. We must get back to the fire."

A second otherworldly shriek rattled the night. Gina wanted to run, but Derrin held her to a slow, silent pace as they made their way back to camp. Once there, he built up the fire to a roaring blaze and settled into his side of the shelter.

"The beast won't approach the flames," he said.

A small comfort, at best.

Gina wedged herself into her corner of the lean-to as the tarma gave a third cry.

* * * * *

Ariek passed his gaze over the single, glittering crystal fragment suspended in the glass vial. His thoughts dropped away, leaving the landscape of his mind unblemished, like sand after a wash of the tide. The precise pattern of the crystal seed leaped into the void, filling his consciousness.

He touched the stone with his mind and circled, searching the surrounding liquid for the elements of the crystal's form. One by one, he drew the grains to the seed's surface and dropped them into place. The crystal grew.

An image appeared in his mind, unbidden, seeping through a crack in his awareness before he had a chance to stop it. A woman with red curls and honey skin, her soft green eyes flecked with gold. The seed trembled. Ariek gripped the edge of the worktable and struggled to maintain the concentration he had so carefully assembled. One grain refused to take its place in the crystal lattice.

Another grain defected, then a stream of particles broke away, skewing the pattern. He muttered an oath. With a wrenching effort, he pushed Danat's image from his mind and tried to sharpen his focus on the crystal.

Before a heartbeat had passed, the leering smile and narrow eyes of Solk sprang to life behind Ariek's eyes. The high priest leaned forward. His smooth hands parted Danat's legs, his long fingers clawed at the delicate skin of her inner thigh…

The particles were spinning in confusion now, the pattern of the lattice damaged beyond repair. Ariek's fist crashed into the glass vial. It skidded across the table and hit the floor with shattering force. This time, his curses rang out against the walls of the workroom.

He pushed away from the table. His existence, once carefree and unencumbered, had become unbearable. A year ago, he'd viewed his liaison with the Bride of Lotark as a challenging game, a thrill he'd assumed would fade quickly enough. It hadn't. Somehow, his heart had followed his passion, until now all that mattered were the few stolen moments he shared with Danat in her attic room.

Leaving the broken fragments of glass where they lay, Ariek went in search of a distraction. A short time later, he entered the Stronghold's common room and scanned its perimeter. Only a few pairs of wizards were positioned at the polished gaming tables, intent on the three-dimensional grids before them.

He approached one of the empty tables and studied its grid, a multi-chambered cube. The games were popular, designed to improve the clarity of mind vital to the practice of wizardry. A match would keep his attention away from Danat until he returned to the Temple that evening.

"Game, Ariek?"

He glanced up, surprised. "Hello, Maator."

The youth took the opposite chair. "Would you do me the honor of a round?"

"You jest." An apprentice rarely challenged a full wizard.

Maator leaned back in his chair. "My work is much improved. Master Balek has submitted my name again for the Wizard's Trial." He produced three crystals. "Shall we begin?"

Ariek shrugged and poured out his own crystals on the table. Not wishing to defeat Maator too badly, he chose three of average clarity and returned the rest to the pouch.

He turned his attention to the game board. Twenty-seven chambers, suspended a short distance above the table, composed a cubic matrix. Twenty-six chambers held white crystals, a blood red stone occupied the very center of the cube. The crystals were crude, and purposely so, to increase the difficulty of the game. A small wire basket was mounted on each face of the cube, awaiting the players' own crystals.

"I'll choose first," Ariek said with an air of condescension. Maator would need the advantage.

"No. The first move is mine, as challenger." Maator dropped a crystal into position on the upper face of the cube. Ariek extended his mind toward the stone and frowned. It was a surprisingly pure specimen.

He set one of his own crystals on the cube's opposite face. Maator made his second move, with another powerful stone. Again, Ariek countered it.

His frown deepened. The quality of the youth's stones was well above that of an average apprentice, but the rules of the game required each player use crystals he alone had created. While Ariek pondered this anomaly, Maator made his third move.

Another flawless crystal. Ariek dropped his final stone into place and leaned forward, considering. It was unlikely that Maator, who had failed the Wizard's Trial a year ago, had improved his concentration to such a degree in so short a time. He thought of the webstone, the mysterious crystal Derrin claimed acted as a catalyst, producing stones of astonishing purity. A five-sided crystal…

Impossible. Ariek returned his attention to the board and signaled the beginning of the game. He sank his will into his stones, using their purity to draw power from the crude crystals set in the cube. Each cubic chamber of the matrix could belong to only one player and would be lit with a white or yellow light when taken. After claiming thirteen chambers, a player could then claim the center, winning the game.

The first chamber filled with white light, sending a jolt through the center of Ariek's concentration. Maator soon controlled a second cube, then a third. Ariek struggled to keep pace with the apprentice, trying to block the force flowing from Maator's crystals by the power he drew from his own.

A bare half-hour later, the apprentice had claimed eight points on the matrix to Ariek's seven. Ariek grimaced. Maator took quick advantage of Ariek's surge of emotion and added another cube to his tally.

Three more crystals fell to Maator, two to Ariek. Ariek struggled, commanding the last drop of power from his crystals. He succeeded in adding another chamber to his credit, then another. Maator also claimed one. The count stood at eleven yellow, thirteen white. Ariek swore softly. The game was slipping away.

The red chamber flared, causing the entire cube to flash with a white light. Ariek sat back, stunned.

Maator cleared his throat. Ariek recovered quickly and rose, extending his hand.

"Congratulations, Maator. I'm sure you'll be a full wizard at the close of the upcoming Trial."

The apprentice nodded as he clasped Ariek's hand. "Thank you." He met Ariek's gaze. "Will Derrin meet you here soon? I'd like to challenge him as well."

Ariek sent the youth a measured glance. He plucked his crystals from the game grid and returned them to his pouch. "Derrin is not in the city." A fact Maator surely knew.

"Where has he gone—to Sirth?"

"I have no idea."

"But he's your partner," the apprentice insisted. "Surely he discusses his plans with you."

"He doesn't tell me everything."

"Will he return for the Wizards' Council?"

"I don't know." Ariek's anger flared, though whether its target was Maator or Derrin, he couldn't say. He turned and strode from the room.

He returned to his chambers, snatched up his cloak and fled the confines of the Stronghold. Danat's arms awaited him. For a brief moment, he allowed the familiar yearning to sweep over him. Soon, very soon, he would lose himself in her heat.

Across the High Plaza, twilight silhouetted the gaudy façade of Lotark's Temple much as the shadows of the Lower City hid the painted faces of whores. Ariek looked up and stopped dead. Danat's lamp should have been visible beyond the carving of the pediment just below the edge of the roof.

His gut twisted. There could be only one explanation for the light's absence. Danat had been called to the Inner Sanctuary to feed the sacred lust of some fat patrician. And Ariek, his wizard's powers notwithstanding, could do nothing to stop it.

White with a rage that stole his breath, he threw himself down a side street. He passed through the Upper Gate into the twisting alleys of the Lower City, not stopping until he reached a grimy tavern huddled along the water's edge. He slammed the door open and shoved across the crowded room to the bar, ignoring the stares of the patrons.

He slapped a coin onto the counter and barked an order. A barmaid hurried to comply. Ariek snatched the bottle from her hand and spun on his heel. A cacophony of gasps and mutterings burst aloud as the door banged shut behind him.

He tore out the cheap cork and downed a huge swallow of the bitter spirits before he reached the end of the alley. He turned, his steps slowing as he waded through garbage and filth. He had no destination.

He wanted only to forget.

Forget that the woman he loved lay under the weight of a man who had paid well for her pleasures while her lover cowered in the shadows.

Chapter Five

The song began as a faint breath.

Balek cocked his head. The strains pulsed again, louder. The flush of triumph heated his skin, as if having heard this particular melody was an incredible feat, worthy of praise. And indeed it was. The song existed only in the webstone, the perfect crystal he had created.

His attention faltered. The music, like a jilted lover, withdrew. He hastened after it, pleading.

He could not bear to contemplate its end.

* * * * *

"That's it. I can't go any farther." Gina lowered herself to the ground and pressed her back against a tree trunk.

Derrin, several strides ahead on the trail, turned. "What do you mean?" A flash in his eyes underlined his sharp tone.

Gina couldn't summon enough energy to care. "Look, you may be used to this kind of thing, but I'm not. I can't take another step." A day and a half of hiking in this God-forsaken wilderness and she'd had it. She rubbed the back of her neck. She'd barely slept the night before, unnerved by the tarma's shrieks and by the man sleeping beside her. At dawn, she'd crawled out of the lean-to cramped and dirty, insects crawling in her clothes and hair.

Derrin came back down the trail. He stood with one hand braced against the tree and glared down at her. Since her escape attempts, his mood had deteriorated.

Well, guess what? So had hers.

She scowled at him. "I'm not going anywhere."

For a moment she thought he would argue, then he straightened and shrugged. "It makes no difference. We'll stay here."

He set about preparing the campsite. She watched him move, all easy strength and masculine grace. Arousal flickered low in her belly, but she quenched the spark before it caught and blazed. She would not allow herself to be attracted to her captor.

Derrin finished starting the fire. As he rose, he sent her a pointed look. "I'm going to fish. This time, don't let the fire go out."

Gina fed the flames grudgingly, wincing every time she shifted her legs. She wasn't cut out for this survivalist lifestyle. Her idea of roughing it was a hotel without room service.

A flicker of movement in some nearby brush caught her eye. Gina went still, hoping whatever animal lurked there was a gentle herbivore. A silent heartbeat passed, then the leaves stirred a second time.

A pudgy creature with blue-green fur waddled into the clearing. It had the size and shape of a rabbit, but looked more like a mouse, with rounded ears and a pointed nose. It snuffled in the dirt, looking, Gina supposed, for insects. After foraging in one area, it moved closer on its six stubby legs, swishing its bushy forked tail behind it.

Six legs. Blue-green fur. A forked tail.

No. It just couldn't be.

But Gina had a sinking feeling that it was. She was no longer on Earth. Or, if she was, it wasn't the Earth she knew.

She jumped to her feet. The furry creature let out a sound like a ringing bell and scampered back into the underbrush. If she were truly in another world, had Derrin told her the truth when he'd said a wizard summoned her here? It was as reasonable a hypothesis as any other she could come up with at the moment.

But which wizard? Derrin's rival? Or Derrin himself? Gina had no way of knowing. Derrin insisted she had been a captive of a high wizard named Balek, but she had no memory of the man. Was he even real—or had Derrin invented him in an attempt to gain her trust?

Yet even if she didn't know who had brought her to this world, she did have an idea why they had done so. It could only be because of her knowledge of crystals.

Crystals were magic in this world. It seemed just a little too coincidental that someone would bring in a crystallographer from another dimension by pure accident. Derrin had taken the rose quartz crystal from her costume. Did he fear she would use it on him? Or did the stone have something to do with how she got here? It had glowed just before the glittering strands Derrin called the web appeared in the forest outside The Wizards' Ball.

Derrin claimed he'd left the rose quartz with Zahta. Gina supposed it was true—he didn't carry a pack and God knew his leather shirt and kilt left little room to hide a stone that size. As far as she knew, the only crystal he carried was the one on a chain around his neck.

He hadn't wanted her to see that one. Why? Could it help her get home?

She needed to get a closer look at it. Perhaps if she held it in her hand, she could figure out how to trigger its power. It was worth a try.

"I'm pleased to see you didn't run this time."

Gina whipped her head around. Derrin was standing nearly on top of her, holding three fish strung on a piece of vine. Again, she hadn't heard him approach. The man moved with the stealth of a cat.

A large, sleek cat, with gray eyes that looked into her soul. A hot flush crept to her cheeks. If this was really another world, complete with magic and telepathy, then the mental orgasm Derrin had forced on her had been real, not a drug-induced hallucination.

He'd been inside her mind, had touched emotions Gina rarely acknowledged to herself, let alone anyone else. The union had been more intimate, more erotic than physical sex. Almost in spite of herself, she met his gaze. His gray eyes darkened, and she knew he remembered. She knew he wanted to touch her that way again. She saw it in the way he raked her body with his cool scrutiny, sensed it in the way he held his limbs taut when she was near him. If he decided to act on his lust, there would be little she could do to stop him. If he had stripped her naked, she would have felt less vulnerable.

He turned away with an abrupt motion and set about preparing the fish. The interminable hours of the afternoon followed. Derrin kept busy, using a round stone to shape crude spearheads from two smaller rocks. He didn't speak. The silver chain that held his crystal gleamed at his neck.

Against the sharp tap of stone on stone, Gina contemplated how to take the gem from him.

That evening, she crawled into the shelter under the deepening dusk and fell into a restless sleep. She woke a few hours later. A silvery moon, eerily similar to the one she was used to seeing at home, hung above the treetops, sharpening the shadows.

A night creature howled. Gina's chest tightened. Beside her, Derrin's breath came deep and slow. She rolled over, stretching her fingers toward him, touching the silver chain. He didn't stir.

Emboldened, she slipped one finger under the links. She tugged it up, gently, gently…

Derrin's hand closed on her wrist even before his eyes opened. A sound like a low growl vibrated in his throat. He jerked her arm, pulling Gina atop him. She dropped the chain.

His grip tightened. She tried to pull away, but he held her fast, the heat of his body burning through the fabric of her dress. His cock hardened, prodding her stomach. She stilled, trying to ignore her racing heart.

After one long, tense moment, Derrin took a deep breath and shoved her off him. He jumped to his feet and strode into the darkness.

Gina stared after him. Was he leaving her? A fierce ache rose in her throat. She swallowed hard. She wanted to escape him, but not before she found a way home. Tears burned her eyes as she built up the fire to a roaring blaze and prayed the shrieking tarma was hunting elsewhere tonight.

Derrin returned at dawn. Gina regarded him with a curious mixture of dread and relief. His expression was no longer angry, but guarded. Almost, she thought illogically, as if he had something to fear from her.

He dropped to one knee and touched her cheek with the tip of his finger. "You've been crying."

"I wasn't sure if you were coming back."

Derrin's eyes clouded before he looked away. "I didn't go far. I'd never leave you alone in the wilderness. I'm sorry you believe me capable of it."

He picked up her hand and rubbed his thumb over the bruise his touch had left on her wrist. "I hurt you. I was angry, but at myself more than at you. I don't blame you for hating me after…after all you've been through." He drew a deep breath and met her gaze. "But I assure you, compared to what High Wizard Balek intends for you, the Na'tahar we shared was nothing."

Gina shuddered. "This really is another world, isn't it?"

"Yes. I promise you, I will return you to your home."

"But why was I called here? Was it really this Balek's doing? Why does he want me?"

"I don't know."

"You can't expect me to believe that."

He sighed. "It might be more accurate to say I'm not sure why Balek summoned you."

"He, or—" she gave him a pointed look "—whoever brought me here must have had a reason."

His expression hardened. "I assure you, Balek has his reasons. He's a wizard of considerable prominence—a member of the Upper House. Recently, he ascended to the High Council, the governing body of the Hierarchy of Wizards."

Gina pressed on. If she was in another world, she needed to gather as much information as possible. "Are you a member of this Upper House, too?"

He gave a short laugh. "No, I belong to the Lower House, a much larger group, I assure you. There are many apprentices as well. Each must have a wizard of the Upper House as mentor."

"And these wizards use crystals."

His gaze narrowed. "Surely the wizards in your world do the same."

She tried another tack. "Are all the crystals in your world magic?"

He hesitated, as if deciding whether to answer. Finally, he said, "No. Only those formed by a wizard's mind. A wizard's skill determines the purity of the stone. The more perfect the specimen, the greater its power."

Gina blinked her surprise. "You can form a crystal with your mind?"

"Yes."

"With a thought?"

"With sustained concentration over a long period of time. Do you not create crystals this way in your world?"

"Hardly," Gina replied. Then, before he could ask more, she said, "Your Hierarchy must be a formidable force."

"It is. The Congress of Lords is hard put at times to contain it. But the Temple of Lotark is powerful as well."

"Lotark?"

"A god," Derrin said. "A hard and unforgiving one. His priests control the Lower City with threats of damnation."

He picked up one of the spears he'd made with the stones he'd fashioned the day before. "Solk, High Priest and Heir of Lotark, wields vast influence. But Lord Forlik, leader of the Congress, is skillful at playing the Hierarchy against the Temple, thereby preserving his own power."

He jabbed the blunt end of the weapon into the fire, releasing a shower of sparks. "Even so, Balek gained powerful allies among the Lords last year when he created a new crystal, one that protects its bearer from the effects of the Madness."

"The Madness?"

"A malady that destroys the mind. There's no cure, but if Balek's crystal is worn, the effect of the disease diminishes. The Lords have purchased piles of the stones. Now the illness plagues only the poor."

"Why? Because they can't afford the antidote?"

"Yes. And even if they had the coin, the lower classes are not permitted the use of wizardry. But it hardly matters, because Balek's remedy is a sham, meant to cover the truth. The epidemic is Balek's doing. He's caused the land to sicken, too. The weather swings from hot to cold with dizzying speed. The forests of Galena wither in the grip of a virulent Blight." He met her gaze, his gray eyes troubled. "The plagues are connected to the rift in the web. The rift you passed through."

"I don't understand."

"Balek has created a crystal he call the webstone. It's the stone he tried to link your mind to. With it, he opens the web that binds the edge of the world. Its structure is incredible. Five faces, each a perfect pentagram."

Gina snorted. "A five-sided crystal, with five pentagonal faces? That's not possible."

Derrin gave her an assessing look. "Why do you say that?"

"This may be another world, but I haven't noticed that the laws of geometry have changed. The angles of a pentagon don't complement each other. The object you described couldn't exist, especially not in crystal form. Crystals never form with five sides."

"True enough," Derrin said slowly. "But the webstone does exist." He paused. "I've given you the information you seek. Now you must answer some questions of my own. What powers do you have? Do you know how Balek planned to use them?"

Gina returned his gaze steadily. She didn't know what use her knowledge of crystals was to Balek, or to Derrin for that matter. Would it endanger her life to tell him of her profession?

"I work with crystals in my world," she admitted finally. "I grow crystallized proteins."

He nodded. "You are a sorceress."

"No! There is no magic in my world. I'm a scientist."

"No magic?" Derrin was clearly taken aback by this pronouncement. "What use do you have for crystals, then?"

"More uses than I can count. The ones I grow are used to develop new medicines. But I don't grow them with my mind," she added quickly. "I just set up the conditions so they can grow naturally."

Derrin was silent for a moment. "Interesting," he said at last. "Perhaps Balek believes your knowledge of crystals will help him control the power of the webstone. Each time he uses the foul gem, the strands of the web weaken, causing a temperature shift. A surge of Blight and Madness follows. But even with your knowledge, Balek couldn't contain the web, not without—" He caught himself, then fell silent.

"Without what?"

He stared into the gathering darkness of the forest. "The web is beautiful, Gina. Beautiful and terrifying."

"You've seen it?"

"Yes. When you appeared in the forest."

"You were there?"

"Not far off, but not close enough to reach you before Maator did. A shining web of pure light and power—just as the Baha'Na stories describe it."

"The Baha'Na know of the web?"

"Yes, it's sacred to them. They say it veils the face of the Goddess."

It veils the face of the Goddess.

Tasa had told Gina a Na'lara's task was to reveal the face of the Goddess. A cold knot of suspicion formed in the pit of Gina's stomach. "Your grandmother can lift that veil and open the web, can't she?" Gina said slowly.

Surprise—or was it guilt?—flashed in Derrin's eyes. He didn't answer.

The knot in Gina's gut tightened. "What's the real reason you kidnapped me, Derrin? Because you know what? I don't believe for a minute it was to save my life and send me home."

Derrin sprang to his feet and closed the distance between them. His hand closed on her wrist with a painful grasp. "You're wrong. I'd like nothing better than to send you back across the web."

She wrenched her arm free. "You expect me to believe that? How stupid do you think I am? First you kidnap me, then you invade my mind, now you're dragging me through this wilderness looking for—"

She blinked. "That's it. The Signs. They have something to do with the web, don't they?"

He avoided her gaze. "The Signs hold power, yes, but not the kind you're thinking of. I'm not your enemy, Gina."

"From where I'm sitting, that doesn't seem likely. You know what I think? I think you need me for something." She snatched up his spear and jabbed it into the dirt at his feet. "I just haven't figured out what it is yet."

"That's not true."

"Then prove it! Send me home."

"I will, as soon as I'm able."

"As soon as you're done with me, you mean."

"No." He held out his hand. "Please, Gina, trust me."

"Is my trust that important to your plans?"

Derrin withdrew his hand, his gray eyes hardening. "Believe what you want."

He tore his spear out of the ground and stalked away.

Chapter Six

The last of the curled, brown leaves lay in the dirt, scattered by a melancholy wind. Danat's gaze climbed the furrowed trunk of the ancient Tree of Lotark, standing with tired grace in the center of the Temple Court. Overhead, its fungus-mottled branches hung like the arms of an old woman. Brittle claws scratched at low clouds, joints creaking.

Far to her left, movement flashed in an upper window of the House of the Servants. An acolyte was watching her, half hidden in the shadows beyond the glass. With measured grace, Danat moved across the courtyard to the door that led to her privacy, her eyes cast carefully downward.

Once alone in her attic room, she peered through the screen into the plaza. The Stronghold jutted into the gray sky, a dark slash of uncompromising severity. The threat of thunder hung above it, but Danat would welcome the storm when it rolled over her roof. It would remind her of Loetahl, of lying on her bed of woven straw while Tarrot, the Rain God, drummed overhead.

Loetahl. Mountains and grasslands. Long sandy beaches where the wild horses ran unfettered and great leaping schools of fish rose from the clear waters. Her life there had been uneventful, lived in rhythm with the sea and the rains, until the day a Galenan schooner appeared on the horizon.

The king showed the voyagers every hospitality. In return, the tall strangers gave him a handful of magic stones. With a thought, the person who held those stones could obtain light, heat and healing.

Enthralled, the king offered horses, sugar and silk in trade, but the Galenan envoy had not been satisfied with those. Galena was in need of strong workers. Before long, the sons and daughters of Loetahl occupied the cargo holds of the Galenan schooners.

Danat buried her face in her hands. A market of misery thrived in Galena. Her father had led a protest before his king, but His Majesty had turned a deaf ear. Or perhaps not so deaf, for raiders had stormed her family's farm within the week, while the king retained Danat's father at court.

Danat and her mother were asleep in their one-room house when they heard the Galenans' approach. Some instinct told them to hide. They had barely concealed themselves when the door crashed against the wall.

Two men tramped in, shouting and laughing, intoxicated by something much more powerful than wine. The first was burly and unwashed, the second stood a head taller. His piercing gaze scanned the room, his thin lips twisting.

Danat crouched, frozen with fear, watching through the slats of a wooden trunk. The boots of one drew closer and she heard his hand on the handle of the trunk's lid. She squeezed her eyes shut.

A shout came, then a low whistle. Danat opened her eyes. The lid of the trunk hadn't moved. Peering through the slats, she saw what drew the raider's attention away from her hiding place. Her mother had stepped from behind the dressing screen.

The men circled the frightened woman, then one reached out and ripped the front of her nightdress, exposing her breasts. Danat wanted to close her eyes, but found she couldn't. She watched, numb, as the pair took turns satisfying themselves on her mother's body. When they'd finished, one of them kicked the senseless woman in the head and laughed. Danat's mother didn't move again.

Danat didn't realize she'd cried aloud until the lid of the trunk swung open.

The burly man dragged her out, muttering in his alien, guttural tongue. Danat shook, mute with terror. He cupped her breast with one dirty hand.

The tall man made a sharp sound of disapproval and a heated discussion ensued. Finally, the burly man released her. His companion produced a length of rope. He tied Danat's wrists and jerked her away from the house while his companion scattered hot coals from the fire over the floor.

Danat's later memories were vivid snatches of fear. The greasy fingers of a trader as he probed to verify her virginity, the endless ride in the dark, fetid hold of a ship, and finally, standing naked before a tall, gaunt man robed in white. At Solk's nod, an acolyte stepped forward and counted coins into the trader's purse. The mark of the One God was burned into her forehead that evening.

The Heir of Lotark consecrated his Bride on the altar of the Inner Sanctuary. Danat had been numbed by the lust of the raiders and the greed of the slave traders, but the righteous piety of the high priest humiliated her beyond anything she'd endured. Solk believed he fulfilled the will of his god as he raped her.

During the first weeks of her captivity, Danat's heart bled with anguish. Then, gradually, a shield of stone formed and it mattered little when men touched her, and even less when she drank the potion that ensured she would not conceive a worshipper's child.

She forgot what it meant to be human, until Ariek forced her to remember.

He came to the Inner Sanctuary in late summer, wearing the Visage of Lotark. The acolytes took her robes and withdrew. Danat waited, but the worshipper made no move to touch her. Instead, the man removed his mask—a forbidden act. He was young and handsome, with kind blue eyes and hair the color of the sun-washed beaches of her homeland.

He unclasped his cloak and offered it to her. "Take it," he said, looking everywhere but at her. "I don't wish to, uh, worship."

Danat wrapped the cloak about her shoulders and frowned. If this man hadn't come to worship, why was he here?

"I hadn't dreamed the new Bride of Lotark was so young, or so beautiful."

Her bewilderment increased. True Believers saw her in the main worship hall each Lotark's Day. Surely this man had been among them. She kept silent, her gaze fixed on the gilded floor.

"Please," the stranger insisted. "My name is Ariek. What are you called?"

She looked up and scanned his face. When he smiled, her heart stirred in its stone tomb. She had learned enough of his language to answer him. "In Loetahl, I was called Danat."

"Danat," the man repeated, not taking his gaze from her face. "It's unusual, but a beautiful name."

Danat's defenses cracked. Her name! When had she last heard it? Her mother had spoken it, just before…

The stone encasing her heart shattered. She sat down on the edge of the altar, hot tears streaming down her face.

Ariek knelt beside her. "I'm sorry. I didn't mean to offend you."

His concern caused her sobs to come faster. Through her tears, she caught a glimpse of his bewildered expression. He sat next to her on the altar and waited, frowning.

When Danat thought she could bear the kindness in his eyes, she raised her head and forced a smile. "You haven't offended me, Ariek," she said. "Just the opposite! I haven't heard my name spoken since I was taken from my home in Loetahl. I'd forgotten what it meant to have one." She studied him more closely. "Why are you here, if not to worship? You must know it is forbidden to speak to me."

Ariek shrugged. "Yes, they told me that, but the rules of the Temple are of no matter to me. I'm here to please my father—he has great faith in rituals such as this, though I doubt he believes in Lotark himself. He insisted I come for good luck."

"You have need of luck?"

He chuckled. "I hope not. You see, I'm apprenticed to a wizard of the Hierarchy. If the High Priest knew that, he would waste no time in throwing me out! As it is, I'm to begin the Wizard's Trial at dawn. If I'm successful, I'll be a wizard of the Lower House."

"A wizard? One who makes the magic stones?"

He nodded.

"I never thought I would meet such a man."

"You haven't, yet. I'm only an apprentice until I pass the Trial."

"Oh, but you will pass it."

"I hope so. It's not an easy task." He grinned. "When it's over, I'll come back and tell you about it. That is, if you want me to."

Danat's heart sank. "How can you? A worshipper may enter the Inner Sanctuary just once in a year."

Ariek snorted. "I won't come *here* again. Is there another place I can meet you?"

She described her attic room. "But how…"

"Don't worry about that—I'll be there. Put a light behind the screen, facing the plaza, when you want me to come."

A bell sounded. Danat's head snapped up. "Put on the mask! Solk is coming." She slipped his cloak from her shoulders and stretched out on the altar. Ariek picked up the mask and strode to the door.

A few days later, Danat lit the signal behind the screen, though she dared not hope Ariek would remember his promise. Even if he did, she thought, how would he be able to enter the locked doors and pass the priests? Four nights later, she gave up what small hope she'd allowed herself. Sighing, she reached up to extinguish the lamp.

A shadow fell across her hand. She turned and found Ariek standing before her, dressed in black, with his cloak thrown across his shoulders. She gaped in amazement. "How have you come to be here? Did you come from the air itself?"

Ariek threw back his head and laughed. "Nothing that exotic. I simply used one crystal to shadow my movements and another to unlock the doors. It wasn't too difficult."

She smiled. "You were successful at the Wizard's Trial, then?"

"Yes. You brought me luck." He remained with her for several hours, describing the stages of the Trial and how he'd mastered each of them.

Danat pushed the memory of Ariek's first visits from her mind and peered once more through the carvings of the Temple pediment. The deserted plaza lay in darkness. He wasn't coming—he would know of the worshipper she served the night before. He'd begun to stay away on the nights following those meetings—at precisely the time she needed his love most. Soon he would not come at all.

That was as it should be. Someday Ariek would want a wife and a family, but there would be no future with the Bride of the One God. She was the property of the temple, and was expected to produce Solk's child. The next Heir of Lotark.

But Danat wasn't sure she could bear a life without Ariek. Every day it grew more difficult to suffer the touch of other men. With Ariek gone, she wouldn't be able to endure at all.

She doused the lamp and huddled on her pallet. Moonlight dipped low on the sloping ceiling before a restless sleep claimed her.

A gentle hand touched her shoulder, rousing her. "Danat? Are you awake? I saw the light was out, but I couldn't stay away."

"Oh, Ariek!"

She threw her arms around his neck. He pressed her into the blankets and covered her mouth with his own. She clung to his warmth, encouraged the hands that swept over her body in hungry possession.

His fingers stroked between her thighs, finding the nub of pleasure hidden in her folds. At the same time, Danat struggled with the ties on her nightdress. When the garment finally fell open, Ariek nuzzled the material aside and drew her nipple into his mouth.

He pleasured her with his tongue, laving and suckling until she thought she would go mad with need for him. She arched into him with a cry, pressing his head to her breast as he drew on her with sweet, aching tugs. Each sent a burst of warmth to her womb, made her aware of how empty she was without him.

Ariek left one breast and kissed his way to the other as he slipped first one finger, then two inside her wet passage. She rocked her hips forward and back. His fingers felt so incredibly good, but she wanted so much more. Needed so much more. She longed for him to be a part of her, to chase away her dark memories.

His thumb teased her nub, causing a moan to tear from her lips. "Oh, Ariek. How I love you."

"As I love you."

His hand withdrew. Danat lay trembling, watching as he undid the laces on his breeches, freeing his sex. He stripped the garment from his body and knelt beside her. She clasped his shoulders and drew him down to her, lifting her hips in invitation.

He groaned as he entered her. For a moment, he held himself still. She reveled in the feel of him inside her, the solid strength of his body, the sound of his quick breathing, the sea-washed scent of his hair. He reminded her of the ocean of her homeland, ever restless, yet ever true.

"Ah, Danat," he whispered.

He began to move inside her, slowly, reverently. Each stroke erased a small bit of the horror of what she had endured in Lotark's sanctuary. In Ariek's arms she was no longer a slave. She felt treasured, whole. Happy.

His slow loving drew her into the night. She clung to him, moving with his rhythm, yielding her body to his love. His shaft hardened inside her, driving her higher into a sparkling bliss. Her peak burst upon her. At the same moment Ariek groaned, gripping her buttocks as his seed spurted deep inside her.

He held her for a long time afterward, not speaking. Their breathing and heartbeats merged. Fierce, futile hope filled Danat's heart, indescribably precious because she knew it would vanish with the morning's first light.

* * * * *

"Here, try it."

Gina examined the fuzzy red stalk Derrin placed in her hand. It hardly looked edible.

He picked a second one and stripped off the speckled leaves growing in clusters along its spine. "The stems are good," he told her, taking a bite, "but the leaves are poison."

"Poison?" Gina eyed the plant with even less enthusiasm than before. "How can it be edible *and* poisonous?"

He shrugged. "It's often the case. I know of a vine that bears both red and black berries. Fruits of one color are powerful medicine, but the others cause a quick death." He nodded toward the stalk. "Go ahead, try it."

Gina ventured a nibble. A cool tang burst on her tongue. Not bad. In fact, it was much better than her last meal, which had been one of the six-legged furry blue-green creatures, skinned, gutted and grilled. *Harta,* Derrin had called them. When he'd returned to camp after their argument the day before, he'd been carrying two of the things. Apparently, he'd killed the fast-moving creatures with the crude-looking spear he'd made, a feat Gina couldn't quite wrap her mind around.

He was a dangerous man. She'd do well to keep that in mind.

By unspoken agreement, they'd settled into an uneasy truce. Derrin was polite, but spoke little, pushing through the forest at a quick pace. Gina trudged after him, thighs burning. Now that she'd accepted the fact she was in another world, she had no desire to be left behind. Her wizard companion was the only link to the web that led to her home.

Her foot caught a root, causing her to stumble. By some miracle, she managed not to fall.

Derrin spun around. "Are you all right?"

"Fine," she muttered.

He shook his head and started back up the trail. Gina scowled at his back. The man barely stirred the foliage. He was as natural in the forest as a wild creature. She, on the other hand, might have been a bulldozer.

He quickened his pace again.

"Wait up!" she called, not bothering to hide her exasperation. "I'm not used to all this exercise in my world."

He slowed his steps. "Is your world very different?"

"I suppose there are places like this, but I've never been to any of them." She leaned against a tree and caught her breath. "I tend to stay inside."

Derrin chuckled, a low, rich sound that caught Gina by surprise. "As I do, in Galena." His expression turned thoughtful. "You've been away from your world for many days. Surely there are those who are worried about you."

She looked away. "Not too many."

"You have no family?"

"My father passed away almost two years ago." The words were still hard to say. "My mother died when I was small."

"Are you not joined with a man?"

"You mean married? No, not any more."

"I'm sorry."

"Don't be. I wasn't." She fiddled with the sleeve of her dress. "I met Michael right after Dad died. He was much older than me, and seemed so much wiser. I needed someone to belong to, I guess, and he was perfect. At least before the wedding, that is."

Derrin didn't answer, and Gina found herself caught by a need to explain. "I couldn't be myself living with Michael. No matter what I did, he never seemed happy. At first I tried harder to please him, but when that didn't work, I just gave up. It was either that or lose myself for good."

"You left him?"

"I kicked him out after I found him in bed with another woman." She laughed, but the memory stung. "I wasn't good at being married. I'm not anxious to try it again."

Derrin shrugged. "You joined with the wrong man, for the wrong reason."

His concise assessment gave Gina a peculiar sort of comfort. "What about you?" she asked, suddenly curious. "Do you have a wife and a bunch of little wizards back in the city?"

He shot her a startled look. "No."

"Why not? Aren't wizards allowed to marry?"

"Yes, many are joined. As for me…" He shook his head. "A family requires time. My work commands all of my attention." He frowned. "Are you ready to go?"

She nodded. They continued along the trail, Gina once again falling behind. She ignored the stabbing pain in her calves and hurried to catch up. Derrin turned to watch her.

A snake-like creature appeared on the trail in a flash of black and red. With one smooth motion it reared and pivoted its head in Gina's direction. A hiss escaped from between two rows of needle-sharp teeth.

Gina froze. The animal's head, as large as her fist, hung in the air an arm's length away. Two lethal-looking spikes protruded from a bony ridge above its eyes. The creature had short, stubby forearms embellished by long, curved claws, but no rear legs, as far as she could see. A rough diamond pattern of scales decorated its back, but its belly was smooth and yellow. A thin black tongue flicked in and out of its mouth. Its head bobbed back and forth with a mesmerizing rhythm.

"Gina." Derrin's voice was barely audible. "Don't move."

In a blur of movement, he scooped up a loose rock and flung it at the creature, striking it squarely on the back of the head. The thing dropped to the ground. Before Gina could react, Derrin sprang over it and spun her off the trail. Her knees buckled.

She clutched at Derrin's shoulders for balance. He lost his footing and they fell. He landed on top of her, the weight of his body pressing her into the dirt. They lay tangled together, not moving, for several seconds.

Derrin propped himself on his elbows and looked down at her. "Are you all right?"

The sensation of his body against hers eclipsed the memory of the serpent's near-attack. His breath tickled her face. His scent surrounded her, an intoxicating mixture of warm earth and warm male. Long legs moved against her thighs. His torso, alive and solid and reassuring, shielded her body. Instinctively, she grasped his upper arms. Sinew and muscle flexed under her fingertips.

Then his cock went hard against her stomach.

She gave a cry and shoved against his shoulders. He slid her an amused glance and pushed himself off her.

Gina scooted back, heart pounding. "What *was* that thing?"

The words had no sooner left her lips than she realized Derrin might wonder exactly which "thing" she was referring to. Heat flooded her cheeks.

To Derrin's credit, he ignored the double-entendre, though when she dared a peek at him, his gray eyes were dancing.

"It was a *kana,*" he told her. "They're very rare."

"Thank God for that. Is it dead?"

"No, just stunned. See—it's gone now."

Gina jumped to her feet and eyed the ground. "Was it poisonous?"

He hesitated, then nodded. "If you had moved, it would have killed you."

Gina's knees weakened. Derrin was beside her in a heartbeat, his hand steady on her arm.

"I don't belong here," she whispered. "Take me back to the city with the pyramid. That's where the web opened. Maybe there's a…a portal or something."

"No. The rift in the web was caused by Balek."

"Then let's go get his crystal and open it ourselves."

Derrin was silent for a time, as if weighing her words. Finally, he sighed. "I can't do that. At least not yet. I promised Zahta I would guide you to the Signs."

"I don't care about the Signs! You claim you want to help me get home, but you don't seem to be working too hard at it. This forest gives me the creeps. I need to get out of here."

"Gina, I know this is difficult for you. You're not of the Baha'Na. How can I explain? The People don't fear the wilderness—they're a part of it. So much so that in Galena the clans exist only in faerie legends." He touched her arm. "I know you don't trust me, but at least let me teach you to survive here."

"I haven't much choice, do I?"

"Oh, there's always a choice," he replied, half to himself. "There's even a choice in not choosing."

Gina huffed in annoyance. "That sounds like something your grandmother would say."

One corner of Derrin's mouth twitched. "Indeed. It was she who told me that, a long time ago."

Chapter Seven

"*Ma hayta*. Welcome. The face of the Goddess shines on your coming." A slim, wide-eyed girl stopped on the path and swept her arm overhead, palm flat.

Derrin returned the gesture. "She shines on you also."

The girl smiled and glided past. Gina watched her slip into the brush, then turned her attention to the collection of huts from which the girl had emerged.

The stone dwellings of the Rock Clan crowded the base of a sheer cliff, their lines merging with the mountain, softening its descent. A large common area claimed the center of the village. There, a handful of elderly women sat in a circle, talking among themselves as they transformed a flowing animal skin into clothing. One crone looked up from her task and gave the newcomers a smile of welcome.

Derrin nodded to the women, bringing his palm to his forehead and dipping his chin in a gesture of respect.

"Are they always so casual with strangers?" Gina whispered.

"I'm not exactly a stranger here, and you don't look so different from a Baha'Na woman."

"But it must be years since they last saw you. Why aren't they surprised?"

He shrugged. "They knew we were coming."

"They knew? How could they—"

"Derrin." A woman, no longer young, stood before the doorway of the nearest hut, her arms folded over an ample bosom. Her black braids framed a serious expression that was belied by a subtle sparkle in her eyes. She wore a headdress set with a stone talisman identical to the one Derrin's grandmother had worn, carved with the same symbol of linked rings and spear.

"Derrin and Gina. Welcome." Her arm traced the gesture of greeting.

Gina gaped at her. "How do you know my name?"

"I am Celia, Na'lara to my clan," the woman replied, as if that were answer enough. She turned and entered one of the huts.

Frowning, Gina turned to Derrin. "How—"

"She knows your name because Zahta knows it."

"What's that supposed to mean?"

"The minds of the Na'lara are linked by the wilderness."

"Linked? Linked how?"

"It's difficult to explain." He motioned toward the hut. "Go on. She's waiting."

Gina's frown deepened, but she drew the hide door aside and stepped under the stone lintel. Derrin didn't follow.

Inside, a ring of tapered columns supported a flat roof, conjuring the image of a forest of stone. The center of the dwelling was open to the sky, allowing a stream of daylight to fall on the coals of a dying fire. Celia stood to one side of the firepit. Beyond her, a young woman sat cross-legged, nursing a small child. Her long braids swung as she rocked. A lullaby floated in the air.

Celia lowered herself onto a straw mat near the firepit and motioned for Gina to join her. Gina sat down a short distance away, tucking her legs beneath her.

The Na'lara gave her a searching glance. The light touch of her mind followed.

Gina drew back sharply.

Celia's eyebrows shot up and a small smile formed at the corners of her mouth. "You doubt the power of the Goddess, Gina. And you do not trust me."

"Trust has nothing to do with it. I just don't understand what your Goddess has to do with me getting back to my world."

"The truth of the Goddess, once seen, vanishes. Her spirit will guide you home."

Gina hid her annoyance. This woman made less sense than Derrin's grandmother had.

"Open your heart to her, my child," Celia said. She rose and left the hut.

Gina watched her go, frustration rising. She sensed this Na'lara would be no more help to her than Zahta had been, but she knew

Derrin wouldn't leave the village until Gina had seen the Rock Clan's Sign, whatever that might be. Derrin had refused to tell her.

Derrin. She hadn't grown a bit more accustomed to traveling with the wizard in the last two days. He had the power to unsettle her. Every time she looked at him she remembered what it felt like having him inside her mind. Remembered the terrifying helplessness and the stunning ecstasy. Every so often she would turn and find his gray eyes watching her.

Thankfully, though Derrin was brooding and terse, he seemed to be under tight control. He kept the beast she knew lived inside him firmly leashed.

Except for those rare moments when his calm façade cracked and his raw, turbulent emotions brushed against her mind.

She knew he wanted her. He wanted to plunge into her mind again, as he had during the Na'tahar. He wanted her body as well, and that realization terrified her. Worse, she felt her body responding to his lust, as though it was a thing totally apart from her rational brain.

How long would he keep his distance? She sensed it wouldn't be forever. Sooner or later that iron control would snap completely. What she would do then, she had no idea.

She let out a long breath. With any luck, she would be home before that happened. She closed her eyes and tried to put thoughts of Derrin out of her mind. When she opened them again, she noticed the young mother had fallen asleep on a pile of furs nearby, one arm flung over her eyes. Her chubby toddler nestled at her side.

Gina wondered why Derrin insisted they travel the path Zahta had set. He didn't strike her as a man who took orders easily. No doubt he would have ignored his grandmother's wishes if they didn't further his own motives in some way. She suspected the answer had to do with the Na'laras' power over the web, but when she had questioned him further on the topic, he'd clammed up. Clearly, he was hiding something from her.

Gina looked up through the opening in the roof to the shadowed cliff face and wondered how far she could trust him. Did he really want to find a path to her home, as he insisted? Or was he seeking something else? Something he needed her help to find?

A hand pulled at Gina's braids. She jumped, jerking around in time to see the toddler, unsteady on his feet, fall to the ground with a hard thump. He let out a howl of outrage. His mother hurried to him, wiping the sleep from her eyes.

"I'm sorry," she said with an apologetic smile. "Torrin has disturbed you." She pulled the boy into her arms. "I am Bera, Celia's daughter."

"I'm Gina."

"I know. Derrin brought you. You seek a path to your home."

"Do you know Derrin?"

Bera nodded. "I was young when he came to the Rock Clan on his quest for manhood, but I remember him well. He did not dwell among us long."

Gina paused, reflecting. "Who else lives in this hut?"

"Great Hawk, my father, and Turtle Man, my partner. Also Black Orna, my grandfather. He is an Elder."

An orna, Gina knew, was a carrion bird similar to a vulture, but much larger. Derrin had pointed one out to her the day before.

"An Elder?" Gina asked.

"They are the oldest of our men and women. Their wisdom leads the clan."

"I thought the Na'lara led her clan."

"No. A Na'lara holds the highest honor of the clan, but she does not lead. She shows the face of the Goddess to the people."

The connection to the web, Gina thought. "She shows the face of the Goddess by lifting the veil?"

"At one time that was true," Bera replied. "But now—"

Little Torrin interrupted, climbing onto his mother's lap and squealing. Gina smiled at him. Emboldened, the boy pitched headlong into her arms. Instinctively, Gina closed her arms around him. He buried his face in her chest.

"Have you children of your own?" Bera asked.

"No." She tickled the squirming boy. He responded with a fit of giggles.

Bera brought her cupped palms to her chest. "Torrin is ever in my heart. Sometimes I think of him as a man and wonder what guardian the Goddess will send to him."

"Guardian? What's that?"

"An animal spirit. It guides a boy to manhood."

"What about the girls?"

Bera looked puzzled. "A girl has no need of a guardian. When her blood flows, she looks within. She stays all her life with her sisters in the clan of her birth. But a boy—" Bera gestured to the sky "—he seeks his manhood outside himself, and finds a home with another clan. When he reaches fifteen winters, he goes into the forest. There he awaits the animal brother who will be his lifelong helper. When it shows himself, he receives its name. A turtle came to my partner, an orna to my grandfather." She smiled at the squirming boy on Gina's lap. "I can only wonder what creature will claim Torrin."

Gina frowned, making a sudden connection. "Why doesn't Derrin use his guardian's name?"

"Derrin has no guardian. Did he not tell you? He left the Baha'Na without completing the rites of his manhood."

"Do people often leave?"

Bera shook her head. "No one leaves the Baha'Na. Who could leave the bones of their ancestors?"

"Derrin did," Gina pointed out.

"Yes, but for Derrin, it was different."

"Why—"

Celia appeared at the doorway. "Come, Bera, Gina."

Torrin wriggled free of Gina and ran to his grandmother, who scooped him into her arms. "You too, my little one. The Clan gathers."

Gina followed the women to the common area, where the tantalizing aroma of roasting meat hung in the air amid talking and laughter. Children darted about, dodging the men and women who were preparing the communal meal. Derrin was nowhere to be seen.

Gina wasn't sure if she was anxious or relieved by his absence.

Celia presented her father, Black Orna, pressing her palm to her forehead when she greeted him. Gina imitated the gesture. The lines of age cut deep in the Elder's face, but he stood erect and moved with ease. A single white braid decorated with the black and silver feathers of his namesake fell almost to his waist. His dark eyes, so like Celia's, sparkled as he clasped Gina's hand.

Bera brought a wooden plate piled with venison and drew Gina into the circle of her family. Little Torrin claimed Gina's lap as his seat.

Gina ate, not speaking much, searching in vain among the villagers for Derrin. Where had he slipped off to, and why?

The sky grew darker, the air cooler. An enormous gibbous moon peeked over the tops of the trees and washed the sky in a soft glow. The villagers gathered closer to the cooking fires, their voices dropping to a low murmur. Torrin lay warm and heavy on Gina's legs, sleeping.

Bera stroked his wispy black hair. "Grandfather, tell us how the Signs came to the People."

"Bera, I cannot count how many times I have told you that story," replied Black Orna, the corners of his eyes crinkling with amusement.

"Yet I never tire of it, and Gina has never heard it. Perhaps the story will aid her journey."

His gaze swung to Gina. "You may be right." He stood and raised his arms.

A hush fell over the gathering. Then, with a voice as solid as the mountain behind him, the Elder spoke.

"Before the wilderness, there existed only the Goddess, the Great Mother of the Baha'Na. She looked into the darkness and thought to fill it.

"She opened herself and brought forth the wilderness. Then she formed a man and set him among his animal brothers. He moved with grace, so perfect in the forest that she longed to be by his side. So she poured her spirit into the body of a mountain doe and approached him.

"The doe was the most beautiful animal the man had ever seen. He longed to possess her. He sharpened his spear, stripped himself bare and set out on the hunt.

"Fear filled the Goddess, but her love was great. She allowed herself to be hunted, fleeing before the man's pursuit for six days. She tired, and he drew closer.

"On the seventh day, the man climbed a tree and waited. When the doe passed beneath him, he dropped to her back and plunged his spear into her heart.

"Her blood flowed over his hands, into the soil. Her breath followed. As the man looked on the still form of the doe, it wavered, enfolded in a shining web of light. When the light dimmed, the man beheld the lifeless form of a woman.

"His spirit shook. He wept bitter tears, and they fell on her wound. He thought to turn his spear on himself, but before the point pierced his flesh, the woman's eyes opened.

"The man's repentance healed the Goddess. She rose and joined with the man. She lived as his partner for many winters and bore him seven daughters. When at last the man died, she gathered her children in her arms one last time, for she had chosen to follow their father's spirit beyond the veil.

"Before she left, she fashioned seven men. To each, she presented one of her daughters. For each daughter, she created a stone talisman, etched with her mark—two rings, linked, pierced by a spear at the space of their joining.

"The Goddess told the men, 'The spear pierces the rings and is caught between them. Your sons will be born of my daughters, and in death they will return to me. Your arms are stronger than your woman's, but remember this. It is only in her you will see my face. I give you the power to destroy her, but in doing so, you destroy yourself.'

"The Goddess divided her body among her daughters. She gave her blood, the Wellspring. She gave her womb and her heart, the Rock and the Fire. She gave her voice, the Wind. She gave her life and death, the Tree and the Skyeagle. To her seventh daughter she gave her greatest gift, all that remained.

"That which has no name."

Black Orna's voice fell from the stars into the dying fire. Later, as Gina lay on a pile of furs in a dwelling crowded with bodies, his words echoed inside her skull, and she wondered why her heart stirred in reply.

*****

Gina upended the vine basket and dumped a pile of herbs on a straw mat in Celia's hut. She'd spent the morning with the Na'lara, mucking along a stream bank in search of the elusive stalks. Not her idea of fun, but at least it had kept her hands busy while her mind seethed.

Derrin had left her with Celia the day before, and had yet to reappear. Gina snatched up the basket and thrust it into place on a high ledge. Where the hell was he? Had he returned to the wizards' city without telling her? If he had, what would she do?

She felt curiously bereft with him gone, a feeling she didn't want to examine too closely. All the time they'd been traveling in the forest, she'd had a sense that his mind had been hovering just beyond hers. More than once she'd been tempted to reach out with her psyche and touch him. But she'd always pulled back at the last minute.

Her gaze swung to Celia, who sat with her head bent over a crude mortar and pestle, pounding a dried root into powder. Gina had avoided questioning her about Derrin's absence, not trusting the woman to give a straight answer. Still, at this point, any information would be welcome.

She forced a note of nonchalance into her voice. "Celia, do you know where Derrin is?"

Celia didn't look up from her work. "He has joined a hunt."

"A hunt?"

"A hunting party left the village soon after you arrived. They will return when they have made a kill."

Gina blinked. Derrin had left her to go *hunting*? What the hell for? Was it some sort of macho competition thing? She almost laughed. It seemed men were the same no matter what world they lived in.

She couldn't fathom it, but Celia's words were proven true the next day when six men returned to the village. They deposited two large bucks at the edge of the village and stood back as a group of old men gathered to admire the kill.

Gina spotted Derrin talking with one of the other hunters, a young man who gestured expansively, then grinned. Derrin responded with a hoot of laughter.

Her mouth dropped open. Derrin—laughing? Impossible. He hardly ever cracked a smile. Most of the time he seemed wound tight as a spring and ready to snap.

Gina stared at him, not quite believing the transformation.

His gray eyes glinted with humor and his lips curved in an easy smile. Even the scar on his cheek seemed less angry. He looked younger, happy and very handsome.

He'd discarded his shirt. Without conscious volition, Gina's gaze dropped to his chest. Hard muscle rippled across his torso under taut skin bronzed by the sun and gleaming with a fine layer of sweat. He shifted his stance, gesturing with one arm.

Her throat went dry.

She looked lower, taking in the tapered lines of his waist and the curve of his butt under sinuous buckskin. His long, strong thighs brushed against the sweep of his kilt. When he shifted, half turning toward her, the bulge under the soft material was difficult to miss.

Gina swallowed hard. The man was gorgeous. And with that easy smile on his lips, he wasn't at all threatening. On the contrary. He was every woman's fantasy come true.

A small boy ran toward him. Derrin let out a shout. Swinging the child onto his shoulders, he launched him into the air. The boy did a flip and landed in the second man's arms briefly before jumping to the ground with a squeal.

Derrin ruffled the boy's hair and grinned his approval. Then, as if finally feeling Gina's inspection, he raised his head and met her gaze.

His smile faded and the laughter in his eyes died. She detected a slight tightening of his shoulders. He nodded a brief acknowledgement before turning away.

I'm the reason he's so grim. He's not really like that.

The realization hit Gina like a blast of icy air. Derrin had attempted to befriend her, but she'd given him nothing but distrust. Had her treatment of him bothered him so much?

She couldn't be sure of his motives. She didn't know for sure if what he'd told her about Balek was true, and she was certain he was concealing important information regarding the web. Yet now, as he squatted at the little boy's level and listened to the child's chatter, Gina found herself wanting to give him the benefit of the doubt.

She pondered her discovery for the rest of the day, while the villagers butchered the hunters' bounty and set about preparing a feast. That evening, Gina once again found herself seated next to Bera. Derrin greeted Bera's family briefly before joining the man and boy he'd been laughing with earlier.

"Black Crow is from the Water Clan, as Derrin is," said Bera, following Gina's gaze. "They were boys together. Shall I ask Black Crow and his family to join us?"

"No," Gina replied. She bent her head and concentrated on her meal.

After sunset, Celia stepped into the center of the gathering. She held a ring of wood stretched with hide in one hand, a blunt stick in the other. The voices of the villagers quieted.

The Na'lara struck the drum, calling forth a simple rhythm, a soft heartbeat that grew until it filled Gina's senses. The beat disturbed, then soothed. It flowed in throbbing currents, seeking response.

A man called, a shout more wild than human. A chorus of men's voices, then women's, answered. The song pulsed into the night sky, rising and falling, one voice, then many. The drum beat on, relentless, not fading until the last voice fell silent.

Later, Gina slept poorly, the echo of the drum still pounding in her skull. She was lying awake when Celia came to her well before dawn, torch in hand.

"Come," the Na'lara said.

Gina pulled on her boots and followed her to a narrow path above the village. The night wind stirred Gina's braids. The stars were so brilliant she thought they might drop from the sky.

Celia halted at a fissure in the cliff face. To one side, carved lines wavered in the torchlight—two rings, linked, with a spear thrust though the space of their joining.

The spear pierces the rings and is caught.

For the third time, a jolt of recognition shot up Gina's spine. She traced the lines with one finger.

"What does it mean?"

"Two rings, the worlds of flesh and spirit. Also, the worlds of man and woman. Where the two meet, life begins." Celia ducked into the portal, holding the torch before her. Gina followed.

The torchlight danced on the rock with primitive frenzy. Celia advanced at a steady pace through the twisting passage, turning so many times it seemed she walked in circles. Smoke from the torch hung heavy in the air. Gina blinked, trying to clear her vision.

The Na'lara stopped in the center of a large chamber and held the fire high, illuminating a rough dome.

"We enter the womb of the Goddess, the Sign of the Rock Clan." Her eyes were deep pools, reflecting the firelight. "Turn away from your doubt. If you must be certain, you cannot know." Bending, Celia picked something up from the floor of the cave and placed it in Gina's hand.

Gina looked down. She held one end of a long cord that stretched into the darkness. She grasped it, uncertain.

Celia's torch sputtered and died. Her footsteps faded into the black depths of the cave.

Gina's unease exploded into panic. "Celia, wait! Don't leave! How am I supposed to..."

Silence answered, complete and deadening. Gina fought the urge to scream. She stood in the absolute blackness, her breath coming in short gasps, her mind scrambling for a means of escape.

With an effort, she quelled the waves of panic. The cord must lead out of the cave. All she had to do was follow it.

The darkness brushed against her, sending a shiver over her skin as she followed the lifeline hand over hand through the dark passage. The path climbed, then dipped, then twisted so sharply Gina was sure she had turned completely around.

The walls narrowed, forcing her to squeeze through a narrow cleft. The sharp rocks clawed Gina's arm. Her breath stuck in her lungs. Thoughts ricocheted inside her skull.

The uneven path led upward, then fell in a slick drop. Gina inched downward, groping for each toe and finger hold. There was no way to tell how far she would fall if she slipped, nor how long it would be before Celia came searching.

She stumbled as she reached the bottom of the slide, flinging her arms wide and losing her grasp on the cord. Dropping to her knees, she scrabbled in the dark until her fingers retrieved the precious thread. She clung to it, fighting back tears.

She continued her journey, a steep climb up what could have been a narrow staircase. After what seemed like hours, light filtered into the passage and the faint sounds of the forest intruded on the cave's brooding silence.

An opening appeared, sharp and bright. Gina lifted one hand to her eyes and stepped into the sunrise.

She found herself on a wide ledge near the top of the cliff. The village lay far below, on the edge of its lush valley. The rising sun peeked between the slopes of the mountains beyond. She'd made it.

Exhilaration lifted her. She stretched her arms skyward as though she could touch the colors of dawn.

Celia stood nearby, a half smile tugging at the corners of her mouth.

"I thought I'd never get out."

"If you had thought that, you would still be in the cave."

Gina considered that. "I guess you're right."

Celia spread her arms wide. "You have passed through the womb and have emerged a daughter of the Goddess. *Ma hayta kolah.* We greet the sun."

Joy, sharp and clear, enveloped Gina. She may be lost in a strange world, but she was alive, and facing a new day. It was an incredible gift.

Celia returned her smile. "Come, *volah.*" *My sister.*

She pointed to a path half hidden in some scrub pines. "This way to the village is much easier than the path you traveled to get here."

They returned to Celia's hut, where Gina fell into a deep sleep on her pile of furs, oblivious to the people stirring around her.

Much later, the low murmur of voices woke her. The afternoon sun streamed through the open doorway where Celia and Derrin sat talking. She couldn't make out their words, but Derrin sounded angry. She sat up, frowning.

Derrin turned toward her, meeting her gaze with a hard expression. Gina found herself wishing for the carefree, laughing man of the day before.

She pushed aside the furs and nodded at Celia's greeting.

"You are ready for the journey to the Fire Clan," the Na'lara said.

Derrin rose. "At the rising of the sun, then."

He turned and strode away, leaving Gina to ponder his retreating form.

* * * * *

Derrin felt as though he'd stepped into a hidden snare and been hurtled him into a bittersweet past. For two clear days, he had joined his kin of the Rock Clan and lived the life that had once been his own.

He had hunted, the bow light in his hands. He had shouted the call of the chase with a voice that had long been silent. His arrows had flown true. He had given the gift of life to his kinspeople.

He had sung the prayer of thanksgiving in the light of the feast fires. Afterward, he had imagined a partner waiting for him, nestled amid the soft bodies of his children. For a moment he had forgotten he was an Outsider, a stranger without the name of a man.

But the dawn brought reality, a reluctant traveling companion, and the continuation of a fool's quest. Celia, like Zahta, had refused to call the web with the Circle empty.

So he trudged the trail leading to the Fire Clan, speaking little. Gina, behind him, seemed lost in her own thoughts. What they were, Derrin hesitated to guess. He knew she doubted him, but when he caught a rare glimpse of her dark eyes, he thought they seemed softer, hesitant.

That evening, he set up camp near a wide stream and cut a fishing spear. He was kneeling on the bank, inspecting his catch, when Gina's shadow fell over him.

"Derrin."

He heard the catch in her voice and looked up.

She fiddled with the sleeve of her dress. "There's something I want to tell you."

Bemused, he put down his knife and waited. Gina avoided his gaze. He'd never seen her so uncertain, not even when she'd been most afraid. He extended his mind slightly, enough to know she was not afraid now. Or if she was, it was not in the same way she'd been before.

"I wanted to say..." She stopped, met his gaze, then forged ahead. "You've been trying to help me and I've treated you badly. I'm sorry. I'd like us to be friends."

Derrin sat back on his heels and regarded her with open amazement. He wasn't sure what he'd expected her to say, but an apology would have been last on his list of possibilities.

Friends. Derrin would have laughed if the thought hadn't been so painful. She wanted to be friends. He wanted to toss her on the ground and ride her until she broke in a wash of bliss. He wondered what she would say if she knew.

"What made you change your mind?" he asked at last.

Gina sat down on the ground and shot him a weak smile. "I had a dream last night. I can't remember it exactly, but when I woke up, I had the strangest feeling. I knew I could trust you."

Derrin raised his brows. She'd fought him for days, not wanting to believe the reality of her crossing, even in the face of the evidence before her eyes. Now she'd decided to trust him because of a dream? He threw his head back and laughed.

A deep flush spread across Gina's cheeks. Derrin struggled to contain his mirth, but failed. This was what came from living on the edge of a sexual knife, unable to find release. He was going mad.

"I thought you wanted proof of my good intentions," he managed finally. "Do dreams pass for proof in your world?"

Gina sent him a scathing look. "Of course not. But we're not in my world, are we?"

He sobered. "No. But a dream, Gina? You're not of the Baha'Na. There must another reason."

She glanced away, hesitant again. "There is, but it seems even sillier than the dream." She looked up, her expression solemn. "I've passed through the womb of the Goddess."

"Ah."

"Have you been through the labyrinth?"

"Of course. All the Baha'Na have."

"Then you understand."

"Yes." Derrin brushed Gina's mind and for the first time, he felt no fear, no anger. Only trust.

"Can we be friends?" she asked again.

Not trusting himself to answer, Derrin leaned forward and took both her hands in his own. Even that small touch made his cock go hard.

He stifled a groan. Friends. She had no idea what she was asking.

Chapter Eight

Music flowed in sweet, endless joy. Balek listened, caught on the edge of an emotion worthy of any sacrifice. When the melody dimmed, a cry of denial burst from his lips.

He pursued the song into the abyss beyond consciousness. He had no choice. He could not risk its loss.

*****

"Race you to the stream!"

Gina took off down the slope, laughter bubbling in her throat. She darted through the brush to the water's edge, tore off her boots and plunged into the blissful, cool water. Derrin splashed in behind her.

"I won," she said, tossing him a smug smile.

His eyes glinted silver in the sun. "You had the advantage."

She shrugged.

His answering grin sent a jolt of pleasure through her body. He'd discarded his shirt on the bank. She watched as he scooped water with both hands and tilted his head back to drink. The muscles in his throat rippled with each swallow. The next handful of water sluiced over his head.

The shining cascade bathed his bare torso, sending rivulets on a path over his navel and into the knotted waistline of his kilt. Gina's gaze followed, despite her best effort to resist the temptation. She could tell he had the beginning of an impressive erection beneath his kilt. Sudden heat curled in her stomach.

Abruptly, she turned away and took a drink from the stream, wishing her attraction to Derrin could be quenched as easily as her thirst. Instead, her fascination with him had grown steadily. Since she'd given him her trust two days ago, he'd dropped his reserved façade. He smiled often, and teased her.

Gina couldn't remember ever being teased. She'd always been the straight-A serious type—not the kind of girl who usually got teased.

And since she was an only child, she hadn't had any brothers to do the job. To her dismay, Derrin's flirtation caused her stomach to clench with a distinctly sexual response. Without underwear, her thighs were wet half the time. Add that to the way his emotions brushed her mind when she least expected it, and the whole situation became just a little too intense for comfort.

She waded to the stream bank. Derrin had already stretched out on the grass. She lay down beside him, not too close, but not far, either.

They'd entered a mountain pass the day before. She blinked up at the great thrusts of stone towering overhead. Peace descended. For the first time since coming to this strange world, contentment eclipsed her fears. The wilderness, once oppressive, was now a source of constant wonder. Even her body had adapted—her legs no longer protested every mile she put behind her.

After a time, she sat up and glanced at Derrin. He lay on his back with his eyes closed. Beyond him a strip of forest crowded between the cliff and the water. Lush, beautiful and—empty. She knew there must be creatures about, because Derrin often pointed out their tracks. Yet she hadn't seen even one since they'd left the Rock Clan.

She leaned over and touched his shoulder. "Tell me something. Where are all the animals?"

He slanted her a glance through half-closed eyelids. "What do you mean? Didn't you see the *leesha* vixen near our camp this morning?"

"No."

"What about the mountain doe with twin fawns we passed?"

"You can't be serious! I didn't see anything."

He shot her an incredulous look. "What *have* you seen?"

Gina frowned. "Trees, of course, with enormous roots. Rocks. Some wildflowers and moss..."

Derrin grinned.

"What's so funny?"

He pushed himself up to a sitting position, resting one forearm across his bent knee. "The creatures of the forest won't run across your feet, Gina. How do you expect to see them if you look at nothing but the trail?"

"If I don't watch where I'm going, I'll fall on my face."

Derrin started to chuckle.

"Stop laughing at me." She picked up a pebble and tossed it at him.

He swatted it away and made an effort to keep a straight face. "To become a part of the forest, you must first be aware of it. Don't let your mind focus. Open it. Do the same with your vision, your hearing, all your senses. See and feel everything at once."

Gina sent him a doubtful look.

"Here, let me show you."

He taught her to walk in the manner of the Baha'Na, each step rolling from the outside edge of her foot to the instep, rather than heel to toe. "This way, you're aware of the ground without having to look at it. Your eyes are free to see the forest."

With a bit of practice, Gina found it easy to move in the way Derrin described. When she did, the forest came alive, flowing past in a ball of fur, a whisper of a white tail, a red flash of feathers at the edge of her vision.

They reached the top of the pass the next morning and after a short, steep descent, the land leveled to a gentle slope into the next valley. Toward late afternoon, they drank from a spring half-hidden by a dip of branches, then followed a deer trail to a grassy clearing.

"We'll spend the night here," Derrin said.

He returned to the forest to collect firewood while Gina cut branches from a copse of evergreens. She built the brush shelter on the edge of the clearing, using her stone-bladed knife for the first time. When she was finished, she stepped back to admire her handiwork.

"Not bad," Derrin commented, dumping an armload of deadwood nearby. "Are you going to light the fire, too?"

Gina sat down on the grass and shook her head. "Later."

"All right." Derrin readied the firepit, then sat and examined a number of thin, straight sticks he'd set aside. He pulled out his knife and cut notches in the wood.

"What are you doing?"

"It's the lazy way to hunt. We'll set some traps tonight and by tomorrow morning we'll have fresh meat. This clearing attracts a good number of *harta*."

"How do you know?"

"Their tracks are everywhere."

"Tracks? I didn't see any."

He pointed with one of the sticks at a slight depression in the ground. "There's a run right there. If you don't focus, you can see it."

Gina opened her vision and found Derrin's words were true. When she looked at the ground the way he'd had taught her, the tracks sprang to life. When she focused on them, they disappeared.

They set several traps, interlocking the notched sticks and bracing large, flat stones against them. A bait of leaves was skewered on a sharp point of each trigger stick. The slightest tug promised to bring a rock crashing down on the prey.

They returned to camp under the spreading dusk. Derrin prepared the firemaking tools and tinder, then reminded Gina of her offhand promise to light the fire.

She gripped the handhold in her left hand, looped the bowstring around the spindle and sawed the bow back and forth. The spindle turned in its socket, but no smoke emerged.

She stroked over and over, until the muscles in her upper arm burned. Ignoring the pain, she tightened her grip on the handhold and whipped the bow furiously.

"Not so hard! The strokes should be fast and even, not brutal."

Derrin's advice only served to annoy her. A spasm struck the muscle in her bow arm and her rhythm faltered. The spindle shot out from the string and skidded across the dirt.

Gina threw the bow after it. "You do it."

He retrieved the tools and within minutes had a lively fire burning. Gina sighed, rubbed her sore arm. Reluctantly, she turned her attention to the evening's meal—a collection of thick roots she and Derrin had dug after setting the traps.

A sudden craving for pepperoni pizza hit. Gina wrenched the thought aside and concentrated on the food at hand. Once the fire had settled into a low blaze, she poked the tubers into the hot coals with a forked stick. They roasted and burst, giving off a tantalizing aroma. By the time they cooled enough to bite into, Gina's hunger had sharpened and she welcomed the sweet, chewy texture of the meal.

The evening air hung low and warm. Derrin scattered damp, fragrant bark on the dying coals of the fire to ward off the worst of the biting insects. Then he stretched out nearby, hands linked behind his head, and shut his eyes.

The bell-like call of a hidden creature came from the treetops. Gina leaned back on her elbows. A sprinkling of stars dotted the swath of sky above the clearing. As she watched, countless more emerged, hanging low like glittering crystals. But Gina's gaze halted on a collection of seven bright stars. Four outlined a lopsided rectangle, three arched in a line from one corner. The Big Dipper.

She stared at it for a full minute, then searched the sky for other familiar patterns. She soon found them. Orion, with his hunter's belt, and the unmistakable "W" that was the reclining figure of Cassiopeia. Her mind raced, trying to grasp the implications of her discovery.

"Derrin," she said slowly, "your sky is the same as mine."

He slanted her a glance. "What?"

"The stars. The patterns are the same as in my world."

He sat up. "Truly?"

She nodded. "I must be on Earth, but in a different dimension than my home. It's mathematically possible. It would explain why so much of your world is similar to mine."

"But much is different."

"Like wizardry. Magic doesn't exist where I come from."

"Perhaps it does, but your people haven't discovered it yet."

She shook her head. "No. There's nothing magic about crystals in my world."

"A crystal isn't magic in itself. Its power is determined by its structure and purity. Magic is a function of knowledge and experience. That's why the man who creates a stone can command the most of it."

"Man?"

"The wizards of the Hierarchy are all men. Women are…" he hesitated. "Not permitted."

"Just great," Gina muttered.

Derrin grinned.

She shot him a dark look. "How did this bastion of masculinity come into being?"

Derrin leaned forward and rested his forearms on his bent knees. "After the earliest wizards discovered the mental techniques needed to create crystals, they compiled information about various crystals and their properties. They formed the Hierarchy in order to share what they knew. Before long, the Congress of Lords became wary of the

Hierarchy's power. The Church of Lotark denounced wizardry as the work of Tarol, the Evil One."

"I'm surprised the wizards were allowed to continue."

"To be sure, they nearly lost their heads to the executioner. At the very least, the Hierarchy would have been disbanded if not for a discovery that allowed untrained minds to use crystals."

Derrin was gesturing now, intent on his subject matter. "It was discovered even an untrained mind can make use of a simple crystal if a trigger element is present. Light, heat and healing became available to all. The Congress of Lords hastened to befriend the Hierarchy. The Church continued to object, but wasn't able to prevent the alliance."

"What are the uses of the more complex crystals?"

"Shadowing and location, of course. Healing of serious illnesses, building structures and transporting heavy materials, and a handful of other uses."

Gina considered his answer. "Why did you take the rose quartz crystal from my costume?"

"It was not like any stone I've seen before. I was afraid you would use it against me."

"Are you still afraid of that?"

Derrin smiled. "No."

"The rose quartz was a natural crystal, of course," Gina said. "So according to you, it wouldn't have any magical power. But it did glow just before the web appeared."

"Truly? Perhaps it reflected the power of the webstone."

"Or maybe it had something to do with the web opening. We should go back and get it from your grandmother."

"No. Once a journey to the Signs is begun, it must be completed. I cannot go back on my word to Zahta."

Gina sighed. "Then tell me more about wizardry. Do wizards specialize in the crystals they produce?"

"Yes. At least that was the case before the Blight became so severe. Now the entire Hierarchy is searching for a remedy. I've nearly abandoned my other research."

"What was that?"

"The creation of twinned crystals. Another wizard and I discovered a way to create identical crystals. We grow them in tandem and they retain their connection even when separated. We can then communicate at a distance using a code of flashes."

Gina couldn't miss the note of pride in Derrin's voice. "You're a regular Alexander Graham Bell," she mused, impressed.

"Who?"

"That's the name of the man who invented a long distance communication system in my world." She recounted a brief history of communications, starting with telephone and radio, and ending with satellites and the Internet.

"Your world is a wondrous place," he said when she finished.

"Some parts of it."

"I'll send you back, Gina, even if I have to steal Balek's webstone to do it."

"What if it doesn't respond to your command?"

He shot her a look that was half-amused, half-affronted. "I won't fail you. You're in danger, and will be until I get you across the web."

"What's to say I'll be safe even then? Balek summoned me once. Couldn't he do it again?"

"After I send you home, I mean to destroy the webstone, but even so..." He reached into the neckline of his shirt and looped one finger about the silver chain that lay against his skin. The crystal swung free, scattering the glow of the firelight. Gina leaned close to look at it. The stone was a flawless gray cube.

Derrin drew the chain over his head. Leaning forward, he placed it around Gina's neck and drew her braids through it.

"This is a shadow crystal. It's the most powerful gem I've ever created. It keeps our movements hidden from Balek. As long as we stay within a half-day's walk of each other, we'll both be shadowed. If you keep the crystal with you, your protection will continue when you return to your world. It will fade only if I withdraw my intention from the stone or it's destroyed."

Gina touched the silver cage. "You didn't even want me to see this before. Why would you give it to me now?"

Derrin shrugged. "I feared you had the power of a sorceress. Now I believe that even if you did, you wouldn't use it against me."

Gina fingered the chain, still warm from the heat of Derrin's body. She slipped the crystal inside the neckline of her dress, where it nestled between her breasts. "I thought you said women couldn't perform wizardry."

"No. I said women weren't allowed in the Hierarchy. Their powers are considered too erratic to control."

"Oh, please."

Derrin sent her a look that was half-apologetic, half-teasing. "I've never met a sorceress, so I can't give you a personal opinion on the subject."

Gina crawled into the shelter a short time later. Derrin didn't join her immediately. He sat by the fire, his back toward her, the muscles of his shoulders clenched in tight lines. Before she considered the wisdom of it, Gina reached out her mind to him.

The wave of raw lust that blasted her caused her to pull back as if scorched. Derrin flinched but didn't turn. Gina's heart pounded in her throat as her body responded to his. Her nipples hardened and ached. Moisture collected between her thighs. She wanted him. And not in a sweet, romantic way. She wanted him wild and hot between her thighs. She wanted to sweat and scream as he drove her, commanding her body as he'd commanded her mind.

Another woman might have welcomed the desire. Another woman might have gone to Derrin and pulled him into the shelter, but Gina lay frozen, unable to move. The Na'tahar had given her unbelievable pleasure, but it had also brought other, more painful feelings. Helplessness. Vulnerability. Those were emotions she had been well acquainted with during her brief marriage. She never wanted to feel them again.

She rolled over and shut her eyes.

*****

A man's hands covered Gina's breasts.

His fingers were warm. Callused. They toyed with her nipples, rolling the sensitive flesh to tight peaks, tugging and squeezing, making her ache. She twisted, arching her spine, wanting more.

She wanted to feel. It had been so long since she'd let herself do that.

A warm, open mouth replaced the hand on her left breast. Briefly, Gina wondered what was happening to her, whether she should resist. In the back of her mind a small voice urged caution, but the waves of pleasure coursing through her body drowned all protest. The scent of earth and musk surrounded her.

She tried to lift her hand, but her limbs were heavy. Weighted. Her eyelids stayed closed, though she willed them to open. In contrast, her body felt light, as if it were floating. She'd fallen asleep in a rough woodland shelter, but oddly, no rough ground caressed her hips now. No cold night air chilled her. She didn't know how that could be, but oddly, the anomaly didn't trouble her.

The man's mouth shifted to her other breast, leaving the first one bare, moist, and needy. His tongue circled her areola. His teeth scraped her nipple, gently at first, then with increasing pressure. Tiny zings of pleasure-pain raced from her breast to her belly, then slid lower. She welcomed the sensation. This was what it felt like to want, to need, to make love. A hint of an old fear rose, but she pushed it away. She wanted to concentrate on the moment. On the pleasure.

The man's hands skimmed over her body. Everywhere he touched, Gina came alive. Her arms, her belly, her hips. It was as though her unknown lover had turned every inch of her skin into an erogenous zone. Her lips parted on a moan. Then lips and teeth left her breast to trail kisses and nips down her torso. His hands moved under her, cupping her buttocks.

She reached into the darkness. Her fingers tangled in her lover's hair. The strands were soft and silky. Long. Much longer than Michael's had been. She toyed with it a bit, liking the feel of it.

His head came up a fraction. She felt his hesitation, his quick intake of breath, then his lips returned to her body. His tongue teased in the dimpled hollow of her navel. Gasping, she pushed his head lower, instinctively guiding him to where she needed him most.

He obeyed, shifting, trailing wet kisses toward her mound. She stiffened a bit as he drew close to her clit. She'd never had a man do this before. In some ways, it seemed more intimate an act than making love the usual way. She hovered on the crest of indecision. Tension coiled inside her like a spring. God, she was close to coming. So close…

The tip of his tongue touched her clit. She writhed, not sure she wanted to yield to the invasion.

His hands on her hips restrained her. *Open for me, Gina.*

The wordless plea was like a splash of icy water. The command had come from Derrin, not some faceless lover. She felt his presence crowding the barrier shielding the deepest part of her mind. If she yielded even a fraction, he would slip inside. Once there, he would become part of her. She wouldn't be able to hide from him.

His tongue dipped and suckled, sending a spike of raw need to her womb. She struggled to shut her legs, shut him out of her body and her psyche. His tongue circled the opening to her body. Clever fingers joined the dance, skating across her clit, teasing the crease of her inner thigh, slipping into the cleft between her buttocks.

Her pleasure climbed. His mind surrounded hers, seeking a weak spot in her defenses. When she lost control and climaxed, would he be able to enter? Would she be at his mercy then?

Cold fear grew, overpowering Gina's dizzying pleasure. Nausea churned in her stomach. The familiar numbness stole through her, weighting her limbs, pressing her down, into the ground. A sharp rock under one hip sent a shock of pain shooting along her nerve endings. The jolt caused her eyes to fly open.

She lay in the brush shelter. Derrin wasn't beside her—in fact, he wasn't in the shelter at all. She was alone, and fully dressed. A warm pulse lingered between her legs and a vague sense of panic squeezed her chest. That was all that was left of what she thought had been a real experience.

Gina let out a long breath.

A dream.

It had only been a dream.

* * * * *

The distance he'd put between them hadn't been enough.

Derrin looped his arms about his knees and tipped his head against the rough bark of the tree he was using as a backrest. The night air held a whisper of ice, but despite his fear the unseasonable weather meant the Blight was advancing, he welcomed the chill on his heated skin. The frosty air didn't affect his cock, though. He suspected the deepest snow wouldn't cool that part of his anatomy.

He'd abandoned his bed in the shelter sometime after midnight, cursing himself for his loss of control. In sleep, his mind had drifted toward Gina's. His spirit had tried to join with hers.

He was still shaken by the experience.

As a boy, he'd known those bonded by the Na'tahar shared experiences beyond the physical, but in his youthful innocence he'd never imagined the erotic nature of those joinings. As he approached manhood, he learned more, but he had left the clans before taking a mate. He'd never experienced the sacred joining of souls.

Until Gina.

But the union he'd forced on Gina in his grandmother's hut hadn't been a joining born of love. It had been a nothing short of an obscenity. If there had been any other way—other than murder—to break Balek's control on her mind, he would have done it. He had vowed afterward to keep his distance, but the lingering bond of the Na'tahar was strong. He was not strong enough to resist it.

He'd pleasured Gina in a dream. Even now, he could feel the sweet surrender of her flesh beneath his lips, taste the pungent bouquet of her arousal as it spilled over his tongue. She'd been soft, open, urging him with sighs and moans to take what he wanted. So unlike the woman she was when the sun was high.

He'd pushed her higher and higher, unable to pull back, wanting more than anything to feel her break under his control. But in a heartbeat, everything had changed. A memory had flashed through her, and in the way of joined lovers, he had felt it in his own mind. In the grip of the same terror and humiliation she'd felt during the Na'tahar, Gina had gone cold. Numb.

Once again he'd caused her pain.

He wouldn't allow it to happen again.

*****

Gina rolled onto her back and stifled a groan. Dawn hadn't yet come, but more sleep was out of the question. The screeching of a thousand birds made sure of it.

Reluctantly, she opened one eye.

Derrin was already up, standing in the clearing a short distance away, his back to her. Despite the chill of the morning her cheeks heated as the memory of her dream flooded over her. Even though she'd managed to fall into a fitful slumber afterward, her thighs were still slick and her clit still tingled. Beneath it all lurked the fear of losing herself, of letting a man cause her to lose control. Michael had done that during her marriage. Derrin had done it when he'd entered her mind. Both memories had the power to immobilize her.

She drew a shaking breath as she pushed herself to a sitting position. If she could feel so unsettled after a mere dream, what would she do if Derrin tried to enter her mind again for real? She didn't want to contemplate it.

He glanced back at her, his gray eyes shadowed. He'd heard her movements, of course, even though she'd been trying to be silent. The man was aware of everything. Sometimes, when she looked up to find him watching her, she had the feeling he could look into her soul.

He gestured for her to join him. She vanquished the last remnants of her dream from her mind and went to him, relieved when he made no move to touch her.

"We need to check our traps," he said.

Three of the stick and stone traps had sprung, including one Gina had set herself. In it, a blue-green harta lay whimpering beneath the stone, its back legs crushed. It writhed in a pitiful attempt to escape.

Derrin hunted around until he'd found a smooth stone the size of a baseball. He held it out to her. "Here. Kill it."

Gina gaped at him. "Me? No way!"

"It's your trap," he said evenly. "The animal's death is your responsibility. Besides, don't you want to eat?"

"Well, yes, but I don't want to kill anything."

"Gina, no creature lives without causing others to die. You're no different. You're not harmless because others do your killing for you." Once again, he offered Gina the stone.

She took it this time, and stared down at the struggling ball of fur.

"Crush its skull. One clean stroke should do it."

She dropped to one knee and raised her arm. The rock struck the animal's head with a sickening crack. Blood splattered on her hands and on the grass.

"There." She tried not to think of how easy it had been.

"Good." Derrin pulled the animal out of the trap and laid it with the others, then pried the stone from her fingers. "Why don't you go back to the camp and check on the fire?"

Gina scrambled to her feet. "Thanks."

They broke camp after eating and continued their journey. At midday they came to a cross trail. A bent tree marked the intersection. Derrin knelt to examine a pile of stones at the base of the trunk.

"What is it?" Gina asked.

"A trail marker. The tree was bent as a sapling, to serve as a signal for the stones. See?" He pointed to a slab set to one side of the mound.

Gina crouched and ran her finger over a crude image of a fire etched on its surface.

"The path leads to the Fire Clan," he said.

They set out in the direction indicated by the marker. By late afternoon they were edging along a narrow path overlooking a sheer cliff. A wide swath of water separated the mountain from the valley beyond.

"We have to cross the river to reach the village," Derrin informed her. "If I remember correctly, we should come to a ravine tomorrow. We'll be able to climb down to the water's edge there."

The hiking was difficult along the ridge. Rock formations loomed above Gina's head. The trail meandered between them, skirting dense patches of thorny brush. There was little that was edible in the harsh landscape, and even less water.

By the middle of the following afternoon Gina's last drink had faded to a distant memory. She relieved her parched mouth by sucking on a smooth pebble. She looked down at the river. All the water she could hope for was less than fifty feet away.

They forged on. The sun dipped low, yet the ravine Derrin had spoken of didn't appear. A stiff wind rose.

"It's going to be another cold night," he muttered. "The Blight is spreading into the wilderness."

A rocky outcropping jutted out over the river. Derrin hiked past the thick bushes clustered on one side of the ledge and surveyed the cliff face. After a moment, he gestured for Gina to join him. She edged toward the precipice and peered over the edge. Far below, brown water swirled, catching the glow of the fading daylight. Hastily, she took a step back.

"Over there." Derrin grabbed a branch and pulled it back, pointing with his free hand to a spot farther along the cliff. "See how the ridge splits? We should be able to make our way down to the river without too much trouble."

"It doesn't look too easy."

He flashed her a grin. "You'll do fine. We won't be able to climb down in the dark, though. We'll have to camp here along the ridge."

Gina turned back to the main trail. She'd taken only a few steps toward it when a menacing growl reached her ears. She halted in her tracks. Less than fifteen feet in front of her, an odd gray-furred creature lumbered out from the shadow of a rock formation.

The beast was the size of a small truck, square and massive, with a shaggy coat that hung in twisted ropes that resembled dreadlocks. A flat snout covered with spiky gray bristles sniffed in her direction. The animal surveyed the human intruders with an air of irritation. Then it rose up on thick hind legs and gave a trumpet-roar.

Gina's insides turned to water. The creature loomed over her, impossibly huge, curved claws unsheathed. She couldn't see Derrin, but she felt his rigid presence at her back. His heat surrounded her. It was the only thing that prevented her from crumpling.

"A tarma," he breathed. "They don't usually hunt this early in the evening. If we don't move, it may lose interest."

A flash of motion caught the corner of her vision. To her right, at the far edge of the overlook, a miniature version of the shaggy beast waddled out of the thicket. It looked past Gina and gave a whimper. The larger tarma roared.

The cub cried. The adult tarma's lips drew back, revealing a pair of sharp, deadly tusks.

"Gina, can you swim?"

"Yes, but—"

The monster charged. Before Gina could react, Derrin grabbed her around the waist and shoved her over the cliff.

Chapter Nine

The impact of Gina's body on the water's surface kicked the air from her lungs. The river closed over her, deadly and cold, pummeling her with rough fists. Rocks bit into her leg as the current drove her into the river's bed.

She kicked hard against it and struggled upward. Icy air blasted her face. She managed a deep, painful breath before the current reclaimed her.

The water rushed in with suffocating force. Terror drove her limbs, propelling her body with desperate strength. Endless moments later, she broke the surface a second time.

"Gina!"

"Here!" She couldn't see Derrin, but his shout told her he was near.

She floundered in the current for what seemed like an eternity before his arm wrapped around her from behind.

"Are you all right?" he yelled over the roar of the river.

"I think so."

He shifted his hold and towed her across the current toward the far bank, where the water broke white against a jagged line of rocks. The daylight was fading rapidly.

"There!" She tried to point to a break in the rocks.

"I see it." He changed course and angled for the cove, but the current drove them past it. He found purchase on the river floor and struggled upstream.

By the time they gained the shore, full night had fallen. Derrin lifted Gina from the water and carried her a few steps before his knees buckled. He sank to the ground, supporting himself with one arm, gasping.

Gina sprawled in the mud, coughing. "Well, we're across the river, and I've swallowed all the water I could want."

Derrin's laugh sounded more like a wheeze. "Gina, if you'd said you couldn't swim, I don't know what I would have done." He pushed himself to his feet and held out his hand.

She gripped it and pulled herself up. Her legs shook. Derrin slipped one arm around her waist.

A violent shiver overtook her. "The temperature—it's dropped so much."

"It's close to freezing." His tone darkened. "It's not normal. It's an effect of the Blight." They stumbled up the bank and into the scant protection of the forest.

Another shudder racked her body. "I've never been this cold." The words stumbled over her numb lips.

"We need a fire," Derrin muttered, "but it will take too long to start one in the dark."

He lowered Gina to the ground and scraped away the forest litter and dirt with his hands and forearms. She wrapped her arms around her torso and squinted at him through the darkness, too exhausted to help.

He burrowed into the soft loam, then pulled Gina in beside him and covered them both with the disturbed debris. "This should keep us until morning," he said, pulling her close.

She snuggled into the length of his heat and breathed a deep, shuddering breath. The scents of earth and strength enveloped her. Her shaking steadied.

She closed her eyes and pressed closer, feeling a comfort she'd never experienced before. In her heart she felt something else, the glimmer of an emotion she dared not name.

* * * * *

Derrin plunged naked into the frigid water. Scooping handfuls of grit from the riverbed, he scrubbed his skin until it burned. He repeated the process with his hair. The last traces of mud dissolved. Finally, even his raging erection drooped.

His thoughts were harder to erase.

He glanced to the edge of the forest, where Gina lay curled in sleep, the heat of his body still alive on her skin. He'd awakened to find her breast under his palm and her round bottom nestled against his cock. Her mind had drifted peacefully in slumber, brushing against his own. How he'd resisted responding, he'd never know. Rock-hard and throbbing painfully, it had taken every shred of his self-discipline to extract himself from the debris-covered hollow and retreat to the river.

He retrieved his clothes from the bank. He scrubbed the tough deerskin on a rock, then stepped out of the river and dressed. His shirt and kilt clung to his skin, his hair stuck to his neck in clammy strands. He shook, dog-like, then dropped onto the narrow strip of beach.

A black mood hung over him. He'd been fighting it for days, and for a time he'd kept it at bay. Now it descended in full force. He turned to face it, grasping it with both hands, turning it this way and that, studying it as he would a rare crystal.

He no longer belonged in the places he had loved as a boy. That fact in itself brought no surprise—he'd known it for years. But though he'd embraced his life in the Stronghold, Katrinth had never become his home. Between the wilderness and the city lay an emptiness too bleak to contemplate.

Derrin suspected it was there he belonged.

He could live with that—indeed, he had endured it for more than eleven years. No, the emptiness itself didn't trouble him. What frightened him was the way it vanished when he looked into Gina's eyes.

He wanted her. He'd dreamed of it every night since they had been Na'tahar, and spent a good deal of his waking hours thinking of it, too. So much so that he'd almost forced his way into her mind a second time.

What would it be like if she were willing?

He closed his eyes and conjured an image of Gina—naked, soft, and open, her clothing strewn at the water's edge. Her parted legs revealed the glistening petals of her sex. He could smell her excitement, feel the touch of her welcome on his mind. He stalked her like a wolf circling its prey. Then he pounced, caging her with his limbs, covering her with his body as he positioned his cock at her entrance and…

Derrin gave himself a mental shake and stood up. He had regain control of his emotions. In the first days after the Na'tahar, he'd entertained thoughts of taking Gina again, body and mind, whether she was willing or not. He knew the desire had been base, but he couldn't seem to keep himself from the fantasy. Then he'd come to know her, trust her, and the vision had shifted. Now he dreamed of her welcoming him into her body and mind. Dreamed she wanted the best within him to possess her. It was all he could think about.

But it wasn't likely to happen.

Holy Lotark's cock. How long had it been since he'd had a woman? He could barely remember. In the past, he and Ariek had hunted female companionship with amazing vigor, but for nearly a year Ariek had restricted his activities to Danat's bed and Derrin hadn't bothered to visit the taverns alone. He tried, but he couldn't quite recall the details of his last sexual encounter. No wonder he'd become obsessed with Gina.

But she didn't belong in either of his worlds and wasn't likely to accept him as a lover after he'd forced her to the Na'tahar. He remembered the shame and humiliation he'd forced her to endure and his gut twisted. Gina had felt the shadow of those same emotions when their minds had touched in sleep. He was very glad she hadn't recognized the dream was a true joining.

A sharp wind blew, sending a shiver across his skin. Last night there had been a summer frost, an extremely rare occurrence. The Blight was worsening, intensified by Gina's presence. Derrin suspected the rift in the web wouldn't heal until she returned to her own world.

It was his task to send her back. It was the only way he could atone for what he had done to her. He dared not forget it.

He pushed to his feet and strode to the tree line. Gina was sitting up, shaking wet leaves and clumps of dirt from her braids. Forest debris clung to her dress and grimy blotches decorated her face and arms. His mouth twitched. She didn't look at all like the Gina in his fantasy.

She shook a clump of dirt from the neckline of her dress and sent him a wry smile. "I must look like a fright."

"Oh no, Gina." His smile deepened. "Mud becomes you."

Her eyes widened. Derrin couldn't repress a chuckle—Gina was so easy to tease.

"Oh, really?" she retorted. "Well, you don't look much better, standing there dripping like a wet rag." Her arm jerked forward. A handful of mud hit him square in the face.

"Tarol's blood!" Derrin made a blind lunge in Gina direction. His fingers slipped on her arm as she dodged past, laughing.

By the time he'd wiped the muck from his eyes, she was wading in waist-deep water. He bolted to the stream and dove in after her.

When he emerged, she'd gone under. He waited, tracking her with his gaze. When she came up, he slammed the surface of the water with his open palm, splashing her full in the face.

Gina sputtered her outrage.

He flashed her an innocent grin. "Just helping you wash off."

She kicked water at him.

He feinted left and dove right, grabbing at her ankle, but missing. She rolled and continued splashing. He laughed and lunged again. This time, his hand closed on her wrist.

He jerked her toward him. She fell against his body, her breasts crushed to his chest, her thighs pressed against his own. His laughter faded as his cock responded, despite the chill of the water. He drew back, intending to release her, but before he could, Gina raised her head and looked at him.

She captured him with her eyes, snared him in the soft darkness of her irises. Once again, he was drowning within her. He froze, his heart pounding, and for an instant the desire to claim her lips was almost more than he could stand.

Warning bells rang in his head. He couldn't afford to forget who she was, where she belonged. What he had done to her. He flung her away in his haste to escape.

Gina floundered in the current. Derrin felt a stab of guilt, but he forced himself to watch her regain her footing without his assistance. She met his gaze with a questioning look. When he felt the tentative brush of her mind, he pulled his own mind back, rebuffing her. She reddened and turned away.

He struggled to keep his tone impersonal. "You finish bathing. I'll go start a fire."

He retreated to the shore, feeling Gina's gaze on his back. By the time she joined him, he had a fire blazing. He nodded to her and headed up the river to fish.

They broke camp at midmorning. The air warmed quickly, then closed around them in suffocating heat. The morning's awkwardness lingered for a time, then, to Derrin's great relief, the easy camaraderie of the day before returned.

Their ascent into the mountains brought cooler air—a change Derrin welcomed at first, then regretted when a chill wind began to blow. They set up camp in a sheltered nook overlooking the valley of Fire Clan, just beyond the highest point of the pass.

That evening, the temperature plunged again. Derrin watched as Gina attempted to light the fire. She sawed the bow across the spindle until her hand blistered, rejecting his offer of assistance. Finally, she gave up. She scowled with undisguised disgust as he sparked the blaze.

"Why does it look so easy when you do it?" she grumbled.

"Practice. I learned as a boy." He stared into the fire. The childhood he had tried so hard to forget burned all around him, tortured by the flames of what had come after.

He looked away. The spindle and fireboard lay nearby. He picked them up and turned them over in his hands.

"Fire is sacred to the Baha'Na," he told Gina. "Its creation is an act of love. The spindle is the male, the fireboard the female. Their child is a gift to the People."

"That's a beautiful image."

"Isn't it?" He gave a cynical laugh and felt the familiar bitterness descend. "In Galena, only the poor use fire. The wealthy don't allow it in their homes. Why should they? Crystals provide the same comfort, without the risks."

He brushed his fingertip over the fireboard's blackened socket. "It's safer, perhaps—but what have they lost?" He let out a long breath. "Why were they so eager to lose it?"

"Derrin..."

He looked up sharply.

"Why did you leave the Baha'Na?"

His throat closed. The emotions rising in the wake of Gina's question were too fierce, too painful. Several heartbeats passed before he trusted himself to speak.

"It's a long story."

Gina offered a small smile. "I have some time."

He sighed and put the fireboard aside, searching for an answer that made sense.

In the end, he offered her the truth.

"I didn't want to leave, Gina. I left because Zahta told me I could not stay."

"Your own grandmother kicked you out? I can't believe that!"

He met her gaze. "It's true. You must have noticed I don't carry the name of a man."

"Yes. Bera told me you didn't receive a guardian from the Goddess. She said you left the Baha'Na before your rite of manhood was complete."

He nodded. "I did, but I began the rites after my fifteenth summer, like any other boy, expecting to become a man. Under the Moon of the Falling Leaves, I stalked a mountain doe. I climbed a tree and waited for her to pass beneath me. When she did, I dropped and made the kill. I brought it to the Elders."

Derrin pushed to his feet and paced the flickering edge of the firelight. Words left unspoken for eleven long winters sprang to his lips, demanding to be set free.

"Afterwards, in keeping with the customs of the Baha'Na, I traveled to the other clans and dwelt with each for a time. I was seeking a partner and a new home. I found what I sought with the Fire Clan. I fell in love with a girl more beautiful than the summer sky. She promised to join with me when I became a man.

"By now I had passed my sixteenth summer. At the Moon of the First Frost, the clans gathered for the final test of the boys who would be men. I went with the others into the forest, to await the animal brother who would be my guardian. One by one the others were chosen, until I sat alone.

"After four nights, Zahta came into my circle of stones and told me the truth of my birth. My father had been a Galenan trapper lost in the wilderness. My mother, a girl of only fourteen winters, saw him and thought to help. He accepted her aid and took her body as thanks. She grew round with the Galenan's seed, and died soon after my birth."

Derrin entered the light and hunkered down, spreading his palms before the flames and hardening his heart against Gina's cry of dismay. After all this time, he would accept no sympathy.

When he spoke again, the lilting cadence of the Baha'Na yielded to the clipped syllables of the Galenan tongue. "Though Zahta had raised me as her own son, it seemed the Goddess herself had rejected me. My grandmother bade me leave the clans and seek my father's people.

"I left the village the same day. In the land of the Outsiders, I joined a large estate and made myself useful in the stables with the peasants and the slaves. I learned the language of the Galenans. I thought it a strange tongue, but stranger still were the customs of my father's people. The rich gorged on plenty. The poor labored as property of the rich. Animals were penned, crops were planted in rows."

He dropped his hands but remained crouching, staring into the flames. "About a year later, I escaped and traveled to the port city of Sirth. Again, I found work in the stables—this time at a large inn. I watched over the patrons' horses at night. A young aristocrat frequented the inn's gambling house. His father, a horse breeder, imported stallions from the island nation of Loetahl. They were magnificent creatures. Ariek liked to visit the stables and inspect the horseflesh of the other patrons. We became friends of sorts.

"One night I heard a scream behind the stables and found the innkeeper's son tearing at a barmaid's dress. The next instant my hands were wrapped around the man's throat and I was pounding his head into the ground.

"I would have killed him if Ariek hadn't stopped me. He understood much better than I the price I would pay if I were caught. He dragged me to his father's estate. There, I received a pallet in the stable loft and a job breaking colts.

"Ariek spent much of his day in the stables or paddocks. Despite the difference in our stations, our friendship deepened. He had four interests—horses, gambling, women, and wizardry. I already shared the first. He soon pulled me into the others.

"Ariek enjoyed his pleasures, but wizardry fascinated him above all else. He traveled to Katrinth and was accepted as an apprentice by High Wizard Niirtor. Some months later, he returned and showed me how wizards create crystals. I sank my mind into the seed, thinking I'd never seen anything so perfect. My thoughts concentrated at its center and the particles surrounding it fell into place.

"I created a crystal of outstanding purity, entirely by instinct. Ariek was astounded. He insisted I accompany him to the Stronghold, but I saw no sense in it. The apprentice fee was staggering and the Hierarchy accepted only aristocrats. I couldn't hope to gain admittance.

"But Ariek wouldn't let it rest. Before a week was gone I found myself in Niirtor's workroom, attempting one of the more difficult crystals. When I succeeded, the old wizard's face cracked in a gruesome smile. 'I'll pay your fee myself, boy,' he told me. 'It will make you some enemies, but I've coddled too many rich lordlings who fancied themselves wearing a black cape.' He seemed to think it a great joke.

"Many in the Upper House—Balek among them—opposed my apprenticeship, but in the end Niirtor prevailed. He was an odd old man, but a brilliant wizard and a good teacher. He died last year, just after Ariek and I entered the Lower House."

Derrin's gaze found Gina's. Her eyes were two dark pools, shimmering with the reflection of the firelight. A fierce emotion surged. He turned it aside, though he ached to grasp it with both hands.

"Gina, when Balek summoned you, my only thought was to take you from him and do whatever necessary to break his control over you—even kill you if that was the only way." He stood and paced a few steps away. His next words would drive her away, but he couldn't leave them unsaid. "I found a method only slightly less abhorrent. I entered your mind against your will. When I did that, I proved myself to be my father's son."

"No!" Gina's denial was swift and vehement. "Derrin, how can you say that? It's not your fault I believed you meant to harm me. You saved my life!"

He shook his head. He wouldn't allow her to cast him in the role of hero. "You don't understand. It's not so much that I entered your mind—it's how I felt when I was inside you. I gloried in it. I reveled in the mastery, the absolute control I had over you. I felt as I do when I create a crystal, only more potent, more powerful." He saw understanding dawn in her eyes and steeled himself to deliver the whole truth. "I didn't have to drive you to your release, Gina. I could have destroyed Balek's control and gotten out of your mind before I gained that last bit of control. But I didn't, because I wanted more than anything to feel you break. To feel that helpless pleasure wash over you."

Gina drew a sharp intake of breath and he looked away. "So you see," he said softly, "the blood of my father truly flows in my veins."

A long moment of silence ensued, growing deeper and emptier with each passing breath. Derrin wanted desperately to bridge the void with his mind, wanted to let Gina feel the depths of his regret and shame for having used her so illy. But he did not. He wouldn't ask her forgiveness. That would be an even greater insult.

Several heartbeats passed, then he heard Gina rise and, incredibly, draw near. Her hands closed, warm and sure, on his upper arms.

"Derrin, look at me."

He did so, turning in her arms, dreading what he would see.

Her face was serious, but he saw no condemnation in her eyes. "Derrin, the Na'tahar was more than either of us could handle. I won't..." A shudder ran through her. "I owe you my life. How can I ask you to be perfect? To resist a force beyond your strength? I can't. And I won't. Let's forget it."

"I won't forget," he said softly. "And you shouldn't, either."

She shook her head, then pulled him into her arms and hugged him tight. He absorbed her comfort for only a brief instant before grasping her arms and pushing her gently away. She retreated to the lean-to. She drew her knees up to her chin and wrapped her arm around her legs, all the while watching him with dark eyes.

Derrin sat for a long while feeding twigs into the fire. Finally, he built up the flames and joined her in the shelter. It was a dangerous move. He should have slept by the fire, but he could no more stay away from Gina than he could command the moon to halt its journey across the sky. Stretched out by her side, not touching her, he felt her every breath as if it were his own.

Her whisper reached out to him. "You may doubt yourself, Derrin, but I see deep goodness in who you are."

He turned to her in the darkness. "As I do in you, Gina."

Chapter Ten

Ariek wrapped himself in the cloak of his shadow crystal and pressed his back against the wall. The door to the workroom hung ajar, allowing a sliver of light to advance a few paces into the gloom of Balek's sleeping chamber. He shifted, seeking a more comfortable position. Long minutes passed.

He could barely credit the fact he had placed himself as a spy. Ariek was unsure what he hoped to learn by adopting Derrin's underhanded method of research, but he was certain of one thing. His friend had been gone much too long. Could Derrin's wild accusations be true? If Balek *had* caused the Blight and the Madness, then…

Then what? He rubbed the bridge of his nose with two fingers. He could take his suspicions to the High Council. High Wizard Rannac's bleary eyes would blink and his hand would shake on his staff. The others would shout at Ariek in outrage, or worse, laugh. Unless Ariek brought solid proof, he would be censured for slander, if not expelled from the Hierarchy.

He rubbed a cramp in his thigh, straining to hear a hint of Balek's approach. Nothing.

Last night he'd been with Danat. His body tightened, remembering her pink-tipped breasts, her soft sighs of pleasure and the musky-slick scent of her arousal. She had filled his senses like the finest wine, and he craved her as he had from the first moment he'd seen her.

She had bewitched him that day. Even so, he hadn't dreamed he would fall in love with her.

His first visits to her attic room were infrequent, weeks apart. He hadn't so much as touched her. Despite her role as the Bride, a fragile innocence clung to her, one he was loath to destroy. Like the petals of his mother's sea roses, he feared she would bruise, then fade, under his touch.

They talked instead, and Danat's innocent company seduced him much more thoroughly than the attentions of a skilled whore or a lusty widow ever had. He told her of his work with the Hierarchy. She listened, wide-eyed, then spoke in halting tones of Loetahl and her family. When her green eyes clouded with pain, his heart twisted. He fought an urge to bury his fingers in her red curls and pull her close, not knowing if she would welcome him.

His desire grew with every meeting, but he held himself in check. She didn't need the burden of his lust.

Then one day, as they sat talking on her narrow pallet, Ariek became aware of a coolness in Danat's manner. Afraid he'd offended her, he asked what was wrong.

She answered without meeting his gaze. "Ariek, why do you come here?"

"What do you mean?"

"There is only one thing I can give you, much sought after. Yet you do not ask for it."

He nearly choked. "I would never shame you that way."

She raised her head and he saw the haunting sadness in her eyes. "Is it pity, then, that brings you here?"

He stared at her. Was it possible she didn't know? "I come because I love you."

Her eyes widened.

"But I don't want to burden you with it, Danat. I know how hard it is for you to endure the Inner Sanctuary."

"The men who come there—they are not men at all, but beasts." Her voice trembled. "You are so different from them."

She leaned forward and kissed him. One slender arm entwined his neck. "Show me, Ariek. Show me how a man loves a woman."

His cock went instantly hard. Her words were the fulfillment of his every dream, yet still he hesitated, fearful of touching her, afraid she would break apart in his hands. He kissed her gently, reverently, framing her sweet face with his hands. He brushed kisses across her brow, her nose, her jaw. He buried his nose in her hair and inhaled her fragile scent.

She responded hesitantly, like a virgin, following where he led. She touched her lips to the hollow of his throat and he felt them tremble against the pulse that beat there. Easing away, he stripped off his tunic. Danat spread her palms on his chest.

Her hands were shaking.

He covered them with his own. "Are you afraid?"

She looked away. "Yes."

He bent and kissed the single tear that escaped her eye. "You do not need to do this thing. Not for me."

"For myself, then. I love you, Ariek. I want to give myself to you, but..." Her voice faltered.

He tipped up her chin with one finger. "Tell me."

"I...I fear a man's weight," she said. "When I am...when I'm in the sanctuary I feel trapped. Smothered."

The image sickened him. Anger churned, but when Danat's tears fell, he put it aside. Anger would not help her in this moment. Only love would do that.

"We can wait," he told her.

"No."

He caught her gaze. "Then you need not suffer my weight. There are other ways to mate."

"Truly?"

He nodded and kissed her. Easing back on her thin pallet, he drew her down atop him. He guided her hand to the arousal straining against the ties of his breeches. When she stroked him, he couldn't suppress a groan of satisfaction.

She raised her brows, her lips curving into the hint of a smile. "Do I affect you so?" Her fingers moved on him again.

This time he moaned aloud. "Wench. You know that you do."

Her smile widened, and he met it with his own. She looked so beautiful sprawled above him, her russet curls tumbling over one shoulder, her robe gaping open at the neckline.

"Do what you wish with me," he told her, lacing his fingers behind his head. "I'm at your mercy."

She laughed at that, tugging at his breeches. He lifted his hips to accommodate her as she pulled them down his legs. When he lay naked beneath her, she loosened the tie on her robe. The silky white fabric slid over her slender shoulders.

His smile faded into awe. Danat was the most exquisite creature he had ever seen. He marveled at her fine, ivory skin, her firm, rounded breasts, the gentle swell of her belly. He longed to thread his fingers through the thatch of blazing curls between her thighs. With an effort, he resisted the urge. This encounter was in Danat's control. He couldn't erase the pain of her past, but he could give her that, at least.

She lifted her hips, guiding him into her body. He hardly felt her weight, only her softness and joy as she sank down on his hard flesh, surrounded him with her slick heat…

A door opened, then slammed. Ariek started, coming back to the present with a sickening jolt. Footsteps sounded in the room beyond the door.

"What have you found out about the woman?" Balek demanded.

"I am sure Derrin abducted her," answered Maator. "I've verified the whereabouts of every other wizard."

"Derrin." Balek spat out the name. "Mongrel scum. Crazy old Niirtor should have been expelled for taking him as apprentice. Tarol's blood! He must have been watching without my knowledge." He paused. "Even now, I cannot penetrate his shadow." He swore a second time. "I wouldn't have thought the insolent pup capable of it."

"Derrin confides in Ariek. I believe Ariek knows where the woman is."

"Find out."

Another pause, then Maator asked, "Master, why not call another woman across the web?"

"Another would be useless," Balek's tone carried an unmistakable note of menace. "I need *that* woman. Find her. Once she is mine, I will see to Derrin."

Balek's footsteps advanced toward the sleeping chamber door. Ariek pushed away from the wall and slipped out the rear entrance, shaken. The situation was far worse than he had imagined.

He swore. Where in Tarol's Inferno *was* Derrin?

Chapter Eleven

The village of the Fire Clan lay nestled in a sun-washed clearing at the valley's edge. Tall grass and wildflowers, heavy with bees and tiny birds, swayed in the wide sweep of open land. The thatched roofs of the clan's dwellings rode low on the landscape, barely visible above the fronds of greenery.

As Gina drew closer, she saw that each hut had been sunk partway into the ground. A walled forecourt with an open hearth fronted each doorway. In a larger mirror of this arrangement, the cluster of dwellings faced an open area ringed with stones. An enormous firepit occupied the center of the community.

The village hummed with activity. At the far end of the clearing a small group of men butchered a mountain deer while women carried the meat to their cooking fires. Small children darted between their legs, laughing.

A young woman broke away from a knot of villagers and hurried toward Gina and Derrin, a smile on her lips. A toddler hovered about her knees and an infant peeked over her shoulder. Her headdress bore the talisman.

Her dark eyes sparkled as her arm arched in the Baha'Na gesture of greeting. Gina swept an arm over her head in reply.

"Welcome, *volah*, my sister, the face of the Goddess shines on your coming. I am Zera. I have been waiting for you." Gina struggled to keep pace with the woman's rapid flow of words. The Na'lara's mind surrounded her like breeze. This time, Gina didn't pull back. She responded with a mental touch of her own and felt the woman's fleeting embrace.

Zera's smile widened. She clasped both Gina's hands in her own. "I am pleased to have you in my home, sister." Catching her breath, she turned her attention to Derrin.

He gave her a flash of a smile, his expression a mixture of amusement and tenderness.

"Derrin." Zera embraced him. "It is good to see you, *vohar*, brother. You are still as handsome as I remember. Those eyes," she added in a confidential tone to Gina. "No woman can resist."

Derrin threw back his head and laughed. "Zera, you haven't changed."

"No, I have not." Zera tilted her head and regarded Derrin expectantly, as if waiting for a question she knew would come.

It did. His smile faded. "How is…?"

"Rahza waits for you," she replied. Her expression softened. "Derrin, you need not be ashamed of what happened at the time of your Seeking."

With a start, Gina remembered Derrin once meant to marry a girl from the Fire Clan. He was asking for her, then. An odd sensation uncoiled in the pit of her stomach. She pushed it away, not wanting to examine it too closely.

Her feelings about Derrin were hopelessly confused. His wrenching confession about the Na'tahar had in some ways drawn them together and in others driven them apart. On one hand, their minds and emotions had become even more entangled—sometimes Gina could hardly distinguish between his feelings and her own, and she suspected he experienced the same unsettling sensations. On the other hand, Derrin wouldn't acknowledge their strengthening bond. He spoke to her very little, and then only on safe topics.

"Rahza is well?" Derrin asked Zera.

"Well enough. She has two strong sons, but her partner was called to the Goddess during the Moon of the Deep Snows. An avalanche came without warning when the weather turned suddenly warm. Go to her, Derrin. She is at the spring. It will do her good to see you."

A painful mixture of emotions flared in Derrin's eyes. He nodded and set out across the clearing toward the forest's edge. The sinking feeling in Gina's stomach intensified.

She dragged her gaze from Derrin's retreating form to find Zera watching her with a thoughtful expression, one that seemed to understand more than Gina was willing to admit. She smiled. "Come with me, my sister."

The Baha'Na woman moved among the huts, guiding the little boy at her legs with one hand. She waved the other toward a group of women.

"Shayla, please take little Mirris—he clings to me so, I cannot walk."

A girl of about thirteen sprang to her feet. Her long braids swung into her face as she took the boy in her arms. Mirris giggled and grabbed at them.

Zera kissed her son's head and gave Shayla a few words of instruction before leading Gina to a dwelling in the center of the village. Inside the hut, three alcoves surrounded a small firepit. A framework of bent wood supported the roof.

The baby slung on Zera's back whimpered. "Oh, Lanya, my precious baby girl, do not worry—Mama has not forgotten you."

Zera adjusted the sling, bringing the baby into her arms, and lowered herself onto a woven grass mat. With a practiced motion, she loosened the neckline of her dress with one hand. Lanya rooted hungrily, then clamped her mouth on Zera's nipple.

Gina looked around the hut. A shaft of light angled through the smoke hole, painting a bright circle on the dirt floor. A rough stone wall rose waist-high behind the sleeping alcoves. Above it, hide wall-coverings stretched over a wooden frame. The scent of the place recalled the tang of woodsmoke and the glow of dawn.

A high, narrow shelf circled the dwelling, supporting an assortment of wooden containers, utensils, and other personal items. Larger tools and weapons hung just below, and from hooks set into the beams of the roof structure. Gina was inspecting a three-pronged stick reinforced with cording, wondering at its use, when Zera spoke.

"You seek a path to your world. At least that is what you tell yourself."

Gina moved to Zera's side and sat down on the pallet beside her. "What do you mean? Of course I want to go home. I just don't understand how this journey will get me across the web."

"Ah, the web. Tell me of it, Gina."

"The web is beautiful, but the passage across it was terrifying. Can you open it? Can you send me home?"

Zera shook her head. "The web has been closed to the Baha'Na since before my birth. The Circle is empty."

"The Circle?"

"The ring of power that draws the glittering threads."

"Derrin says a Na'lara can see the web. Have you?"

"Yes. Sometimes at a difficult birth or a painful death. And once..." Her eyes clouded. "When Derrin left us." She smoothed her hand over the fuzzy head of her infant.

"Tell me."

Zera looked at a point above Gina's right shoulder, as if she were watching the scene replay in the dim light of her home. "Derrin meant to join with my sister, but he never came to claim her. When Zahta told us he had left the People, Rahza pleaded with me to go after him. I followed a trail heavy with his grief and caught up to him the next day. I begged him to return, but he would not."

She sighed and shifted Lanya to her other breast. "My tears flowed. Derrin turned from me, but not before I saw that his own eyes shone with his sorrow. As he walked away, the web shimmered around him, though he took no notice of it."

Zera caught her baby's wandering hand in her own and met Gina's gaze. "I knew then the Goddess had not abandoned Derrin, but had set him on this path for a purpose I could not fathom. Now, after so many winters, he has returned with you—a woman who has crossed the web, yet knows nothing of the Goddess." Her dark eyes regarded Gina steadily. "You will find the answers you seek, my sister. You need only desire, nothing more. It is a simple thing."

The infant gave a soft sigh and closed her eyes. Zera eased the sleeping child onto the ground and retied the laces of her dress. "The face of the Goddess shines on you, little one." She nestled the baby in a hanging cradle of rawhide and furs and set her rocking.

"Would you watch her for me, Gina?" Before Gina could answer, she was gone.

After a moment, Gina pulled aside the hide door covering and stepped into the forecourt. Not far beyond the low stone wall, a pair of village woman worked a deerskin stretched on a frame. Zera stood to one side, speaking in low tones.

Gina's gaze roamed further until it came to a tall figure at the edge of the forest. She tensed, then berated herself. She'd been looking for him all along.

Derrin stood at the edge of the forest talking with a slender wisp of a woman. He gestured earnestly, then gripped her shoulders. The woman raised her hand and touched his cheek. Gina willed herself to turn away, but she couldn't tear her attention from the intimate scene.

At that moment, four boys crashed like a storm into the forecourt. They rolled within inches of Gina and fell to the dirt in a grappling, shouting heap. Inside the hut, Lanya let out a wail.

Gina stepped around the melee and hurried to the infant. The little girl howled and kicked in her cradle. Gina lifted the squirming bundle to her shoulder and murmured what she hoped were soothing sounds. The cries subsided to whimpering.

She stalked back to the forecourt, where the good-natured brawl continued in full swing.

"Quiet!"

The boys froze. Four pairs of dark eyes stared. Gina's mouth twitched at their sudden attack of calm.

The largest boy scrambled to his feet. "Uh… I am sorry. I did not know my sister slept." As an afterthought, he added, "Welcome to the dwelling of my parents. My name is Natis."

He gestured toward the others, who came to stand beside him. "This is Lorrin, my brother, and my cousins Maran and Geris."

"I'm Gina. I'm staying here for a few days."

A woman's voice sounded behind her. "Maran… Geris…"

Gina turned. The slender woman Gina had seen with Derrin was gliding down the stone steps into the forecourt. The image of a willow tree sprang into Gina's mind.

The woman's delicate features were framed by wispy curls that had escaped from her braids. Pink flushed her cheeks and her dark eyes glowed. A smile sprang to her lips.

A girl more beautiful than the summer sky. Eleven years hadn't dimmed her beauty.

Maran and Geris detached themselves from their cousins and went to her. Gina clutched the infant in her arms.

"The face of the Goddess shines on you," the woman said. "I am Rahza, Zera's sister. I see you have met my boys."

"I'm Gina."

"I know. Derrin told me of you. Come," she said to her sons. "There is someone I want you to meet. Goodbye, Gina."

I'll bet there is, Gina thought, doing her best to ignore a stab of annoyance. Rahza guided Maran and Geris from the hut. The other two boys trailed after them.

Lanya's sudden squeal brought Gina's attention back to the bundle in her arms. The infant was wide awake now, arms flailing. She gave Gina a toothless grin.

Gina couldn't help but smile back at her. With an effort, she pushed the image of Derrin and Rahza from her mind and gave herself up to the entertainment of the tiny girl.

They were still playing when Zera returned with a basket over one arm, followed by a husky man carrying a huge portion of roasted venison. Trailing them were Zera's three sons—Natis and Lorrin, and the toddler Gina had seen earlier, Mirris.

"This is Swift Tarma, my partner." Zera settled her basket near the firepit. Gina thought of the beast that had run her and Derrin off the cliff and suppressed a shiver.

"You have already met my oldest sons," Zera said. She shot a stern glance at the sheepish boys, then smiled and took her baby from Gina. "Oh, Lanya, you will never know the joy of a quiet home, with such brothers as you have."

Gina eyed Zera's partner. He was tall, standing a full head above his wife. His broad chest bulged with muscles. He nodded to Gina, then bent to stroke his daughter's cheek with exquisite tenderness. Lanya batted at his necklace of claws and feathers.

The Baha'Na man produced a long stone knife and proceeded to cut the venison into smaller portions, which he placed in a wooden bowl. Zera laid Lanya on a blanket and emptied her basket of curled fern tips onto a rawhide platter. The ensuing meal was hectic, overwhelming Gina with its clamor.

Afterward, the older boys roughhoused with their little brother and Zera retired to nurse Lanya. Swift Tarma sat by the hearth, rubbing a soft bit of hide dipped in grease over a new bow stave. Gina watched him, noting the smooth movements of his large hands, as gentle on the wood as they had been on his infant daughter's skin.

"How long have you been working on this bow?"

"Two winters. Since before Zera's womb stretched with Lanya."

"Really?" Gina took a closer look at the bow stave. It was beautifully wrought, and long, almost as tall as the man who held it, but she found it hard to believe it had taken two years to make. It was, after all, just a piece of wood.

"Why does it take so long?" she asked.

He looked at her, clearly perplexed by her ignorance. "A bow is sacred. Before I made this one, I asked the Goddess if my need was true. In reply, she brought me to the place where the bow hid in the heart of a young tree crowded by her sisters. 'Little One,' I told the tree, 'if you are willing, I will transform your weakness into strength for my People.'"

Swift Tarma stroked the bow stave again, beginning at one end and moving along the graceful curve of the wood with the reverence of a lover. "I cut the sapling in the Moon of the Deep Snows. For three seasons it hung in my dwelling."

He dipped the cloth in the bowl of grease and continued his labor. "At the Moon of the Falling Leaves I began to shape the bow. I worked most of the winter, first with a knife, then with fine-grained rocks. I steamed the ends and curved them as the snows receded, during the Moon of the Bitter Herbs. Now, with this grease, I add the strength of the tarma, my guardian. When I string the bow, my arrow will fly true. The spirit of the tree will provide food for my clan."

Gina touched the fine grain of the stave. "Do Baha'Na women ever hunt?"

"Of course. Zera is an excellent shot, but it is a rare woman who has the strength to draw a longbow such as this. A woman uses a smaller weapon."

He stood and hung the unfinished stave from a hook overhead. Then he retrieved a smaller bow and a quiver of arrows hanging a short distance away. "Come outside. I will teach you, if you wish."

"I'd like to try."

An hour later, Gina's forearm was bruised from the impact of the bowstring and she had a high opinion of anyone who could actually hit a running animal with the weapon. She couldn't even strike the hide target hanging on a tree at the edge of the clearing. A group of children, Natis and Lorrin among them, shouted instructions and encouragement, and gave eager demonstrations of their prowess. Finally, Gina's arrow pierced the target. A cheer erupted from the onlookers.

Zera joined the group. Her partner greeted her, then turned his attention back to the children. The Na'lara's gaze lingered on his broad back. "He is a good man."

"Yes," agreed Gina, smiling. "Did you enjoy your rest?"

Zera rolled her eyes. "How I wish every day for such peace! But as soon as it is quiet I want everyone back again."

That evening, the clan assembled for a communal meal. Zera kept Gina by her side, presenting her to at least thirty pairs of curious eyes. Derrin was nowhere to be seen. Gina's heart sank when she realized Rahza was also absent.

A huge pile of deadwood had been stacked in the central firepit, arranged in a pattern of radiating lines. When full night had fallen, the clan circled the pit, drawing close.

Zera's partner appeared at her side and claimed the bundle that held his daughter, then joined his sons a short distance away. He gestured for Gina to join him. She did, but sat to one side, not feeling a part of the boisterous family, yet not wanting to be alone.

Zera stood before her people and raised her arms to the sky. "The Fire Clan gathers. The Goddess burns with love for her children."

She knelt and took up the spindle and bow. The tinder sparked and burst into flame. Zera eased the bundle into a nest of kindling and fanned it with a long breath.

Gina watched, mesmerized by the grace of the ceremony. Though she had seen Derrin perform the same task many times, Zera's fire and its making seemed more intimate, as if the Baha'Na woman had lit it from a spark of Gina's soul. Flames rose, flinging red stars into the sky. Waves of heat rolled.

From a place outside the light, a drum beat a rolling rhythm, rising and falling with the flames. Zera backed away from the fire and joined her family.

Across the flames, Gina caught a glimpse of Derrin sitting with Rahza and her sons. An uneasy sensation rose in her chest, and she could no longer deny its significance.

She was jealous.

Long tongues of flame danced, enveloping logs of deadwood in orange sheets of wind. Gina pushed the unwanted emotion away. Despite the Na'tahar and the mental connection they shared, she and Derrin were friends, nothing more. She had no right to his attention. If he had rekindled the love he'd lost long ago, she would be happy for him.

Even if it hurt.

A crackling rattle joined the drum. The villagers danced, chanting, their long shadows thrown to the ground by the flames. A primitive drama unfolded, an ancient story that renewed its truth in the telling.

A hand touched Gina's shoulder. Startled, she looked up into the cool gray of Derrin's eyes.

Her surprise must have been obvious, for Derrin met it with a half-smile. He dropped to the ground next to her, but didn't speak. Gina gazed into the rippling heat of the fire, acutely aware of his presence, of his body only inches from hers, and wondered why he'd left Rahza's side to come to her.

After a time, the bonfire burned low and the coals crawled with the memory of the flames. The gathering dispersed.

Gina turned to face Derrin. "I met Rahza," she said without preamble. "She's beautiful."

"Yes." His gaze traveled to the Baha'Na woman, still seated with her sons. The tightness in Gina's chest returned, but she ignored it. It was nothing to her if Derrin was still in love with Rahza.

Zera appeared and they rose to greet her.

"My two little ones have already shut their eyes," the Na'lara said. "I will soon join them. Derrin, will you sleep by my fire this night?"

"No. I leave Gina to you. I am promised elsewhere."

With a nod, he strode away. Gina couldn't keep her gaze from following him to Rahza's side. A moment later, the family disappeared into the shadows beyond the firelight.

Zera watched them, then turned to Gina. She made no comment, but the sympathetic expression in her eyes sent the heat rising to Gina's cheeks.

The Na'lara showed Gina to her sleeping place, a pile of furs in one of the alcoves of her hut. "The space belongs to my older sons, but they are glad to give you use of it. They will sleep in the forest while you are here." She yawned. "Sleep well."

Gina smiled her thanks. She lowered herself onto the furs and rolled on her side, facing the wall.

A number of niches had been hollowed into the stone. In them lay the trappings of a boyhood spent in close contact with nature—small stones of various colors, sticks bent into interesting shapes, a bird's nest, a snakeskin, a collection of bones, even the skull of an animal whose identity Gina could not guess. She touched a long, blue feather. Had

Derrin collected such treasures as a boy and hoarded them in Zahta's hut?

Thinking of Derrin brought a host of images to mind, most of them unwanted. Gina lay awake long after the fire had subsided to a soft glow, then slipped into an unsettled sleep. When she awoke, the edge of the sky blazed with color.

After a cold breakfast of leftover meat, an elderly villager came to Zera seeking relief from a toothache. Zera dispensed an herbal poultice and a steady stream of conversation. Then she placed her cupped palm on the old woman's cheek. The crone's shoulders relaxed, and she gave Zera a smile.

"What did you do to her?" Gina asked when the patient had left, remembering how, at the Wellspring, Zahta had cured Gina's headache with nothing more than a touch.

Zera regarded her with an inscrutable expression. "A Na'lara is called to heal," she said. "I drew the pain into my own spirit, then released it to the Goddess."

Gina spent the rest of the morning in the forecourt with Zera, pounding roots with a stone mortar and pestle while Mirris stacked gourd bowls and Lanya cooed on her blanket.

At midday, dark clouds piled on the horizon and moved swiftly to blanket the sky. Zera and Gina moved to the doorway of the hut with the children and watched as the fury of the storm broke. White sheets of rain pounded the village. Across the clearing, three figures emerged from the forest at a run.

A moment later, Derrin burst into the hut with Natis and Lorrin on his heels. Gina tried to avoid the spray of water as the three shook off the worst of the rain.

The boys were in high spirits. Natis dropped to the floor and opened a hide pouch. He spread out several additions to his store of treasures—a songbird's tailfeather, a turtle shell and a bright red stone.

Derrin spent the afternoon making arrows with the boys, then joined Gina and the others for the evening meal. Afterward, Zera and her family retired, and Gina found herself alone with him. Derrin stirred up the fire and settled cross-legged nearby, his dark head bent over a small piece of wood.

He passed the tip of a sharp bone through the fire and etched the fine grain, first lightly, then with a stronger hand. Precise strokes scraped away the ash. A cluster of mountain wildflowers emerged.

Gina marveled at his skill. "Where did you learn that?"

Derrin didn't look up from his work. "As a boy, from an elder of my clan. Do you like it?"

"It's beautiful. What's it for?"

"It's a gift for someone I care deeply about."

"Oh." Then, with forced lightness, she said, "I'm sure Rahza will like it. She must have been happy to have you with her last night."

The hint of a smile played at the corners of Derrin's mouth. His gray gaze captured hers. "I wasn't with Rahza last night. I was with her sons, and Zera's, in the forest."

Gina's rush of elation was so strong she didn't trust herself to answer. Derrin returned to his carving, working long after she had retired to her pile of furs. In the morning he was gone, as was Swift Tarma and the boys. Zera glided about the hut, gathering items into a pouch. Lanya lay on a fur, cooing and staring cross-eyed at her tiny fists.

"We have much to prepare today," Zera said. "The dark of the moon approaches."

"What happens then?"

"The *Na'salah*, the time when the women and men part. We will go to the women's grove. It is a time much treasured by the women. No matter how much we love our men, it is good to be apart from them for a time."

"What do the men do?"

"They do what men always do. They try to discover who is best among them. They hold races, contests of skill with the bow and spear, perform feats of bravery and strength. They teach the boys how to become men." She chuckled. "At night they tell the men's stories—tales they would not dare speak to a woman." Her dark eyes danced.

She produced a rawhide bucket and asked Gina to pack the food and herbs she'd prepared for the short journey. With Lanya cradled in her arms, she hurried from the hut.

Gina knelt and began layering gourd bowls and hide pouches into the bucket. A noise came from the doorway. When she looked toward it, her breath left in a rush.

It was Derrin, but she hardly recognized him.

He was naked, or nearly so, a scrap of a loincloth his only clothing. A dark, twisting tattoo snaked up his arms and legs, across the hard planes of his chest to his neck and face before disappearing into the glossy blackness of his hair. Curved feathers hung from his headband. A cord strung with animal teeth dangled from his neck.

She sat back on her heels and stared.

The muscles in his powerful thighs flexed as he moved toward her. Then he grinned. The familiar expression helped her regain her wits.

She shook her head. "I am not even going to ask."

"The Na'salah," he said by way of explanation. "All the men have prepared in this way." He glanced at his chest. "Don't worry, it's only dye made from *calah* root. It comes off."

Gina snorted. "I certainly hope so."

He dropped to one knee beside her. "I wanted to give you this before I left." He placed a small object in her palm and closed her fingers around it before drawing back.

She opened her hand and looked down at the carving she had watched him work the night before. The fine grain of the wood shone amber against her palm. Delicate blossoms hung from a knot in their stems, through which passed a braided cord.

Her breath caught. "You... You were making this for me? I thought—"

"I know what you thought."

"But Rahza—you care for her still, I can tell." She didn't look up at him.

He eased away a fraction. "It was difficult to see her again. You can't imagine how I dreamed of her in my first years among the Galenans. Now..." He let out a long breath. "I've been gone so long, and changed so much. She understands nothing of the man I've become."

He paused. She looked up to find him watching her. Tentatively, she reached her mind out to him. She could feel nothing. As always, he kept a tight leash on his emotions.

"I knew we'd be parted during the Na'salah," he said slowly. "Most of the women will carry a small token given to them by a father, a brother or a partner. I know I'm none of those things to you," he added quickly, "but I thought you'd like a reminder of your journey. From a friend."

Gina placed the circle of cord over her head and watched the wildflowers fall between her breasts to nestle beside Derrin's shadow crystal. The dark wood lay in stark contrast to the stone's silver cage.

"What do the women give their men as a token?" she heard herself ask.

"Nothing, Gina." A note of humor crept into Derrin's voice. "Except, perhaps, a kiss."

Heat rose to her cheeks. "You're teasing me," she muttered, staring at the ground.

"Am I?"

She looked up sharply, expecting to see his gray eyes flash with humor. Instead, they pierced her with absolute sincerity. Her breath went and her heart pounded into her throat.

Derrin rose, drawing Gina to her feet. She swayed toward him. Hands framing her face, he bent and brushed a slow, lingering kiss across her lips.

She leaned into his warmth, palms flat against the bare skin of his chest. His life's blood pulsed against her fingertips. He kissed her again, deeper, his lips parting hers, his tongue teasing. The rough pad of his thumb stroked her cheek. Sparks sprang to life at his touch.

The shield on his emotions cracked. Just a tiny sliver, but the hint of the longing that seeped into Gina's mind was enough to make her knees go weak.

Derrin slid one hand to the back of her neck. The other traveled a slow, heated journey across her collarbone and along the outside contour of her breast. It roamed lower, touching the sensitive dip at the base of her spine and pausing on the curve of her buttock.

He groaned and pulled her closer. His cock hardened against her stomach, sending a jolt of electricity coursing through her. Heat exploded in her breasts and stomach. It pooled as a dark ache between her thighs.

She twisted, trying to move closer, wanting to feel his cock against her throbbing clit. But Derrin eased back, steadying her with his hands on her shoulders and touching her once with his gray gaze.

Before Gina could gather her scattered emotions, he was gone.

Chapter Twelve

The song demanded everything, more than Balek could give. He needed others to tend it, men and women who would give their lives. When they were bound to the melody, it would never end.

He found it easy to enslave. Easy, because those he snared did not wish to be free. The webstone gathered all in its embrace.

Each conquered soul strengthened the song.

* * * * *

The fire danced in the clearing, throwing shadows into the treetops. The women—daughters, mothers, grandmothers—gathered close. Gina stood between Zera and Rahza, fingering her wildflower pendant. Derrin's gift helped her feel less foreign, and she was grateful for it.

The other women and girls wore similar tokens—pendants, bracelets or hair ornaments. Zera's were the most striking. A pair of bracelets, carved as snakes, circled her forearms. Their eyes, translucent yellow stones, gleamed in the firelight.

A festive mood prevailed. Women who had lived their entire lives together laughed and chattered. Lanya, nestled in Rahza's arms, was the youngest among them. Gina could only guess how many winters the elders had seen. One of the wrinkled crones stood nearby, conversing in low tones with a woman and a teenager, the same girl who had tended Zera's toddler.

The trio approached Zera. "My granddaughter is a woman," the elder said. "Her first blood flows with the new moon."

Zera brought her palm to her forehead and bowed to the old woman. Then she smiled and embraced the girl. "I rejoice with you, Shayla. Your woman's power cannot be contained, but must be released with each moon. When you accept the seed of your partner, your power will become so great a new life will emerge from your body."

Shayla's mother stepped forward and placed what appeared to be a loop of rope over the girl's head. The circlet, an odd twisted braid, fell over Shayla's shoulders.

"What is it?" Gina whispered to Rahza, who stood nearby.

"The cord that joined Shayla to Deehna in the womb. It can never truly be severed. When a boy is born, the cord is buried. A girl's cord is braided with rawhide and returned when her first blood flows."

A fine tremor shook Rahza's voice, drawing Gina's attention. Tears lay glistening on the Baha'Na woman's cheeks. She clutched the bundle that held her tiny niece.

Gina touched her arm. "You want a daughter."

"Does not every woman? I love my sons with all that I am, but when they are grown they will seek homes with another clan. Running Fox and I hoped our next child would be a daughter, but now..." She pressed her cheek against Lanya's downy head. "I have my sister's daughter—I love her as my own."

"You still may have a daughter someday. I mean, you're very young..." Gina inwardly cursed her tactlessness.

Rahza gave her a small smile. "Perhaps I will join again with another. Wading Heron has been courting me, though he knows I still mourn the loss of my partner. It will be some time before I am ready to love again in that way." She paused. "It was much the same when Derrin left."

A flood of emotions burst upon Gina at the mention of Derrin's name. Memory poured through her. The exquisite pull of his lips, the pulsing heat of his touch. She shifted, suddenly restless. She'd wanted more, so much more that it terrified her.

He'd backed off. Why? Why had he kissed her at all if he wasn't going to finish what he'd started?

Maybe he'd wanted her to pursue him. The thought made her go cold. She'd chased a man once before, given him her heart and the promise of a life together. Michael had thrown it away for a quick screw. Gina wasn't eager to put herself in such a vulnerable position again.

Besides, Derrin had vowed to send her home. He'd made it clear more than once there was no place for her in his world. Her very presence was sickening his homeland. One kiss hadn't changed that fact.

Night fell, drawing the shadows inward. Several girls threw more wood on the fire. Tongues of flame shot hissing into the sky. Small children scrambled back, to hover at their mothers' knees. Rahza, like the other women who carried infants, secured Lanya in a snug sling, leaving her hands free.

Sparks darted past, vanishing into darkness. Zera stepped forward and raised her arms. The talisman on her headdress gleamed. Her snake armlets seemed to hiss.

She threw her clear voice into the gathering. "We stand together before our Mother. Of her, all are born. To her, all return."

Rahza grasped Gina's hand and lifted it. The woman on Gina's right did the same, as did all the women, forming an unbroken circle around the fire. Waves of smoke and heat rolled over Gina. She fought a sudden dizziness.

Zera threw her head back and let out a loud cry—a rich primal note that pierced Gina's brain, scattered her thoughts. An instant later, the clanswomen joined Zera's call.

The chant ran through Gina's body like a jolt of electricity. It continued, unbroken, a single note repeated over and over by each voice, the whole never fading, always strong. Gina added her own voice to the cry.

The call caught her in the center of its energy and lifted her into the wind. She shut her eyes and gripped the hands of the women on either side, her heart pounding in her ears. The voices grew louder.

Then, abruptly, silence.

Gina opened her eyes and looked down on the clearing. The circle of women danced around the fire, framed by the treetops. Zera stood with her arms raised and her head flung back. She clasped the heads of two live, writhing serpents.

Gina blinked, dazed, trying to understand. Her gaze found Rahza, then herself, far below on the ground. Yet she felt no fear. Instead, a sparkling euphoria embraced her. The women danced, swirling and leaping around the fire. Their lips moved, but Gina couldn't hear their song. Silence still surrounded her, deep and fathomless.

She watched herself spin around, then suddenly she was there, in the midst of the women, dancing, and the wild song was on her own lips. Pure joy burst from deep within her and spilled into the night, into the flames.

Hours later, when the fire had burned low, Gina lay in the warm embrace of the earth and listened to the soft breath of the women around her. A breeze touched her face. She looked up into a sky hung with more stars than she'd ever imagined. She drifted to sleep, carried on the love of her sisters.

* * * * *

Zera slipped through the forest, making her way to a hidden place she loved, where a stream spilled into a deep pool. Lanya whimpered in her sling.

"Almost there, my little one."

It was a rare moment when Zera could be truly alone with her babe, away from the call of the people who depended on her. But a Na'lara needed silence, needed to take herself away from time to time. Zera learned this as a girl, from her grandmother, but had not understood. Why would she wish to go apart? She loved people, loved to be with them, loved the talk of the women and the laughter of the men.

But now, Grandmother lived beyond the veil and Zera better understood her wisdom. She could not show the face of the Goddess to the clan unless she sought strength in silence.

It was, in a way, her most difficult duty.

She had left the other women in the hour before dawn. Her daughter would not disturb her meditation, and the little one needed feeding as much as Zera needed to feed her.

Her breasts were hard and aching by the time she settled on the sandy bank. Lanya waved her fists and howled. Zera loosened the neckline of her dress and guided the small mouth to her dripping brown nipple, letting out a sigh of relief when Lanya latched on. The milk tingled and flowed. Her daughter's small mouth worked furiously to keep up.

The familiar rush of peace washed over her. She gazed at Lanya's bright eyes, focused in unblinking concentration as she concentrated on her meal with single-minded determination. A smile played on Zera's lips. She brushed her finger over the babe's silky dark hair and felt her love flow with her milk.

Lanya drained one breast then continued feeding, a little less urgently, on the other side. Soon after, her eyes closed and the sucking slowed. The nipple slid out of her mouth, spilling white drops across her small chin. With a sigh, Lanya settled her cheek on the pillow of her mother's breast and sank into a heavy slumber.

Zera's thoughts turned to Derrin. He had spent so many seasons among the Outsiders, and had changed in a way she didn't understand. A man of the Baha'Na would never ask her to call the power of the talisman. True, six Na'lara stood at the edge of the Circle, but the Center was empty. The Seventh was lost. The veil could not be lifted. The web could not be called.

Yet last night Zera had seen a vision in the night shadows. Derrin did not need the aid of the Circle—he would open the web himself and Gina would cross.

Why would the Goddess bring Gina to the People only to take her away so soon? Zera pondered the question. She found no answer, but she did not question the wisdom of the Mother. And she would not let Derrin's tales of waste in the Outside Lands frighten her.

The People lived in the heart of the Goddess. Nothing else mattered. Zera was sure of it.

* * * * *

A high-pitched wail, a woman's voice, pierced the air. Gina froze in the act of unpacking a rawhide pouch, her body tightening with instinctive horror.

Zera's gourd bucket thudded to the ground, spilling its contents onto the earthen floor of the hut. Rahza stifled a cry, her palm pressed against her lips.

Outside, in the village, a second wail joined the first. Lanya, disturbed, whimpered in protest.

"What… What is it?"

"The death song." Rahza's voice came in a trembling whisper.

Lanya let out a howl. Zera, half-dazed, moved to the cradle and lifted the infant into her arms. "Someone has died," she said, looking into her daughter's face. "One of the men, or the boys… We must go."

The impact of Zera's words knocked the breath from Gina's body. A moment earlier they'd been laughing and talking, preparing for the return of the men after four days of separation. Now…

Please don't let it be Derrin. Gina struggled to pull air into her lungs. She followed the Baha'Na women out of the hut, dreading every step.

A group of men huddled on the far side of the village. Women streamed toward them, adding their voices to the death song. The men stood silent.

Gina scanned the gathering for Derrin. She soon found him, standing next to Swift Tarma. The husky man held little Mirris in his arms. Zera's and Rahza's other sons pressed close on either side.

Relief, stunning in its intensity, washed over her. She paused and drew a deep breath before hurrying after Zera and Rahza.

The mourners cleared a path for the Na'lara. Gina glimpsed a man lying on a rough stretcher of branches. His chest had been crushed. Blood caked his body, splinters of bone protruded from his skin. Two glazed eyes looked out from a gray, twisted face. Gina shuddered, feeling suddenly sick.

Zera handed Lanya to her sister and ran forward to look at the man's face. She turned, searching, then ran past Gina to Deehna and Shayla. Deehna caught a glimpse of Zera's face and stiffened.

"No." Her voice cracked. "It cannot be."

Zera halted before them and spread out her arms. Her dark eyes brimmed with tears. "It is Red Hawk."

"No!" Deehna pushed past Zera. She ran to the fallen man and dropped to her knees. With a trembling hand, she touched his forehead, his cheek, his wounds. Then she raised her face to the sky and let out an animal's scream.

Shayla launched herself through the crowd and flung herself on the body. "Father! It cannot be...you cannot leave me..." She clawed at the dead man, grabbed his hair. She shook his head from side to side, as if, with enough force, she could wake him.

Gina watched, her chest dragging with each breath. Would no one step forward to restrain the girl? The men stood still and silent, their expressions set in stone. The smaller children sobbed while their mothers continued the wail of the death song.

The high-pitched keening grated along her shattered nerves. By now every village woman had joined her voice in grief, but Gina couldn't have forced a sound from her lips if her life had depended on it.

She backed away, stomach heaving, memory clamping her throat like a vise.

*****

The wait at the hospital emergency room was much too short. The instant the closed door swung forward, the truth flooded every cell of her body.

Her father was dead.

"Massive heart failure." She accepted the words with a nod and turned away.

Dry-eyed, she inspected the corpse. Its face—frozen in a final, desperate gasp—stared back at her.

She noted the aspects of death with the precision of a scientist. Sightless eyes. Bent neck. Rigid joints. Skin that had taken on the color of the sky.

A brilliant, nauseating shade of blue.

*****

Derrin tore his gaze from the grieving girl and scanned the huddle of mourners. He found Gina soon enough, looking like a lost child. She stood apart from the others, her arms wrapped tight about her torso. The pain in her expression was fierce, personal.

Her need drew him.

He went to her without a second thought. She didn't seem to notice his approach. He halted in front of her and examined her pinched expression, at a loss for words.

After a moment Gina looked up at him, then glanced away. "What happened?"

"A rockfall," he replied, his chest tight. "It came without warning. Natis and Mirris were in its path and Red Hawk was closest to them. He flung them out of the way, but—"

A sharp wail from Shayla cut him short. He followed Gina's gaze to the girl, then turned his attention back to Gina. She was shaking, as if suffering from a shock much greater than the death of a man she didn't know. A flash of understanding struck him. She grieved for a more personal loss, one she hadn't made peace with. Her father's death had thrown her into the arms of a man she hadn't belonged with. As Shayla mourned her father, so Gina mourned hers, the pain as sharp as they day she had lost him.

He touched her arm. "Is it still so hard, then, even with the time that has passed?"

She turned to him, raw pain in her eyes. "My father was my only family. I was there when his heart gave out, but it was so sudden, I couldn't do anything but watch him die." She made a helpless gesture. "I didn't even have time to say goodbye."

Derrin drew her close, settling her cheek against his chest and stroking her hair as if she were a small child. She pulled away and met his gaze.

"I didn't cry at all. Not even at the funeral. I was afraid if I gave in I would shatter into a million pieces and never be whole again."

She buried her face in his shirt, but not before he saw the shimmer of tears in her eyes.

Derrin pressed his cheek to the top of Gina's head and smoothed her braids with his palm. "Cry now, Gina," he whispered. "As much as you want, as much as you need. I won't let you break apart."

A tremor shook her. He tightened his arms and felt Gina's emotions break. She clung to him as the storm of sobs buffeted her. Derrin absorbed the pain with his own soul, holding her until she quieted and for a time afterwards, reluctant to let her go. She fit perfectly in his arms, as if she weren't a woman from an alien world at all, but a part of himself he'd long ago given up as lost.

That evening, flames consumed the body of Red Hawk, releasing his spirit to the Goddess. The corpse, wrapped in a hide blanket, fell into the center of the fire. Once again, the women wailed the death song. Derrin felt Gina stiffen at his side.

He drew her closer as a gust of wind sent up a whirl of sparks. A man gave a shout, pointing upward.

A hawk sailed in slow circles above the gathering. It pulled back, wings flared, then dove toward the fire. For an instant, Derrin thought the flames would consume it, but at the last moment the great bird veered away. Long wings beating, it mounted up into the sky and flew toward the setting sun. Exclamations of wonder followed it.

"What does it mean?" Gina asked in a hushed voice.

"It's a good sign. Red Hawk's guardian has taken his spirit to the Goddess," Derrin said.

"She's real, isn't she?"

"Who do you mean?"

"The Goddess—she's real. I thought it was just a story, but now…" She paused, as if not quite sure how to continue. "I can feel her. I feel her love, even in the sadness, or maybe…because of it."

Derrin shot a sharp look at Gina. Her last words had been spoken not in the unusual cadence of her alien language, but in the lilting tones of the Baha'Na. He wondered if she'd even realized the change in her speech.

A fierce emotion washed over him. His gaze touched on her smooth, sun-browned skin, her straight nose and high cheekbones. Her eyes were the deepest brown, almost black, wide and honest. Vulnerable, yet unafraid. Every day he wanted her more, until he thought he would go insane with longing and loneliness. He'd wronged her deeply, but incredibly, she'd forgiven him. He didn't deserve her acceptance, but he hadn't the strength to reject it. All he could do was protect her from more hurt, by denying himself what he wanted most, until he could send her back across the web.

But each day that task grew more difficult, because each day it became harder to remember Gina was not of his world. Hard to remember she was not of the Baha'Na. She wore the clothing and spoke the language of his mother's people. The sun had kissed her pale skin and turned it golden. She held her head high and moved through the forest with a grace she hadn't possessed at the start of their journey.

Still, he would not forget.

"When I was a boy," he told her, "Zahta often told me the People live in the heart of the Goddess."

"Yes." Gina swept her arms outward, then brought her palms together. Derrin's chest tightened. He'd seen his grandmother make the same gesture countless times, a sign showing the relationship of the Baha'Na to the wilderness.

His senses filled with the memory of Gina's kiss. A kiss he had so unwisely teased from her, while he'd been swept away in the fantasy of once again belonging to the Baha'Na.

He pushed the illusion away. It was time he accepted reality. Neither he nor Gina belonged here in the wilderness. Yes, he ached to love her, but no good could come of it. Her presence fueled the Blight. Any bond between them would only serve to make their parting that much more difficult.

He couldn't afford to lose sight of his goal, no matter how confused his feelings had become. He would open the web and send Gina home—the fate of his world depended on it.

He stepped away. "Come. We will be needed in Zera's dwelling. She'll stay with Deehna this night."

Gina nodded. Together, they left the dying flames.

*****

The pale blue crystal flashed a pattern. Three long bright bursts, then two shorter sparks. Ariek ran one hand over his head and waited, his gaze intent on the stone's blank surface. After several long, pulsing seconds, he muttered a curse and turned away.

Derrin had promised to send a signal from the mate of the blue crystal, but now it seemed as if he'd vanished into thin air. Ariek stared sourly at the lifeless crystal, his apprehension flaring into fear. What in Tarol's Inferno had happened to Derrin?

He slammed out of his workroom and entered the hallway, trying to remember the details of Derrin's accusations concerning Balek—accusations Ariek had once dismissed as fancy, but now was beginning to credit. The Madness and the Blight were aspects of the same malady, Derrin had insisted. It seemed unlikely, yet...

"Master Kaltir! Meerak!" Ariek hurried to catch up with the two wizards who had entered the passageway a short distance ahead. They turned at his greeting.

"You've been scarce, Ariek," the younger man remarked.

"I've been busy." Ariek fell into step beside Meerak and his mentor. "I've developed a hypothesis. I'd like your opinion. You've both spent a good deal of time studying the Blight. Is it possible the Blight and the Madness are one disease, springing from a common source?"

Kaltir raised one bushy gray eyebrow. "There is no reason to think it. Do you have evidence to support such a theory?"

"Uh...nothing definite," Ariek faltered, "just a feeling." At the sight of Meerak's incredulous stare he added, "They appeared at about the same time."

"My dear Ariek," Kaltir said, "if two men arrive in Katrinth on the same day, it does not necessarily follow that they journeyed from the same town. The Blight and the Madness are two very different maladies. One affects the forest and fields, the other strikes the minds of men. It is not probable that they arise from the same source."

"It is an interesting theory, though," put in Meerak. "One that could be studied. If you wish, we could work together to devise a series of experiments. My schedule is full until after the next Lower House Council, but afterwards—"

Ariek cut him short. "Thank you, Meerak. I'll give that some thought."

Kaltir snorted. "Set your mind to more pressing matters, Ariek. Such simplistic reasoning is beneath you."

Chagrinned, Ariek turned away. He had wanted to test Derrin's theory and had feared just such a reaction. It would take months of research and analysis before he could hope to present enough evidence to convince the Upper House to consider Derrin's idea. How much longer would it take to prove Balek's activities were the cause of the Blight?

On the other hand, maybe Derrin was mistaken. Ariek had to agree with Kaltir—precious little in the way of hard fact existed to support his friend's speculation. Derrin, however, had a talent for uncanny leaps of perception. His improbable prediction of communication via twinned crystals had proved accurate. But a five-sided crystal? Impossible. Such an object couldn't exist. Still, there *was* the question of Maator's amazingly pure crystals...

Without allowing himself time to reflect on his actions, Ariek turned his steps in the direction of Balek's chambers. The High Council was in session, and Ariek had seen Maator leave the Stronghold a short time earlier. He might as well take the opportunity to have a look around.

He unlocked the door and eased himself into the long workroom. Once inside, he searched every shelf and storage area, fighting back a feeling of utter foolishness. Did he expect to find the improbable stone? His gaze passed over countless crystals of all types. Some were incredibly pure, but none resembled Derrin's description. Ariek turned to leave. As he moved toward the door, the faint outline of a pentagram caught the corner of his vision.

He moved closer to get a better look at the pattern etched in the center of the gleaming black worktable. His fingers touched it. The ebony slab slid back. The shallow compartment below contained a single yellow crystal.

Ariek blinked and bent closer. Each sharp plane of the crystal had five edges. He slid the stone from its resting place and turned it over in his hands. An uneasy feeling of wonder clawed at his stomach. The crystal did indeed have five sides, each a perfect pentagram.

His throat went dry. Somehow the impossible, the insane, fit together with perfect logic.

He studied the anomaly, but could not fathom its structure, and his mind refused to acknowledge it. There was only one way to understand the nature of the stone. Ariek stretched his mind toward it. His concentration flickered on the surface of the paradox before plunging inside.

Madness exploded, flinging fragments of reason to the outer reaches of his consciousness and beyond. The room spun. He stumbled against the table, gasping, his sanity reeling in the maelstrom. With a desperate effort, he grasped at the last shred of his will and wrenched his mind free.

He stared at the crystal, chest heaving. Raw power shimmered in waves around the stone, a wild, primitive force unmoved by logic. Ariek's doubts vanished. Derrin was right. This obscene crystal was indeed the source of the sicknesses ravaging the land. He would stake his life on it.

Footsteps sounded in the hall. Quickly, Ariek returned the crystal to its niche and closed the pentagram. He pulled out one of his own crystals and uttered a silent command. He faded into shadow as Balek and Maator entered the room.

He dared not remain. His concentration had been shaken by his plunge into madness and wouldn't sustain the shadow for long. He edged toward the open door. Once safe in the passageway, he breathed a sigh of relief.

*****

"He's gone." Maator stole a glance at Balek. His mentor was in a particularly foul mood.

"Tarol's blood! I cannot believe he broke free of the webstone." Balek's tone was sharp. "What have you learned? Does Ariek know where Derrin has hidden the woman?"

Maator knew better than to show fear in Balek's presence. He stared at the faint pentagram etched on the worktable and shrugged with a nonchalance he did not feel. "I've been watching him. The man knows something." Maator dared a glance in Balek's direction. "He will be the first person Derrin contacts when he tires of hiding."

Balek did not answer, but his displeasure showed in the cold glint of his eyes. Maator racked his brain for some scrap of information to keep his master's anger at bay.

"Ariek is concealing more than Derrin's whereabouts, Master."

"What do you mean?"

"He spends many of his nights in the Temple of Lotark."

Balek's brows shot up. "The Temple? How curious."

"But true. Ariek is the Bride of Lotark's secret lover."

Balek stared at Maator for one startled moment. Then he started to laugh.

The mirthless sound sent a shiver up Maator's spine.

"Brilliant." Balek chuckled, stroking the gray-gold strands of his beard. "Brilliant indeed. That information, Maator, may prove quite useful."

Chapter Thirteen

The night was hot.

Gina gave up on the pretense of sleep. There'd been no need for a shelter, but Derrin hadn't extinguished the fire at nightfall, choosing instead to let it smolder as a deterrent to insects and other, more dangerous beasts. As a result, rivulets of sweat pooled between her breasts. Her dress clung limply to her sticky skin.

Rolling onto her back, Gina watched the stars wander in and out of the clouds, keenly aware of Derrin stretched out little more than an arm's length away.

She concentrated for a moment on the rise and fall of his breath. Still awake. She'd been his sleeping partner long enough to tell. Odd, having spent so many nights with a man who wasn't her lover.

Her lover. Slow heat infused her body at the thought. She rolled onto her side and peered at Derrin. He lay with his back facing her, one arm tucked under his head. She extended her mind to him, but as usual, she could feel nothing. He was guarding his emotions well. She sighed. She wished she could do the same.

They'd left the Fire Clan early this morning. Once alone with Derrin, Gina had been plagued by the memory of his kiss. It had awakened every cell in her body and set them vibrating, clamoring for more. Unfortunately, though there'd been plenty of opportunity, Derrin hadn't kissed her again. He hadn't even drawn close enough for her to touch. She'd tried more than once to ask him about it, but the words had stuck in her throat.

An owl hooted, somewhere far above. Despite her vulnerability during the Na'tahar—or maybe because of it—Gina wanted Derrin. She wanted him with a longing she'd never before experienced. And when she thought of making love to Derrin, she didn't think of candlelight and flowery declarations. She didn't think of tenderness and respect.

She thought of raw power and possession. She thought of being helpless in the face of his lust and reveling in it. She thought of giving him everything, holding nothing back, letting him drive her harder and further than she'd ever gone before.

The thought was both exciting and terrifying.

Gina focused on his motionless form and imagined reaching out to skim her fingers over the corded muscles of his shoulders and over his powerful biceps. She almost extended her hand to try it.

But at the last moment, she pulled back. A biting apprehension stopped her from offering herself to him. What if he refused her? Even worse, what if he accepted her offer and found her lacking? Michael had.

As Gina's relationship with her ex crumbled, he'd never lost an opportunity to point out her deficiencies in bed. Gina had come to dread sex. She tried to avoid it, claiming she was too tired or had too much work to do. Unfortunately, Michael wasn't a man to take no for an answer, especially when he had a hard-on.

He told her it was her fault their marriage was falling apart. She hadn't tried hard enough to please him. His accusations rang true, so she'd closed her eyes and tried to respond to his advances. It didn't work. Stretched out under him, her body had turned numb. When he entered her, it hurt.

She kept trying until she came home early one day to find Michael in bed with one of his students.

After their breakup, she'd tried a few times to date, but found herself going numb when her date tried to kiss her. It was as if her body had relearned its response to sex. What if she tried to have sex with Derrin and her body shut off? What would she say to him? What would he think? Traveling with him afterward would be a nightmare.

Gina rolled over onto her back and shut her eyes. Best to play it safe.

* * * * *

Derrin came to her in a dream.

This time Gina knew it was him, and knew it wasn't real. He stretched out beside her, pressing every inch of his hard body to hers. Bare skin, slick with sweat, caught and slid, creating delicious friction. The spark of desire in Gina's belly caught and blazed.

It was only a dream.

Derrin's hands moved down her back to cup her buttocks. His thigh parted her legs. The rough hairs on his leg scraped her tender skin, pressed hard against her clit. She bucked against him, a satisfied moan tearing from her lips as she rode his leg. His palms on her ass guided, urged.

His teeth caught on her neck, igniting small bites of fire along her shoulder. He smelled of woodsmoke and loam, mystery and darkness. His cock was hard—she could feel it nudging her hip as she moved against him. But when she would have shifted to take him in, his grip tightened, holding her back.

Her arousal spun higher. Her rhythm quickened. She rubbed her clit against his thigh, mindless with the pleasure of it. For once, her body did not betray her. This was a dream, nothing more. She was safe. She could let herself go, let herself imagine, and Derrin would never know.

Her climax broke swift and hard, leaving her gasping. She came awake as it washed over her, her own hand pressed on her pulsing mound. *Oh God.* It took all her will to keep from crying out.

She lay still, struggling to keep her breath even, waiting for the trembling of her limbs to subside. When it did, she rolled to one side, trying not to rustle the dried leaves under her.

She darted a glance at Derrin, and let out a sigh of relief.

He was asleep.

* * * * *

The midday sun beat down on the still landscape, dropping its weight like a blanket over the valley. The staccato rhythm of insects battered Derrin's skull. He scowled at the blue sky, then quickened his pace through the thick underbrush, lengthening the distance between himself and Gina.

The most sensible course of action would be to wait out the hottest part of the day near a shady stream, but Derrin couldn't bring himself to stop walking. It would mean having to talk to Gina, and after the mind-shattering dream they had shared the night before, he wasn't sure he was up to the task.

The night joining had been awash with Gina's pleasure—pleasure she had no idea he'd given her. After the dream had faded, he lay awake, unwilling to risk closing his eyes again. He'd never been so happy to see the dawn.

But it hadn't taken long for a black mood to descend. The result, no doubt, of his restless night. Vivid images of Gina, naked beneath him, had haunted his waking moments as thoroughly as their dream had permeated his slumber. In his mind's eye he saw her writhe as he drove himself into her body so powerfully his balls slapped against her buttocks.

He hadn't been able to look her in the eye once she'd risen. If he had, he would have taken her in the dirt. His control was that fragile.

All morning, he kept a careful distance between them—it was the only way he could resist his craving to touch her. Even so, the memory of her kiss on his lips was driving him insane. His palms tingled. He wanted to kiss her again, to slip his hand beneath the hem of her dress and stroke upward. He wanted to part her slick folds, find the hard bud where her pleasure centered and urge her to…

No.

With a foul curse, he reminded himself again that Gina was from another world. She was a woman who would soon be gone from his life. A woman he had already violated. A woman who by all rights should despise him in the flesh, even though she welcomed him in her dreams.

His efforts were useless.

He could no longer think of Gina as a stranger to his world. She moved through the forest with stunning grace. She laughed and cried with his mother's people. She no longer spoke in her own alien tongue, but in the language of the Baha'Na. Yet Gina understood Derrin's life in Galena as no woman of the clans ever could. She knew all that he was, all that he had lost. She had seen the worst part of him, suffered because of it, and forgiven him for it.

He wanted her. The intensity of his desire staggered him. He wanted to tear out his heart and offer it to her. He wanted to feel the rise and fall of her breath against his body as they lay beneath the stars. He wanted to suckle her breasts like a newborn babe.

He wanted to throw her on the ground and fuck her like a Galenan whore.

But how could he form a bond with Gina when her very presence fueled the destruction of his world? New evidence of the Blight confronted him everywhere. The symptoms were not as obvious as in Galena, where entire forests had been stripped of foliage, but the signs were clear to anyone who knew the wilderness. Sudden shifts in temperature, trees and shrubs that hadn't set fruit, a particular birdsong absent from the chorus at dawn.

Anger and frustration gripped him. Each Na'lara in turn had refused to aid him in opening the web. They accepted the changes in the wilderness as the will of the Goddess. They would wait patiently for the Great Mother to rescue them, but Derrin knew better. No miracle would be forthcoming. The source of the Blight was a man's greed. The plagues would not abate until Balek's webstone was destroyed, and Derrin was the only man capable of doing it.

He would stop the high wizard, no matter the cost. Sending Gina home was his first step. Zera had told him she had dreamed Gina would cross the web at the next full moon. Though he dreaded the hour of Gina's departure, he hoped, for the sake of his own sanity, the Na'lara's vision had been true.

"Derrin, wait!"

He stopped and turned. Gina was struggling through a dense patch of brush. He watched, torn between a desire to help and a reluctance to place himself so close to her. As a compromise, he shouted instructions to duck under the higher branches and follow the animal trails close to the ground.

Gina crawled from the thicket flushed and panting. Her arms were scratched. Thorns had snagged her braids and dress. Perspiration dripped from her forehead and down her cheeks, leaving trails on her dirty face.

He turned without a word and continued on the trail. The thick vegetation soon gave way to a steep, rocky slope. Waves of heat rose from the rocks as he climbed.

"Derrin!" Gina yelled again.

He stopped and waited for her to catch up.

"Why are you in such a hurry?" she said, panting.

"I'm not hurrying. You're slow."

She glared at him. "I'm doing the best I can."

"That may be true, but it's not much." He was baiting her, he knew, but he couldn't seem to stop himself. His sexual frustration, combined with his fear that the Blight would soon consume the wilderness, battered his tenuous control.

"What is your problem? You've been in a rotten mood all day."

He didn't answer.

"Did you hear me? What are you so mad about?"

"Nothing." He turned and started walking.

"Fine."

He heard her trudging behind him. A sudden, irrational anger blasted him. He whirled around so quickly that Gina stumbled into him. "I'll tell you why I'm angry," he said. "It's you."

"Me? I didn't do anything!"

"Maybe not, but I'm stuck here with you, aren't I? I should have been back in Katrinth weeks ago." His hand closed in a fist. "Everywhere I look I see the edges of the wilderness dying. I can't afford to forget what your presence in this world means."

Gina stared at him, surprise and hurt naked in her eyes. Then she turned away and dropped her head, her braids swinging forward to hide her face. Guilt stabbed Derrin's gut. He took one step toward her, then stopped and held his ground.

"Are you, Derrin?" she asked.

"Am I what?"

She looked up. "Forgetting why I'm here?"

He gaped at her. He could feel her emotions brimming, threatening to overflow. Her dark eyes, wet with tears, ripped at his heart and her mind hovered just a hairsbreadth from his own. He knew if he let down his guard for even an instant, she would look into his soul and see everything he fought to hide.

"No," he snapped. "I'm not forgetting."

He continued the journey, Gina's angry silence pursuing him. If he'd succeeded in matching her mood to his own, it was just as well. Still, he dreaded setting up camp for the night. The temptation to move their union from dreams to flesh was entirely too great.

They hiked across a landscape of rocks, skirting the base of a steep ridge scarred with caves and ledges. The village of the Wind Clan lay on the opposite face of the mountain. It would take two or three days to negotiate the valley trail.

Derrin shut his eyes and let out a long breath. He was certain to go mad in that time. Unless…

He squinted at the mountain. There was another path to the village—a steep trail that zigzagged across the face of the cliff. He could easily make the climb alone, but could Gina manage it? He thought so. Leaving the valley trail, he headed straight up the slope.

"We aren't going to climb that, are we?"

Derrin could tell Gina's anger was still simmering. He turned and nearly winced at her expression of hostile disbelief.

"It's not as bad as it looks," he lied. "The village of the Wind Clan is just beyond the ridge. We can be there before nightfall."

Gina's scowl deepened, but she didn't comment further. They crept up the face of the mountain, inching from one rocky outcropping to the next. A steady breeze rose, cutting through the worst of the simmering heat.

By late afternoon, Derrin regretted his hasty decision. The wind had turned gusty, and much cooler. Dark clouds crowded the horizon.

He glanced at Gina. The effort of the climb was etched on her face. "We have to hurry," he told her.

She hoisted herself up beside him and grimaced.

A jagged finger of lightning flashed. Overhead the sky shone blue, but the black edge of a storm was advancing at a rapid pace. Too fast, Derrin thought, trying to gauge its speed as he climbed. A low rumble of thunder reached his ears.

He muttered a curse. "We won't make the top before it hits." Beside him, Gina clutched the rock with a white-knuckled hand, chest heaving. The sky went dark.

Derrin pointed to his left. "There's a cave over there. We'll take shelter until the storm passes."

"Derrin, there's nothing but sheer rock between us and that cave! We'll never make it."

"We'll make it," he replied grimly. He found the first handhold. He began the sideways climb, the first heavy drops of rain stinging his face.

*****

The dark, pounding wall of water flattened Gina against the cliff. She must have been insane to let Derrin talk her into this climb. She tightened her death grip on a narrow crevice and hung on with all her strength. The sky flashed white.

Thunder rolled like an avalanche. Panic squeezed her lungs. Derrin's form had dissolved in the torrent.

"Gina! Give me your hand!"

Cautiously, Gina extended her left arm toward his voice.

Her foot slipped. She made a wild grab in Derrin's direction, then lost her footing completely. The rock under her right hand crumbled.

Her body slammed into a ledge. Before she could get hold of it, a gust of wind knocked her backward. She fell, hit the rocky slope and skidded.

The wind blasted Derrin's shout into the storm. Gina slid down the rocks, scraping the face of the mountain with increasing speed, arms flailing.

A second ledge broke her slide with a painful jolt. She managed to anchor one hand to a jagged stone while she struggled to find a foothold. Her legs swung forward, meeting air.

She attempted to lift herself onto the ledge, but the effort only caused her fingers to slip. Panicked, she clung to her meager support.

I'm going to die. In a strange way, the thought seemed almost a comfort. At least she would be able to stop fighting. The storm faded a bit. Her grip loosened. It would be so easy to let go…

"Gina! Where are you?"

Derrin's voice pierced her daze. She renewed her hold on the rock and gathered her remaining strength into an answer. "Here…"

"Hold on." Derrin's voice sounded closer, but how far away, she couldn't tell. Her arms burned. Her fingers slipped a fraction lower.

A grip like a vise closed on her forearm and then Derrin was hauling her upward. He flung her onto the ledge and crouched over her, blocking the worst of the storm.

The wind whipped his dark hair into his face. "Are you all right?" he shouted. "Did you break anything?"

She sucked in a painful breath. "I…don't think so."

"Good. Gina, listen to me. We can't stay here. It's too narrow. There's a cave just overhead. It's not far—I'll get you there."

He wanted to move? "No." Her chest constricted. "I'll never make it."

"You have to." He urged her to her feet and turned her around, pressing her palms to the face of the cliff and covering them with his own. His chest pressed against her spine. "I won't let you go again. If you fall, I'll fall with you."

He guided her hand to a crevice. Somehow, she managed to raise her leg and find a foothold. She felt Derrin behind her. His voice sounded in her ear, urging her upward, praising every inch of progress. His low tone steadied her, kept her sane.

She started to believe she would make it.

Endless moments later, she reached the mouth of the cave, a ferocious downdraft at her back. Derrin caught her around the waist and dragged her forward, out of the worst of the wind.

The shallow depression afforded minimal protection, but even that was welcome. Derrin slumped against the back wall and pulled Gina close, his breath coming in short gasps.

Rain battered the meager shelter. Gina shivered against the chill and Derrin's arms tightened around her. She pressed her forehead against his chest, concentrating on his solid strength.

"I almost lost you..." His voice was raw.

The sky went white with lightning. Gina raised her head in time to catch a glimpse of Derrin's eyes. They were fierce, filled with a longing so great it took her breath.

Then the darkness returned and he kissed her.

His lips took hers with the power of a tempest—wild, ruthless, primitive. He drove deep, claiming her mouth with his tongue, turning to shove her spine against the wall of the cave. She met his assault with equal fury, riding the aftermath of her fear and drawing reassurance from his response.

He drew back and pulled her into his lap. His hands turned gentle, stroking her hair. She wrapped her arms around his chest and pressed her cheek against his wet shirt. His lips brushed her forehead. His mind touched hers with a light, calming stroke. She sensed he exerted a great effort to keep it that way.

Gina tried to speak, but Derrin eased her to the ground, and told her to rest, to sleep. Too exhausted to resist, she closed her eyes and sank into oblivion.

* * * * *

Gina woke to the light of a brilliant half moon. She groaned, rolling away from the intrusion and flinging one arm over her eyes. Every muscle in her body protested.

Her elbow ached, her shoulder throbbed and a sharp pain stabbed her chest with each breath. Her dress clung to her skin like clammy seaweed. Wincing, she propped herself up on her uninjured arm.

"I'm alive," she said. It seemed the only explanation for all the pain. The words were little more than a croak.

"Did you think you weren't?" Derrin's voice was strained. With an effort, Gina turned her head and focused on him. He sat a few feet away, leaning against the back of the cave. She extended her mind to him, but felt nothing. The shield was back in place.

"No, I guess not." She gritted her teeth and pushed to a sitting position. "I hurt too much to be dead."

Derrin looked out on the valley, where the moonlight fell on a low shroud of mist. "I'm sorry, Gina. I never should have brought you up the cliff path."

She tried to conjure a remnant of the previous day's anger, but found she couldn't. She was just too tired, and the pain in Derrin's voice destroyed any thoughts of a sarcastic retort. She tried for a light tone. "No kidding. Next time I'll take the long way around."

He gave her a sharp glance, as if judging her mood.

She reached over and laid her hand on his arm. "What's happening to us, Derrin?"

He pressed the back of his head against the wall of the cave and let out a long breath. "I don't know, Gina, but I nearly killed us both by fighting it."

"Maybe you should stop fighting, then."

The muscles in Derrin's arm tensed under her fingers. He turned his head and met her gaze. His eyes, caught in the light of the moon, were searching, guarded.

For a moment, Gina thought he would move away. Then his shoulders relaxed. He reached out one arm. At the same time, she felt his silent invitation brush her mind. She scooted closer, into the shelter of his body.

His arm tightened around her. "Maybe you're right," he said, his breath at her temple. "Maybe I should stop fighting,"

Gina pressed her cheek into the hollow of his shoulder and let the silence of the night wash over her.

Mist appeared in the valley as dawn approached. It crept into the cave in white swirls, then rose into the sky. The moonlight disappeared.

Gina floated on the edge of mystery, where every shape lay hidden. The mood lingered even after the new sun dispersed the worst of the fog.

They left the cave and made the short climb to the crest of the ridge. The terrain on the opposite side of the peak sloped gently into a lush forest, then disappeared once again into the mist. Morning birdsong sounded from the shrouded greenery.

Derrin led the way into the dream world. Vapor swirled around Gina's knees, then rose to obscure her vision. Drops of rain, delayed by the trees, beat a patternless tempo around her.

She reached for Derrin, barely visible at an arm's length in front of her. "Couldn't we wait until the fog lifts? I can't see a thing."

"There's no need to—"

A songbird called to its mate, a high, lingering note, followed by a run of shorter tones at a lower pitch. Derrin tensed.

"What—"

"Shh..."

The song came again. Derrin listened intently, then, to Gina's surprise, he cupped his hands around his mouth and answered with an identical call. Before she could question him about his curious behavior, he caught her hand and gestured for her to remain silent.

They continued along the trail at a snail's pace. The mist lightened, allowing Gina to peer about a dozen paces ahead. Derrin continued his curious behavior, stalking, then motioning for Gina to halt as he listened. Gina strained her ears, but she could discern nothing out of the ordinary.

An icy shiver ran the length of her spine, coupled with a growing sense of uneasiness. What—or who—was Derrin listening for? Had the bird's call been a warning?

Gina could feel tension radiating from Derrin's shoulders. He crouched low and motionless like a wildcat set to pounce.

A screech shattered the air as a man dropped from a branch overhead.

Chapter Fourteen

Gina screamed and staggered backward as Derrin went down under his attacker's weight. An expression of deadly intent contorted the man's face. He wore the clothing of the Baha'Na, but Gina knew the men of the peaceful clans didn't fight among themselves. Was he an outcast?

The man's corded muscles flexed as he rolled Derrin onto his back. With an agile twist, Derrin flipped over and broke free. The man lunged for Derrin's neck.

Gina grabbed a rock the size of a football and hefted it with both hands. She took a step toward the grappling men, watching for her opportunity to heave her crude weapon into the melee without hitting Derrin.

Derrin spun about and dove for the assailant's waist. He caught it and rolled, crashing through the underbrush. When his arm came free, he braced it on his opponent's shoulders and tried to slam him into the ground. The burly Baha'Na man took advantage of a muddy patch of ground and threw Derrin over.

He landed flat on his back. With a wild cry, the attacker pounced. Gina hoisted her stone over her head and aimed it at the wild man's skull.

Her gaze locked with Derrin's. His eyes widened as the stone began its plunge.

He shouted and rolled to one side, taking his assailant with him. Gina's rock thudded into the dirt.

The combatants sprang apart, chests heaving. Gina swung her gaze from the stranger, who crouched with his head propped in his hands, to Derrin, who leaned against a fallen tree.

The men exchanged glances and burst out laughing.

Derrin flung himself onto the ground, shoulders heaving. The Baha'Na man bent over and hooted with mirth. Gina, her legs suddenly unsteady, grabbed for the nearest tree.

After a moment, Derrin regained his composure and sat up, still chuckling.

The Baha'Na man grinned, showing even white teeth. "You have to admit it, Derrin. I won that contest."

"I admit no such thing. It wasn't a fair match." Derrin gestured in Gina's direction. "I had a severe disadvantage."

The burly man snorted. "She makes almost as much noise as an angry tarma."

Gina snapped out of her daze. "Just one minute— "

Derrin pushed himself to his feet, ignoring her. "She almost split your skull open. You didn't even know she was there."

"Oh, I knew she was there. My skull was never in danger."

"That's true enough. She would have needed a rock twice that size to put a dent in your thick head."

Gina stepped into the space between the two men and fixed Derrin with an icy stare. Scratches covered his forearms, mud smeared his clothing, and a nasty cut over one eye was already starting to swell.

"I'm sorry if I'm interrupting," she said, "*but what the hell is going on?*"

Derrin looked at her and blinked, as if just remembering her presence. Then he gave a sheepish grin and jabbed his thumb at the stranger. "Gina—this is my cousin, White Otter." He paused. "Tasa's brother."

"Tasa's brother," Gina repeated dubiously, thinking of the slim, gentle girl from the Water Clan. This hulking beast was her brother?

The man's snarled, shaggy mane flew in every direction. He wasn't as tall as Derrin, but his shoulders were massive, barely contained by his hide shirt. His legs were like tree trunks. He grinned at her, then winced and touched the trickle of blood flowing from his split lip.

Gina's irritation faltered. For all their physical differences, the dancing laughter in White Otter's eyes was indeed a mirror image of his sister's. She arched her arm in the Baha'Na gesture of greeting.

White Otter returned the gesture, his smile widening. "I heard of your coming. I thought to meet you before you came to the village."

"You have strange way of greeting visitors."

Derrin snorted. "It's a game we played as boys to improve our skill at stalking. We take our position and signal by birdcall, then try to catch the other unaware." An apology clouded the clear gray of his eyes. "It didn't occur to me you would think it was a real attack. You know the Baha'Na don't fight."

"Fighting is real enough in my own world, though."

White Otter stepped closer. "I am sorry I frightened you. My curiosity got the better of me. I was eager to meet the woman who had come through the web." He turned to Derrin with an impish grin. "I must confess, though, I had not expected her to look so ordinary. I would have thought such a woman to be more..." He made a gesture of exaggerated womanly proportions.

Gina's eyes narrowed. She was about to make a choice retort when she caught the two men looking at her with identical expressions of male mischief. She rolled her eyes instead. "Is it much further to the village?"

White Otter let out an exaggerated sigh. "I have this effect on all women."

Derrin regarded his cousin with mock sympathy. "It's hard to imagine what Kaila saw in you."

"That is true enough." White Otter laughed, then sobered. He regarded Derrin for a long moment, and Derrin returned his gaze steadily. A palpable emotion flared between the two men, a mixture of past unity and painful loss, and the unexpected renewal of both.

"By the stones and the sky, it is good to see you again, *vohar*," White Otter whispered.

"And you, my brother."

Then, as suddenly as the emotion had swelled, it vanished. White Otter turned to Gina, a smile on his lips. "You must come to my dwelling to dry your clothes. Derrin, Kaila is even more beautiful than she was at our joining—do you remember? We have two daughters. They are the image of their mother."

Derrin clapped him on the shoulder. "I'm happy to hear it, my friend. No girl should be burdened with your features."

White Otter grinned and started toward the village.

The morning fog had vanished. Sunlight slanted through the green canopy and sparkled on foliage still bedecked with drops of water. Derrin's cousin led the way along a narrow, twisting route. The terrain was difficult in some areas, but much less steep than the slope Gina had scaled the previous day.

She looked ahead, searching for signs of the villagers' dwellings. It wasn't until she stood in the center of the village common area that she realized the Wind Clan didn't live in huts at all, but in a series of caves carved into the rocky mountainside.

Terraces of the higher dwellings formed the roofs of those below. An intricate arrangement of stairs cut into the hillside, providing access to the upper levels. The lowest tier of dwellings faced a level common area. Beyond the gathering space, the ground sloped toward a wooded valley.

White Otter's partner, Kaila, greeted the travelers and exclaimed over the men's injuries, shaking her head as she tended the worst cuts. Her older daughter, a girl of about nine, brought food and water. Another girl, a few years younger, stationed herself next to Gina and chattered cheerfully.

Gina met Derrin's amused gaze over the top of the girl's head and smiled.

*****

The Voice of the Goddess called into the midnight sky.

Gina fought the urge to shift her legs. She peered across the flames at Patah, Na'lara to the Wind Clan, and wondered when—or if—the crone would speak.

Patah was ancient, older than any woman Gina had ever seen. Her slight frame was ethereal, more spirit than flesh. An expression of pure peace illuminated her wrinkled features, framed by thin braids that had long since turned the color of the morning mist. Her eyes were clear and dark, but sightless. Even so, Gina suspected Patah could see the spirits of her people, if not their physical forms.

Blue beads decorated the Na'lara's dress and the band at her forehead. The talisman glowed in the light of the fire.

Patah's granddaughter, a stout woman already well into her middle years, sat in impassive silence at her grandmother's side. The night wind surged, whipping the flames. Sharp shadows danced past the women to the edge of a stone field pockmarked by pits and crevices.

Eerie music rose from the depths of the mountain on the arms of the wind. It wrapped around the women, strengthening, probing, then dissolving into a whisper. A scant heartbeat later, the melody began anew.

"I have waited long to greet you, Gina," said Patah at last.

"The face of the Goddess shines on our meeting, Grandmother," Gina murmured. She pressed her palm to her forehead, though she knew the Elder couldn't see the gesture of respect.

The old woman smiled. Her mind pulsed across Gina's consciousness. Gina inclined her head, allowed her thoughts to be touched and understood.

"Long ago, a man of the Baha'Na thought to find his heart outside the wilderness," the crone said.

A sharp hiss from the fire answered her words. Patah nodded, then continued. "One day, many winters past, a man of the Seventh Clan left his village. He returned many moons later and told of a wondrous land beyond the wilderness. Its fields were flat and fertile, its winters mild, its waters sweet and plentiful. A great lake, filled with fish, stretched further than the eye could see. He wanted his clan to leave the wilderness and settle in the new land."

The keening melody poured from the depths of the mountain. Patah tilted her head, bird-like, and listened. When the ghostly whistle faded, she continued her tale.

"The People argued among themselves. Some wished to leave the wilderness and go to this place of endless ease. Others believed a life far from the Signs was a hardship not to be borne. The factions could not be reconciled. The Baha'Na were cut in two. Some stayed in the wilderness, others traveled to the Outside. The children of those who left forgot their kin, forgot the Goddess."

Patah rose, surprising Gina with the fluidity of her movement. "The Great Mother speaks to all her children, Gina. Follow me to her Voice."

The old woman skirted the dying flames and glided to the edge of the rocky field. Despite her age and blindness, she moved with unerring grace across the maze of openings. The melody seeped from the rocks like a magic spell.

It sank into Gina's soul. She yearned to catch the heart of the song, but it danced beyond her reach. The route through the sea of crevices grew treacherous. Gaps in the rock widened, shrinking the path to a mere ribbon of rock.

Patah walked as if unaware of the danger at her feet. She continued without pause to the center of the field.

The Voice grew louder, driving away all thought.

"Stay and await the dawn," Patah said. The old woman retreated, retracing her steps to the fire circle.

Gina sat cross-legged on a smooth patch of stone, feeling uncomfortably exposed beneath the endless sweep of the sky. The eerie song undulated around her.

She found it easy, at first, to lose herself in it. But then the minutes stretched and the melody grew disturbing. Haunting tones rose and fell outside any pattern or harmony Gina could discern, leaving her bruised and unsettled.

It probed her consciousness with relentless fingers, peering into each dark corner of her soul, merging with her joys and sorrows. She floated with it, weightless in time, until the first glow of dawn crept over the horizon.

*****

The winged creatures of the wilderness called to the Day Traveler, urging the shining orb to peek above the edge of the world and begin its journey across the sky. Derrin lay motionless, stretched out on his stomach on a low rise just beyond the bank of the stream. The forest was awakening. Soon its creatures would make their way to the water's edge.

He brought one hand up to the quiver on his shoulder and closed his fingers on the shaft of an arrow. Moving so slowly his progress was barely detectable, he fit the arrow in his bow, drew back on the bowstring and waited.

White Otter's consciousness brushed Derrin's mind. The clansman lay on the opposite bank of the stream, so well hidden Derrin couldn't make out his position. The first clear rays of the sun glistened, casting pools of golden light on the stream. Derrin's nostrils flared with the crisp, sweet scent of morning.

Still, he waited.

He knew the exact spot at which the buck would appear even before it stepped from the cover of the thicket. The Feathered People had told the forest of the mountain deer's journey and Derrin had listened to their counsel. He slid forward on his belly, using his quarry's movement to cover the sound of his own. He pulled the bowstring taut, and waited.

The animal took a few steps in Derrin's direction. It was one of the smaller bucks in the herd, partially lame. The People did not take the largest deer from the herd, no matter how great the need. The Deer People needed the strength of their leaders to thrive.

The buck jerked its head upward and looked into Derrin's eyes. "Forgive me, brother," Derrin whispered.

He let his arrow fly.

White Otter loosed his arrow in the same instant. The projectiles struck their target, one through the neck and the other just below on the opposite side. The buck collapsed with a shudder.

Derrin leapt from his hiding place. His cousin was already halfway to the stream, a cry of triumph on his lips. The two men pulled the carcass from the water and removed the arrows. Thick red blood pulsed onto the ground.

White Otter found a long, stout pole and whittled its ends to a sharp point. Derrin pierced the legs of the deer, just above its hooves, passing his knife between bone and tendon, then inserted the ends of the shaft, securing the carcass for its journey to the village.

When they had finished the task, Derrin and White Otter waded into the deepest part of the stream. White Otter took a handful of grit from the streambed and scoured the mud he had smeared on his body as camouflage. Derrin bent and sluiced the cold water in armfuls over his head, scrubbing his hair with handfuls of sand.

White Otter slapped Derrin's shoulder. "It was a good hunt."

"Yes."

"It has been too many years since we last hunted together."

Derrin met his cousin's gaze. "In some ways, *vohar*, it seems as though no time has passed at all."

"Will you stay then, and join the Wind Clan?"

An unexpected yearning washed over Derrin. What would it be like to stay, with Gina as his partner?

He pushed the thought away. "No. I must return to the Outside, and Gina must return to her own land beyond the web."

"And what of your heart, Derrin?"

Derrin froze in the motion of scrubbing his arm. "What of it?"

"Do not think you hide your feelings from me, little brother, even as you try to hide them from Gina."

Derrin stared at a point downstream. "Is it that obvious?"

White Otter laughed. "It is. And it is clear she returns your regard. Make her yours, Derrin."

Derrin's heart clenched. "To what end? We will be parted soon enough." He scooped up a handful of grit and scoured his other arm. "Despite what you say, White Otter, I'm not so sure Gina would have me, even if I were to ask."

His cousin sent him a look of disbelief. "Then you are blind," he said. After a silent moment, he continued. "Derrin, the wilderness changes always, yet peace exists in each moment. Once Gina is gone you will regret the moments you let pass."

Derrin was silent for a time. "Gina doesn't need a bond with a man she must leave," he said at last. He trudged up the bank and took hold of one end of the branch holding the deer carcass.

White Otter lifted the opposite end and together they heaved the weight of the deer onto their shoulders. "It is not for you to make Gina's choices," he said. "Think on that before you push her away."

*****

Kaila lifted a rock from the fire with a forked stick and dropped it into a hide pouch filled with water and herbs. The mixture sizzled. Above, the familiar patterns of the stars emerged. Derrin glanced back at the doorway of the cave dwelling, where his cousin's daughters slept on their bed of furs.

White Otter kept up an easy banter of conversation. Derrin gave an occasional response, but his attention was focused on Gina. She lifted a gourd ladle and stirred the herb tea. The simple movement of her arm enticed him. She glanced up and blushed, then looked away.

A restless energy battered Derrin—a surge of fear and exhilaration, as if he were walking a narrow log spanning a deep gorge.

Kaila handed Gina a wooden cup. Gina filled it and passed the drink to White Otter.

He took it and said, "Last night you heard the Voice of the Goddess. Is it not a most beautiful sound?"

"Yes." Gina returned White Otter's smile, then offered a second cup to Derrin. His fingers brushed hers as he accepted it. He didn't miss the small catch of her breath.

White Otter sighed. "When I first heard the Goddess sing, I was so overwhelmed I did not speak for a whole day."

Kaila and Gina laughed. Derrin shot White Otter an amused look and opened his mouth to speak.

"No comment from you, little brother," White Otter said. "Is it not enough that you bested me in almost every game we played as boys? Now you seek to embarrass me in front of two beautiful women."

The women in question laughed harder.

"I never beat you at anything!" Derrin protested. "You always let me win."

"Is that true?" Gina asked.

"It is not," said White Otter. "Why, I remember the time I challenged Derrin to a race to an old skyeagle's nest..."

"Oh, no." Derrin groaned. "Don't tell her that story."

White Otter gave Gina a broad wink. "Not tell her? Why not? Do you not want her to know of your bravery in climbing to the top of the tallest tree in the forest?"

"I was all of seven winters," Derrin muttered.

"Derrin was fearless, as always," continued White Otter. "But I was no fool—I abandoned the race halfway. He laughed at my cowardice and scrambled up to the nest. Then he looked down and realized just how high he had climbed." He chuckled. "He sat there and bawled. It was a full day before my father could coax him down."

Derrin's face grew hot and he avoided Gina's teasing gaze. To his chagrin, White Otter recounted several more tales of their boyhood exploits, each one more embarrassing than the last. Derrin had no choice but to retaliate with some stories of his own, ones Kaila found quite interesting.

The laughter died as the last story came to an end. Derrin stirred up the fire a bit, but left the flames low, since the night was warm. White Otter disappeared into the cave.

He reemerged a moment later, carrying a long wooden flute. It gleamed a rich gold in the firelight. Feathers and beads hung from strips of leather wrapped around its barrel.

White Otter raised the instrument to his lips and blew a long, steady breath. Clear notes danced in the night air, rising and falling with delicate grace. Derrin watched Gina's face as the melody swept over her. Her eyelids fluttered closed and her expression grew languid, as if she'd just made love.

His cock responded.

Derrin shifted, bending his knee and drawing his leg up to hide his arousal. His efforts to resist Gina had been doomed from the start. He could avoid being drawn to her no more than a moth could avoid a flame. At first his desires had been born of pure lust. Those needs hadn't dimmed. If anything, they'd grown stronger. But at the same time, they had merged with other, deeper emotions—respect, friendship.

Love. Yes, he loved Gina, though the emotion was not the tender feeling he had once held for Rahza. No, his love for Gina was fierce, uncompromising. The sheer power of it frightened him. And yet he could not push it away.

White Otter's soft notes continued. *You will regret the moments you let pass*, he had said. Derrin had a feeling his cousin was right. He'd already known too many regrets in his life.

Deep inside his heart, a decision slipped into place.

The flute song ended. White Otter placed his instrument on the ground, nodding at Gina's exclamation of praise. With a decisive motion, Derrin picked it up and ran his hand over the smooth wood. Bringing it to his lips, he blew a few experimental notes. His fingers moved over the air holes.

He looked up to see Gina regarding him curiously. "Can you play?" she asked.

"A little." He blew a note, low and haunting, and held it until it faded. Out of the corner of his eye he saw Kaila's head come up. She exchanged a meaningful glance with her partner.

Derrin blew another note, a companion to the first, then a third. A melody formed, sprung from his hope. With his heart's breath, he fashioned a slow, aching song.

Each note hung in the air, nearly visible, before yielding to the next. The tune rose and fell and rose again, wrapping itself in the velvet darkness of the night.

He dared a glance in Gina's direction. His gaze met hers over the trembling notes of the flute song, notes that had become a question.

The last, trilling breath faded into the night. Only then did Gina look away, but not before Derrin thought he'd seen an answer in her eyes.

Chapter Fifteen

"Come, Gina, let me comb out your braids." Kaila held up a bone comb.

Gina ran one hand over the plaits Tasa had fashioned at the Wellspring. The intricate hairstyle was unraveling in several places.

She sat down in a patch of sun, facing the deep stream where she'd come with Kaila to bathe. The Baha'Na woman settled behind her and loosened the tangled braids. Gina closed her eyes. Kaila's soft humming melded with the laughter of the women and girls already splashing in the water.

She joined them in the stream a short time later, after stripping off her dirty dress and washing it out. She left the garment draped on a boulder and swam, cheered by the warmth of the summer afternoon, and marveling at how natural it felt to be frolicking naked with women she barely knew. When she stepped onto the shore, Kaila approached her with a white dress.

A pattern of red and black beads danced across the front. "Do you like it, Gina?"

"It's lovely."

"Wear it for today, while your own garment dries."

Gina thanked her. She ran her fingertips over the intricate beading, then shook out the dress and slipped it over her head, relishing the cling of the soft material on her damp skin. Kaila once again produced the bone comb. She pulled it through Gina's wet hair and left the dark strands to dry unbraided.

The sun was low in the sky by the time Gina returned to the village with the women, still wearing the borrowed dress and carrying her damp clothing over her arm. Kaila stopped to talk with an elder, leaving Gina to accompany her daughters to their home.

The girls each carried an armload of vines they had gathered on the stream bank. When they reached the terrace at the entrance to their dwelling, they sat in the sunlight and sorted the vines into various lengths and thicknesses. Gina spread her dress in a patch of sunlight and went to join them.

The older girl, Liana, gave a shy smile. "Do you like to weave baskets?"

Gina sat down next to her. "I don't know. I've never made one."

"No?" Liana looked shocked. "Don't people use baskets in your world? How do they carry what they gather in the forest?"

Gina grimaced. "Yes, well, there are baskets, and…um…other things that are used for carrying. I'm just not one of the people who make them."

"Oh." The Baha'Na girl considered this information, then brightened. "Would you like to learn?"

Gina picked up one of the vines and gave it an experimental tug. It was surprisingly tough. Liana showed her how to lay the thicker strands as ribs while weaving the thinner ones through them. When dry, she told Gina, the basket would be very strong.

Two baskets quickly took shape under the girls' nimble fingers. Gina did her best to reproduce Liana's technique, but somehow the larger vines wouldn't stay in place when she pulled the smaller ones tight. And when she tried to tie off each end, it unraveled as if it had a will of its own.

She was comparing her poor results to the perfectly shaped oval baskets produced by the girls when Derrin appeared on the stone stairway, his face thrown into shadow by the late afternoon sun. Gina blinked up at him. A tingle of awareness shuddered up her spine, leaving her slightly breathless. She hadn't seen him since the night before, when the notes of his flute song had left her with a fierce yearning.

Afterwards, she'd fallen asleep in White Otter and Kaila's dwelling and dreamed of dark pleasure, of possession and surrender, of a lovemaking that was as violent as it was glorious. She'd awakened flushed and needy, glad that Derrin had slept elsewhere. He would have taken one look at her and known.

A flick of his fingers sent the girls scampering into the cave, giggling. When they had gone, he picked up Gina's basket and examined it solemnly, turning it over and scrutinizing it from all directions. His eyes glinted and the corners of his mouth quirked.

"I know, I know," muttered Gina, finding her voice. "I better not quit my day job. But it was kind of fun to make."

He flashed a smile and set her basket with the others. His gaze touched her, sweeping slowly over the fall of her unbraided hair, then dipping lower.

When he raised his head she saw the teasing light in his eyes had been replaced by a much more primitive expression. Her heartbeat accelerated.

He extended his hands. "Will you come with me, Gina? There's a place I want to show you."

She gazed at his palms, strong and calloused, and at his fingers, agile and tanned dark by the sun. She had watched those hands spark fire, craft tools, prepare food. They had comforted her while she wept, protected her from danger. She remembered their touch on her face.

Now he held them open before her. She hesitated a brief moment, then reached up and placed her hands in his, sensing as she did so that she accepted far more than a simple offer of assistance.

His easy strength lifted her, pulled her close—so close she could feel the tense energy rippling in his muscles. She sensed the turbulence of his emotions easily, as if he no longer felt the need to shield his mind from her. A tendril of heat uncurled low in her stomach, and with it came a wash of uncertainty. What did he want? What would she be able to give?

Belatedly, she tried to extract her hand from his, but Derrin didn't allow it. He laced her fingers securely in his own.

*****

The narrow ledge meandered up the steep slope through several turns and switchbacks. The village had long since dropped out of view below a scattering of pines. Derrin climbed steadily, paying more attention to the trail than was necessary. He was thankful for Gina's silence behind him. Truthfully, he didn't trust himself to speak.

"Where are we going?" she asked at last.

"You'll see." He glanced back at her and caught a glimpse of wide dark eyes. Her sun-browned skin glowed and her dark hair flowed over her shoulders like a shining cloak. Her soft panting called an erotic image into his mind.

She regarded him quizzically, but gave no indication of what she thought of his request for her company, or of the fact that her hand was still clasped in his own. He sensed her nervousness, and her trust. He fixed his gaze on the trail and forged ahead.

He halted at a low opening in the face of the hill, the entrance to a narrow tunnel forming a link to the sheer cliffs on the opposite side of the mountain. Ducking inside, he drew Gina after him.

They emerged from the passage and entered the glow of the setting sun. A smooth platform of moss-covered rock overhung the valley. The scent of pine drifted from the gnarled trees perched above the mouth of the cave. Directly ahead, on the far side of the valley, the sun sank into the embrace of the mountains. Tufts of amethyst clouds scattered over a dusky rose sky.

The colors deepened into liquid indigo and smeared the crimson blaze of the sky. Too quickly, they faded into twilight. Derrin turned his gaze to the clear line of Gina's profile. A breeze caught a silky strand of her hair and flung it across her lips. He caught it, letting it slid through his fingers before letting go.

He swallowed, his throat suddenly dry. He'd been unable to stop himself from wanting this woman, from needing her, if only for the short time she would be in his world. If she didn't share his feelings, would he be able to retreat to the edge of his emotions?

Unsettled, he eased his hand from hers and strode forward, stopping at the very edge of the cliff. A hoarbat darted through the shadows below. He leaned forward, tracking it with his gaze.

"Watch out! You'll fall," Gina cried.

He turned toward her, a smile playing on his lips. She stood with her arm half-extended, as if ready to snatch him from the jaws of death. Seized by an impulse to make her laugh, he flailed his arms with exaggerated drama.

She let out a cry and lunged for him. He tried to head her off but stumbled, pitching forward and knocking her to the ground. He landed on top of her, his forearms braced on either side of her head. She stared up at him, stunned.

Unaccountably, Derrin started to laugh.

Her eyes narrowed. "You weren't falling."

Another wave of mirth overtook him. He pressed his forehead into the curve of her neck and let it wash over him. It was too absurd.

He'd brought the woman who haunted his dreams to the most romantic spot he could think of, set on seduction, only to knock her flat on her back.

Gina thrust, unlover-like, against his chest. Derrin struggled to regain a measure of control.

When at last his shoulders stopped shaking, she lay still beneath him. Her scent brought to mind the peace of the valley, the hidden mysteries the wilderness. He raised his head and looked down at her.

And fell into the twilight pools of her eyes. Doe's eyes, wide with wonder. Startled by the sudden appearance of danger, yet fascinated, unable to move to safety.

Her hands inched up his arms, brushed his throat, then one finger traced a trembling line along the scar on his cheek. The surprise in her eyes changed to something else, but Derrin did not dare give it a name.

"Would you care so much if I fell?" he asked.

She went very still. A slow blush crept across her cheeks and her eyelids fluttered shut. He gazed down at her, mesmerized by the feathered shadows cast by her lashes.

"Yes," she whispered. "You know I would."

He lowered his head a fraction, until he felt her breath on his lips. A fine tremor ran through her. Yet he waited, not wanting to take what she would not give freely.

His unspoken question hung for a trembling beat of eternity in the space between their bodies. Then Gina's fingers wove through the hair at the back of his neck and he had his answer.

He kissed her softly at first, molding his lips to hers, drinking in her response to his slow insistence. Then her lips opened on a sigh and he dove deeper, tasting her.

Her body drew taut beneath him. Like dry tinder swept into a new fire, his desire exploded. All the weeks of denying his need rushed at him like thunder. His cock throbbed harder than he would have thought possible. He was certain he would die if he couldn't plunge it inside her.

All thought of restraint, of tenderness fled. His hand closed on her breast in a punishing grip. He pinched its peak through the soft fabric of her dress. Gina gasped and twisted, trying at once to accept and evade his possession. Her arousal, laced with a thread of fear, brushed against his mind. It called to the predator deep within in him.

The fevered need to know all of her consumed him. He wanted to feel her impaled on his cock, helpless beneath him as he drove her past the barriers of her control. The memory of the Na'tahar and the dreams they had shared swept through him like a wildfire. He longed to do to Gina's body what he had done to her mind. When he had, she would be his, utterly and completely.

A sane fragment of his mind called for him to stop, but its voice was lost in the rush of lust that gripped him. He ripped at the laces of Gina's neckline, baring one breast. With a growl, he drew her nipple into his mouth and scraped the tender flesh with his teeth.

"Derrin—"

He shoved the hem of her dress to her waist and sank his knee between her thighs. His hardened shaft prodded her folds, but couldn't sink in. She wasn't wet. Wasn't ready.

Gina struggled beneath him. He could sense that her thread of fear had grown wide and overtaken her desire, but he fought to ignore the knowledge. He was drowning in her, struggling to drink her essence as desperately as a man mad with thirst. A man who, after not daring to hope for an end to the drought, had found himself plunged into deep water.

"Derrin, no." Gina grabbed a fistful of his hair and pulled hard.

He struggled to regain control. He left her breast and kissed her lips again, less roughly, willing her to come with him.

Her body went rigid beneath him. She tried again to push him away. "Derrin. Stop. Just stop. Please." A burning river of shame and revulsion poured from her mind into his.

His chaotic senses reeled with the obscenity of it. What was he doing? What kind of man was he?

Summoning his last shred of willpower, he shoved himself off Gina's body and braced his weight on one shaking arm. His chest heaved.

"I—" The single word was all he could manage. He drew a ragged breath.

Gina rolled out from beneath him. She yanked her dress into place and hugged her legs to her chest. "I'm sorry. Oh, God, Derrin, I'm sorry!"

A suffocating tide of self-disgust washed over him. "Tarol's blood." She was sorry? After he'd fallen on her like a rutting buck?

He forced his breathing to steady. Even so, some time passed before he trusted himself to speak, and he couldn't bring himself to look at her at all.

"Don't you dare apologize to me."

"Derrin, I—"

"I all but forced myself on you. It won't happen again."

"No!"

He raised his head. He could make out little of her expression in the falling dusk, but now that the craze of his lust had abated, he sensed the fear and shame pouring from her were not directed at him, but at herself.

"Derrin, it's not you—it's not what you did. I want you that way, too. Not gentle. Wild. Brutal, even. I've dreamed of it. But when you touched me..." Her voice faltered.

"What, Gina?" He started to move toward her, but stopped when she looked away.

"Something's wrong with me, Derrin. It's why my ex-husband found another woman." She swallowed hard. "He was a lot older than me, and very particular about having things a certain way. About me being a certain way. When I didn't meet his expectations, I could tell how I'd disappointed him. It began to interfere with our sex life. He'd want me to respond in a certain way, and I couldn't get turned on. Everything he did hurt. I let him do it anyway. I pretended it was good, but he could tell I was faking. Finally he gave up. It was my fault he had to find someone else."

"Is that what he told you?" Derrin asked hoarsely.

Gina nodded. "I thought it would be different with you, because I want you so badly. I've even dreamed of us together. But when you get too close, I can't handle it. My mind wants one thing, but my body goes numb."

At that moment, Derrin would have gladly beaten Gina's former partner to a bloody pulp. "Your partner was a swiving fool," he said evenly. "Gina, you don't have to try with me. You don't have to pretend to be something you're not. There isn't anything about you that doesn't please me."

He knelt in front of her, running his palm over her shoulder and down her arm. Then, when she didn't protest, he took both her hands in his own and massaged her palms with his thumbs.

She raised her head. He waited, not speaking, wishing he could see her face more clearly, but the mountain hid the rising moon and he could discern little more than the outline of her body against a sea of darkness. He searched for the words that would call her back to him, but discarded each phrase that rose in his mind. He couldn't bring himself to offer her flattery or sweet endearments. Not when his feelings for her were so raw and primitive.

He could only offer himself, with all his regrets and imperfections, and hope it was enough.

He reached for her with his voice and his mind. "Gina, I brought you to my mother's people to hide you from Balek, but I dreaded every step that brought me here. I meant to return to Galena the next day." He drew back, releasing her. "But I found I couldn't leave you, not after we'd been joined in the Na'tahar. I needed you too badly. So I stayed, and led you into the heart of everything I had fought so hard to forget."

He rose and paced a few steps away. "At times, I could see what I had lost so clearly, feel it so acutely that I thought every breath of the wilderness would drive me mad." He fought to keep his voice steady. "But it didn't. Because you were by my side. You showed me the place I belong. With you, Gina. Even if it's for only the briefest of moments."

"Oh, Derrin."

He brought his cupped palms to his chest, though he was unsure if she could see the gesture in the dark. "You are in my heart, Gina. It may not be wise for me to ask, but will you have me this night? This night and for as many nights as we are given before you return to your world?"

The silence lay fragile between them. "I… I don't know what to say," she whispered at last.

"Say what's in your heart. Say what you want."

The stillness swelled again until it threatened to swallow the night. Then, through the velvet blackness, he saw her arm sweep forward. Her open palm came to rest on her breast.

"I want you, Derrin. You're in my heart. And somehow…it seems you've always been there."

A fierce joy unfurled and soared. Derrin took a quick step forward and pulled Gina into his arms, tangling his fingers in the silky weight of her unbound hair. His mouth covered hers. He dropped to the mossy ground, her arms tightening around him.

Hot desire flooded his veins, flinging him beyond any emotion he'd ever experienced. His tongue sank between her lips, explored the contours of her mouth.

But after one wild drink he retreated. He traced the outline of her lips with his tongue and trailed hot, openmouthed kisses along her jaw and neck. Easing her dress over the smooth curve of her shoulders, he freed her arms from the sleeves and let the soft material pool at her hips.

One finger traced a featherlight circle around the tip of her breast. He dipped his head, taking the hardened nipple into his mouth, gently this time. Gina moaned and arched against him, her fingers tangling in his hair, pulling him closer.

"Don't tease," she whispered. "Not now. I'm not afraid any longer."

Fire exploded in his loins at her words, but he forced it to a slow burn. He sucked her nipple deeper into his mouth, his heart catching when a small moan of pleasure escaped her. She held his head tight against her breast, traced circles on his scalp.

Her skin was soft and welcoming. Her scent was that of the forest, a warm mystery, alive with promise. She was all he thought she would be, and he wanted to savor every moment of their lovemaking. He kissed his way from one breast to the other, then, still licking and suckling her nipples, he rolled onto his back and pulled her atop him.

When his mouth finally left her breast, Gina whimpered and rubbed against him, urging him to return. Instead, his hands moved over her torso, cupped her breast and belly. His fingers combed through the soft triangle of hair between her thighs. He found her damp center and teased into it. The wild, musky scent of her desire reached out to him, beckoning. Moisture flowed over his hand. He smeared it on her soft folds.

A low moan vibrated in Gina's throat. "Come inside me, Derrin."

But he remembered his earlier loss of control and clamped down on his desire. Forcing himself to a slower pace, he grasped the bunched fabric of her dress and slid it up, over her head, careful not to tear the soft doeskin. Gina's fingers tugged at his kilt. By the time he'd stripped off his shirt she'd untangled the knot at his hip.

She straddled his bare thighs, fingers wrapped around his rigid cock. It leaped in hot pleasure. He lay motionless, shuddering, while she teased him. She drew his foreskin up, then back, over the outer ridge of his head. Her hand tightened with each successive stroke. She wet her fingers with moisture gathered from her own sex and lubricated his shaft. Her hand slid again on his cock and he thought he would go mad with wanting her. A low growl emerged from his throat, a sound more animal than human.

He suffered her attentions for as long as he dared, then hauled her into his arms and rolled her beneath him. He covered her, trapping her with the length of his body, pressing her into their bed of moss-covered rock.

Her nakedness felt so glorious against his body. His damp skin clung to hers. He began a slow exploration of her curves, his tongue plunging into the honey-scented hollow between her breasts, then dipping lower, to dart into her navel. Her arousal was an earthy perfume, drawing him to her center.

He breathed a hot trail to the curls between her thighs and inhaled the aroma of her body's nectar. He tasted her there, his tongue plunging deep. Gina gripped his hair, her hips writhing as he feasted on her. He sensed she had little experience being pleasured this way. She wanted to retreat from the intensity of the sensation, but he refused to allow it. He held her thighs open with his palms, not yielding even when she cried out. His tongue moved in hard, deliberate strokes, building a hot, wet fire.

When she was panting with need, he drew back a fraction. "You taste sweeter in the flesh than you did in our dream."

"Our…our dream?"

"The first one we shared. I had but a small taste of you then, but now—"

"Those dreams were real?" He heard the dismay in her voice. "You were really there?"

"Yes," he said. "Those joinings were as real as this physical one."

"But…how can that be?"

"We bonded during the Na'tahar. I could not prevent it. Now our minds are linked."

"I've felt you," she said. "I sensed you tried to keep your mind separate, but there were times…"

"I can no more keep myself from you than the river can keep itself from the sea." He bent his head, blew a stream of air over her glistening folds.

Her buttocks flexed. "Oh, God."

He slid one finger, then two, into her tight sheath. His thumb circled the hard nub hidden in the slick folds.

Gina's hips bucked. She gripped his hair and pulled. "Now," she whispered on a ragged breath. "Come inside me now. I want to feel you there."

He raised his head and gave a tight smile. "Not yet."

His tongue began a slow journey up her body, while his hand continued its pulsing strokes. By the time his mouth claimed Gina's lips, his own breath was coming in gasps.

The tempo of his fingers increased. Gina clutched his shoulders and pressed against him, panting.

"I can't take much more of this, Derrin. I need you."

"I need you as well, Gina. More than you know."

He eased his hand from her body and shifted, coming over her, supporting himself on his elbows. His aching erection settled between her thighs, bathed in soft, slippery heat.

With one hard thrust, he drove himself into her.

She let out a strangled cry. He withdrew until their bodies barely touched.

"No!" She grasped his hips and tried to pull him back.

He teased at her entrance for a brief moment, then surged forward again, burying himself in her welcoming heat. Sharp currents of pleasure raced along every nerve in his body. He braced himself and thrust deeper, again and again, letting the endless waves of sensation overtake him.

He stroked hard, his buttocks flexing, his arms rigid as he pounded into her with all his strength and all his longing. The slide of his cock in her slick passage was a sensation he craved more than breath, more than sanity.

Gina's breathing hitched. "Derrin. Oh God, Derrin, I want—" A tremor pulsed through her core as he surged into her.

"Let go, Gina."

He picked up his pace, moved faster, more urgently, wanting—needing—to hear her cry of release. He bent his head and nipped at the sweat-slicked skin of her shoulder and neck. "Let go."

She stiffened, even as he stroked into her. "No. You don't understand," she said on a half-choked sob. "I never…came this way. I can't do it."

"Yes, you can. You can do it for me."

He doubled his effort, driving her without mercy, drinking in each whimper, each gasp, each moan. Now that she had welcomed him into her body, she would have no choice but to surrender to his will, as she'd had no choice when he'd entered her mind. He would drive her to her peak, and follow after.

Her frantic whimpers and writhing body told him her climax was near. As was his own. A place lay ahead, just beyond the crest of a mountain of exquisite sensation, a haven where Derrin's past, his doubts, and his duties held no meaning. A place he wished for more than anything else.

He looped his arms under her knees and pulled her legs higher, changing the angle of his invasion. "*Now*, Gina." He plunged deeper, touching her womb.

"Now. Throw your heart to me."

She shattered beneath him, her fingernails tearing a path across his shoulder. The pain merged with her cry and vibrated through every muscle of his body. Her hot inner spasms milked his cock. The exquisite torture threw him into the chasm, into an endless gulf of stunning bliss.

He landed in a place he'd never dreamed he would find.

Home.

Chapter Sixteen

High Lord Forlik fac Dallor was no longer a young man, yet he had never felt the full weight of his years as he did this night. A lone crystal cast its glow over the polished stone of the council table, chasing the shadows to the far recesses of the room. It did little to erase his unease.

Reports from Sirth and the Eastern Plains littered one end of the long table. At the opposite end, Forlik bent over maps of the Galenan coast and countryside, searching for a pattern, some clue he could use to avert the impending doom. He found nothing but a bone-deep weariness.

In less than a fortnight, the Blight had swept from the forests between Katrinth and Sirth into the rich farmland of the Eastern Plains. This morning, a courier had brought news of massive crop failures at the larger estates. A very small portion of the spring grains would be harvested, and the outlook for summer was even bleaker. The Plains had seen little rainfall. Seeds had been sown in dust, only to rise in great clouds and disappear with the winds.

Reports from the coastal towns were little better. The Congress of Lords had counted on the bounty of the sea to replace what had been lost on the farms. But two days ago, a warm current had swelled the tides and left thousands of rotting fish on the shore. Fishermen running smaller boats had seen the amount and quality of the fish they brought in plummet. Only the larger, seagoing vessels still managed a decent catch.

The jeweled sleeve of Forlik's robe dragged across the parchment as his finger traced the path of ruin. The Congress would need to release large portions of the emergency grain stores, even before winter. And if conditions did not improve…

The prospect was grim indeed. He ran a palm over his sparse hair, then straightened and started to pace. An enemy that could be seen—a human enemy—could be fought. But this? Forlik was not a superstitious man, but even he had to admit the rumors circulating about the city held a ring of truth. Lotark had hurled a curse at Galena.

"The One God is displeased, my Lord."

Forlik turned, his face set in the careful mask that enabled him to retain the position of High Lord. He knew only one man who would dare intrude unannounced at so late an hour.

Solk, the Heir of Lotark, stood with regal stiffness in the doorway, his golden robes falling in perfect folds around him. His hands were clasped in a gesture of humility.

If Forlik had been in a better mood, he would have laughed.

The high priest inclined his head with conscious grace. "My Lord Forlik. Forgive my intrusion."

Forlik gave an inner snort as he nodded. "Your Grace. To what do I owe the pleasure of your visit?"

"A dark hour has fallen upon Galena, my Lord. Lotark is displeased with his children. They have turned away from his teachings. In his anger, the One God has withdrawn his protection." His lips pressed together in a thin, straight line. "There is only one remedy."

Forlik leaned back against the table and folded his arms across his chest. "Which is… ?"

"Penance. Penance and a return to the Old Ways. The Congress of Lords must renounce the Hierarchy. This Blight is the wizards' doing."

"How so?"

"The spawn of Tarol have taken the privileges of Lotark into their own hands."

Forlik regarded the High Priest evenly. "There are many who would say such talk is naught but superstition, Your Grace. Many believe wizardry is our lone weapon against the Blight. Have you forgotten the crystal cure for the Madness Balek brought to the people last year? You predicted the entire populace would be deranged by now, yet that has not come to pass."

Solk frowned. "The holy works of the True Believers turned back that crisis. Their sacrifices can save us once again, if it be Lotark's will. Yet all efforts are for naught if the evil of wizardry remains in our midst."

Forlik fought an intense surge of loathing. Solk delighted in inflaming the masses against the Hierarchy and the Congress. Privately, Forlik would have liked nothing more than to burn the Temple of Lotark to the ground, with all its Servants inside. But he was too well aware of the power the Temple held over the common folk to act on his inclinations. Solk was a vastly powerful man. He could precipitate a riot among the peasants with alarming ease.

But the commoners were not the only ones who clung to the Old Religion. While Forlik and the most of the Lords on the coast did not put much stock in divine retribution, many aristocrats from the Eastern Plains held Lotark's wrath to be a very real possibility. Forlik had walked a fine line between the two factions for almost a generation.

He assumed an appropriately reverent expression. "What do you suggest, Your Grace? The feast of the Bride's Rising will be upon us in a fortnight. Surely this is an unpopular time to talk of sacrifice. The people will not react kindly to a cancellation of the usual revelries."

"No. The feast will go on as usual, as a demonstration of faith in the midst of uncertainty. The Season of Atonement follows. The Temple will command the True Believers to fasting and prayer beyond the usual observances. It is to be hoped that the noble families will embrace the devotion."

Forlik's mouth twisted. "It will be done. I pray Lotark will hear our supplication and send relief. If not," he added, "at least the asceticism will be good for our dwindling food supply."

Solk drew himself up to his full height. "You jest, Lord Forlik. It does not become you. The devotions are necessary to our salvation, yet they will be useless if the Hierarchy is not abolished." He cast a withering glance at the crystal of illumination glowing on the council table. "True Believers have no use for wizards and their abominations, my Lord. When the people realize their lives depend on the destruction of this repugnant cult of evildoers, I can assure you they will take action in the name of the One God."

The high priest turned and left the chamber without waiting for a reply, his precise footsteps echoing in the long hallway. Forlik stared at the empty doorway. Never before had the Temple issued such a direct threat. Solk knew full well the Hierarchy was too powerful a group for the Congress to wish away.

Was the high priest so sure of the mobs, then? Did Solk really imagine the True Believers could destroy the Stronghold? Forlik's shoulders sagged. Faced with the twin threats of starvation and political upheaval, it would be a miracle if the city survived intact.

Unless a cure from the Stronghold saved it first. Forlik rolled up his maps. High Wizard Rannac lay on his deathbed, and it was common knowledge that Balek would be elected his successor. Balek had devised a cure for the Madness. Perhaps a cure for the Blight followed.

It was the only hope of avoiding bloodshed.

* * * * *

Gina woke to the first wash of dawn. Rolling over, she closed her eyes and snuggled deeper into the furs, relishing the luxurious texture on her bare skin. She felt happy and alive in a glorious way she'd never before experienced.

Then the last remnants of sleep scattered and the memory of the night before rolled over her like a small earthquake.

Oh. My. God.

She sat up abruptly. Morning mist blanketed the valley, filling it to the very edge of the cliff, leaving Gina with the odd sensation of being adrift on the rocky perch. She shut her eyes and forced herself to take a long, deep breath.

She dared a look around. Derrin knelt nearby, nursing a new fire. He hadn't bothered to dress. His muscled back and bare buttocks looked so enticing she had to hold herself back from throwing herself at him.

He sent her a cautious smile over one shoulder. "Good morning."

She clutched the furs to her bare breasts, keenly aware that it was much too late for modesty. He'd licked and sucked just about every part of her body last night.

The thought unnerved her. "Oh, God, Derrin, what have we done?"

"You don't remember?" His voice was teasing, but his eyes were guarded by shadows. "It couldn't have been very good, then."

Heat flooded Gina's cheeks as she remembered just how good losing herself to him had been. "Very funny."

"I would have sworn you were enjoying yourself," he continued in a conversational tone. He glanced at his shoulder. "I've got the claw marks to prove it."

Claw marks?

Gina stared at the angry red lines. Her face grew even hotter. "Oh God, I'm sorry. I—"

"I'm not." Derrin left the fire. With two swift strides he closed the distance between them and kissed her, hard. "Do you regret our joining, Gina?"

"No!" She stared at him, stricken by the pain she could feel flowing from his mind. Their lovemaking seemed to have intensified the mental connection between them—or maybe Derrin had stopped shielding his emotions from her. She wasn't sure which thought unnerved her more.

"I don't regret it," she said slowly. "It was wonderful. I never knew it could be like that. It's just…" Just that she hadn't been ready for it. Wasn't sure she ever could have been. And now that it was done…

Tears stung her eyes. "It will be so hard to leave you now."

Derrin stood and paced back to the fire. He picked up a dead branch and snapped it in two, then threw the pieces into the flames and sighed. "It will be no easier for me." He returned and sat beside her. "Gina, we have no idea when we will be parted, but neither does anyone else. Did Deehna know Red Hawk would be taken from her so suddenly?" His eyes, gray and piercing, held hers. "If you were to cross the web today, I wouldn't regret what we shared."

His gaze dropped to her breasts, still hidden behind the furs. She gripped the skins tighter. Derrin's lovemaking had been amazing, yet at the same time it had terrified her. He'd shattered every one of her defenses. She'd been so vulnerable, so open. Everything she'd promised herself she'd never be again. He could hurt her now, worse than Michael ever had, and there would be nothing she could do to stop him.

She cast about for something to say. "Where did these furs come from?"

"I went back to the village after you fell asleep. I borrowed these from Kaila."

Her head jerked up. "Kaila. I was supposed to give her dress back! She'll wonder where I am, and if she knows you're gone, too—" Gina grabbed for the dress, but Derrin snatched it up first.

"She won't be wondering," he said casually as he shook out the wrinkles and folded it. He set the garment aside, out of her reach. "She knows where you are, or at least who you're with and what we're doing."

"What? You told her we were going to—" She choked, then tried again. "You talked to Kaila behind my back about this? Were you so sure I'd say yes?"

"I let Kaila know my intentions, but it wasn't behind your back. You were there."

Gina stared. "What are you talking about?"

"My flute song told her. It was more than a simple melody I played for you two nights past. It was a question. Kaila and White Otter knew what I asked, even if you didn't. As for being sure of your answer—" He gave her a wry smile. "I hoped, but I wasn't certain at all. Kaila must have been, though."

"Why do you say that?"

"Your hair. A Baha'Na woman always leaves her hair loose when she joins with her partner for the first time. And the dress. It is a first joining dress."

Derrin's words settled into Gina's brain slowly, and a few heartbeats passed before their full import hit. When it did, she felt as if she'd been tossed into a raging river heading for a steep waterfall.

"Derrin." Her voice held a dangerous note, and she enunciated each word. "Are we—" she swallowed hard "—married?"

He avoided her gaze. "I'm sure Kaila would say we are."

"But...but..." she sputtered. *Married!* She didn't want to be married! After Michael, she'd sworn she'd never be trapped that way again.

Derrin dropped to one knee before her and gripped her bare shoulders. His gray eyes glittered with an emotion much less complicated than love. It was the same emotion that had ruled both of them last night. Gina's reaction came swiftly and completely, an erotic response so raw and wild it threatened to shatter her. Her first impulse was to strangle the feeling, return it to the murky depths of her psyche from which it had risen.

His fingers dug into her flesh. "Gina, I didn't want to join with you the way Galenan men take their women—as a servant or an afternoon's dalliance. I wanted to follow the customs of my mother's people." He searched her eyes. "But you're not of the Baha'Na and I'm a wizard of Galena." He released her. "Our joining is what you want it to be."

He half turned away and Gina understood he was leaving the choice to her. She'd been mistaken. She hadn't given him everything. There was still one small part of herself that she had kept safe. She could keep it from him, or she could accept him completely, along with all the risk and pain such a love brought.

Was there really a choice at all?

"I love you." They weren't the words she'd meant to say, but once spoken, Gina found she had no desire to call them back. Her heart had already chosen, without asking her blessing.

He turned back to her and she placed her palms, fingers splayed, on the hard muscles of his chest. "I love you," she repeated, savoring the words as they left her tongue. Her hand stroked his skin, dipped to his flat belly and lingered. His breathing quickened and the muscles in his stomach tightened. Her fingers quested lower and closed around his cock. It was already hard, and very, very hot.

Only then did Gina realize the furs covering her had dropped away. Derrin's gaze was fixed on the taut peaks of her breasts. She smiled and eased onto her back.

He followed, coming over her. He caged her body, filled her vision. He caught her wrists in his hands and spread her arms wide, pressing them into the furs. Gina felt a small stab of panic at the restraint. Michael had held her this way once when he'd been angry at her. She'd felt used. Humiliated. She tried to free herself, but Derrin didn't allow her to cover herself.

Finally, she gave up and lay still, heart thudding with a dull rhythm. He held her in place as his gaze tangled with hers, then traveled past the shuddering rise of her breasts to the arc of her belly and the dark curls below. The thought came to her that being under Derrin's control was a world of difference from being under Michael's. The intimate scrutiny sparked a tingling, burning ache between her legs. She trembled with desire, not shame. Her body was coming alive, not going numb.

She flushed under his open gaze. The intensity of last night's lovemaking had shaken her to the core, but at least in the darkness she'd been shielded from seeing his reaction to her surrender. Now, awash in the slanting rays of the morning sun, she felt unbearably exposed by the completeness of her body's response to her lover. But, oddly, she had no desire to break free of his hold.

Derrin didn't release her, and Gina lay still, barely breathing. The fire spread from her loins to her stomach, then to the tips of her breasts, ignited by her lover's attention as it caressed the length of her body. She felt a fine tremor run through the muscles of his arms. His heated gaze caught hers.

She struggled to take her next breath. Overwhelmed, she shut her eyes and twisted her face away.

He released her and rolled to one side, propping himself up on one elbow. His free hand traced a line across her cheek. "Gina, are you embarrassed?"

She forced herself to answer. "A little."

"Why? I love looking at you. You're so beautiful—even more than I imagined."

"You imagined me like this?"

Derrin rolled onto his back and laughed. "Of course. I've thought of little else since we left the Fire Clan. And even before."

Gina sat up. "You weren't picturing me naked the day we got caught in the storm. You were miserable to me!"

"All I could think of that day was throwing you down on the trail and ripping your clothes off. If you hadn't been so angry, I would have done it."

Gina laughed. Her self-consciousness fell away. Derrin was her friend, after all, the best one she'd ever had. Now he was her lover as well. Maybe she didn't need to protect her heart from him. Still smiling, she reached her arms around his neck and pulled him into a kiss.

Derrin rolled her onto her back and pressed the length of his body to hers. His fingers roved over her breast, gently scraping the hardened peak. His teeth followed, drawing on the sensitized nipple with a series of sharp tugs. Gina moaned and clutched handfuls of his hair. The unbearable ache between her legs had returned. She rubbed her clit against the hard muscles of his thigh, seeking relief.

"I hated fighting with you," she said.

His cock pulsed hot and heavy against her thigh. She lifted her hips. Derrin rocked forward and filled her. He loved her with slow, agonizing strokes, pulling wave after wave of response from her body. Gina shuddered. She gripped his shoulders and shut her eyes.

"No, Gina." His voice was husky and cajoling. "Don't close your eyes—look at me."

Gina fought the urge to obey, unwilling to reveal to Derrin how completely she'd surrendered to his erotic onslaught. What would she see in the shadowed mists of his eyes? Triumph? Or the self-absorbed expression she'd seen so often on Michael's face?

Derrin moved again, deep inside her, tearing a moan from her lips. His fingers stroked the cleft between her buttocks, circled the opening there.

The tempo of his rhythm increased. "Look at me, Gina. Please, look at me."

She drew a trembling breath and met his gaze. There was nothing of triumph, nothing of selfish gratification in his expression. Instead, she saw all he offered her. His strength, his heart, and—most precious of all—his vulnerability. His inner self stripped naked before her, given freely. Her heart split open.

It was a gift beyond her wildest imaginings. Could she offer him anything less?

The endless waves buffeting her body intensified, a storm reaching its full fury. She met each thrust. Derrin's eyes darkened. He called out her name and she spun out of control. Her heart pitched toward the center of the maelstrom, all reason, all resistance gone.

His hips bucked with frenzied power. Still locked in his gaze, Gina felt all her senses rush into the place of their joining and explode, flinging her into the center of the storm. She cried out as the world dropped away, gripping the anchor of Derrin's body.

Her name tore from his throat. His body went rigid, then sank atop her. She welcomed his weight, his ragged breathing, the wild pounding of his heart.

She closed her eyes and clung to him.

Chapter Seventeen

The song continued, lilting strains that caressed with a feather's touch. Balek exulted. Another soul had fallen to its promise. Life traded for sanctuary. Breath given in exchange for peace. Each tiny soul strengthened the delicate mosaic of his power.

The golden mesh crept across the land.

* * * * *

Ariek strode across the upper plaza, cutting a diagonal across the shadow of the Stronghold. His boots echoed on the broad cobblestones. Ducking down one of the smaller side streets leading out of the square, he made his way past the staid palaces of the Upper City, barely glancing at their chiseled stone façades and sparkling multi-paned windows.

Following a path he could have walked in his sleep, he emerged from the press of town and swung onto a road leading to the high bluffs. Here, the villas of the wealthiest Galenans overlooked the sea. At the end of the road, he veered to his right and strode up a stone staircase. The gleaming black doors adorning the villa's main portal were carved from a single piece of wood carried from the rainforests of Loetahl by one of his father's ships. He lifted the clapper of an enormous bronze doorknocker, cast in the shape of a horse's head. It fell with a thud.

The door swung inward to reveal a tight-faced elderly man, his back frozen into a vertical line. A tailored dark blue coat was devoid of the merest wrinkle. The man fixed a disapproving stare on Ariek, but moved to one side to allow him to pass.

"Master Ariek," he acknowledged with a slight bow.

Ariek grinned, prompting a further scowl from the butler. "It's nice to see you again as well, Rorric. Would you be so kind as to tell me where my mother passes this day?"

"The Lady Kalana is walking in the gardens."

Without a backward glance, Ariek strode through the entry hall past the grand staircase and through the doors leading to the ballroom. He let himself out one of the glass-paned doors opening onto a broad marble terrace and paused, his gaze drawn to the wide expanse of sparkling water stretching to the horizon. Though he, like his father, preferred the family's country estate on the outskirts of Sirth, his mother chose to spend most of her time here in the capital city. Both villas overlooked the sea. Ariek wouldn't know how to live without the sound of the surf in his ears.

He spied his mother's trim form, encased in a yellow silk gown shot through with pure gold thread. He'd always thought his pretty, buxom mother mismatched with his wiry father. The difference in their ages, as well as their personalities, was great. His father kept a close eye on his fleet of ships and his horse breeding and didn't shrink from the dirtier aspects of either. His mother, in contrast, disliked the least bit of dust or grime. She lived for fine food and clothes, expensive jewelry and an active social life.

Lady Kalana strolled through the searose garden, stopping every so often to smell a bloom. She expected him—he came every Lotark's Day at this time. He took the stairs from the terrace to the gardens two at a time, his cloak billowing behind him as he descended. His mother turned toward him, a smile lighting her delicate features.

He was struck by her beauty, barely dimmed by the passing of the years. He thought of his hook-nosed father, ensconced in his estate near Sirth, and wondered if his mother had a lover in the city. Most noble wives did—he had personal experiences with such liaisons. Then, since the thought was disturbing, he pushed it aside. He returned his mother's smile and fell into step beside her.

"Ariek. It's good to see you." Lady Kalana placed a small white hand on Ariek's arm. "I'm glad at least one of my sons bothers to visit me."

He shrugged. "Mother, you know Berak is weighted down with business regarding Father's imports and Galek is training with his troops on the Eastern Plains. I'm but a short walk away."

"And you know even if they lived here in the villa, they wouldn't seek my company. You're the only one who does." She gave a delicate pout.

"Why shouldn't I?" Ariek teased. "You're a beautiful woman. Last month, after I accompanied you to the market, several people asked whether I'd found a girl to court at last." He grinned. "I told them you were my sister."

Lady Kalana laughed delightedly, her blue eyes sparkling. Ariek knew his own eyes matched his mother's, a mirror of the sea. "But truly, Ariek, when will you bring a girl home for me to meet? It's time you looked for a wife. I want my garden filled with the laughter of my grandchildren." Her expression turned thoughtful. "Lady Tirania's daughter is of marriageable age..."

"Mother." Ariek looked out across the waves, his chest suddenly tight. "I'm but a third son. Not the best prospect for a girl of good family."

Lady Kalana's expression showed what she thought of Ariek's excuses, but she didn't press further. They continued their stroll down the garden path, halting at the stone wall edging the cliff. Far below, waves crashed in a white froth against the rocks. A gull called. Ariek picked up a rock and flung it into the sea, trying to erase the mental image of Danat's red curls tumbling across her pillow. The deep green of her eyes was an endless, lush forest drawing him in...

He cast a sideways glance at his mother, who stood looking at him with poorly masked concern. He forced a smile. "Let's not spoil the afternoon discussing my marriage prospects."

"As you wish."

A flash of sunlight caught on a golden crystal hanging from a chain at her throat. He started. "Mother, you wear the Madness antidote—are you..."

Lady Kalana glance down at the charm, then waved her hand. "It's not what you think, Ariek. You know Rorric would summon you if I fell ill."

"There must be some reason you wear such an ornament."

She rolled her eyes. "Your father. A preventive measure, he said." She unclasped the chain and dangled the gem between them. "Don't you remember me asking you if they were used as such? I told Vaaltor what you said—that the antidote wasn't engaged unless the Madness had already entered one's mind—but he paid no heed. He insists I wear it." She frowned. "Though I must confess, Ariek, I find this crystal rather unsettling."

"Unsettling? In what way?"

Lady Kalana caught the stone in her palm. "It's hard to describe," she said, peering at it fretfully. "There's a chill vibrating around it, like the shattering of thin ice on a pond. I feel my soul turning numb." She shivered. "I know it's foolish. It's just a stone."

Ariek took the antidote and held it up to the sunlight. He knew his mother to be extraordinarily sensitive to the delicate power fields encircling crystals. He suspected she could have been a sorceress.

He sank his mind into the crystal. It flared, then took on a steady glow. He explored its structure, tracing each line of symmetry from center to outermost edge. There was nothing remarkable about the pattern, and that in itself disturbed him. How could a crystal so simple suppress the Madness? What was it about this stone that had so alarmed his mother?

A numbing of the soul. He'd felt an instinctive response when his mother had said those words. Ariek steadied himself and drove deeper into the crystal's structure, seeking... What? He couldn't say. He searched, goaded by an intuition, a fleeting sensation.

"Tarol's blood!"

"Ariek, what is it?" Lady Kalana gripped her son's arm. "What do you see?"

Ariek bit back a second oath. "Mother, may I borrow this crystal for a while?"

"Of course, but...is something wrong?"

He forced a smile. "No. I simply wish to study it further. These crystals are hard to come by, even in the Stronghold." At her nod, he pocketed the stone.

He walked in the garden at his mother's side, reining in his impatience until he was able to excuse himself without rousing her suspicion. It was only when he stood alone in the street outside the villa that he dared to contemplate the implications of what he'd seen.

Buried deep within the crystal's simple primary structure, he'd discovered a second crystal lattice. It was submerged in the first, well camouflaged, yet Ariek could sense its power—subtle, but at the same time utterly compelling to anyone who accepted its control. The same force he'd felt once before, in Balek's workroom, while linked with the crystal Derrin had called the webstone.

It was a power beyond reason, beyond logic.

Insane, insatiable power surging through an impossible web of five-fold symmetry.

Chapter Eighteen

Pure fury raced through Solk's veins. High Wizard Balek—Spawn of Tarol!—dared to enter Lotark's house on the eve of a holy day, demanding a private audience. If it were not for the fact that the man had clothed himself in ceremonial white, Solk would have had him thrown into the back alley.

"Your Grace," said Balek, bowing from the waist as humbly as any supplicant. "I know my presence here is highly unusual, but I come regarding a matter of great import."

"Go on."

"I am very much saddened by the enmity that exists between the Temple and the Hierarchy. I've often thought we should put our differences aside and work together, for the good of— "

Solk did not bother to hide a flash of irritation. "Master Balek. Surely you have not come here on the eve of the Bride's Rising to discuss ideology."

"No, Your Grace. I have not." The wizard's expression was grave, but his eyes gleamed like a forbidden crystal. "I am a wizard, true, but I respect Lotark's law. I've come to warn you."

"Warn me? Of what?"

"Blasphemy. An abomination committed here, in the House of Lotark."

Solk's gaze narrowed on the man. "How so?"

"The sanctity of the Temple has been desecrated."

The high priest drew in a sharp breath. "That is impossible. Lotark's Temple cannot be violated—even by the black forces of wizardry. The One God is jealous. To mock Him in His house is to suffer immediate death."

Balek's expression shifted from earnest sympathy to the amused gaze of a father surveying his child's folly. "I only wish that were the case. I bring you proof. Proof that the Bride of Lotark has taken a lover, a wizard named Ariek. He visits her chambers at will."

The blood drained from Solk's face. His hands grew cold and trembled, fisting into the folds of his robe. "Wizard filth…you lie," he rasped.

Balek produced a scarf and draped it casually over his arm. The Mark of Lotark shone in blue thread on the white silk. "I found this in the young man's workroom."

Solk snatched up the cloth and examined it. It was genuine. The Bride did not wear such items during ceremonies—it must have come from her chamber.

A black fury descended on him. "The blasphemer must pay for this outrage with his life." He eyed the wizard suspiciously. "But you… Why would betray one of your own kind?"

"I count as my 'kind' men who are honorable, not any who would defile what the people hold as sacred."

"This man. Show him to me."

Balek drew a flat crystal from the pouch at his belt. He cupped it in his palm, then extended it toward Solk. The high priest hesitated but an instant. Surely Lotark would not condemn him for making use of wizardry in so grave an instance.

A face appeared on the glassy surface of the crystal. Solk stared at the image, an old memory tugging at the corner of his mind. "I remember this man. He worshiped the Bride at the altar a year ago." His mouth twisted. "He will pay for his deeds. Before the sun sets on tomorrow's feast, he will be dead." He drew himself up to his full height and swept from the room.

Balek smiled at the priest's retreating form. "No, Your Grace," he murmured. "I very much doubt he will be. A wizard of the Hierarchy is not so easily defeated."

* * * * *

Derrin watched Gina's face. They had taken leave of White Otter and Kaila in the morning amid tears and good wishes for their joining. Now, at midday, they'd reached the start of the canyon trail that would carry them to the village of the Tree Clan.

Waves of green-gold grass carpeted the canyon floor, diamonds of light sparkled on the surface of the wide, shallow river. Steep walls of stone rose on either side, sometimes carrying the forest with it, other times casting off the trees to reveal layers of brown, red and tan. A brilliant slice of blue sky arched above.

Gina's eyes swept closed. The sunlight dusted her expression with gold, and her lips parted. His heart contracted at the sight.

She turned to him. "I never dreamed such a place existed."

"I know." Then, since any further words seemed inadequate, he pulled her close and kissed her.

Gina's stomach growled. Loud. She buried her face against his shoulder. "How embarrassing."

He chuckled. "Let's find something to eat. I can't have you scaring away all the game, or our traps will be empty in the morning."

She swatted him on the shoulder. "If the traps are empty, I'm sure it won't be *my* fault."

She set to breaking off the furled tips of the ferns clustered at the edge of the forest, gathering them into her skirt. Derrin, still smiling, made his way to the water's edge. He searched a jumble of rocks, lifting each stone and pulling tiny shelled creatures one by one from their hiding places.

After they'd eaten, Gina made several trips into the forest to gather deadwood and edible plants, while Derrin set about making up the camp. He'd chosen a grassy site well above the stream, with a sheltering wall of rock rising behind it. He cleared a large area, laying the long sheaths of cut grass in a pile nearby. The afternoon grew hotter, and he found himself sweating. He stripped off his shirt and tossed it to one side.

He built a round shelter a short distance from the firepit. It was larger and afforded more headroom than the hasty lean-tos he and Gina usually constructed. He sunk saplings into the ground, forming a circle and lashed them together with strong vines. He covered the frame with overlapping sheets of bark, leaving a smoke hole in the center of the roof.

When he had finished, he turned to find Gina eying his handiwork. "This camp's a bit more elaborate than usual," she commented.

"We've been traveling at a fast pace. I thought we'd stay here for two or three nights."

Gina threw him an amused glance. "A honeymoon, Derrin?"

"A what?"

"A marriage trip," she explained dryly. "Taken after a wedding so the bride and groom can have some privacy."

"You can call it that if you like." Derrin settled himself on the bed of cut grass and stretched out with his hands behind his head. He grinned up at her. "By all means, take advantage of our privacy."

But Gina was already turning away, and he caught only a glimpse of her back as she disappeared into the trees. "Where are you going?" he shouted after her.

"I'll be back."

He considered following her, but the sun's warmth on his bare chest made him comfortably drowsy, and the bed of grasses was soft and fragrant. He closed his eyes and drifted between slumber and awareness.

A rustling noise sounded in the brush. He opened his eyes in time to see Gina emerge from the thicket. Every muscle in his body tensed.

She was completely naked, wet from a swim in the stream. Water dripped from her braids. His gaze followed the path of a droplet as it rolled down the curve of one breast and crested the tip of her nipple. Another danced over the swell of her belly and disappeared into the dark curly triangle between her thighs.

He watched the movement of her legs, the placement of her bare feet as she moved closer. Her shadow fell across him. A wren called from the brush. Its mate answered, distant.

Gina looked down at him for endless moments, measured only by the faint rushing of the water and the soft roar of the wind in the treetops. Then she gave a slow, secretive smile. Her gaze swept down his body, alighting on the bulge under his kilt. Her smile deepened and she moved closer, close enough for him to touch. He reached for her.

"No," she said. Her eyes were dark. "Don't move."

His hand fell away. She knelt beside him and leaned forward, brushing the tips of her braids across his chest. His breathing quickened.

"Kiss me," he said.

She covered his mouth in a deep kiss, stroking with her tongue. She bit his lower lip, gently at first, then harder. He groaned and caught her about the waist, pulling her atop him. She fell astride his torso, palms braced on his chest. Her arousal moistened his skin, and his cock grew even harder.

He locked her gaze in his. Her pupils darkened. She scored his flesh with her fingernails, dragging them down his chest to his stomach.

She followed the trail with her mouth, painting him with her tongue and with droplets of water as her body shifted back. When she was astride his thighs, she tugged at the knot of his kilt. His breathing quickened and his fingers tightened on her shoulders.

Her hand, warm and damp, closed around his swollen flesh, stroking upward over the sensitive ridge, sending shockwaves through his body. He closed his eyes, lost.

The sensation of her mouth on his cock, scalding, tight and alive, caused his eyes to fly open again. Gina flicked her tongue across the tip of his shaft. She glanced up, her expression wicked, her red lips framing his head. He watched, fascinated, as she drew him in completely. She worked him with her teeth and tongue, leaving him gasping, hurtling toward the precipice.

He endured it as long as he dared. With his breath coming in short gasps, he gripped her upper arms and hauled her off him. He captured her lips with bruising force. A feral, primitive enveloped him. He wanted Gina under him. Wanted to mark her with his scent, brand her as his mate. Giving her no chance to escape, he turned her in his arms, pressed her to her knees. A low growl rose in his throat. Caging her with his arms, he covered her body, his chest pressed to her spine, her round buttocks nestled against his groin. His breath bathed her neck. He inhaled deeply and scented his mate's surrender.

His tongue flicked over the swell of flesh where Gina's neck joined her shoulder. The taste of her sweat-slicked skin intoxicated him. He caught the soft mound of flesh at the base of her neck between his teeth and bit down, hard. She whimpered and ground her ass into his cock. He slid his hand around her torso and plucked at her nipples, first one, then the other. He loved the feel of her bare skin under his hands, loved the sounds of Gina's submission. He passed his fingers between her legs and found her wet with her body's juices. Ready for his possession. She was so soft, so accepting of his brutal passion. Her surrender went beyond his wildest imaginings.

He could think of nothing but the need to be inside her welcoming core. To hold her helpless while he took his pleasure and gave her pleasure in return. Panting, he caught Gina's hips. His fingers sunk into her flesh in a punishing grip, holding her steady, slightly away from him. She ground her buttocks frantically, trying to move closer. He did not allow her that satisfaction.

He filled her slowly, deliberately, thrusting forward as she writhed until his full length was embedded deep in her hot, slick passage. Holding himself motionless for several heartbeats, he savored the rush of sensations that flowed from his cock to his body. Gina's inner muscles were alive, clamping down on him, milking him with tiny spasms. He'd never felt anything like it.

He withdrew and surged into her again, pausing once again at the peak of his stroke to feel her response.

"Oh, God," Gina groaned. She tried again to move her hips.

His grip tightened.

"Fuck me," she gasped. "Oh, God, just fuck me."

He granted her wish. He withdrew and thrust himself back inside her, over and over, moving with increasing urgency as Gina moaned her acceptance. Waves of intense pleasure swept over him, burgeoning upward from a well of need so profound it threatened to consume him.

*****

Gina let out a shuddering sob. Derrin's passion had broken her open, swept her past any coherent thought. He drove deeper, his cock hard inside her body, invading her, marking her as his own. Flexing his hips, he urged her up the spiral, following her as she climbed. She braced her arms on the ground and met each thrust gladly, savoring the fevered growls of her mate, the power of his rut, the painful grip of his embrace.

Her climax rushed at her. She threw herself into it and heard Derrin's shout as he followed. He fell atop her, pressing her into the bed of cut grass, his chest heaving against her back. She welcomed his possession, welcomed the earth caressing her body. She lay still beneath him until she felt him move.

He rolled to one side and gathered her into his arms. He kissed her, then drew back and met her gaze. His gray eyes were soft, with a touch of an apology.

"Did I hurt you?" he asked.

"No." She traced one finger along the angry scratch on his chest, where she had marked him. "Did I hurt *you*?"

Derrin chuckled. "I love you, Gina." His tone grew serious. "I was afraid my need to possess you had become too great for you to accept."

She touched his cheek, looked into his eyes. "Never think that, Derrin. I love you. I love the way you need to be with me."

She lay with her head on his chest for a long while, listening to the steady beat of his heart mingle with the sounds of the forest, no longer fearful of the power of their physical joining. It was a part of them, part of their love, and she gloried in it. The past and the future receded. Her peace was complete, perfect in that moment.

Sometime later, she pushed herself to a sitting position. She thought of her clothes, drying on a boulder near the stream, but the sun was still warm and she felt no need to retrieve them. Derrin lay with his eyes closed, one hand resting on her leg. She'd never been so close to another person, had never trusted anyone so much. They'd be parted soon, but even if she left this world tomorrow, she wouldn't regret her decision to become his lover.

She would give him more, if she could. "Derrin?"

"Hmmm?" He opened one eye and focused on her.

"The Na'tahar. How is it done between lovers?"

Derrin thrust himself into a sitting position and regarded her seriously. His eyes were troubled, and Gina knew he was remembering the trauma he'd inflicted on her when he'd entered her mind to destroy Balek's control.

He looked away. "I wouldn't ask that of you."

"And if I asked you? If I told you I wanted to feel you inside my mind as I've felt you inside my body?"

He met her gaze. His eyes were gray smoke, concealing a smoldering fire that threatened to erupt at the barest touch of wind. "I would give you anything you asked of me, Gina, even my soul, but are you sure? We have shared our dreams and our bodies, but the Na'tahar is so much more than that. When it is freely and completely accepted by a man and a woman, it is a true joining of souls. More intimate than anything we have experienced. Partners often mated for many seasons before they trust each other enough to join in that way."

"We don't *have* many seasons. Or even many days, for that matter." Gina fought back the grief that accompanied the thought. She wouldn't give in to it until they parted. "All my life I've hidden in my lab and my work, wondering how other people could plunge into love with so little regard for the pain it could bring. I couldn't do it. I wanted to be safe more than I wanted anything else."

She paused, searching for the right words. "Now I realize every moment, every breath of life is a leap of faith." She touched his hand. "I love you, Derrin. I never imagined loving anyone this completely.

When I return to my world I don't want to wonder what the Na'tahar would have been like. I want to know." She drew a deep breath. "Even if it hurts to remember it."

Derrin covered her hands with his, then lifted them to his lips and kissed the back of her fingers.

"Then let me show you, Gina."

* * * * *

Derrin brushed Gina's mind with the lightest of touches. He felt her soften, inviting his entry. A fierce longing gripped him. *Na'tahar.* To know and be known in the deepest recesses of being. Gina offered him that bond in love, even after he'd forced her to accept it in terror. The thought humbled him.

He opened his mind and let his love for Gina flow toward her, holding nothing back. No secrets, no longings, no dark corners of his soul. He exposed every flaw, every shortcoming, and offered it to her. She accepted his gift and sent him her own love and fears in return. Their life essences touched, retreated, touched again. They danced in this way for a time, learning each other, discovering nuances that had until now gone hidden. Finally, Derrin gathered his will and extended it toward Gina. He felt her surrender.

He pulsed on, and they were joined.

They had joined in Na'tahar once before, but that first, hurried joining was but a pale shadow of the union they experienced now. Gina's emotions flowed over him in waves. Joy, wonder, trust, surrounding him in a willing embrace. Her spirit touched each of his memories, each emotion, knowing him in the essence of his inmost self. He immersed himself in her, floating through a tide of dream images, seeking to know, to understand.

Gina's mind poured into his soul, filling it with endless love. The power of it overwhelmed him. She surrounded him, touching every part of his mind as thoroughly as he touched hers. No thought, no emotion lay hidden. His soul was stripped to its bare essence, revealed in all its imperfections. Letting go of his last fears, he shared all of himself, letting Gina see him for what he was. He allowed her to feel all of his life—the wonder of a boy who had sparked his first fire, the shame of a youth who had failed the test of his manhood. His brotherhood with Ariek, his sorrow at Niirtor's death.

He had never imagined the power of such a surrender.

In return, Gina opened the gates to her deepest emotions. The pain of losing first her mother, then her father. The shame inflicted by her marriage to a selfish, manipulative partner.

Once their pain was shared, it vanished. Only love existed. Derrin filled Gina with his passion, reaching deep within himself to draw out that which was most pure. She did the same for him.

Then the dream images faded, leaving them swathed in darkness. A blankness lay ahead of them, a huge field of nothingness. Derrin advanced to its edge, uncertain.

When he would have pulled away from the void, Gina urged him forward. Joined as one, they gathered courage and plunged ahead.

Together, they fell into the place beyond the mind, into pure emptiness. They surrendered their joined souls to a force beyond their bodies, beyond their emotions, beyond every uniqueness. The white center of the hottest flame engulfed them, burning away everything. Only the essence of their love remained.

They touched infinity and shattered.

A force beyond anything Derrin could comprehend flung them back into the physical world like a crashing sea disgorging a scrap of jetsam onto the shore. He fell back into his body. Gina was wrapped in his arms, her legs encircling his torso, her emotions still tangled with his own. He sensed her wonder of the lingering rapture.

Suddenly, it was unbearable their minds were joined when their flesh was not. He shifted and slipped into her body. Into his home. He fell back, pulling her atop him, guiding her movements as she rode his cock to her peak.

He met her in the darkness.

*****

Two nights later, the weather turned frigid.

Gina edged closer to Derrin. They sat by the fire after dark, sheltered by a nook in the canyon wall. The night winds had chilled her to the bone, but her heart was even colder. Each step she took brought her closer to her own world. She was no longer certain she wanted to return, but if her presence was, as Derrin believed, harming his world, she had no choice but to go back.

She hunched as close to the fire as she dared, seeking comfort. The wind whistled through the hidden cracks in the rocks of the canyon walls, calling out threats she couldn't name. Bottomless shadows crept from the stone, sprung to life by the flickering flames. She shivered. Derrin's hand stroked, firm and comforting, on the back of her neck.

"It sounds like evil spirits are all around us," she said.

Derrin gave her an odd look. "For the Baha'Na, there are no evil spirits, but the Servants of Lotark have dealings aplenty with them. Do they exist in your world?"

Gina gave a short laugh. "I'm just jittery. There are plenty of evil people in my world, but evil spirits? I think they're a matter of people projecting their fears outside themselves."

"What are you afraid of, Gina?"

She chewed on her lower lip. "That's the problem, Derrin. I don't know. All day I've felt unsettled, as though something important had changed." She cast about for words to describe the fleeting tendrils of fear. "Something isn't right, or... someone's in trouble." She raised her head, her heart suddenly pounding. "That's it! Someone's in danger! But who? It's not you or me. Or anyone of the clans."

Derrin was regarding her intently. "Someone from your own world, perhaps?"

"I don't know." She shook her head. "Just listen to me—I can't believe I'm talking like this. It's my overactive imagination."

"Perhaps," he allowed.

A piercing wail tore through the night, sending Gina crashing into Derrin's arms. She pressed her back into his chest, gripping his arms.

A second cry came close behind the first. Starting low, it rose in pitch, passing through the notes of a mournful scale. It peaked, then descended, fading, slipping into the night.

"What...what was that?"

"Direwolves."

"Wolves!" A paralyzing panic poured into her limbs. "Will they attack? Oh, God—where can we hide?"

Derrin's body shook. Several moments passed before Gina realized he was laughing.

She twisted in his arms. "What's so funny?"

"They won't harm us. The People don't hunt direwolves."

"What has that got to do with it?"

"Direwolves are the brothers and sisters of the Baha'Na. They taught the clans how to hunt. To kill a wolf is unthinkable, and the wolves know this. They don't threaten their human relatives, but neither do they seek us out. They are cunning and elusive, difficult to track, rarely seen."

Gina didn't feel reassured. "Are they close?"

"Yes." He shifted back onto his heels, easing Gina from his arms. Cupping his hands around his mouth, he threw his head back and let out a howl. He added a series of short yips at its end, just before the call faded into a whisper.

Her scalp prickled. The minutes stretched out before her, silent and intense. Derrin peered past the circle of firelight. A breath of smoke drifted past him. Gina held her breath.

The direwolf call came again, beginning so subtly it seemed it hadn't been born at all, but had sprung fully alive from the darkness. It rose to a crescendo, then subsided, ending with a series of short yips identical to the ones Derrin had uttered.

Gina gasped. "It answered you!"

Derrin flashed her a smile, his eyes sparkling. He tipped his head back and repeated the call. They waited, but no second reply came. Gina supposed the animal had retreated. She breathed a sigh of relief. Despite Derrin's nonchalance, she couldn't shake the image of a slavering beast ready to devour a helpless pig or a little girl in a red hood.

Beside her, Derrin tensed and laid his hand on her arm. She followed his gaze into the forest. She could see nothing out of the ordinary, but Derrin's posture indicated something was there, and not far away.

A pine bough gave a soft sigh as a shadow brushed past it. An enormous gray wolf padded toward them, firelight reflected in its golden eyes. A male, so huge that its front paws were easily bigger than Gina's hands. Long tufts of shaggy fur streamed over its powerful flanks.

It sat down less than an arm's span away. Derrin stared at the animal. The creature gazed back with an almost wistful expression. Long moments passed, then the direwolf rose and faded into the night as silently as it had emerged.

Gina would have spoken, but the aching sadness in Derrin's eyes stopped her. Instinctively, she knew he needed solitude. She eased away and crawled into the shelter, where she lay awake for a long time, listening to the wind.

Chapter Nineteen

The tree rose higher than Gina would have believed possible, spreading its limbs in a cloud of green. At the canyon floor, its gnarled trunk was so wide a dozen people with arms outstretched could not have encircled it. Overhead, the tips of its branches reached nearly to the crest of the cliff. Its roots pulled at the earth in great waves, entwining huge boulders in its grasp. Younger, straighter trees gathered close, like grandchildren at the feet of an ancient matriarch.

The Tree Clan lived in a large hollow at the base of the main trunk, in four communal roundhouses. The bark-covered dwellings merged with the skin of the great tree. The familiar curl of smoke rose above the rooftops.

Gina and Derrin made their way toward the village, negotiating waist-high roots and rain-scoured gullies. A group of about a dozen barefooted children ran out to meet them, calling the traditional Baha'Na greeting amid much laughter. Gina smiled and waved in response. A moment later, upturned faces surrounded her, and she could go no further.

One small girl caught Gina's hand. "Come, I will guide you to my mother."

"Your mother?"

"She is Malia, Na'lara to the Tree Clan."

Gina went with the girl, the other children trailing behind. Derrin nodded, but didn't follow. He angled toward the far end of the village, where a cluster of men stood.

Her tiny guide chattered away, a disjointed font of information. "I am Lasha. My brothers are Tolin and Sarrin. They are almost men. Our father is Standing Deer. We live over there." She pointed to the nearest roundhouse. "Father calls me a *rama* because I am such a good climber."

"What's a rama?"

Lasha giggled and pointed to a long-tailed creature scampering overhead.

They neared the massive trunk. Stout vines wrapped around it, climbing high, sliding along the trees limbs, then dipping to the ground. Lasha grabbed one curled end. With swift grace, she hopped up on the wide curve of a low-hanging branch and scrambled up to the nearest vee.

"Come on!" she called.

Gina gaped at her. "Up there?" she asked, feeling foolish.

"Of course!" Lasha giggled. "Where else? My mother is waiting for us." She cocked her head, her eyes bright, and Gina could well believe the little girl was kin to the rama. "It is easier with your feet bare."

Gina untied her boots and followed, gripping the vine and hoisting herself into the tree. Foliage enveloped her, pulling her into its embrace with the ease of a mother gathering her young. She climbed higher, easily finding her footing, her hands always within reach of a hold.

The branches were wider than her outstretched arms. Deep furrows wandered over the bark-like lines on the face of a woman so old she has forgotten her age. Leaves—huge sheets of green—rustled as she climbed.

Gina looked down at the crisscross of limbs below her. The ground had disappeared.

Overhead, Lasha giggled. She was perched on a limb near a woman whose face was a mature version of her own.

Gina pulled herself up beside the pair. Malia greeted her with a graceful arc of her arm. "The Goddess shines on your coming, Gina."

"She shines on your home," replied Gina, returning the gesture. She extended her mind to the Baha'Na woman, touching her in a brief embrace. "Your little rama is a good guide."

Malia smiled. "Scamper away, now, little rama," she told her daughter. Lasha jumped from her perch and disappeared into the foliage. "My daughter loves the tree, as do all the People. The path of each clan joins with ours in the grandmother's embrace."

The strength of the Tree radiated from its rough skin. "I feel her embrace, as well," Gina said. "I'm glad my path has crossed yours."

"Your journey cannot help but be one with ours. All paths lead to the Goddess. Truly, there is nowhere else to go." She rose. "Stay here for a time, Gina." She slipped through the branches and disappeared.

Gina let out a slow breath and looked around. Scattered patches of ground and sky flashed between the leaves. She settled into the seat Malia had vacated and felt her limbs grow heavy with peace.

A light breeze wafted through the branches, rustling the leaves and making the smaller branches sigh. Patches of brilliant blue played around edges of green, breathing with the wind. A large black ant walked a torturous path along a ridge of bark. Three others soon followed it. A small bird darted past, sure in its flight between the leaves, calling to its mate. A glint of sunlight illuminated a spider's thread. A chattering rama undulated along a thick branch.

By the time Gina thought of descent, daylight was beginning to fade. Her mouth was dry and the air had grown cooler, but she pushed those discomforts from her mind. The night creatures would soon begin their twilight cries. She waited, listening.

Moon shadows passed over her. An unseen animal brushed her leg in the darkness. A night hunter called.

A birdsong signaled dawn. Gina sat up and blinked. She didn't remember falling asleep, but somehow the night had flown past. A vibrant scent filled the air. Soft pink, then crimson filled the spaces between the leaves. She left her perch and climbed to the ground.

The village was awakening, but Gina wasn't yet ready to join the morning's activities. A narrow path on the bank of a winding creek led deeper into the forest. She followed the trail, drawn toward the sound of falling water. The creek grew wider and flatter, then disappeared over a small cliff.

Gina waded across the stream and peered over the edge. A shining pool of water, churning with the impact of the falls, lay a short distance below. It was the perfect spot for a morning swim.

She scrambled down the rocks beside the waterfall. A brilliant sky, adrift with clouds, arched over the pond. Morning sunlight played on the rippling water. Rainbow colors shimmered in the spray of the falls, then disappeared into the shadow of a shallow cave, barely visible behind the curtain of water. Gina picked her way across the rocks to the far end of the pool, where the water washed in faint ripples upon a strip of sand. She untied her boots and slipped out of her dress. She left them on the bank and waded into the deepest part of the pond, sighing with pleasure.

Far off in the forest, a songbird called to its mate. Gina sluiced the clear water over her braids. Scooping up a handful of clean sand, she scrubbed her skin all over until it tingled. Then she dunked her head under the surface again and washed off the grit.

It wasn't a hot shower and she didn't have any soap, but she emerged feeling clean and refreshed. She retreated to the tiny beach and lay down on the sand. The sun felt so good on her naked body that she left her dress on the boulder while she looked up at the sky. Huge white clouds passed lazily across an impossibly blue canvas. Did the sky at home ever look this perfect? She didn't know. She'd never taken the time to look.

The clouds enthralled her. Gina had always thought of a cloud as something colorless and static, sharply delineated, like the lumpy bubble of a child's drawing. She'd never noticed a cloud's fluid movement, the swirling mists of blue and pink and gold at its edges.

Eventually she closed her eyes. The sun was warm pleasant, the chatter of birdsong peaceful. She wondered where Derrin had spent the night, and if he was waiting for her.

Thinking of Derrin caused an ache to spring up between her legs. She let her hand drift toward it. She touched herself, circling one finger around her clit, imagining it was Derrin who touched her. The thought made her thighs go damp. She slid her fingers through the slipper folds, gathering the moisture. Then she returned to the tight, aching nub, stroking with an increased tempo.

The pleasure spiraled, grew. She shifted her hips, moving in time with her own rhythm. She was close, very close. Her free hand came up to pluck at one nipple.

Her climax spread over her in a sweet slow wave. She rode it, rocking her hips. All too soon it passed, leaving her warm and relaxed, but not quite sated. She lay still, her eyes closed, until a pebble dropped with a soft thud onto the sand beside her.

Startled, she sat up to see Derrin standing a short distance away, a hungry light in his eyes. Heat infused her cheeks. She picked up the stone and tossed it back at him. He caught it with one hand, then turned and skipped it neatly across the water's surface.

"How long have you been spying on me?" she asked.

He grinned. "Long enough."

He shrugged out of his shirt and began to unknot his kilt. When his clothes were in a heap on the ground, he turned to her.

"Let's go for a swim."

Her gaze dropped to his impressive erection. "Looks like you're ready for more than swimming."

He moved toward her. "I want you again, Gina. Now." His voice dropped to a hoarse whisper. "Come to me."

Her legs felt suddenly weak. Derrin moved closer, his gaze dangerously intent. Gina's choices were simple—fight or flight.

Or surrender.

She ran her hands up her body, from thighs to hips to breasts. Derrin watched, but made no move toward her. He was waiting, she realized. Waiting for her to go to him. She took one step, then another.

A third brought her into his arms.

He lifted her and settled her on a large boulder, legs parted, bare buttocks pressed against the warm stone. He stroked the sensitive skin of her inner thighs, circled his thumbs over the aching tingle her self-induced climax had left. Gina couldn't find her balance on the boulder's sloping, uneven surface. She slid toward Derrin, hands braced on his shoulders.

His fingers teased, featherlight in her curls, just beyond her aching need. Gina wriggled. Why wouldn't he touch her where she craved it? She arched her hips, silently pleading.

His hands shifted, sliding up under her thighs until her buttocks were nestled in his palms. He lifted her higher, to the highest part of the boulder. His head dipped and he tasted her, his mouth hot, his tongue seeking.

"*Oh, God.*" Gina gasped at the burning intimacy of the contact. Derrin seemed to love to make her come this way, but Gina still found it hard to accept. His tongue seared her at her core, left her no place to hide. She tried to twist away, to control the flood of sensation. She succeeded only in sliding more fully into Derrin's mouth. His hands burned, his lips and tongue played urgently upon her. She was tossed into the storm inside her, battered by waves of pleasure so intense they left her gasping for air. She twisted again, this time welcoming, pleading, reaching toward the goal that hovered just out of reach. It came closer. Her senses blurred.

Then Derrin's cock was inside her, hard and pulsing. His scent was all around her, powerful and male. His mouth closing over hers and Gina tasted herself on his lips. She clung to his neck, felt the scrape of his skin beneath her fingernails.

Suddenly she was weightless. Derrin lifted her off the boulder, into his arms, pressing her firmly onto his erection. She wrapped her legs around him, moaning as he slipped deeper. He strode to the water, rocking inside her as he entered the pond. The cool current shocked Gina's skin. She sighed as the clear water covered her legs, lapped at her breasts.

Derrin maneuvered them across the pool. The rush of the falls sprayed across them, taking Gina's breath with it. Derrin pressed her into the shadows beyond the waterfall, pinning her against the slick wall of the cave. He drove into her with slow, powerful strokes.

Gina melted around him. She gave herself up, opening wide to his need and to her own. He took all she offered and demanded more. She moaned and twisted as Derrin went deeper and deeper into her, unrelenting. The rush of the falls sounded in her ears. She could feel nothing but his possession of her, think of nothing but her surrender to it. She clung to him, breathless, riding to the top of the spiraling eddy, her emotions twisting around her.

Derrin's cry came at the edge the vortex. She called out his name as she fell with him.

Together, they crested the fury, and emerged onto gentler waters.

*****

By the time they reached the village, the midday cooking fires were blazing. Derrin took Gina's hand and guided her to Malia and her boisterous family. The Na'lara greeted the newcomers warmly. She introduced her partner and sons to Gina, then turned her attention back to her oldest boy, who was describing his morning hunt with great enthusiasm.

"It was the best throw I ever made," Tolin said. "The rama was quick, but I aimed just ahead. It landed at my feet." He held up his catch. "Sarrin would have seen it if he had not been in the cave of the ice stones."

"Your skill honors the clan, my son," replied Standing Deer.

"It will make a fine stew, Tolin, with the new shoots I gathered at the sun's rising." Malia dipped a gourd ladle into a wooden bowl and poured a mixture of pounded grains and water onto a flat rock at the edge of the fire. The batter sizzled, giving off a sweet aroma. Using a wide wooden spatula, Malia transferred the golden ashcakes onto bark plates and passed them around the circle. A bowl of berries followed.

"I can throw, too," declared Lasha, who flitted like a butterfly between her brothers. "But I hate killing things." Her bottom lip trembled.

"The animal and plant people give their lives for us," replied her father. "Their bodies sustain us, and their spirits join with ours. We honor their sacrifice and ask their forgiveness."

The little girl nodded. She looked at the dead animal. "I am sorry you had to die. Thank you." She turned to Sarrin and gave him a bright smile. "Did you bring me an ice stone?"

"Of course, little one." He picked up a small buckskin bag at his side, and drew out a flat prism about the size of his palm. Lasha took the stone and ran her finger along the smooth surface. She tilted it to catch the light and giggled. "It is like looking through ice."

"May I see it?" Gina struggled to keep her voice calm.

Lasha placed the stone in Gina's palm. Gina held it up to the light and scrutinized the jagged imperfection along one edge. She could hardly believe what she saw. Incredibly, it was a selenite specimen identical to the one in Madam Rose's workshop. Which, in turn, had been identical to the one Gina had placed in her father's coffin.

Impossible.

She brushed her fingers across the crystal's glassy surface. Her hand tingled and her vision blurred.

Power. She sensed it, pulsing through the stone.

She touched the stone again, but this time felt nothing. Had she imagined the sensation?

"You can have it." Lasha pushed her head up under Gina's elbow, snuggling into her side.

"I wouldn't want to take the gift your brother brought you."

"I want you to have it. I like you."

Gina put the selenite aside and pressed her hands together in the Baha'Na gesture of thanks. After the meal, she stowed the crystal among the fur blankets of her sleeping area. Later, as she and Derrin were wading through the stream, she asked him about the ice cave. He pointed to its entrance, high in the canyon wall.

"It's a difficult climb, but worth it. The walls and ceiling shine. The crystals are never cut by the People, but many have fallen and are piled on the floor of the cavern."

"The stone Lasha gave me looks like one I saw in my own world, just before I traveled through the web." She told him about Madam Rose and her predictions.

Derrin was intrigued. "The old woman must be a sorceress," he said. "Perhaps she created the crystal."

"Not likely," Gina replied. "But even if she had, that doesn't explain why it has a twin in your world."

Derrin could offer no explanation.

"Could you use a crystal like Lasha's ice stone to perform wizardry?" Gina asked.

Derrin shook his head. "The power of wizardry springs from the intention of the wizard as he creates the stone. Any power a natural crystal holds is hidden from human thought."

"Are you sure? Have you ever tried it?"

"I don't need to try it, Gina. The first wizards experimented with natural crystals, but failed to draw any power from them. A crystal becomes magic only after it is dissolved and rebuilt. The wizard's will must be part of the lattice structure."

The sun had disappeared over the top of the canyon wall by the time Gina and Derrin returned to the village. The clan had assembled for the evening meal. Two men called to Derrin, gesturing for him to join them.

He grinned and returned the greeting. "They're my kinsmen from the Water Clan," he said, angling toward them. At that moment, Malia caught her gaze. Gina left Derrin to the men and cut across the open center of the village to greet the Na'lara.

A very old man stood near her. Deep furrows accented the long line of his nose and the sharp slant of his cheekbones. Strips of hide bound his long white hair into a long queue. He turned his attention to Gina, black eyes glittering. Malia introduced him as Sleeping Harta, an elder of the clan. Gina pressed her palm to her forehead.

"Welcome, my child. I have heard of your journey from beyond the golden web. It is good you have come to seek the Goddess."

Gina murmured her assent.

A shadow passed over his face. "You have known the Goddess in five of the Signs, and will soon know the sixth as well. But it is when you reach the Seventh that you will truly understand the loss of the People."

"I don't understand."

"No clan dwells at the Seventh Sign. The Circle is empty."

"The Circle?"

"The spirits of the Na'lara are linked," Malia said. "We form a Circle of six around the Seventh. She who stands in the Center unites her sisters. When the talismans are linked, the web opens."

Gina started. "Then it's true—you *can* open the web!" Had Zera lied? She could hardly believe the Na'lara had possessed the power to send her home, yet hadn't offered to do so.

"No. Without the Seventh, the life of the forest weakens. We cannot reach the veil."

"Where is the Na'lara of the Seventh Clan?"

"There is none. The Seventh Clan dwells with the Skyeagle Clan."

"Why?"

Malia's eyes clouded. "Many winters ago, when I was a girl, a young man of the Seventh Clan loved a girl of his own clan. He refused to seek a partner elsewhere. Danala, Na'lara to the Seventh Clan, did not allow the joining." She shook her head. "Anger turned his heart to stone. That night he set fire to the Na'lara's dwelling. The next morning, Danala and her son-by-joining lay dead in the ruins. Her daughter's body had been consumed completely. The talisman was never found."

"The man stole it?"

"Perhaps. He was never seen again."

Sleeping Harta extended his hand, palm up and fingers spread, the Baha'Na gesture signifying emptiness. "A clan cannot live apart from a Na'lara, and there can be no Na'lara without the talisman," he said. "The Seventh Clan left their home and journeyed to the village of the Skyeagle Clan. They dwell there still, awaiting the return of the lost talisman."

Malia swept her arm to one side. "That day approaches. The Circle has dreamed the return of its Center."

A shiver ran the length of Gina's spine. "You have?"

Malia nodded. "Seven winters have passed, not once, but four times since the talisman was lost. At the last full moon, the night visions came to me. The time is not far off."

She touched her thumbs to her forefingers, making two circles. Slowly, she brought her hands together, until the circles were linked.

"The People will soon be whole."

Chapter Twenty

A fat hand slapped Ariek on the back.

"Tarol take me, boy, if they ain't the finest tits I ever seen. Bring that Bride wench here. I'll make her moan fer it. My cock's bigger than Lotark's, ye know."

Ariek turned and slammed his fist between a pair of red-rimmed eyes. The drunk staggered backward into the arms of his equally sotted companion.

"Swiving idiot," Ariek muttered.

Choking on his rage, he shoved his way through the crowd until he reached one of the side streets leading away from the frenzied celebration. Throwing himself down on the marble stoop of a stately mansion, he cursed again, this time at himself, for venturing into the streets for the festival. He'd come because he'd known he would see her. He should have stayed away for the same reason.

The Feast of the Rising marked the holiest celebration of the Temple, the day when Lotark and his Bride ascended to the heavens. The feasting had begun at noon the day before and would continue unabated through the following night and day.

Food dominated the revelry. It had been the focus of solemn ritual and of frantic merrymaking. It had been blessed, thrown in the air and trampled. Now the putrid remains of the celebration decorated the cobblestones. Masses of flies swarmed in blissful gluttony.

The frenzy rose as the night descended. True Believers crowded the Upper Plaza, clad in white. There were few women about. Any with virtue to guard had been locked away.

The male revelers wore masks, cheap imitations of the Visage of Lotark. Ariek wore white as well, though he was unmasked. His wizard's garb would have attracted an angry assault. No one wore black on this day.

An hour before sunset, the tall doors of the Temple had swung open, and a high ceremonial platform had rolled into the center of the plaza. Solk towered above the mob, masked with the face of the God. A brilliant white robe draped his lanky frame.

The high priest glimmered in the light of the ceremonial torches. The Bride stood at his side. A sheer netting of white lace revealed the pleasures in which Lotark had reveled during his earthly stay. Danat had stood erect, her expression calm and serene, as if unaware of the effect her figure had on the swarm of drunken men at her feet.

A cheer echoed from the plaza, piercing Ariek's tortured memories. He dropped his head into his hands. The culmination of the ceremony was beginning. The God would join with his Bride before the people, then rise to Paradise. Self-loathing burned like acid in his throat. How could he allow Danat to endure this humiliation? Was he not man enough to rescue her?

He squeezed his eyes shut and tried to block the sordid images from his mind. Raucous jeers surged from the plaza as the ceremony unfolded.

After an eternity, a deafening roar told Ariek the farce had ended. Lotark and his Bride had once again ascended to Paradise.

Streams of revelers poured down the street, voices loud with swaggering bravado. One youth staggered and fell across Ariek's knees, retching a day's culinary excess onto the marble steps. Ariek sprang to his feet and threw the boy to one side.

He ducked into an alley leading to the rear entrance of the Stronghold, giving wide berth to a pair of fornicating True Believers. Dark passions consumed him. His hands tingled, yearning for the feel of Solk's throat. Ariek ached to kill the swiving hypocrite for the humiliation he'd inflicted on Danat. No, not just kill, but torture, until the arrogant bastard broke and begged for mercy.

Intent on his imagined revenge, he stumbled on a heap of rubbish. A cat screeched and darted through his legs. He whirled in time to see a stiletto poised in the air above him, its thin blade glistening in the shaft of light cast from a nearby window. It was held by a man dressed in white, masked with the face of the One God.

Ariek lunged to one side. His attacker's arm sliced through empty air. The masked man stumbled, thrown off-balance by the force of his fruitless blow.

Ariek grabbed for his own dagger and cursed when his hand came away empty. Lost—or stolen? He floundered in the trash heap, searching for something to serve as a weapon. Grasping a broken table leg, he spun around and met the second attack.

The man slashed, then dodged Ariek's counterattack and slashed again. Ariek lunged, swinging the table leg at the man's head. The attacker ducked. The brittle wood glanced off the stiletto, knocking it to the ground, then hit the wall and splintered into fragments.

Ariek dropped the remnants of the table leg and threw himself at his opponent. They fell in a wild grapple of limbs onto a heap of slime.

They rolled across the alley, skidding through excrement. The masked man shoved Ariek onto his back. Iron fingers closed around his neck, cutting off his breath. The Visage of Lotark leered down at him.

Strength, driven by primitive fear, surged through Ariek. He gripped his assailant's arms and twisted, gaining the upper position. He hauled the man to his feet and drove him against the wall. The man's skull hit stone with a sickening crack. His grip on Ariek's throat loosened.

Ariek sucked in a rasping breath and watched, chest heaving, as the man's limp body slid down the wall and dropped face-down into a slimy puddle. Patches of black swarmed his vision. He dropped to one knee.

Who had attacked him? A commoner overcome by the Madness?

Ariek rolled the still body onto its back and removed the mask. His breath seized, almost as if the man's hands were once again wrapped around his throat.

He recognized the face beneath the mask. A Servant of Lotark, one of Solk's most trusted acolytes. That this man had been sent to kill him could mean only one thing.

Ariek staggered to his feet and set out at a run toward the Temple.

*****

The tall doors swung shut with a dull thud, shutting out the worst of the manic cheering. The chill of the main worship room touched Danat's skin through the white lace of her Bride's robe, recalling the touch of Solk's cold fingers. The crowd had watched him take his pleasure of her. Her heart had turned to ice. Would she ever feel warm again?

An acolyte pushed a short flight of stairs to the platform. The high priest descended with regal grace. Danat followed, turning at once toward the Inner Sanctuary. Despite all she had endured, the ceremony was not yet complete.

The holiest of rooms lay in darkness, relieved only by the thin light cast by a torch above the altar. Danat covered her ears with her palms, trying to block the howls of the mob. But the shouts were in her head and could not be erased.

"Come to me." Her spine stiffened at the sound of Solk's voice. She turned.

The high priest removed his mask and set it in its niche by the altar. The cold angles of his face twisted into a tight, cruel smile.

"Come," he repeated. Danat's blood froze in her veins.

But she knew well enough there was no place to hide. She obeyed, stepping closer, every fiber of her being shouting in protest. She dropped her eyes and turned her palms outward in a gesture of submission, waiting for Solk's next command.

The force of his blow sent her sprawling across the altar steps. Pain exploded under her eye. Solk loomed over her, his body rigid, his pale eyes blazing with righteous fury.

"You slut," he spat. "You harlot! You are honored above all women, yet you defile the name of the Lotark in his own sanctuary with a wizard lover!" He leaned toward her, his face contorted with rage.

Danat shrank back against the altar. Solk knew of Ariek? How?

"Lotark's Temple must be cleansed in blood. Already your lover has paid with his life." Solk reached inside his robe and drew forth a silken scarf.

A scarf she'd last seen in Ariek's hand.

"You have...killed...Ariek?" Grief burst over her, eclipsing the pain under her eye. Solk gave a horrible laugh.

He raised his hand. Danat twisted and the high priest's second blow crashed on the altar. He howled his outrage.

Danat scrambled over the altar and dropped to the floor on the other side. Ariek was dead. The words echoed in her head, tore at her heart. She, too, would be dead before long—of that she was certain.

Suddenly, it didn't matter.

"You hypocrite," she hissed. The high priest's face flushed—the Bride was not permitted to speak in Lotark's sanctuary. "You *dare* call me a defiler. You, who took me from my home and used me as a whore."

"What blasphemy is this? You have been honored with the highest place a woman can hope to attain." Solk's voice grew deathly quiet. "It is insufferable." He darted around the altar and grabbed Danat by the wrist.

She drew herself up to her full height and spat in his face.

"You will pay for your insolence," Solk thundered. He raised his free hand and struck her again, across the cheek already swollen from his previous blow. Danat cried out. She brought up her free arm to ward off his fists.

The door to the Sanctuary burst open and Danat caught a glimpse of a reveler covered in the filth of his merriment. The high priest's head jerked around. Danat took advantage of his distraction and wrenched her arm free.

The man lunged for Solk. The high priest fell under his attacker's weight and rolled toward the altar. Danat backed away, sending a prayer of thanks to whatever fortune had led a madman to her rescue.

The man's hands went for Solk's throat. Solk rammed his attacker into the side of the dais, into the light of the altar torch.

Danat's heart leapt. "Ariek!"

Ariek let out a curse and fell on Solk, landing a blow to the high priest's jaw.

"You bastard. You sent your lackey to kill me while you stayed here to abuse a woman. I'll kill you for what you've done to her!"

"Blasphemer! It is Lotark's will that you be destroyed."

A metal blade flashed between the men. Before Danat could cry out a warning, Solk struck. Ariek's blood spread in a dark stain across his chest.

Ariek's struggle became even more crazed. He squeezed Solk's wrist in a crushing grip and smashed it against the altar. When the knife dropped to the floor, his hands shot toward the high priest's neck.

Solk dealt a blow to the side of Ariek's head. Ariek dropped to his knees, grunting when Solk's kick connected with his gut. He fell backward, gasping for air.

Solk slid a second, smaller knife from his sleeve and bent low, a wild laugh emerging from his throat.

He will kill him. He will kill Ariek.

Danat lunged across the floor. Her fingers closed on the hilt of the high priest's fallen dagger. Vivid colors swirled before her eyes. She leaped up behind Solk, brought the weapon high over her head, and drove it downward with all her strength.

Blood spurted from the high priest's neck, spraying her in the face. She pulled the blade from his flesh and let it fall a second time, then a third. "I will not let you kill him! I will not!" The knife plunged into Solk's flesh, hitting bone and sinew with a satisfying whack. "I. Will. Not."

Ariek shoved the limp body of the priest aside and pulled himself upright, gasping. Danat doubled over, shaking. "I…will…not…"

Ariek's arms closed around her from behind. He pried the dagger from her fingers.

"It's all right, Danat. He's dead."

She stared at the body sprawled face-down on the floor. Blood was everywhere—on her hands, her body, the altar. She knelt in a warm puddle of the priest's fading life.

"I killed him," she whispered.

"You've given him what he deserved," Ariek replied grimly, turning her toward him. "You saved my life."

Blood soaked his shirt. "Ariek, you're wounded! How bad is it? Let me see."

"I'm fine. We have to get out of here. I took care of the two at the door, but there will be others." He rose, staggering slightly, and pulled her to her feet behind him. "Is there another way out?"

"Here." She led him to a passage hidden by a tapestry. "It leads to Solk's private chambers. There's a doorway to the street."

"Wait." Ariek fumbled at his belt for his pouch of crystals. "I'll shadow us." Once outside, he threaded a dizzying path through the drunken revelers, descending to the Lower City.

"Where will we go?" Danat whispered as soon as they were clear of the crowds.

"I don't know, but we can't stay in the city." He turned and gave her a quick, hard kiss. "I'll find a place where you'll be safe, Danat." His tone hardened. "I should have done it long ago. Now I'll kill anyone who tries to touch you."

They followed a narrow alley to its juncture with the waterfront. With the aid of a crystal, Ariek eased open the door of a long, low building. It opened onto a tack room, perfumed by manure and hay. Along one wall hung saddles, bridles, and riding crops. Wooden bins were lined up opposite. The snicker of horses could be heard from behind a heavy door.

"This is my father's stable," Ariek whispered. "The stable boy is probably dozing on the other side of that door. I'll make sure he doesn't wake up."

Ariek ducked through the doorway and returned a few moments later. "He's out." He opened one of the wooden bins and pulled out an assortment of riding clothes. "Some of these belong to the jockeys. They might fit you." He tossed her a bundle. "Try these."

Danat stripped off her bloodstained gown without a word. The shirt and breeches fit well enough to wear, though the boots Ariek handed her were too large. He'd found clean clothing for himself as well. He shrugged out of his shirt and bit back a gasp of pain.

She flew to his side, horrified to see the deep slash across his shoulder and upper chest. Undressing had torn it open. She pressed her bare hand over the wound, trying to stem the flow of blood.

"You need a healer! We must go to the Stronghold!"

"No. We haven't time."

"Let me bind it then, at least." She tore one of the jockey's tunics into strips and bound Ariek's wound, then helped him into a new shirt.

They entered the stables, stepping around the unconscious stable boy. Ariek chose a horse from one of the stalls and threw a saddle over its back, straining at the effort. Danat, afraid he would injure himself further, refused his attempt to lift her into the saddle. Using a stool she found in a corner, she scrambled onto the horse's back unaided.

He took a package and a flask from a low table. "Food. Not much, but better than nothing," he said, stashing the bundle in a saddlebag. He opened the stable's main door and led the horse into the street, then swung into the saddle behind Danat. They inched across the crowded market square.

The night's revelry showed no signs of abating. Danat's heart pounded in her chest as they negotiated a path through the mob. She bit down on her lower lip, not daring to distract Ariek with her fear. She sensed he needed every bit of his concentration to keep them hidden.

He kept a steady pace. When they had passed the last staggering drunk some distance from the city, he slowed the horse.

"We're safe enough for now."

Danat looked up into the glaze of his eyes. "You need to rest."

"For a few minutes. We need to put a good stretch of road between us and the city."

Danat unwrapped the stable boy's bundle and found several hearty slices of bread and cheese. The flask contained dark ale.

"Here," she said, offering both to Ariek, "drink this, and eat. You are near to collapsing."

He accepted the flask. "You're right." His voice shook. "I barely held the shadow while we passed through the crowd." He took a deep draught and bit into a wedge of cheese. "I won't be able to hide us from a dog unless I get some rest."

His face was deathly pale. Danat could tell his injuries had drained him even more than he'd admitted. She took the food he offered and choked down a swallow of ale. Icy tendrils of dread curled in her stomach.

"Do you hear that?" Ariek asked suddenly.

Danat cocked her head. "Horses, coming from the city," she whispered, her gaze fixed on a dark curve in the road. They drew their mount into a thick copse and waited.

Five riders appeared. Two men, dressed in white, held torches aloft, while the others peered into the thick undergrowth along the road's edge. Danat caught a glimpse of their faces and shrank back into the shadows, not daring to breathe. They were Servants of Lotark.

After what seemed an eternity, the priests moved on. Ariek grimaced and turned the horse to the open countryside. The moonlight cast a deathly pall over his features.

"I'm going to cut across Lord Garlik's estate and pick up the road to Sirth where it cuts inland. With any luck, the priests will abandon the chase before then."

They made slow progress through the open country, across fields ravaged by Blight. It was well past midnight when they rejoined the road.

"We'll go to my father's estate. There's a lodge in the hunting park. We can hide there for a few days."

Danat twisted in the saddle. Blood soaked the shirt he'd taken from the stable. "Is it far, Ariek?" she asked, wondering how long it would be before he collapsed.

"Farther than I'd like it to be." He urged their mount forward.

The road skirted the edge of a forest decimated by the Blight. The odor of decay hung in the air. Ariek tried to stay hidden in the shadow of its bare trunks and splintered limbs, but his mount skittered, shying away from the smell of death.

Danat bent over the horse's head and whispered in her native tongue. Though the animal had most likely been bred in Galena, she was sure it understood the language of its sire's homeland.

They rounded a sharp turn in the road. Ariek uttered a foul oath and jerked back on the reins. Danat's head snapped up. Three men on horseback, Servants of Lotark, had halted on the road some distance ahead, and were talking among themselves. One looked up and gave a shout.

"Tarol's blood." Ariek dragged the reins to the left, grunting at the effort. The horse took two steps toward the dead forest then reared up on its hind legs. Danat clung to its mane. The priests whirled their mounts about and plunged after them. Ariek brought his crop down hard on the horse's flank. The beast shot forward into the trees.

Brittle branches clawed at Danat's clothes as the Blighted forest flew past. The priests gave chase, but Ariek's mount tore through the trees in a panicked frenzy, slogging into an oily swamp. By the time he was able to bring the animal under control, Danat had lost sight of the pursuers.

"The priests say the Blighted forest is cursed by Lotark," she whispered. "It is blasphemy to enter."

"I've heard that as well." Ariek's breathing came in short bursts. His grip on the reins loosened and he sagged against Danat's back. The horse shied to one side and shifted. She grabbed the reins. The moon cast a dim light through the tangled black lace of the dead canopy and shone dully on the stagnant water. She guided the horse to a lone patch of dry land. Once there, Danat slid from the saddle and pulled Ariek down after her, staggering under his weight.

He dropped to his knees. His face had gone from white to gray, and he was so weak he could barely hold himself upright. Danat eased him to the ground. Ariek tried to smile, but the effect of his effort was closer to a grimace. "I'm sorry, Danat. I just…need to rest."

Terror squeezed her heart. Ariek needed much more than rest, of that much she was certain. He closed his eyes. When she pressed her head to his blood-soaked shirt, Danat could barely make out the beat of his heart.

"Please don't die, Ariek," she whispered.

Far above her, a dead branch snapped, sending an echoing crack through the forest. The horse reared, then bolted, crashing through the swamp in a blind panic, until she could hear it no more.

Danat kissed Ariek's cold lips. She curled up by his side, silent sobs racking her body.

Chapter Twenty-One

A woman's laugh, low and sultry, brushed across Derrin's awareness like an intimate caress. He shut his eyes and tried not to listen. The enticing sound yielded to a moan. A man's voice this time, hoarse with need. Derrin gave up. It was impossible to escape the muffled rhythm of the lovers, slow at first, then growing in urgency.

It was impossible as well to ignore his own painful arousal. Stifling a groan, he rolled onto his back and stared at the sloping roof of the roundhouse. Soft light fell through the smokehole, illuminating the cross of beams and ties. He scrutinized the pattern of light and dark with exaggerated interest, but to no avail. He couldn't help but be acutely aware of Malia and Standing Deer making love under their furs less than three strides away.

He turned toward Gina. She lay beside him, her breath rising and falling with a deep, even rhythm. Her lashes cast dusky shadows on her cheeks. He thought of rousing her to make love in the crowded roundhouse, where the cover of darkness afforded the barest privacy.

Derrin had a good idea what his partner would say to that.

His partner. His wife. It was so easy for him to think of Gina that way. So easy to pretend a lifetime spread out before them—days of joys and sorrows, children and laughter, trials and tears stretching into the future, vanishing far in the distance. A dream that had little to do with who they were—two people who never should have met, let alone become lovers.

Malia and Standing Deer neared their climax. Derrin let the muffled sounds of their final pleasure wash over him, then let out a sigh of relief as the silence of sleep overtook the lovers. He willed his eyes to close, but after a futile attempt to find a comfortable position, he gave up any pretense of rest. Rolling onto his side, he propped himself up on one elbow and watched Gina while she slept.

She kicked off her covers and rolled onto her back. The soft doeskin of her dress clung to her skin, rose and fell with her breasts.

The hem had bunched at her thighs, leaving her legs bare. Her knees fell open. Derrin sucked in a breath.

Experimentally, he touched Gina's arm, tracing a featherlight line down the inside of her elbow to her palm. She shifted in her sleep with a soft sigh, but didn't awaken. Her lips parted, revealing the pink tip of her tongue.

Derrin's need grew unbearable.

He eased the hem of Gina's dress higher, until the dark triangle between her thighs and the silky moist petals of her sex were exposed to his view. He gazed at her for a time, enjoying the play of moonlight and shadow on her skin. Then he loosened the lacings at her throat and drew the soft material back, revealing one breast. Gina looked so beautiful and vulnerable lying exposed while she slept. Lust and a fierce need to possess her raced through him.

His breathing quickened. He caressed Gina's breast with feathering strokes, then moved his palm lower, to her soft inner thigh, tangling his fingers in the dark thatch of curls before easing away. She shifted and sighed. He watched her for a moment longer, wavering on the point of indecision. Then, his mind made up, he loosened the knot of his kilt and tossed the garment aside.

He covered her, his body braced above hers, but not touching. Bending his head, he brushed the lightest of breaths across her lips. Gina arched against him. He deepened the kiss, running his tongue along the contour of her lower lip. She stirred again. One arm came up around his neck, pulled him closer. He lowered himself slowly, surrounding her, pressing his body to hers. She sighed, rubbing against him, her slumber unbroken.

He shifted to one side, settling his hip on the ground beside her, still raining kisses on her lips. His hand slid over her bared breast and teased the dusky pink nipple into a tight nub. She let out a soft moan against his mouth and kissed him back.

His good fortune didn't last. An instant later, Gina stiffened. She broke the kiss and tried to push him away. Derrin didn't retreat. He continued stroking, his fingertips brushing over her hips, teasing between her legs. She was slick there, ready for him.

"Derrin! What are you doing?"

"Can't you tell?" He sank one knee between her legs and kissed her again, sucking her lower lip, trailing kisses across her jaw, burying his head in the hollow of her neck and licking the salt of her skin. He eased his other leg between her thighs and pinned her against the furs with his lower body. His arousal throbbed against her cool skin.

"Are you crazy? We can't do this here!" She struggled to free herself.

Her efforts made him grow even harder. The head of his cock prodded the creamy softness of her sex. He gritted his teeth held himself still. "Why not?"

"Let's go outside."

He raised his head and focused on the outline of the doorway. Impossible. He'd never make it that far.

"There are at least ten people between us and the door," he said. He returned his attention to her breast, taking her nipple in his mouth and grazing it with his teeth, hoping to distract her. No such fortune favored him. Gina stifled a gasp and renewed her struggle.

Derrin fought an urge to bury his cock inside her with one swift stroke, making any further discussion pointless. He contented himself with suckling her breast instead.

She shoved at him. "Cut it out! Someone will hear us."

His head came up. "They will if you don't stop talking."

She went still at that. Derrin drew a deep breath and pressed his forehead against hers.

"Gina," he whispered with a patience he didn't feel. "Please. I've lain awake half the night. At least three other couples took their pleasure. No one will care if there's a fourth." He gave a tight smile. "Besides, it won't take long, I assure you."

He was rewarded with a low laugh. Gina's arms came around him, stroked his back. She softened and he slid into her, losing himself in her heat. She pulled him closer and wrapped her legs around his waist.

The roundhouse and the sleeping clan dissolved. A dark fire enveloped them, pulsing and returning over and over, the promise of forever trapped in each instant. He felt Gina's climb, mirroring his own. He caught her cries with his mouth and surrendered himself to the flame.

* * * * *

A woman sobbed. Gina fought through a fog of terror, desperate to reach her. But when she did, the figure vanished and Gina realized the shout had come from her own lips.

A strong hand shook her shoulders. "Wake up. Gina, wake up."

She struggled to the surface of her dream, gasping at the effort it took to disentangle herself from its snare. She opened her eyes and tried to focus.

The world outside her nightmare undulated in a sickening wave. She squeezed her eyes shut again. "Give me a minute."

Derrin's arm tightened around her. She drew a deep breath and the dream images retreated. When her eyes opened a second time, everything stayed put.

Sunlight streamed through the smokehole of the roundhouse, casting an oval patch of light on the far wall. Derrin and Malia sat on either side of her, wearing twin expressions of concern.

"I'm sorry." She gripped Derrin's arm and fought to keep the hysteria out of her voice. "It was just a dream, but it seemed so real. I'm all right now."

Malia laid one hand on her shoulder. "What made you cry out so, Gina?"

She shuddered. "Nothing, really."

"A strong vision must never be ignored."

Gina waited for the worst of the terror to drain away, then raised her head and nodded. "There were trees," she said, her voice trembling, "dead trees. Oily muck covered the ground. I heard a woman sobbing."

She drew a deep breath before going on. "I saw her sprawled in the mud, clutching an injured man. Blood soaked through his shirt. He tried to talk, but couldn't. The woman was so young—just a girl. She had long red hair, and an odd mark on her forehead that—"

Derrin's fingers bit into her arm. "A mark? A blue circle?"

"Yes! How did you—"

"The man—was he blond, with blue eyes?"

"I...I think so. Yes. Yes, he was."

Derrin swore under his breath.

A rush of dread twisted Gina's stomach. "It was only a dream," she whispered.

Derrin and Malia exchanged glances. "Not a dream, Gina," Malia said. "A true vision."

"A vision?"

He nodded. "Blight decimated the bogs near the city of Sirth last spring. I know the woman you described. The man with her is Ariek."

"Your friend? The wizard you shared an apprenticeship with?"

Derrin rose with a swift movement. "Yes. I don't know what's happened, but I must find him before…" He started to pace.

"Wait a minute." Gina's voice shook. "Are you telling me I dreamed something that's happening right now? That's impossible!"

"No," Malia said. "The People often have such dreams."

A sharp tingling began in Gina's palm and ran up her arm. She looked down at her hand. Her fist had closed on something sharp. She uncurled her fingers and saw Lasha's selenite crystal pulsing with white light.

She gasped and jerked her arm back.

The prism rolled across the ground. Derrin snatched it up, but the light was gone. Gina stared. Derrin had insisted a natural stone couldn't be used for wizardry, but he'd been wrong. She was sure the selenite had precipitated her vision.

He frowned at the stone. "The dead swamp lies on the edge of the wilderness. If I go by river, I may be able to reach it by nightfall."

"All will be ready for your journey within a hand of time," Malia said. She hastened toward the door.

Gina stood up. "I'm going with you."

"No. Sirth is too close to Balek's power."

"But you can't go alone! Balek would find you once you traveled beyond the range of the shadow crystal."

Derrin's jaw clenched. "I'll take that chance."

"No. I won't let you. Besides, you'll find Ariek quicker if I go with you. I can lead you to him."

He gave her a searching glance. "Are you sure? How do you know?"

"I can't explain it." Gina repressed a shudder. "But I feel the red-haired girl's pain, even now. I know I can guide you to her."

Derrin nodded. "All right, then. We'll go together."

* * * * *

A short time later, Derrin pushed a small bark canoe into the river, his chest tight with worry. Provisions of dried meat, roots and berries, along with firemaking tools and several full waterskins, were stowed behind the bow. He sat in the stern and stroked the paddle into the clear water. *Hold on, Ariek, just a few hours longer.*

Gina knelt in front of him, paddling with the second oar, the muscles in her arms and back flexing as she added her strength to his own. His shoulders relaxed a fraction. Her presence steadied him, gave him hope.

The riverbank moved past at a swift pace. By midday, the canyon walls had yielded to a wide valley, but the journey's speed wasn't enough to stem Derrin's near-panic. From Gina's description, Ariek had been close to death. Would his friend be alive when they found him? He stabbed the water with the paddle.

Gina shifted, looking back at him. "Why does the red-haired girl have a tattoo on her forehead?"

"Danat is no ordinary woman. She's the Bride of Lotark."

"Lotark? You mean the god?"

Derrin nodded. "Danat is a slave of the Temple. She bears the mark of the One God and the high priest, masked as Lotark, lies with her in church ceremony. For an exorbitant price, any True Believer can wear the mask and take his place."

"That's horrible!"

"Yes." He told her of Ariek's secret visits to Danat's chamber. "He talked of stealing her from the Temple. He must have done it." He gave a short, humorless laugh. "It appears the Servants of Lotark didn't approve."

He thrust his paddle into the water, working the oar without pause until the afternoon sank into a dull twilight. At last, he paused long enough to light a torch.

He handed it to Gina. "Feed the strip of bark through the slit in the stick as it burns. It should last well into the night. The dead forest isn't far. Already the trees show signs of Blight."

The canoe sliced through the water. Derrin paddled close to the shore, searching for signs of an inlet. After several long minutes he found one. He steered his craft into the shallow waterway.

The torch filled the night with flickering shadows, black against a darkening sky. Bare branches hung low, scratching the surface of the water. The smell of decay grew stronger and the edges of the channel took on an unnatural sheen. A fallen tree slowed their progress. Derrin muttered curses under his breath.

The banks of the channel widened until the passage spilled out into an oily swamp. An acrid stench rose from the mire. The scent of death.

Derrin pushed the thought from his mind. "Which way?"

Gina pointed into the darkness on her left. He sank the paddle into the muck, steering the canoe through the deeper channels of the swamp. Once or twice he called out, but silence absorbed his shouts.

"They're nearby," Gina whispered. "I feel it. I wish this light cast further."

Derrin pulled a thick tangle of dead vines from a branch overhead and wrapped it into a tight knot. "They're damp," he muttered, "but maybe they'll burn." He touched the vines to the torch, and with some difficulty managed to ignite them. The knot blazed for several seconds, illuminating a wide circle of barren swampland.

"There!" He peered in the direction of Gina's outstretched arm, but saw nothing. "That high patch of ground. That's where they are."

Derrin shot her a piercing glance and dropped the smoking clump into the water. Her intuition was uncanny, yet he didn't question it. Had Gina indeed drawn power from the ice cave's crystal? If so, the implications were vast.

He poled the canoe through the thickening quagmire until the craft dragged in the mud. Abandoning the paddle, he jumped out and slogged to drier ground. Gina followed close behind with the torch.

Dead branches reached from the body of an ancient tree like the broken arms of a corpse. Tangled roots bubbled to the surface. Derrin scanned the scene, his hope fading. How could he hope to find Ariek in this wasteland?

"There," Gina said suddenly, pointing.

Movement flashed at the periphery of his vision. He leaped in its direction, toward a man sprawled in the muck. Ariek. He reached for his friend's throat, praying he would find a pulse.

The unexpected force of Danat's small body knocked him into the mud. Gina cried out. Danat screeched and dug her fingernails into Derrin's face.

He twisted and caught the girl's arms against her side. She struggled like a madwoman, screaming in a language he didn't understand. Bruises mottled one cheek and her green eyes burned with rage and grief. She drew a long breath and spat in his face.

"Don't touch him," she shrieked in Galenan. "He will die without the dirty hands of a bastard priest defiling him."

He gave her a violent shake. "Danat, stop! I'm not a swiving Servant of Lotark, I'm Derrin. I've come to help."

Her eyes widened and she stilled. "Derrin? Ariek's friend?"

He released her cautiously. "Yes."

"Ariek…tried to contact you, but you didn't answer. How did you find us?"

"I'll explain later." He turned back to Ariek. Gina moved closer, raising the torch. He felt under Ariek's jaw and caught a faint pulse. Relief crashed through him. His friend still lived—for now.

He drew his knife and cut away Ariek's blood-soaked shirt, then hacked at the bandage. Red, swollen skin bordered the ragged gash. He groped about, searching in the dark for Ariek's pouch of crystals.

"Can you save him?" Danat's voice shook.

"I don't know." He dumped Ariek's crystals into his palm and probed each one in turn. If only one was strong enough…

Behind him, Danat let out a low keening moan. His nerves, already stretched taut, began to fray. Turning, he saw Gina had thrust the torch into the mud and knelt with her arms around the hysterical girl.

"Please," he whispered, meeting Gina's gaze. "I need to concentrate." She nodded and pulled Danat away. Danat pressed her head against Gina's breast, muffling her sobs.

He chose one of Ariek's stones and returned the rest to the pouch. It held minor healing power. Not enough for Ariek's wound, but he had little choice. He sank his mind into its center, pushing away a surge of sickening doubt.

He slammed the door of his will on every trace of emotion. A core of calm, the fruit of many long hours of discipline, filled his consciousness. A sharp red light sprang into the center of the crystal.

The dead forest faded from Derrin's awareness. He descended into the perfect symmetry of the stone, drawing what he needed from its logic, its perfection. Power flowed into his mind, then poured into Ariek's body, where the dimmest flicker of life remained. He gathered his friend's remaining strength and linked it to the crystal.

Ariek's life force flared, but the power of the stone was not great enough to sustain it. The red light faded. With grim determination, Derrin sank further into the crystal, running along the lines of its lattice, seeking its essence. The crystal flickered.

Derrin drove forward, commanding the last drop of its potency. The stone flashed in response. Ariek's life force surged.

A shock of intoxicating power shot through Derrin's body. He dove into the void and anchored his mind to Ariek's. Slowly, he pulled his friend from the grip of death, knowing with icy certainty he would not fail.

Then, unbidden, a thin, sharp knife of revelation pierced his concentration.

The power is not yours to command.

His mind reeled as if from a blow. The truth beat down on him. The crystal power he wielded—the power that would save Ariek's life—was the same power Balek used to create the webstone. The same force that had torn open the web and loosed the plagues of Blight and Madness. The fundamental tools of wizardry were force of will and absolute control—qualities that violated the very essence of life. Derrin's power as a wizard aided the land's destruction.

Truly, he was no better than Balek.

The wall separating his mind from his emotions crumbled. He recoiled from the crystal's power, dropping the thread that held his friend's life.

Ariek's life force shuddered and slid toward the void.

Derrin stared at the still, gray face of the only true friend he had found in Galena. Danat's quiet weeping curled around him and Gina's fear brushed against his mind. Derrin possessed the power to save Ariek. But could he use it knowing the harm it would bring to the land?

The choice beckoned and he made it. Reclaiming the center of the crystal's power, Derrin bound his mind to Ariek's life force and wrenched his friend from death's shadow.

Derrin's triumph blazed, then sputtered and died. Nauseating shame washed over him. He tried to stand, but the ground lurched to one side. His legs refused the weight of his body.

Gina's arms broke his fall as darkness rushed in. He closed his eyes and surrendered to it.

*****

Gina cradled Derrin's head in her lap and stroked her fingers across his forehead. Heat flushed his skin. He stirred, caught in a nightmare. She cupped his cheek. It had been hours since he'd collapsed.

"Derrin, can you hear me?"

He didn't answer.

The cobwebs of a gray dawn covered the sky. Gina glanced at Ariek, sleeping a short distance away with Danat sprawled beside him. Fatigue stung Gina's eyes, but she'd been unable to rest.

Dark clouds hung low, blanketing the dead forest with silence. A wave of stench rose from the greasy mud. She shifted, stifling a prickle of fear. Her nerves hummed. Every minute she spent in the Blighted forest bit into the thin shroud of her sanity. She would go mad if she stayed much longer.

"Derrin," she said, giving him a shake. The dry pallor of his skin frightened her. He'd saved Ariek's life, but at what cost? "Wake up. Please, wake up! We've got to get out of here."

His eyes opened, but stayed blank for a long moment. Finally, recognition sparked, along with something Gina wished she could erase.

"Gina." He winced and pushed himself up on his elbows.

"I'm here. Are you all right?"

"I will be in a few minutes."

Beside her, Danat stirred. The girl pushed a long strand of hair from her face and smiled at Derrin.

"Thank you. You saved his life. We've never met, but I feel as though I know you. Ariek speaks of you often."

An answering smile flickered on Derrin's lips. "I can imagine what he says."

"He says your talent is remarkable, perhaps stronger than any wizard of the Hierarchy."

Gina glanced at Derrin and caught the shadow of pain on his face.

"Ariek exaggerates," he said.

They fell silent. The stillness of the Blighted forest grew unbearable. Gina thought she would choke on it. She caught Derrin's gaze and tried to keep the panic from her voice. "I can't stay here much longer."

Derrin expression told her he understood how close she was to breaking. "We'll leave this cursed place as soon as we can." He pushed himself to his feet and crossed the short distance to Ariek. "He won't be able to walk, but we should be able to move him in the canoe." He bent and called his friend's name.

* * * * *

Ariek forced his eyes open, wondering why someone had poured sand into them. His throat burned. An unholy stench assaulted his nostrils.

A face came into focus. It looked like…

"Tarol's blood, Derrin. It *is* you." With an effort, he hoisted himself on his uninjured arm. "How did you find us?"

"Don't worry about that now. We have to move on."

Ariek's gaze swung to the dark-haired woman at Derrin's side. "You're the woman from the web."

She nodded. "I'm Gina."

"Can you stand?" Derrin offered him an arm. Ariek gripped it and managed to rise, despite a stab of pain. His shoulder throbbed and his head spun, but his legs held out for the short walk to a boat mired in the mud.

He climbed into the odd craft. Derrin helped Danat settle in front of him. Ariek leaned forward and kissed her, then touched the angry welt under her eye. "I'm sorry I didn't arrive in time to prevent this."

She offered him a tremulous smile, her eyes shimmering with tears. "It could have been much worse."

Derrin handed him a full waterskin. Ariek offered it to Danat, then tipped his head back and drank as Derrin shoved the boat into deeper water. The craft accommodated only two passengers. Derrin and Gina waded alongside, guiding it through the oily water.

The swamp gave way to an abandoned farm field covered by a sparse scattering of weeds. A hedgerow of yellow-leaved trees lined the far side.

The boat ran aground. They abandoned it and set off across the barren land. Sharp pain stabbed Ariek's chest, but he gritted his teeth and ignored it. Even so, he was thankful when they reached the relative shelter of the trees. He sank to the ground, his breathing rough.

Danat and Gina halted a short distance away. Gina rummaged through a sack of provisions she'd carried from the boat.

Derrin sat down beside him. "Tell me what happened."

Ariek recounted the details of Solk's attacks, then stopped Derrin's questions with his raised palm. "What of you, Derrin? Where in Tarol's Inferno have you been? You didn't answer my calls." He gestured at his friend's odd clothing. "What are you wearing?"

Derrin shifted and looked away. "I took Gina to a place where I knew she would be safe," he said, then fell silent.

Ariek's gaze narrowed. "You can trust me," he muttered.

"I know that."

But nothing could have prepared Ariek for the tale Derrin told. Hidden people living in the Northern Waste? It was a fantastic story from his childhood sprung to life.

He shook his head. "I often wondered where you came from, Derrin. I thought you a runaway slave. I never imagined you were one of the faerie folk!"

A glimmer of amusement crept into Derrin's eyes and the corners of his mouth twitched. "Have a care you don't cross me. You might find yourself put to sleep for a hundred years or deluded into thinking you're a dog." He sobered. "I must have your word you'll tell no one of my mother's people."

"You have it. It's a small price to pay for my life." Ariek rubbed his temple, frowning. "Much has changed since you left Katrinth. The Blight worsens. Most of this year's crops have failed, even on the Eastern Plains. The news has been kept from the commoners. The Lords fear a riot."

"And Balek?"

"You were right about him. I saw the obscene stone he wields. What's more, I've discovered its pattern hidden in the crystal antidote to the Madness. Half the Upper City wears it, and the Lower City is demanding it as well. I fear Balek is able to control a man's mind through it, much the same way he attempted to control Gina's."

He glanced at the dark-haired woman. She caught his gaze and moved closer, drawing Danat with her. They sat down facing him.

"Balek wants you," he told Gina. "You seem to figure prominently in his plans. He's incensed by your disappearance." He turned to Derrin. "When he finds her, he intends to kill you because of what you know."

Derrin shrugged. "I expected as much. The ironic thing is I know very little."

"I suspect he wants to become the sole leader of the Hierarchy," said Ariek.

"He already controls the High Council and hold influence with the Lords. It must be more than that. Perhaps he wishes to command the True Believers as well."

"That's not likely to happen."

"It could. When the Lower City is starving, the threat of Tarol's Inferno will mean little. The people will trade loyalty for bread. Does Balek know you suspect him?"

"I couldn't say for sure, but I don't think he regards me as much of a threat. He's been too busy looking for you. Why didn't you answer the signal I sent to the twin crystal?"

"I never saw it. I left all my crystals—except the shadow—at my grandmother's village."

"You left them!" Ariek head snapped up. A wizard didn't leave his crystals.

Derrin said nothing. Ariek frowned. "I lost a huge amount of blood. I was nearly dead when you found me, yet here I am, alive. How could that be, if you have no crystals?"

The question fell unanswered.

"He used one of yours," Gina interjected.

"One of mine? How? I have no healing stone." He fumbled at his belt, but found his crystals gone.

Gina retrieved the small leather bag from the pouch of provisions and handed it to him.

He dumped the stones into his palm. "Which one?"

She pointed to a red crystal. Ariek shook his head. "You must be mistaken. This crystal couldn't cure a toothache."

"She's not mistaken." Derrin met his gaze. "That stone holds more power than you think. Forget it."

Ariek puzzled at the sharp edge in his friend's voice, but didn't question further.

"Let's return to your predicament," Derrin continued. "Are you sure Solk is dead?"

Ariek mouth tightened. "Yes, I'm sure."

Danat drew a sharp breath. Before he could reach for her, she jumped up and hurried away. Gina sprang to her feet and followed. Ariek watched the two women walk a short distance into the stand of trees. Worry gnawed at his stomach. Danat's strength was nearly gone, but at the moment he had little of his own to offer her.

With an effort, he turned his attention back to Derrin. "The priests of Lotark won't publicize the blasphemy of their Temple," his friend was saying. "The faith of the True Believers has been weakening for years, especially among the aristocracy. This misfortune could lay it in ruins for good."

"The Servants of Lotark will seek revenge."

"Perhaps, but there's nothing the Temple can do openly, and little they can attempt in secret against a wizard on his guard." Derrin gave Ariek a pointed look. "I can't say the same about Danat. She's marked, and the unusual color of her hair will be hard to hide."

"I won't leave her, Derrin, if that's what you think."

"I never said that."

"You didn't have to. I'm a pampered aristocrat. It's true I've never possessed your discipline or strength of will, but I'd cut off my right arm before I'd abandon her." He spiked his fingers through his hair. "She deserves far better than me. Another man would have freed her from those bastard priests long ago. I know the whole thing started as a game, but now…" He met his friend's gaze. "I'd give my life for her. I know that's hard for you to understand, but—"

"No," said Derrin sharply, "it's not."

Ariek gaze followed Derrin's to the woman from beyond the web. Gina stood at Danat's side, just out of earshot. As he watched, she turned, almost as if she'd felt Derrin's attention upon her.

All at once, Ariek understood. He looked back at his friend with new interest.

"I see," he said.

*****

Gina put her arm around Danat's shoulders and drew her into the shade of a tree, out of sight of the men. The girl had lost the battle with her emotions. Tears streaked her face and her slender frame shook.

"Do you know," she said between sobs, "You are the first woman I have spoken with since..." Her voice cracked and she buried her face in her hands.

Gina could think of nothing to say, couldn't imagine the horrors of Danat's captivity. She wished she could ease the girl's pain...

A wave of vertigo spun around her, leaving her with a sensation of buoyancy, as if she were floating above the ground. Her vision blurred. An aura of light appeared, surrounding Danat's body, a glow fringed with pain.

Instinctively, she reached out to Danat with her mind, sensed her agony, sharp and suffocating. Gina flinched, but didn't draw back. She grasped Danat's hand and pulled her pain into her own mind. A raw stream of burning loneliness and humiliation poured through Gina.

The intensity of Danat's emotions threatened to shatter Gina, but she held fast. She gathered the girl's trauma in a fleeting embrace, then released it to the sky. It vanished beyond the clouds.

Gina released Danat's hand and lowered her gaze. The girl was staring at her. "Thank you," she whispered, her hand shaking as she shoved a tangled red curl out of her eyes. "I don't know what you did, but thank you. It doesn't seem so...overwhelming now."

Gina's mind spun. What had she done, and how? "I'm glad I could help," she murmured, dazed.

At that moment Ariek called to Danat. The girl gave Gina a parting smile and went to him.

Gina gave herself a mental shake and looked about for Derrin. She spotted him some distance away, inspecting a scraggly tree. She made her way to his side. "Danat is much calmer now," she said.

"Good." He pulled one of the tree's branches closer and scrutinized it.

"What is it?"

"It suffers from the Blight. It hasn't set fruit." His voice sounded odd.

Something troubled him. She suspected it concerned Ariek's healing, but couldn't imagine why that should be. Her mind reached out and brushed against his. She felt a glimpse of his consciousness, enough for her to feel his turmoil before he jerked his mind away.

She caught his gaze. "What's wrong?"

"Nothing."

"Don't lie to me, Derrin."

He stiffened. Gina waited.

"It was wrong for me to save Ariek's life," he said finally.

For an instant, she thought she'd misheard him. Then she grabbed his arm. "Wrong? How could saving your friend's life be wrong?"

"I blamed Balek for the Madness and the Blight." He gave a humorless laugh. "What a hypocrite I am."

"Derrin, what are you talking about?"

"Wizardry. Wizardry itself is the cause of the plagues. I realized the truth just before I pulled Ariek back from the edge of death." Derrin shook off her hand. "Don't you see? Each time a wizard's will changes what should be, the land sickens."

"You can't be sure of that. Things change all the time."

"Ariek should have died, but I wouldn't allow it. I used my power to change the natural course of his life."

"Derrin, listen to yourself! You're not making any sense. How can it be wrong to save your friend's life? He wasn't supposed to die—someone tried to kill him. Would you feel better if they had succeeded?"

He shot her a dark look. "Of course not. I'd feel worse."

"Then you made the right choice."

"I can't know that. My feelings are not a true reflection of what's right and what's wrong."

She threw up her hands. As far as she was concerned, his logic was flawed, but it wouldn't do any good to argue about it now. "Look, what's done is done. Let's not debate it. We have more immediate concerns. We're out of water, and this field hardly seems like a good place to spend the night."

Derrin nodded. "You're right. We need to move toward the coast, where the forest is healthier."

"Then let's go."

*****

They forged downstream, making camp in a rare scrap of green forest. Derrin pondered his next move. The worsening Blight troubled him more than he cared to admit. Even this far from Katrinth, the land cowered under the ravages of the plague. How much longer before the villages of the Baha'Na succumbed to the Blight's ravenous hunger? He needed to confront Balek soon, with Ariek's help.

He went in search of his friend. He found him sitting near the fire, bare-chested, flexing his shoulder. His color had improved and the open gash on his shoulder had faded to a thin red line.

"I'm a credit to your healing powers, Derrin," he said, shaking his head. "Amazing."

"That's good, since there's no time for you to lounge about. Will you be able to travel hard today?"

Ariek nodded.

"Then I suggest we part ways. I'll take Gina to the nearest Baha'Na village. Leave Danat in Sirth, then meet me at your mother's villa in Katrinth."

"Sirth! Hide her on my father's estate, you mean? It will be crawling with Lotark's Servants."

"Not there. In town, in the last place the priests would dream of searching for their sacred Bride."

Understanding dawned in Ariek's eyes. "Do you think Beltha would—"

"I'm sure of it," Derrin said. "All you need to do is ask."

Chapter Twenty-Two

Power, sweetened by the terror of innocents, sang in Balek's veins. The people sought shelter from madness in the depths of the webstone's song.

The golden strains of music swelled.

*****

Needles of sleet stung Danat's face. She clutched the edges of the bloodstained stable blanket and pressed her spine against Ariek's chest, wishing their stolen horse could manage something faster than a feeble trot.

Ariek leaned forward, shielding her from the worst of the wind. "This is the sorriest piece of horseflesh I've ever had the misfortune to encounter," he muttered. He set his heels to the dappled mare's flanks.

The nag pitched forward, then dropped back to its accustomed gait. Danat's stomach lurched with every uneven step the exhausted horse took. She gripped Ariek's arm and willed the nausea to settle.

"It's not much farther," he said. "I see the first lights of the city already."

The scattered dwellings on the periphery of the city plodded past. Danat drew the edge of the blanket over her head, praying no one would pass them on the road. Even within the protection of Ariek's crystal shadow, she dared not show the Mark of Lotark.

But the few travelers on the road kept their heads bent against the sleet. Ariek bypassed the most direct route into the city, circling the outskirts until he met the sea road.

The roar of the surf brought memories of Loetahl. Danat blinked back a sudden wash of tears.

Ariek shifted, pointing to a manor house set high on a bluff overlooking the sea. "My father's estate."

"Will we go there?"

"No. The priests may be watching for us." His arms tightened around her. "I'm taking you to another place. You'll be safe there."

They reached the docks, where the skeleton masks of the tall ships scratched the charcoal sky, and the stench of decay overpowered the scent of the sea. Danat's nausea intensified. She bit back the taste of bile.

A ramshackle collection of buildings crowded the far end of the waterfront, belching music and shouts into the night. For a moment, Danat thought Ariek meant to approach one of the bright doorways, but he drew up short and turned into a narrow alley. High stone walls loomed tight on either side, leaching the warmth from her body.

Despite the near-total darkness, Ariek didn't slow his mount. He threaded the back alleys with single-minded purpose, ignoring the stench. It was clear he'd traveled the route many times. Danat closed her eyes and pondered that fact. Why would the son of a wealthy lord frequent such a place?

The freezing rain had penetrated the wool of the blanket, leaving her soaked to the skin. The fabric hung heavy on her arms, its musty smell mingling with the scents of salt air, rotting garbage, and human waste. Another wave of nausea hit her, more urgent than the last. If not for Ariek's steadying arm, she would have fallen.

They turned into a narrow passageway and the beleaguered horse set its hooves and refused to advance. Ariek muttered a curse. He dismounted and pressed between the animal's flank and the rough wall, grabbing the reins close to the horse's head. When the beast could not be coaxed forward, he reached up and pulled Danat off the saddle.

"We're almost there." He peered down at her through the gloom. "Are you well?"

"Well enough, Ariek."

He drew her farther into the fetid alley, skirting a pile of muck and turning into an even tighter passage. Overhead, stone arches pressed the leaning walls outward. The night sky was a dull slice of gray far above.

Ariek pulled her into a shallow doorway. "I've brought us around the back way. I didn't want to risk the main entrance." He groped at his belt for his crystals. A stone glowed white in his palm and the lock of the heavy door clicked. He pushed it open. Its hinges groaned in protest.

He stepped into a dim passageway and motioned for her to follow. Danat blinked as the door thudded shut behind her, grateful for the wave of warmth that swept over her. A hanging lamp cast a flickering glow over walls tinted the color of wine. A thick rug lay beneath her feet.

"Whoever you are, don't take a step. I have a knife and I know how to use it."

A woman appeared at the end of the hallway, the promised blade poised in her raised hand. The weapon provided an odd counterpoint to her gown of red lace over watered silk, cut low to reveal the swell of her ample breasts.

Danat clutched Ariek's arm.

He chuckled. "Darcy, think what your employer would say if you were to murder me."

The woman faltered, dropping her arm a fraction. "Ariek?"

Ariek stepped into the light.

"It *is* you!" The woman bent and lifted the hem of her gown, sliding the dagger into a sheath strapped to her calf. "What are you about, sneaking in the back door? Does Beltha expect you?" She regarded Danat with frank curiosity. "Who's the wench?"

Danat shrank back, gripping her blanket, an uneasy suspicion forming in her mind.

Ariek gestured to a nearby door. "We'll wait here, Darcy. Bring Beltha, and tell no one you saw us."

The woman hesitated a moment, then nodded. Skirts rustling, she disappeared around a turn at the end of the hall.

"In here." Ariek guided Danat to a small chamber and closed the door behind them. A huge bed filled the room with a froth of scarlet lace. A washstand and wardrobe crowded one wall. A fireplace, unlit, occupied the other. An oil lamp flickered on the mantle, illuminating a collection of silhouettes—men and women engaged in various positions of coitus. A tight knot of dread coiled in Danat's stomach.

"Ariek. Have you… Have you brought me to a whorehouse?"

His face reddened. "I can explain."

At that instant, the door flew open and a truly stunning woman entered the room.

She was tall, nearly as tall as Ariek. An abundance of golden blonde hair coiled atop her head in elegant disarray. Her features were exquisite—wide blue eyes, flawless skin and full, pouting red lips. A gown of wispy yellow silk clung to her lush curves, hinting at the peaks of her breasts, the swell of her hips and the soft mound between her thighs.

The woman's gaze fell on Ariek and her eyes lit up. With a graceful flurry, she threw her arms around his neck and kissed him. The full length of her body pressed against his, arching like a cat. An instant later, she jumped back.

"Tarol's blood! You're soaked through!" She glanced down at her dress. Rainwater soaked the front, leaving even less to the imagination than before.

"It's ruined." She sighed, then gave Ariek a wicked smile. "But it was worth it. You've been away much too long, Ariek."

Ariek sent a pointed look in Danat's direction. "It's always good to see you, Beltha, but this isn't a casual visit."

The woman frowned, taking in Danat's form for the first time. "What's this? Have you brought me a new girl? You could have come in the front with her, you know. A new girl is always good for business. There's no harm in her being seen."

A sudden, wrenching nausea swept over Danat. The room spun and her legs turned to water. She pitched forward.

"Danat— " Ariek's voice vanished into a black void.

* * * * *

"Sweet Lotark's cock, Ariek! This girl is the Bride!"

"I know that," muttered Ariek, lowering Danat onto the bed. Thankfully, he'd caught her before she hit the floor. He struggled with the fastenings on her cloak.

"Damn it all to Tarol's Inferno. I should have realized she was exhausted." And he should have warned her about their destination.

Beltha rummaged through the wardrobe and appeared a moment later with a pink dressing gown, soft and somewhat frayed at the hem. Not something the girls wore while they worked, he noted with relief.

When the last of Danat's wet clothes were removed and the coverlet tucked around her, Ariek sank down on the edge of the bed. His wounded shoulder ached. He lifted the sodden curls from Danat's face and spread them across the pillow.

Beltha laid one hand on his arm. "She's only fainted, Ariek. She'll come around soon enough. In the meantime, why don't you tell me what in Lotark's name you've done this time?"

He studied her expression and felt a stab of guilt. Beltha still loved him, though she was far too practical to admit it. She didn't deserve this.

He pushed himself off the bed and moved to the hearth. Crouching, he stacked the logs and kindling, then struck the flint and coaxed the spark to life. He stared into the new flames, thinking how best to plead his case.

"It's a long story," he said finally.

She folded her arms and regarded him steadily. "Start by telling me how you fell in love with the Bride of Lotark."

Ariek's mouth twisted into a wry smile. He rose to his feet, wiping the soot from the fireplace on his breeches. "You know me far too well."

"I don't need to know you well to see how much you care for her, Ariek. Any fool could tell as much."

In terse sentences, Ariek told her of his liaison with Danat and the events of the night of the Bride's Rising festival. Beltha gazed down at Danat with an inscrutable expression.

"So you found another lost soul to save. Like me."

Ariek spiked his finger through his hair. "I've succeeded in endangered her life, not saving her." He turned and leaned on one arm against the mantle, staring at the flames. "What news have you heard from the capital, Beltha? Are the Servants of Lotark searching for me?"

"No, not openly, at least. I'm quite sure I would have noticed your name in the news couriers' reports."

"What's being said?"

"The Temple claims the Heir and his Bride have been lifted body and soul into Paradise. It's a miracle," she added dryly. Her gaze narrowed on him. "Did you kill Solk, Ariek?"

Ariek closed his eyes against the image of Danat's frenzied attack. No matter what happened, he would not allow her to take the blame for the high priest's death.

"Yes, I killed him." He told her of his flight into the dead forest and of Derrin's timely appearance. He followed it with a brief account of Balek's experiments with the webstone.

"I promised to meet Derrin in Katrinth once I've hidden Danat. The crystal must be destroyed if Galena is to be saved." He spread his palms in a gesture of supplication. "I know it's much to ask, but will you hide Danat here? You're the only one I can trust, and this is the last place the Servants of Lotark would think to look. I'll pay you well."

Beltha regarded him, scowling, and Ariek knew she was remembering another dark night, nine years past, when a foolish young aristocrat had fought a pimping slaver for a young girl's life.

"Keep your money, Ariek. You know any girl in trouble is welcome here." She tapped her finger against her mouth. "I can't let her be seen, though—not with that brand on her forehead. It's a good thing it was Darcy who came across you in the passageway. Of all my girls, her lips are the tightest."

At Ariek's raised eyebrow, Beltha laughed. She licked her fingertip and ran it across his lower lip, her eyes flashing with wicked fire. "Take that any way you like, love."

He chuckled. He caught her hand and pressed it. "Thank you, Beltha. I'm in your debt."

She pulled away, a wistful expression clouding her eyes. "It's nothing. Now, if you'll excuse me, there's a gentleman waiting for me in the salon."

His gaze followed the provocative swing of her hips as she moved to the door. "I don't doubt it," he said. "I don't doubt it at all."

*****

"I'm going with you to Katrinth."

"No."

"But you need me there!"

"No, I don't." Derrin spared Gina the briefest of glances, but didn't slow his swift pace. "You'd be in the way."

He winced at the invective Gina hurled at him in reply.

She halted. He kept moving, sure she would follow.

"You're a stubborn idiot," she yelled after him. "The best way to set a trap for Balek is to use me as bait. I'm going."

Derrin turned and paced back down the path, until he stood less than an arm's length from his belligerent companion. She stood with her hands on her hips, eyes flashing.

He looked up at the sky and counted to ten. "Pay attention, because I'm only going to say this once. You will not go within a day's travel of that bastard." He held up one hand to head off her reply. "You will stay with the Skyeagle Clan. When I return with Balek's crystal, I'll send you home."

Gina expression told him what she thought of his plan. "I'm not going to wait on some mountaintop, wondering whether you're alive or dead! Besides," she persisted, "why are you so sure I'd be safer there alone than I'd be with you in Katrinth?"

"Gina—"

A jay, hidden nearby, screeched. Birds in every direction took up its cry of alarm.

Her head came up. "What is it?"

"Perhaps a predator, come to hunt. A wildcat, or a skyeagle." But the pattern of the birds' cries didn't fit. Danger lurked close by, to be sure, but he sensed it was a threat alien to the wilderness.

Laughter sounded, low and intimate, flowing with genuine amusement. Derrin froze, scanning the forest around him. He could see nothing out of the ordinary.

Gina touched his arm. "Derrin, what's wrong?"

"Didn't you hear it?"

"Hear what?"

"The laughter..." Derrin's whisper died on his lips. The voice echoed inside his head, growing stronger.

Did you think I wouldn't find you, you pitiful guttersnipe? Your gutless friend led me to you. The woman is mine.

He probed the shadows. Balek couldn't be far away.

"Derrin, what is it? What are you looking for?"

"Balek. He's nearby. I can hear his ranting in my mind."

She will be my queen, mongrel, ruling over all my subjects, even as I rule her soul. From this day on, she will exist only inside the web. Through her, all will be One.

The laughter erupted again, striking like lightning. Derrin fell backward and slammed into the ground. Pain spiked up his spine.

His limbs froze, snared by invisible shackles. At the periphery of his vision, he saw Gina caught in shining waves of golden air. Balek's laughter grew louder.

Gina's eyes flared. "Get out of my head!" she screamed.

Derrin strained with all his strength, but Balek's unseen bonds held firm. Desperate, he hurled his consciousness outward, searching. An aura of obscene power drew him. He followed it to a sheltered hollow where the high wizard stood, holding the webstone aloft.

Derrin flung his mind into the stone and entered a yawning chasm of insanity.

Balek's attention shifted from Gina. A slight frown creased his forehead. "You are but a minor nuisance, mongrel. Do not doubt my power."

A screeching melody invaded Derrin's brain, whittling away fragments of his sanity. Power focused and exploded, sending a thousand shards into his skull.

He ignored the agony. With his last scrap of reason, he anchored his will in the heart of the webstone and called forth the golden strands.

He pulled them taut, trading sanity for power. The skewed lines twisted and turned, resisting, sending sharp vibrations through his brain. He wrenched the web forward. He could see the path inside, a pulsing tunnel of light. With a final, desperate thrust, he dropped it over Gina. *Go!*

She spun around and reached for him through the glittering strands. "No! I won't leave you!"

Balek's mind slammed into Derrin like a fist. The tunnel wavered. *Gina, go!* Madness swirled into his vision. He wouldn't be able to hold the passage open much longer. *Go now!*

Gina's hand dropped. She nodded, tears streaming down her face. Her image wavered in the golden light.

The next instant, she was gone.

* * * * *

Pain, coupled with an unnatural silence, lifted Gina into consciousness. She lay face down on a surface she couldn't identify. Flat. Hard, but covered with a thick layer of a softer material. A dusty, stale scent hung in the still air.

She pushed to a sitting position and opened her eyes. A perfectly flat, perfectly blank wall came into focus.

Oh, God. She was home.

She lurched to her feet, then bent double over the arm of her sofa and willed the room to stop spinning. When it did, she staggered into the kitchen. The porch light glared through the window above the sink. The clock on the microwave blinked red. 3:23 a.m.

How could I have left him?

A wave of nausea broke hard. She stumbled to the sink and retched, reaching for the faucet with a shaking hand. The shock of cold water on her face cleared her head. After a moment she felt strong enough to climb the stairs to her bedroom.

Everything was just as she'd left it—how long ago? She forced herself to calculate. One month. It seemed like a lifetime. If not for her clothing and the tangled braids falling over one shoulder, she might have thought it a dream. The scent of woodsmoke clung to her, recalling clan fires rising to the stars.

She stripped off her clothes and unraveled her braids, as if removing all traces of her crossing would erase the pain in her heart. She dressed in jeans and a T-shirt, then sank onto the bed.

She tried not to think about Derrin. She couldn't bear to remember his gray eyes sparking with laughter or his mouth hot on her bare skin. She didn't have the strength to examine Balek's final attack and the desperate voice in her mind that had ordered her across the web. Most of all, she didn't want to wonder what had happened to him after she'd gone.

But unwanted images battered her mind with savage clarity and would not fade. Giving up the fight, she curled up in a ball and sobbed herself into an exhausted sleep.

Some time later, a car alarm shattered her fitful slumber. Sunlight streamed through the window and ran across her legs, illuminating swirls of dust motes. Hunger throbbed in her gut, reminding her that, despite not caring, she was still alive.

She located some crackers and peanut butter, but couldn't manage to force much down her throat. She fingered Derrin's wildflower carving and his silver-gray crystal. She squeezed her eyes shut, but a tear escaped anyway.

She missed him with a ferocity that gnawed a hole through her chest and choked her every breath. Had he defeated Balek and destroyed the webstone? She refused to consider the alternative.

She dumped her uneaten meal in the trash and retreated to the shower, blasting the water as hot as she could stand. A bitter laugh escaped her. How many times in the last month had she wished for a hot shower? She let the last traces of dirt melt from her body, then dried herself with a towel.

The white cloth came away from her body carrying an angry red streak. With a shaking hand, Gina touched the thin stream of blood trickling down the inside of her thigh.

Overwhelming loss shook her to the core. She hadn't until that moment realized how much she'd hoped a part of Derrin was living inside her. She dropped the towel and sank to her knees, sobs racking her body.

Now, irrevocably, every trace of him was gone.

Chapter Twenty-Three

Danat retched into the chamberpot, but her stomach had given up its contents long ago and the act brought little relief. She reached for a cloth and wiped her face. The ache in her heart rose into her throat. She squeezed her eyes shut. She would not cry.

The scent of woodsmoke lingered in the cold hearth, and dim light filtered through the wooden slats of the single window. Dawn. She'd waited all night for Ariek, but he hadn't come. Had he spent the hours with Beltha?

She moved gingerly to the bed, thankful the ground didn't lurch under her feet. A tear trickled down her cheek. She couldn't deny the intimacy between Ariek and the stunning woman. She was sure they were lovers.

He'd brought her to a whorehouse. Why?

Because that's what you are. A whore.

She buried her face in her hands. What did she know of Ariek, really? He'd told her of the Hierarchy and his duties in the Stronghold, but little of his personal life. Danat had always avoided dwelling on Ariek's past, preferring instead to live each moment with him as it came. Perhaps she was a fool to believe he loved her.

A brisk knock sounded at the door. Before Danat could react, Beltha entered, dressed in a morning gown of pale green silk. She carried a tray of food. Danat eyed the thick slices of bread and cheese, and the accompanying pitcher of ale.

Her stomach lurched. She gripped the bedpost and lowered herself onto the lace coverlet.

Beltha set the tray on a small table near the door and turned an assessing eye on her. "Are you ill?"

"No." She pulled the edges of the pink robe tight around her.

Beltha's gaze narrowed. She moved to the bed and put her palm to Danat's forehead. "Like ice," she muttered.

Danat pulled away.

"Ariek left before dawn. He didn't wish to wake you."

Bile rose in Danat's throat. "He left?"

"He'll return soon enough."

"Oh."

"He went to his father's estate to borrow—or steal—a new mount."

"I see."

Beltha frowned. "Why don't you eat while you wait for him? You must be half-starved."

The mention of food brought a surge of nausea. Danat threw a surreptitious glance at the chamberpot. "I'm not hungry."

Beltha gave her an assessing look. "How far along are you?"

"What?"

"Don't pretend with me. I've seen the signs often enough. When was your last flux?"

"I can't remember."

"Does Ariek know?"

"No!" Danat leaned forward and gripped Beltha's wrist. "You must not tell him!"

"Lotark's cock, girl! Why not? Ariek has a right to know you're carrying his child."

The tears Danat had struggled so hard to deny flowed hot on her cheeks. "I don't know that it's his." She dragged the back of her hand across her eyes. "You must give me a draught."

"A draught?"

"Yes. A place such as this... I mean I am sure you must have need of such a thing from time to time..." Danat faltered under Beltha's hard gaze. "Please," she finished weakly. "Ariek need not know."

"Needn't he?"

"Do not pretend to misunderstand!"

Beltha snorted. "I understand. You want to do away with the babe before Ariek finds out you're carrying." She paused. "Is it the high priest's child?"

"It could well be." Danat's voice hardened. "I will not bear the Line of Lotark."

"Yet you're not sure. It may be Ariek's."

Danat couldn't bear to contemplate that possibility. "Please, Beltha, you must help me. I will leave when it's done. You will have Ariek. I know you have been intimate with him."

The older woman's frown deepened. "What is it? Has Ariek outlived his usefulness now that you're free? Did you plan all along to put him in danger of his life and then abandon him?"

Danat sprang to her feet. "No! But how could he have a life with me? I am marked."

Beltha eyed her. "Where would you go?"

"Home. To Loetahl."

"Ariek would be furious."

"He will forget soon enough."

"He loves you."

"He pities me. He enjoyed the challenge of meeting with me in the Temple, passing unseen within arm's length of the Servants. But now—he will tire of hiding me soon enough and then what will he do?"

She squared her shoulders and met Beltha's gaze. "I was brought to Galena as a slave. I will never be free here, and I will not ask Ariek to leave his home. Please. Help me, for his sake."

Beltha moved to the window and peered through the slats as if there were something to see outside in the alley. "Girl, Lotark knows I'd do almost anything for Ariek, but doing away with his child is not on the list."

"Then I will leave this place and deal with the babe on my own. Please, I beg you. Will you help me gain my freedom?"

Beltha turned and regarded Danat for a long moment, her expression inscrutable.

"Yes," she replied.

*****

"I'm sorry my errand took so long." Ariek drew Danat into his arms and buried his face in her soft curls, inhaling deeply. She'd bathed in his absence and smelled of sea roses.

"Beltha told me where you had gone." Danat drew back and looked up at him, her fingers playing with the short hair at his nape. Her green eyes clouded. "You will leave, then?"

"At nightfall. I prefer the cover of darkness in addition to the shadow of the crystal."

"Be careful, Ariek. Promise me."

"I do. I'll be back soon, I swear to you. And then—"

"Shh..." Danat pulled his head down and captured his lips in a kiss. "Do not speak of it. Do not speak at all." Her hand slid down the front of his tunic and slipped below his belt, her hand boldly stroking his cock. He tensed in surprise, then groaned.

"Love me, Ariek," she whispered.

He needed no coaxing. He caught her up in his arms and tumbled her onto the bed. The wooden frame creaked as his body came over her. Her robe fell open, freeing her breasts. Her fingers reached again for his belt.

Long red curls fanned out over the pillows, mingled with the crimson lace of the coverlet. He kissed her deeply, then, rising up on his knees, dropped his belt and pulled off his tunic.

Danat tore at the laces of his breeches with an urgency she'd never before displayed in their lovemaking. She bit her bottom lip when the knot wouldn't come undone.

Ariek covered her hand with his. "What's wrong?"

She stilled. "Nothing."

He pressed the length of his body against hers. She kissed his chest, but when she looked up, her eyes held a note of fear.

"Are you afraid because I'm leaving?" he asked. "Don't worry. I'll be back before you have a chance to miss me."

Tears crowded her eyes. "That would be impossible. I will miss you every second we are apart."

He caught one salty tear with a kiss. "Once Balek's crystal is destroyed, we'll never part again. Think on that." He rocked his hips against her thighs, letting her feel his desire. Her arms entwined his neck. "I'll make love to you every day, Danat, and surround you with our children." He dipped his head and nuzzled the curve of her neck. "Let me show you how it will be."

"Oh, Ariek..." Her lips touched his temple, skimmed across his brow. He claimed them, framing her head with his hands and pulsing gently inside her with his tongue.

She arched against him, riding his thigh, pulling again at his laces. He shed his breeches and boots, then lowered his head to her breast and circled one nipple with his tongue.

Danat moaned. She clutched at him, pressing him closer as he suckled. Her thigh rubbed against his throbbing erection. "Do not be gentle," she whispered and slipped the robe from her shoulders.

Ariek hesitated. He'd always made love to Danat with the utmost tenderness. He treated her like a precious flower, one he took care not to bruise. Now, suddenly, she spilled over the garden fence and ran wild on the shore. Her fingers closed on his cock, demanding his attention.

"Danat, I—"

"Now, Ariek. I want you inside me." She guided him to the thatch of red curls between her thighs. A moment later he was lost.

Danat wrapped her legs around his waist and pulled him close, claiming his mouth in a searing kiss. She tasted of the sea, of white froth on the breakers, of the sand washed clean by the tides. He gritted his teeth and forced himself to a slow, gentle pace.

"Do not hold back, Ariek, not now."

His resolved wavered. "I don't want to hurt you."

"You could never do that." She kissed his jaw, bit his shoulder. "Take me, Ariek. Take me hard. Give me all your strength."

Her sweet urging broke him. With a shudder, he abandoned all pretense of control. He drove his flesh into her, flexing his buttocks, anchoring her hips in his hands. Danat moaned his name and sank her teeth into his neck. He answered by hauling her legs up over his shoulders.

He trapped her in the prison of his arms and doubled his efforts. "You're mine now," he gasped as his body branded its claim on her. "Do you hear me? Mine. I will kill any man who dares to touch you."

Her release came sharp and quick, driving him over the edge. He emptied his soul inside her, offering all that he was, all that he ever would be. The maelstrom drove him down, then tossed him, beaten and sated, onto the shore.

But later, on the road to Katrinth, Ariek couldn't shake a feeling of foreboding. As he caught sight of the Stronghold perched high on its peak, he realized why.

Danat had given herself to him as if for the last time.

*****

You will lead me to her.

Laughter drove through Derrin's skull like a spike, leaving him gasping for breath.

"No." He jumped up and paced the confines of his cell, a deep pit of precisely five strides square. A patch of blue sky hovered far above. His fist slammed into a wall of sheer, flawless stone, sending a shock up his arm. The shaft had been formed by wizardry and it caged him more effectively than bars or chains ever could.

Show her to me.

Blinding pain, a sword between his eyes, struck with swift brutality. He slumped against the wall, shoulders braced for the next assault. Dirty fingers probed the recesses of his brain. Balek's breath sounded in his ears.

You will not protect her. Withdraw the shadow.

"No. I will not."

The laughter surged anew, louder, hammering his skull. A vision of the webstone filled his mind with aching perfection. The impossible was more beautiful than he dared to imagine. The five sparkling faces lured him closer.

He reached out with his will and touched it.

Euphoria shot through him like a bolt of lightning. A song soared, a melody sweeter than any he'd ever known. It wove through his mind, caressed his secrets, claimed his trust.

His limbs grew heavy. Warm waves of pleasure bore him into eternity.

Give her to me.

"No," he whispered, though he choked on the word.

Laughter rang in his ears. *I will wait.*

*****

Derrin stroked into Gina's body, forcing a sharp cry of pleasure from her lips. He drank in her joy, reveled in her eager acceptance as he filled her again and again, driving toward his own release. But at the final moment she twisted away, her moans frozen in a silent scream.

Her fists pummeled his chest. Derrin felt his limbs go cold, saw blood flowing between their bodies. His skin fell away, exposing muscle and sinew. His rigid cock, still thrusting between Gina's thighs, separated from his skeleton. His bones dropped, one by one, onto her body...

Derrin jerked upright, heart pounding in his throat, breath coming in spurts. The nightmare shattered.

A low snigger sounded. It grew in depth and fullness until deep-throated laughter, mingled with pain, rang in his mind.

He staggered to his feet and paced like an injured wildcat, avoiding the corner where his excrement lay. He'd been two days without food. A trickle of morning dew on the sides of the pit had provided his only drink. The fetid odor of waste gagged his every breath. Balek's wild laughter rang in his head without ceasing.

At times, he laughed with it.

Show her to me and you will live forever. A whisper, followed by blessed silence. Derrin drew a shuddering breath.

A hot slice of agony pierced his skull. He dropped to his knees and bent forward, covering his head with his arms. The pain evaporated, leaving him breathless, awaiting the next assault.

A stunning, erotic pleasure coursed though his body and pooled hot and insistent in his groin. Derrin twisted onto his back. His hips arched, his hand grasped his rigid shaft.

Give her to me and you will have her for yourself as well. I will allow you to join her in the web for all eternity.

The glittering faces of the webstone spun into Derrin's mind. The exquisite song stroked his soul. His arousal hardened under his fingertips. He stroked himself, seeking release from the sweet torment.

He moaned, struggling to remember why resisting the melody was so important. The crystal drew closer, tantalizing him with its beauty. Why shouldn't he have it? Why should he fight when surrender seemed the better choice?

The song rose on a soaring wave. He longed to join with it and become a part of its vast, glittering sea. His mind surged forward, searching for the dark crystal that held Gina in its shadow. He would remove his protection and they would enter the melody together.

Yes. It is the only way.

Long, silken strands of light appeared and opened. He caught a glimpse of his lover's spirit, hidden beyond the web. He flew to her, reaching out to touch her crystal. Its shadow would vanish in the light of the webstone.

The song's tempo increased, compelling him forward, but he faltered at the last moment. The melody hit a sour note.

"No!" He recoiled and wrenched his mind free, shuddering with the knowledge of how close he'd come to giving Gina to Balek.

The music shattered. Derrin flung his spirit out of the web and back into his body.

Blinding pain erupted behind his eyes.

* * * * *

"Where the hell have you been?"

Gina opened her apartment door a little wider. "Hi, Mikala."

Mikala blew past Gina like an angry tornado. She was halfway across the living room before she whirled around. "'Hi, Mikala?' Is that all you have to say for yourself? My God, Gina, everyone thinks you're dead!"

Gina shut the door and leaned against it. "How did you know I was back?"

"I saw the light. I've been driving by every night, hoping…" She all but collapsed on the sofa, blinking back tears. "Despite what the police said, I just couldn't shake the feeling that you were alive. That you would be back."

Gina sighed. Mikala looked almost as bad as Gina felt. "I'm sorry."

"Where did you go?"

"I wish I knew."

"You mean you don't remember?"

Gina shoved away from the door. "No, I remember well enough. Do you remember what you told me that day we were in Crystal Shadows?"

"The New Age shop? When we were shopping for your costume for The Wizards' Ball?"

"Yeah. You said it was mathematically possible for other universes to exist. Well, you were right. I went to one."

"What?"

Gina sat down across from Mikala and leaned forward, one elbow resting on her thigh. "I know it sounds crazy, but it's true. I spent the last month in another world." She gave Mikala a brief account of her experience while her friend listened, wide-eyed and silent.

"The worst part is, I don't know what happened to Derrin after I left him," Gina finished. "He could be dead." The word stuck in her throat.

"Maybe not. Maybe he kicked the bad guy's ass."

If Gina hadn't been so miserable, she might have laughed. Only Mikala would accept a story like the one Gina had just told her. "Maybe. But I'll never know for sure. And I need to. Not only about Derrin, but about all the people I met there."

She rubbed the throbbing ache in her right temple. "I felt a weird connection with them, Mikala. I don't know how to describe it. It started the moment I saw Derrin's grandmother. She wore this white stone disk with an odd symbol etched on it—two rings and a spear. It's the symbol of Derrin's people. Every time I saw it, I got a chill."

Mikala gave her an odd look. "Were the rings linked? With the spear passing through the overlapping part?"

Gina looked up. "Yeah. Why?"

"Gina, you have a stone like that. In that box of antique costume jewelry that you got from your father's house when he died. Do you remember? You asked me if I wanted to wear any of it to the Wizards' Ball."

Gina stared at Mikala for several seconds, her heart pounding into her throat. Then she lurched off her chair and into her bedroom.

Her mother's jewelry box was where she had left it, on the top shelf of her walk-in closet. Mikala crowded close as Gina lifted the lid and sifted through a jumble of necklaces, bracelets and broaches. Gina's fingers closed on a stone disk strung on a thin black cord.

A million stars burst in her head.

She stared, dazed, at the delicate lines etched on the surface of a milky-white stone—two rings, linked, with a spear thrust through the place of their joining. Gina had seen five stones identical to this one—each had been sewn onto the headdress of a Na'lara.

There could be no mistake.

The stone nestled in Gina's palm was the lost talisman of the Seventh Clan.

* * * * *

Death waited in patient vigil.

Derrin had lost count of the days since his capture. A quarter moon, perhaps more, perhaps less. No food. Only a few drops of water. He sprawled on the floor of the pit, drifting in and out of an endless nightmare.

The muscles in his arms and legs twitched, and the slightest movement brought exquisite pain. His skin hung limp, bunching like soft leather over his bones. Pain pounded his temple, tightened in bands across his chest. He existed, waiting—hoping—for the end.

The voice in his head, inexplicably, had fallen silent. He struggled to make sense of this fact. Had Balek found Gina without Derrin's cooperation? Had the high wizard dismissed him as an insect unworthy of a boot heel?

A stream of lurid images flowed through his consciousness. Derrin opened his eyes, but nightmare didn't disappear. Perhaps he was already dead, awaiting entrance to Tarol's Inferno.

The visions spun faster. Gina's face contorted in terror. Niirtor dead in his coffin. Rahza standing beyond his reach. Zahta's wrinkled hand, reaching for him, then drawing back.

Then, finally, nothing.

Derrin drew a burning breath. The sheer walls of his prison wavered in his failing vision. Far above, a direwolf howled.

The walls of the pit took on a faint luminescence. He squinted, certain he had gone mad at last. Waves of pulsing light washed the air, spread across the floor of the pit, creeping toward him.

His skin tingled at its touch. A shower of sparks sprang from the rock, dipped low and entered his mind.

Place yourself within me.

A woman's whisper sounded in his ear, so close he could feel her breath on his skin. He turned his head, gasping at the effort, but saw nothing.

Place yourself within me.

The command stirred a response from the deepest recesses of his mind. Derrin gathered the shadow of his fading life and offered it.

A raw bolt of lightning seared the air.

"Derrin."

He rolled over and pushed himself to his knees, stifling a moan of agony. Less than an arm's length away, draped in light, stood a woman.

She wore a buckskin dress, dyed the color of midnight and decorated with rows of red and black beads. Furrows of age lined her face, silver braids hung to her waist. Her eyes held the mystery of the universe.

Derrin forced his swollen tongue to move. "Who are you?"

"Who do you believe I am?"

A grandmother from the spirit world. Another of Balek's tricks. Either choice seemed likely.

"I don't know."

The crone took a step forward. "Your power is great. It lives in the stones you create with your spirit."

Her words fell like a blow. "The power I wield is a curse. It sickens the land."

"No, my son. The land is held in the heart of the power, how can it be harmed by its own spirit? Only one who is apart can harm it."

"I don't understand."

"Place your spirit in mine. All else will follow." Her breath passed over him like the mist of a summer night.

The outline of her body wavered. Derrin blinked. "Who are you?" he asked again.

I move in all things. Give me your spirit.

Her light flared. Derrin shielded his eyes with his hand and watched as the grandmother's form thinned, then scattered in a sparkling rush. Sparks spun, then reformed in a pattern of skew lines, spun with golden light. Unable to bear the beauty of the web, he shielded his face with his hands.

A moment later, the light dimmed and Derrin raised his head. A she-wolf stood before him, watching him with eyes of silent gold. She tilted her head, as if asking a question, before padding to the wall of the pit. The beast met his gaze once more, then turned and walked into the rock.

Derrin stared as the tip of the direwolf's tail disappeared. The light fled, and what little strength he possessed vanished with it. He sank to the ground, gasping with the weight of the darkness.

The warmth of the direwolf-goddess lingered. His mind sank into the bedrock and touched the raw grains of crystal entombed there. He held himself still, demanding nothing, waiting for his last moments to pass.

A wave of pure power, at once agonizing and ecstatic, squeezed the breath from Derrin's body, emptied every corner of his mind. He surrendered without question, without struggle. The force intensified. His senses screamed, his flesh crumbled. A roar like the crash of a tidal wave broke over him, driving him into the void. Then, nothing.

It was over.

* * * * *

"Stop pounding, Gina. The shop's not open yet. We'll just have to wait."

Gina glared at Crystal Shadows' locked door. "Madam Rose is in there, I know it. And she owes me some answers."

"Do you think she had something to do with your…uh…trip?"

"I hope so. I want to go back through the web."

Mikala paled. "You're joking."

"Hardly." Gina cupped her hands around her eyes and peered through the shop window into the gloomy interior. "I *need* to go back. Because of the stone."

"I don't understand."

Gina rattled the door handle. "Mikala, the talisman wasn't something my mother picked up at a yard sale. I'm guessing it came from my birth mother."

"Your birth mother? I didn't know you were adopted."

"I was. But it wasn't a normal situation. My father was an ER doctor. One night they brought in a pregnant woman who'd been hit by a car. The trauma sent her into labor. My father delivered the baby."

"You?"

Gina nodded. "The woman died. No ID, and she didn't fit any profiles of missing persons on file with the police. No one ever came looking for her. My parents had been trying to adopt a child for a while. My father pulled some strings and got me." She gave a final glance at the store window. "Come on, let's try around back."

She strode for the street corner, Mikala nearly running to keep up. "But why would your birth mother have a stone from another world?"

Gina reached the end of the row of shops and turned the corner. "She brought it with her when she crossed the web."

"You mean you think you're—"

"Yeah. I'm one of them. And they knew—I'm sure of it. Not Derrin, but the wise women I told you about. One of them told me the talisman of the Seventh Clan disappeared in a fire with the daughter of the clan's wise woman. The daughter was pregnant."

She turned the corner into the alley and backtracked toward the rear entrance to Crystal Shadows. "That happened four cycles of seven years ago. And guess what? I'll be twenty-eight on my next birthday." She reached Madam Rose's service entrance and pounded on it. "The return of the talisman has been foretold. And it's not going back without me." She raised her hand.

Before she could knock a second time, the door swung inward on rusty hinges. Madam Rose stood on the threshold.

"Welcome, my daughters. Come in."

Incense hung heavy in the air of Madam Rose's cluttered back room. Gina turned to face the woman, feeling suddenly foolish. "Madam Rose, you may not remember us, but—"

"I remember." She shuffled into the main section of the shop and parted the curtain of beads veiling the crystal room. Gina and Mikala squeezed into the small space.

"You come to my shop. Choose ice crystal." She lifted a trembling blue-veined hand, palm up. "Stone gone now."

"Where?" Gina asked.

"Other side. I send it to you there."

Gina steadied herself with one hand on a tall wooden cupboard. "Then you know how to call the strands. You can open the web."

"Yes, I can call."

Gina's gut tightened. "Can you send me across?"

Madam Rose shook her head. "Only you can choose. Dark man waits."

"I know. I have to go back. I have this." She drew the cord holding the talisman out from under her shirt.

Madam Rose's eyes gleamed. She extended one claw-like finger and touched the stone. To Gina's amazement, the disk began to glow. A milky-white mist swirled just below its surface. Mikala gasped.

A rushing noise, like the wind in the treetops, filled the tiny room. A single strand of shimmering gold hung in the air. It split, then multiplied, weaving a skew of light.

Come. The unspoken syllable echoed in Gina's mind. *Come now.*

Now? Gina's resolve weakened in a rush of panic. She wasn't ready.

You have all you need.

The web encircled her, beckoning. She took a step toward its center.

"Gina." Mikala's voice was trembling. "Are you sure you want to do this?"

Was she? An hour ago Gina's answer would have been unequivocal, but now, faced with the reality of stepping through the web a third time, her courage faltered. Where would the shining strands take her? To the Baha'Na? Back to the wizard's city? She would be ill-prepared in any case. She had nothing but the clothes she wore.

Gina's throat went dry. She didn't have to go. She could stay in the world she knew best. She was safe here. But if she did that, she would never know what had happened to Derrin. Never know what might have been.

Inside her, something shattered. She took a deep breath.

"Gina?"

"I'm sure, Mikala." She turned to her friend and saw tears in her eyes. "Wish me luck."

"I do."

The web sang to her heart. She took a deep breath and crossed the shimmering strands.

Chapter Twenty-Four

Derrin lay on his back in the middle of a shallow stream. Cool water flowed over his body, infusing his limbs with life.

He had no idea how he'd gotten there.

Green branches floated overhead, framing snatches of the dawn sky. A flock of small birds darted across his line of vision. He turned his head a fraction. Water trickled into his parched throat and burned a trail to his gut.

He sat up and coughed. When the fit eased, he drank again, careful not to take too much into his shrunken stomach. With shaking arms, he pushed himself to his knees. He stripped off his clothes, then caught a handful of grit and scrubbed the filth from his body.

The wolf-goddess had led him to the natural crystal imbedded in the walls of his prison. Somehow, he'd triggered its power and escaped, though he had no memory of it. He murmured a prayer of thanks for his deliverance. Would he prove worthy of the favor?

He tried to stand, but found his legs unequal to the task. He pulled himself into a patch of sun on the riverbank and considered his dilemma. He was too weak to gather food, but if he didn't eat, he would die.

Across the water, a shadow darkened the underbrush. A heartbeat later, a male direwolf emerged from the foliage, the leaves silent in his wake. The animal advanced at a slow pace, head raised, tail straight. It halted on the opposite bank of the stream and regarded Derrin with calm eyes.

He recognized the creature. It had approached him once before, the night the wind had howled through the canyon and Gina had spoken of evil spirits. The wolf picked its way across the water, placing each foot with precise care. It halted at Derrin's side.

Sharp teeth loomed over him, then dipped closer. Every muscle in Derrin's body clenched. Hot, blood-sweet breath bathed his cheek, fine whiskers tickled his chin. Pink lips curled over long fangs.

The beast flicked its tongue over the corner of Derrin's mouth and brought one giant paw down on his chest. A howl pierced the air.

A she-wolf emerged from the underbrush, her teats swollen with milk, a fresh kill dangling from her jaws. She trotted to Derrin and draped the carcass on his lap, then pushed it with her nose.

Both direwolves turned and bounded out of sight.

"Thank you, my sister, my brother," Derrin whispered.

A sharp stone lay within his reach. He hacked at the direwolves' gift, chopping strips of meat from the carcass and eating it raw.

He slept. When he awakened, he found he could walk without stumbling. He caught a few fish and built a fire. After eating, he rested by the stream and waited for his new companions.

They arrived in the long shadows of late afternoon. The male dropped another kill at Derrin's feet, but his mate disappeared behind a rocky outcropping with a lifeless harta. Derrin spitted the wolf's bounty and cooked it.

A short time later, the she-wolf returned, leading her pups. Five bundles of fur launched themselves at Derrin as if he were a long-lost uncle, pouncing and nipping at his arms with needle-sharp teeth. He wrestled with the direwolf-children, barking and snarling in play.

One small female clamped its jaws on a stick. Derrin grabbed the stick and hauled it into the air, laughing when the pup refused to let go.

When night came, the little she-wolf was still at his side. She nestled under his arm and dropped off to sleep.

* * * * *

Branches clawed Gina's face and snagged her clothes, leaving thin trails of blood across her bare thighs. Her breath came in white gasps of cold mist. She kept moving, clinging to the illusion she had someplace to go.

An icy wind whipped her T-shirt. A fine drizzle, hardened to sleet, pelted her bare limbs. Daylight dimmed with each passing moment. A violent shudder racked her body. She had to get warm.

Why hadn't she worked harder at learning the skill of firemaking? She'd failed to spark a blaze under the best of conditions, even with Derrin by her side, coaching. Her chances of succeeding during a storm, with night falling, were slim. She would have to do without it.

She dragged a deadwood branch to a sheltered hollow and propped up one end on a boulder, then built a rough frame of sticks around it. She dumped armloads of leaf litter on top. Inside, she huddled in the darkness, amid the odor of decay, wondering if she'd survive the night.

The next morning Gina woke shivering, but alive. She crawled from the shelter and foraged for the little food that had been spared by the night's freeze. In the morning, the temperature rose, warming her briefly, but the relief was short lived. Come late afternoon, the temperature plummeted to freezing. If she couldn't manage to make a fire, she would die.

She cracked a stone on a boulder and used the sharp edge to fashion the tools of firemaking. She gathered tinder and firewood, then, with trembling hands, she looped the bowstring about the spindle.

The spindle whirled in its socket. Her arm burned, but she ignored the pain, focusing on the birth of the fire.

Black dust poured into the tinder. The smoke thickened. A spark flashed. With shaking hands, Gina lifted the tinder bundle and blew long streams of breath across the red coal.

I cast my breath into the flames.

The coal flared briefly, then shrank. Her chest tightened. She blew again, keeping her breath steady, using her body to shield the worst of the wind.

Flames burst to life.

The fire is born. It fills my heart.

* * * * *

Derrin arrived at the village of the Water Clan under the low stars of midnight. When he pulled the buckskin drape of Zahta's dwelling aside, he was not surprised to find his grandmother awake, and waiting for him.

She sat by the glowing remains of a fire, her eyes two dark pools. He lowered himself to the ground beside her and watched an ember die.

"The Goddess shines on your coming, Gray Wolf."

His head snapped up.

Zahta pressed her palm to her forehead and dipped her chin in the Baha'Na gesture of respect.

Derrin gave a short, bitter laugh. "So. It seems I am a man at last."

"You have long been a man, my son."

A charred log collapsed, showering sparks.

"You know Gina has returned to her world," he said at last. It was not a question.

Zahta inclined her head.

"I've come for my crystals and clothing. I must return to Galena."

"The Goddess is near you, Gray Wolf, even when you walk with the Outsiders. Listen for her call."

Derrin nodded. "I will do what I must."

*****

The body of an unrecognizable creature lay in the stream, alive with maggots. Gina gripped her stomach and bent double, retching into the frost-blackened grass. She'd felt ill since early morning, after drinking downstream. Now she knew why.

The stench of death assaulted her, driving her from the writhing carcass. She'd been wandering for days, searching for a signs of human life, but she'd found none. No hunting party had crossed her path. No familiar landmark jogged her memory. She hadn't even seen a trail marker.

She vomited again. Her gut had turned to water. Unnatural cold seeped into her bones. At sunset, she crawled into a shallow cave and covered herself with a blanket of forest debris. Shaking, she closed her eyes.

Ripe berries hung heavy on the vine like tiny stars, hidden by round leaves covered with fine hairs. The fruit glistened with dew, swayed gently in the early morning breeze. Some black, some red.

Choose.

She found the berries at dawn, near the entrance to the cave. A spindly vine with twisted branches hung from a crevice, bearing two colors of fruit. She dug deep into her memory, recalling Derrin's words from her first days in the wilderness. One fruit would save her, the other would kill.

Which should she choose?

A whisper brushed her mind, a voice telling secrets. Gina stilled. The murmuring grew louder. Not a human voice. It belonged to…

The voice belonged to the vine.

Choose.

She touched one of its leaves, stroking gently. Which? She closed her eyes. The warm skin of a fruit brushed her finger. She plucked it and ate.

*****

Derrin slipped into the shadow of the forest's edge. An ornate carriage, accompanied by four outriders, rattled by at a brisk pace, headed toward Katrinth. One horseman called to the others with a jolly shout. Derrin couldn't make out his words, but the sally must have been a fine bit of wit—the man's companions erupted in raucous laughter. In the carriage, a slender female hand drew back a silver filigreed curtain. He glimpsed a flash of golden hair and a dimpled smile.

The merry procession glided by, framed by the ravaged landscape of what had once been the lush farmland skirting the Galenan capital. The destruction left in the wake of the Blight staggered Derrin's imagination. Fields, denuded of its crops, swarmed with insects. Rivers flowed thick and slow, choked by fetid slime. The rain seared his skin.

Exhausted and burning with thirst, he made his way toward the capital. The land's ruin increased with every step and he feared what he would find once he reached his destination. Yet in the hours since dawn, several groups had passed him, not fleeing the city, but riding toward it. Each set of travelers smiled and laughed, as if headed to a festival. His head throbbed. What in Tarol's name was going on?

The devastation swept outward from the city on a relentless path to the wilderness. For the first time, Derrin considered the possibility the Baha'Na would be destroyed. A brutal rage smoldered inside him. The People trusted in the Goddess. How could she allow her children to come to such an end?

He continued his slow trek to the city, through the remnants of the world he once knew. The shadows of the ravaged tree line shielded his journey. He suspected Balek had found a way to bring the entire populace under the control of the webstone, showing them only what he wanted them to see. It was possible he could see through their eyes as well.

Derrin crossed the river and entered the Lower City. No crystal shadowed his movements, but the lack of cover didn't concern him. His boyhood in the wilderness had taught him the art of hidden movement. Compared to stalking a forest creature, moving unseen among the Galenans was a simple task. Only a wizard actively searching would see him. He hoped Balek thought him dead.

He moved without difficulty across the market square. The Galenans, busy with their daily affairs, saw little of their surroundings. They clung to familiar routes, heads lowered, their awareness locked into the world behind their eyes. He passed unseen within a hand's breadth of many of them.

An atmosphere of merriment prevailed in the market square. Women jostled at the stalls, picking over piles of half-rotted produce with bright smiles on their faces. One vendor did a brisk business selling moldy cheese, another had no trouble attracting buyers to a mound of stinking fish. Bile rose in Derrin's throat. The air blew in putrid waves from the sea.

He threaded the maze of alleys leading to the Upper City. Once in the shadow of the Stronghold, he detoured toward the cliff road. Above him, the sun cowered behind a yellow haze. Below, the sea rolled as if a storm approached.

The wall encircling Ariek's mother's villa stood well over Derrin's head, but he dared not risk the gate. Taking advantage of a gnarled pine, he hoisted himself over the barrier and dropped onto the soft ground beyond.

He remembered Lady Kalana's garden as a beautiful place, a lush oasis in the confines of the city, where the tang of sea air mingled with the perfume of the flowers. Now the scorched patch of ground displayed blackened stalks, and what little life remained was yellowed. The orchard trees had lost most of their leaves, revealing a few pockmarked fruit. The ornate fountain spurted a sour white trickle from a sea nymph's shell.

Derrin crossed the ruins, making his way toward a cellar door hidden behind a tangle of brittle shrubs. Bending, he grasped a heavy iron ring and heaved the door upward, then descended the stone stair.

Ariek was waiting for him.

His friend sat at a small wooden table, his hand curled around a silver goblet. Casks of wine filled with Galena's finest vintages lined the stone walls behind him.

Derrin dropped into an empty chair. "It's not yet midday, my friend."

Ariek shrugged. He rose and produced a second goblet from a rack overhead. Uncorking one of the casks, he tipped it on edge. A stream of burgundy liquid spilled into the cup and dripped over the edge. He presented it to Derrin with a flourish.

"Waiting in the wine cellar has its advantages," Ariek said.

"So I see." Despite Derrin's weariness, a smile played on his lips. He took a long draught of the wine.

Ariek's eyes struggled to focus. "Gina…?"

Derrin's smile abruptly faded, replaced by a twist of pain. "Gone. She has returned to her home."

"How?"

"I sent her back. I used the webstone to open the path."

His friend's eyes widened. "Tarol's blood. You put your mind into that cursed crystal?"

"The effort cost me dearly." Derrin recounted the story of his capture and imprisonment, and what he could recall of his escape.

Ariek sat up, sobering rapidly. "In truth, I feared you were dead before I received your signal."

"We must stop Balek. I'll go before the High Council."

Ariek laughed. "Balek *is* the High Council, my friend. The other Councilors stepped down when he produced the cure for the Blight. Now that the city has returned to normal—"

"Normal?" Derrin stared at Ariek, dumbstruck. "Katrinth is a cesspool!"

Ariek's brows drew together. "What do you mean? It's a paradise! Within minutes of Balek's announcement of a cure, the waters cleared. Green returned to the forest. It's nothing less than a miracle!"

"Ariek—"

"The commoners worship Balek as though he were Lotark returned. The Lords have pledged him their allegiance. Even Solk's successor has bowed to him. The city is crazed with joy."

Derrin stared at his friend, dread twisting his gut with an icy hand. Ariek grinned and raised his goblet. "The crisis is over, Derrin. Perhaps it would be best to acknowledge Balek's success."

Derrin wrenched the goblet from Ariek's grip and slammed it onto the table. Red liquid sloshed over the rim and sunk into the wood, darkening it.

"Can you not see the truth?" he said, his voice deadly calm.

"I see what everyone sees."

"Come." Derrin grabbed Ariek by the arm and hauled him up the stair to the garden. The odor of rot hammered his nostrils when he pushed the door open.

He shoved Ariek into the barren plot. "What do you see?"

Ariek turned to him with a bemused expression. "My mother's sea roses."

"I didn't ask what you *want* to see. Look again."

"I don't understand."

Derrin's hand clenched into a fist. "See what is real, Ariek. Understand what you have lost."

Ariek blinked, studying the scene. Derrin watched him. Was his friend blind, mad like all the rest?

Ariek's gaze roved over the contours of the garden he'd known since boyhood. Derrin noted the exact moment the illusion vanished. Grief, then anger flooded his expression.

"So many will die," Ariek said, his voice distant.

"There will always be more."

"Tarol's blood! Why did I not see it?"

Derrin couldn't reply. His own anger swelled, reaching unbearable proportions. A realization, one he'd avoided facing, smashed into his gut like a fist.

"I will kill him, Ariek. There is no other way."

Chapter Twenty-Five

The young tree stood at the edge of the clearing. Its trunk was deformed—it bent at head height and ran parallel to the ground for an arm's length before straightening. Gina had noticed it two days ago, but hadn't until now realized its significance.

She ran across the meadow and searched the ground at the base of the tree until she found what she sought—a pile of rocks with a flat stone set to one side. A crude representation of a bird had been cut into the slab, pointing the way to the Skyeagle Clan.

The path sliced through a section of barren land littered with bones. They lay strewn across the hardpan, bleached white by the sun. In the sky above, graceful ornas rode the spiraling updrafts, their black wings spread wide. One of the creatures dipped low to the ground, searching. It landed and advanced on its goal with a waddling gait, the purple feathers of its head catching the rays of the morning sun.

Gina wondered what had died in the night.

She followed the trail across the field and began a steep ascent, the rising sun at her back. The Day Traveler hung high in the sky when she came upon the village.

The laughter of children rang from a rough collection of stone huts. She caught sight of a small group of them throwing sticks at a target set to one side of the communal firepit. Several women worked hides amid cheerful chatter. The steady ping of stone on stone rang from the center of a group of men. The community was larger than the other Baha'Na villages Gina had visited, for here the Skyeagle Clan dwelt with the Seventh.

The Seventh Clan. Her family. Gina caught her breath at the sudden, visceral realization. For most of her life, her father had been her only relation. Now, she wondered if one broad-shouldered man could be her cousin, or if an older woman with a lilting laugh had known her mother. Drawing a deep breath, she walked into their midst.

All work and play came to a halt. The villagers rose and formed a circle around her, joined by several more who emerged from their huts.

Gina felt a presence in her mind, fleeting and soft, touched with love. She snapped her head around.

A gray-haired woman stood before her. A talisman shone at her forehead. Gina's hand shook as she slipped her mother's stone from the braided cord at her neck. She held it out, drawing reverent murmurs from the villagers.

A name echoed in Gina's head. "Dahra," she whispered.

"Welcome, Gina." The Na'lara embraced her.

Several more villagers emerged from the forest and gathered at the fringes of the crowd. One woman slipped through the others and took Gina's hand. "The Goddess shines on your coming, *volah*."

A snatch of a memory danced behind Gina's eyes. The face she remembered from a faded photograph was younger, but the almond-shaped eyes and quiet smile were identical.

"You…you look like my mother," she whispered.

The woman nodded. "I am Lana, her sister. Your mother was the elder by three winters, but it was often said we were like babes who had shared the womb." She took the talisman of the Seventh Clan from Gina's fingers and cradled it in her hands. "Now you are home."

As if she'd given a signal, the villagers pressed forward and embraced Gina. She returned their joyful greetings, awkwardly at first, then with tears of happiness. After the last child hugged Gina's legs, she followed Lana into one of the dwellings. She replaced her torn T-shirt and shorts with a doeskin dress while her newfound aunt set about preparing a meal.

The Baha'Na woman looked up and smiled when a younger woman entered the hut. The newcomer gave Gina the smile of a girl, but the fabric of her dress strained to accommodate a belly swollen with child. A grunt escaped her lips as she lowered herself to the ground.

Lana was beside her in a heartbeat. "Are you well, my daughter?"

"The babe is restless," the girl said. As if in answer to her words, her stomach bulged out on one side.

Gina stared, fascinated and horrified at the same time. "Does that hurt?"

The girl cradled her belly between her palms. "There is no pain, but much tightening since midnight."

Lana's eyes gleamed. "Does the rhythm quicken with each pass?" At the girl's nod, she smiled. "Pasha's babe has begun the journey. Gina, we will welcome our new kin together, before the next dawn."

Gina's mouth dropped open. "You want me to attend the birth?"

Lana inclined her head. "You and I are the nearest kin to the babe. It is our task. Pasha's partner, Sleeping Kana, will assist us."

The memory of a terrifying junior-high health class video ran through Gina's mind. She choked. "But...I couldn't. I wouldn't know the first thing to do."

"You will soon learn." Lana helped her daughter to her feet. Her tone turned brisk. "Walk in the forest, Pasha, but do not stray far. Gina will stay with you."

She turned to Gina. "I will fetch Sleeping Kana and prepare the birthing hut. When the pain becomes too strong for walking, bring Pasha to us."

She left the hut. Gina watched the door flap drop, too dazed to reply.

*****

Pasha moaned. Her soft sigh evoked images of lovemaking and dark passion. It was not at all a sound Gina associated with childbirth.

The contraction eased. The expectant mother lifted her head. She'd gone down on all fours and rounded her back during the worst of the pain. Now she sat on her heels and cradled her stomach, rocking back and forth. Her eyes glazed, watching some inner vision, then cleared. She gave Gina a tremulous smile.

"The babe is eager, I think." She held out one hand.

Gina took it. She gave her young cousin what she hoped was an encouraging smile, and wondered how much longer it would be before the baby put in an appearance. She'd spent most of the morning walking with Pasha in the forest, her heart pounding every time the pregnant girl groped at the branches for support. Well past midday, the pain increased, leaving Pasha gasping with each contraction.

The birthing hut, a small shelter covered with woven grasses, boasted a single door facing the sunrise. In the center, a pit held rocks that had lain in a fire just outside the door. Upon entering the heated air, Pasha had shed her clothes. Her swollen breasts hung low, brown-tipped pendants brushing an impossibly huge belly.

Sleeping Kana threw a dipper of water over the rocks. A burning cloud of steam seared Gina's face.

"It is too hot." Pasha twisted away from the pit. Her partner lifted a stone with a forked stick and ducked out of the hut.

Another contraction began. Gina eyed the covered doorway, wishing Lana would appear. Pasha's shoulders tensed. She bent her head to the ground and emitted a guttural sound that made Gina's heart skitter. Gina rubbed Pasha's lower back, trying to ease her pain.

Sleeping Kana reappeared. He knelt close to his partner and bent his head to hers, whispering something Gina didn't hear and smoothing the wet strands of Pasha's hair. His own long hair was plastered against his upper torso.

The girl offered her partner a tight smile, then tensed and humped her back. Her groaning started anew.

The outside world ceased to exist within the womb of the birthing hut, yielding to the rhythm of tightening and release, sharp moans and soft sighs. When the daylight filtering through the grass roof faded, Sleeping Kana lit a torch. Shadows flickered over the laboring woman's face and licked at her belly. A dipper of water splashed on the rocks. Steam rose with a hiss.

Pasha tensed, then screamed. A spasm racked her body, wringing her dry. When it passed, she collapsed, sobbing and whimpering. Sleeping Kana moved from the steam and gathered her in his arms.

"Our babe is eager to lie at your breast, Pasha." Gina's heart ached at the tenderness in the young man's voice.

Pasha stared, wild-eyed, into his face. Gina knelt beside her. The girl's shoulders were slicked with sweat and shaking. Gina massaged the tight muscles.

The next contraction came nearly before the last had subsided. Pasha screamed and clawed at Gina's arm.

A sense of utter helplessness washed over Gina. The swell of a wave bore her with relentless energy to a rocky shoreline. There would be no hope of stopping it.

Lana appeared at the doorway. She knelt by her daughter and stroked Pasha's forehead.

"Good, my precious girl. Good. You are a fine mother already."

Pasha's gaze clung to Lana's. "Am I?"

"Yes, of course. The babe will soon pass the door."

"My babe..." Another powerful contraction gripped Pasha, squeezed a keening moan from her throat.

"Stand, Pasha."

Pasha gulped for air. "No... I have not...the strength."

"You have my strength, Pasha," murmured Sleeping Kana. He caught Pasha under the arms and lifted her to her feet.

"You have all you need, daughter."

A drum sounded outside the hut, the steady rhythm of a beating heart. With it came the voices of the women.

"Do you hear, Pasha? Your sisters sing your babe into the world."

Lana draped one of Pasha's arms across Gina's shoulders. The girl sagged. Gina braced for the next contraction.

Pasha twisted and screamed, bucking against the ground, grasping Gina's neck so tight she nearly choked. A river of bloody water coursed down Pasha's thighs into the bed of dried grasses. It came again, trickling in rivulets.

"The babe comes." Lana's fingers massaged between Pasha's legs, easing the opening wider. "Push, Pasha."

Pasha drew a shuddering breath and pushed, her face contorting with the effort. It took all Gina's strength to support her kinswoman's weight. "Almost there, Pasha," she murmured. "You can do it."

The minutes stretched out, measured by the slow rhythm of the baby's descent and the beat of the drum outside the hut. Gina supported her cousin's weight, echoing Lana's words of encouragement. Her shoulders and arms burned. She could only wonder at the unflagging strength and determination of the birthing woman.

"I see your babe's head," said Lana. The older woman knelt before her daughter, her fingers smoothing the opening, urging the taut skin to stretch.

Pasha howled and pushed again.

A small head emerged, caught grotesquely between Pasha's thighs. Wrinkles distorted its face. Gina watched in riveted fascination as the infant twisted. Beside her, Pasha gathered her strength for her final effort. She grunted and pushed.

The baby slid into Lana's waiting hands. She lifted the child into the torchlight.

"A girl," she said.

*****

Gina emerged from the birthing hut and blinked against the glare of the morning sun. She hadn't slept and she barely remembered the meal she'd eaten the day before, yet a fierce elation gripped her.

Everything was sharper, clearer. The dark earth under her feet and the brilliant sky above circled a world of wonder. Several women called to her, asking after Pasha and the baby. She answered with a broad smile, remembering.

Lana had placed the little girl in her mother's arms even before Gina and Sleeping Kana lowered Pasha to the ground. The baby opened her mouth for the breast. Pasha reclined in her partner's arms and nursed her child while Lana bathed the blood from her thighs. When the infant finished, Lana lifted her granddaughter and Sleeping Kana cut the umbilical cord with his knife. He helped Pasha settle on a bed of furs while Lana washed the baby and swaddled her in a doeskin blanket.

Gina hung the cord from the roof of the birthing hut. The kinked rope dangled over the fire, swaying. Later, Lana would braid it with vines and Pasha would keep it for her daughter.

Gina recounted the details of the birthing to several women of the Seventh Clan, who nodded and exclaimed at her words. The men, they told her, had gone on a hunt in honor of their new clanswoman. A feast and naming ceremony would take place when they returned. The women drew Gina into their circle, telling of their partners and children, offering her food and drink.

One woman asked Gina to look at a cut on her small son's arm. The skin around the wound was puffy and red.

Gina frowned. "You should let Dahra look at it."

"But why? You have come." She swept her arm in a circle, then brought her palm to her heart. "At last, we will return to our home."

It took several moments for the meaning of the woman's words to sink in. When it did, Gina took a step back, stunned. She'd brought the talisman to her mother's people, but somehow she hadn't anticipated they would expect her to wear the stone. She'd seen a fraction of the duties of the Na'lara. She was quite certain she wouldn't be able to fill the role.

"Dahra will know what to do for your son," she told the woman. She backed away, then fled into the shelter of the forest. She ran up a narrow footpath, her thoughts spinning.

She'd been caught up in the discovery of her mother's family, but try as she might, she couldn't imagine a permanent future living with the clan in the wilderness.

Not, at least, without Derrin.

She caught her breath and sagged against a boulder. Derrin had to be alive—she wouldn't allow herself to think otherwise. He wouldn't know of her return, though. He'd have no reason to come seeking her.

She had to go to him.

The screech of an orna sounded. She looked up, through the limbs of a dead hemlock. The blackened branches spun a pattern of brittle lace against the sky. She continued the climb to the crest of the ridge. When she looked out over the valley, her stomach twisted.

Blight had claimed the forest. Wide swaths of yellow and brown streaked what should have been a lush carpet of green. Entire stands of trees were stripped bare. The remains of a lake, shriveled within a cracked shoreline, showed a lifeless reflection on its gray surface.

It won't stop. Blight would consume the wilderness and the People. Already, an unnatural silence cloaked the land. A faint odor of death hung heavy in the air.

A skyeagle swept into view below her, golden wings spread wide. It circled the desolate landscape in a slow, sweeping spiral. Catching an updraft, it rose, coming level with Gina's position on the mountaintop. With each pass it drew closer. Gina discerned markings of white on its tail and wings. Sunlight gleamed on it talons.

It dropped, hovering, then dove, plummeting earthward with dizzying speed. A moment later it reappeared, prey struggling in its claws. Its talons flexed rhythmically until the unfortunate creature hung limp. The skyeagle flew toward Gina and alighted on the branch of a nearby tree.

One black eye turned toward her, unblinking. The skyeagle's head dropped. The tip of its hooked beak tore into the flesh of its victim. It devoured the meal leisurely, spewing drops of blood and bits of fur and bone on the ground. When the carcass was gone, the creature spread its wings and rose into the air.

"Terrible, is it not?"

Gina started. Turning, she saw Dahra on the trail behind her. "Yes."

The older woman drew closer and watched the raptor disappear over the crest of the ridge. "Also beautiful. The skyeagle allows the wilderness to renew itself."

"The forest is dying."

"The Goddess has given us the gift of death. Without it, life would have little meaning."

"But the Blight isn't a natural part of the wilderness, Dahra. It was created by a man—a wizard. If it worsens, the Baha'Na will die."

"Everything dies, Gina."

Gina's fist clenched. "You must fight, Dahra, don't you understand that? The Baha'Na must fight for the life of the forest. We must go to Galena and confront Balek."

Dahra shook her head. "It is not our way."

"You would rather die? Think of your children—do you want them living in a ruined world? Or dying before they have a chance to grow up?"

"The future is not for us to see. We must live in the present, in the body of the Goddess. Life and death are but different expressions of her being." Dahra's gaze searched Gina's face. "You and I are Na'lara. We seek the will of the Goddess in the present. We do not ask for her reasons."

"I'm not Na'lara—how can I be? I didn't grow up in the wilderness."

"It matters not."

"It does! There's so much I don't know, even more I don't understand. I've never even seen the Seventh Sign. I don't know what it is."

"Then you know as much as your grandmother before you. The Seventh Sign is never seen, or understood. The Na'lara of the Seventh Clan stands within the Circle of her six sisters. In bonding with them she connects the Baha'Na to the Goddess. This is your task, Gina. This is the way in which you will aid your people. Not by killing a wizard, or any other man."

"But—"

"Think on it, Gina. Ask the Goddess to speak, and listen well."

* * * * *

Little Tania slept through her naming ceremony.

How she could have done so was a mystery to Gina, since the noise of the revelry echoed into the forest without pause as the gibbous moon rode the night sky. The celebration continued until dawn, in spite of the fact there was little to eat.

The hunting party had not seen a single mountain deer. The smaller game they brought to the village showed signs of stress and disease. Women foraging on the mountainside met with a similar lack of success. Frost had killed many of the food plants. Roots formed the largest portion of the food collected for the feast.

Two men built up the fire at sunset, and a circle of elders gathered around a wide drum. As the sky darkened, the rhythm of the drum quickened. A chant rose. Lana brought her granddaughter into the firelight and raised the infant above her head. The voices of the villagers hushed.

"Tania, a daughter of the Goddess."

The singing started anew. Lana lowered the child into the arms of an old man. He spoke in low whispers to the baby, then handed her to a woman at his side. The infant traveled the circle of her relations.

"What are they saying to her?" Gina asked Dahra, who stood at her side.

"A greeting."

A man approached and placed Tania in Gina's arms. Gina gazed at the red, wrinkled face of the newborn. The infant's eyes were dark, like the night sky. They held an expression of worldliness, of a soul who had seen many lifetimes. Gina touched the soft velvet of the baby's cheek and stroked her tiny fist. The infant grimaced.

"Hello, little one," Gina murmured. Tania responded with a yawn. Smiling, Gina handed the baby to a woman standing nearby.

Dahra drew her aside. "Will you take your place among your people, Gina? You are Na'lara to the Seventh Clan. As such, you are the Center of the Circle." She extended one hand, draped with the headdress of a Na'lara. "Without you, the power of the Goddess cannot reach the wilderness."

Gina stared at the talisman. "I can't."

"Walk with me, then."

They moved away from the crowd, into the forest, not speaking. Dahra led the way through the Blighted trees, circling the village. The sounds of the revelry followed.

Their trust is complete. Gina touched the talisman with her mind. She saw a smoky image of herself, alone in a clearing, sitting near the remains of a stone wall. Somehow, Gina recognized the setting as the ruined dwelling of her grandmother. The image sharpened and she looked closer. She wore the headdress of a Na'lara.

Gina came to an abrupt halt. Dahra paused beside her and sent a questioning look.

She sighed. There was really no choice for her to make. "All right, I'll do it. I'll wear the talisman." It was the only means she had with which to fight Balek.

Dahra nodded and led Gina back to the firelight and lifted the headdress. A hush settled over the villagers. The stone glowed with an inner light.

Gina took the headdress and placed it on her head. A tingle touched her scalp, moved down her spine and raced to her fingers and toes. Dahra's mind touched hers and Gina returned the embrace. She shut her eyes. Together, they entered the darkness beyond consciousness.

Zahta's touch came first, calm and reassuring. Zera embraced her next, threading her spirit through Gina's as easily as she'd linked arms with her in the village of the Fire Clan. Celia and Patah, then finally Malia joined them. The Circle was complete.

Gina stood in its center, surrounded by her sisters. A shimmering strand of light appeared. It wrapped itself around her, then exploded outward, touching the six who stood at the edge. Gina's body tingled and for one brief moment, time dissolved. She saw her life in its entirety, one pure pulsing spark connected to all others, bound by the web.

She opened her eyes. The web illuminated the village, covered the people, spread into the valley, disappeared into the darkness of the Blight. The dark shadow extinguished the shining threads one by one. Gloom settled on Gina, deadening her senses.

The shadow crept closer, moving with unerring purpose, and suddenly, she understood that she was its goal. The darkness would not stop until it anchored itself to the Center. Once there, it would draw on the endless power that had no name. Balek must have known this, must have sought Gina because of her connection to the Circle—not for her knowledge of crystals.

The high wizard's blighted spirit moved in the wilderness. Death trailed in his wake. Only she held the power to stop him.

Her fingers touched Derrin's shadow crystal, nestled at her breast. If she destroyed it, Balek would find her.

She tugged the silver chain over her head and flung the stone into the fire.

Chapter Twenty-Six

"He's dead." Derrin rolled the body onto its back. Maator's features had frozen in a ghastly grimace. "A day, at least."

"The Madness," said Ariek.

Derrin nodded. He'd seen enough victims of the malady to recognize its ultimate price. The tracks of Maator's fingernails furrowed the blue-tinged skin of his face. Derrin muttered a curse and let the body drop.

"And Balek's gone." Ariek paced one end of the high wizard's workroom. "His horse was saddled yesterday at dawn. Now we'll have to wait until he returns."

"We can't afford to wait. We'll follow."

The next morning, Derrin knelt in the dust of the road, examining the print of a horse's hoof. The stable boy had pointed out the stall of Balek's favorite mare. Once Derrin had seen the marks on the dirt floor, it had been a simple, though time-consuming matter to track the animal's progress.

He raised his head and stared into the distance. "He's heading north."

"He must be at least a day ahead of us," Ariek said.

Derrin noted the depth of the fine dust that had fallen from the edge of the track to pool in the shallow depression. "Almost two. He's riding hard."

They followed on their own mounts. Derrin kept his vision unfocused. The pattern of the horse's hooves spread out before him as if it had been painted in red. They traveled through most of the night by the illumination of Ariek's crystal. They slept for a few hours after midnight, and after a hasty breakfast, were back on the road before dawn.

"Tarol's blood, Derrin, are you sure we're going in the right direction?" Ariek asked at midday. They'd left the road and traversed miles of barren cropland. Now, sharp cliffs loomed above them.

"I'm sure."

"But there's nothing out this way. We've already passed the turnoff to Sirth and the river trail to the Plains. We're headed straight into the Northern Waste."

Derrin shrugged, frowning. Ariek was right—Balek had set a direct trail into the wilderness. Why? Derrin dismounted and examined the patterns in a wide patch of the broken grasses. "He spent the night here, then abandoned his mount. His tracks lead into the mountains."

Ariek squinted at the dirt and shook his head. "If you say so." He dismounted and began to unbuckle his pack.

"Leave it. It will only slow us down."

* * * * *

The woman from beyond the web stood in a soft hollow circled by boulders. Balek exhaled on a note of triumph. His gaze traveled the spill of her braids and the swell of her breasts. He approached her as a lover would his bride.

"Do not be afraid."

She looked into his eyes. "I'm not."

"Good."

He drew forth the webstone. Already it crackled, sending shocks of heat across his palm. The power he had created would bind all of creation to his command. Light arced from its shining facets and spun a pulsing snare around the woman.

Triumph coursed through Balek's veins. He flung his head back and laughed, lifting the stone to the sky. At last, he would claim the power of the web. Exultant, he sank his mind into the woman who would provide the link.

A shudder raced through him. She was not alone.

* * * * *

Clouds hung low, dulling the night sky. Derrin crouched behind a boulder at the highest point of the ridge and peered into the shadowed valley.

"He's here." A chill wind blew, stirring the trees.

Beside him, Ariek shifted, leaning forward. "I can't see a thing."

"The web touches the wilderness at the Seventh Sign," Derrin muttered, half to himself, "but how could Balek have known?"

"Perhaps the webstone led him here."

An unnatural silence pressed close. Derrin's jaw clenched. "When the web opens, its power will be absolute. If Balek is able to control it—"

A light flashed, then held. A soft glow spilled from deep in the trees.

Ariek rose. "Let's go."

They descended, moving toward the light. Derrin's hand closed on the hilt of his dagger when he heard Balek's voice.

"You knew I would come."

No answer came. A knot formed in the pit of Derrin's stomach.

"We will live forever as part of the One."

He caught sight of the high wizard at last. Balek stood in the center of the ruined village with his back turned, speaking to someone Derrin couldn't see.

A strand of white-gold light arced from Balek's hand. It twisted and shattered, spewing a whirlwind of golden threads. Derrin circled to his left, intent on discerning the object of the high wizard's attention. When a woman's form came into view, his lungs seized.

Gina.

She stood facing Balek, the talisman of a Na'lara shining on her forehead. Her white doeskin dress bore a circle of red beads with a burst of gold in the center, a design peculiar to the Seventh Clan.

Derrin swore under his breath. He'd sent her home. Why had she returned?

Balek's web dropped over her like a net. Gina fell forward, onto her hands and knees, head bowed.

"Tarol's blood, Derrin, I thought you said she was gone."

"She was."

The web streamed through Gina's body, infusing her with pulsing light. Her arms buckled, sending her face down in the dirt. In his mind, Derrin heard her soft moan.

His control snapped. He sprang at Balek, a savage cry on his lips. The high wizard turned toward him and frowned. He swept one arm in a dismissive gesture.

Derrin crashed into an invisible wall and crumpled to the ground. Unseen bonds snared his arms and legs. He twisted, trying to break free. The webstone spun in Balek's hand, throwing strands of light outward.

"So the guttersnipe has returned. This time I will not make the mistake of leaving you alive."

Balek strolled to Derrin and flashed a leering smile. "You will die, of course, but first you will watch me make love to my queen. Is she not beautiful? She will rule in eternity by my side."

Derrin glared up at him. "You're mad."

"What is insanity, but a spirit set free?"

He moved away, toward Gina. Derrin strained, but could move no more than a hand's breadth. He fell back, gasping.

Balek passed through the shining strands and stopped at Gina's side. His booted foot nudged her body, then thrust harder. She rolled onto her back. He leaned close and touched her face, molding his palm to the curve of her temple.

No! Derrin hurled his consciousness outward, desperate to reach Gina before Balek entered her mind. He slammed into the force of the web. Balek stroked Gina's face, ran one finger over her chin and down her neck. His hand came to rest on the swell of her breast.

Derrin's mind battered the barrier of light, struggling to reach Gina within the violence of Balek's web, even as the web sought to divert his attention. He flung off its assault and, one by one, forced the shining strands apart.

He slipped past Balek and entered her mind. In the chamber of her consciousness, Gina stood with arms raised. A storm raged around her, a distortion of the web revered by the Baha'Na, an abomination of the sacred light. Derrin wrapped his mind around Gina's. He positioned himself between her and the obscenity, absorbing the strands of light into his own psyche.

Six delicate threads sprang from Gina and disappeared into the darkness beyond the tempest. Pulsing energy returned. Derrin sensed Zahta's spirit first, touching him. Zera met him next, then each Na'lara in turn. Derrin struggled to grasp the meaning of their presence. He nearly lost his hold on Gina's mind when he did.

He had entered the Circle.

Balek's rage washed over him in hot, suffocating waves. From a vantage point somewhere above the struggle, Derrin's spirit-body saw the high wizard abandon his position beside Gina. Still holding the webstone, he drew his dagger and advanced on Derrin. Derrin tensed, trapped outside his body, waiting for the blow.

*****

Ariek tore out of the trees, intent on reaching Derrin before Balek planted a dagger in his back. The high wizard whirled, laughing.

"Another one? This grows tiresome." He waved in Ariek's direction. An arc sprang from the webstone.

Ariek shot his will toward the line of light. The arc slowed, then wavered, then stopped in midair. His mind pulsed forward, forcing the strand back. When it reentered the webstone, he followed it into insanity.

Balek laughed again, with true mirth. "Will you command the One with your mediocre talent, Ariek?"

A song more beautiful than anything Ariek had ever imagined teased at the edge of his consciousness. He advanced, seeking, needing to hear its full essence. The melody wove a pattern of promise. Freedom, safety, comfort. Ariek's head, suddenly heavy, dropped. Overwhelming desire plucked at his heart, carried him forward. It would be so easy to surrender.

In the deepest reaches of Ariek's memory, he saw his mother's garden sinking from glory to ruin.

See what is real. Understand what you have lost.

The illusion snapped. Ariek peered through the mesmerizing light and saw the webstone for what it was—the warped ambition of a madman. The melody played false. He twisted free of its grasp and the glittering strands dissolved.

The five-sided crystal burst into flames in Balek's hand. Balek howled. The stone hit the ground and skittered across the dirt.

"Ariek! Watch out!"

At Derrin's shout, Ariek spun to face Balek's dagger. He blocked the blow with his arm, then turned his body and smashed his shoulder into Balek's gut. The high wizard staggered, arms flailing. The blade sliced into Ariek's thigh.

Ariek went down on one knee, cursing. Derrin wrenched himself free of the ground and rolled, grabbing for Balek's leg. Balek twisted out of his grasp. Snatching up the smoldering remains of the crystal, the high wizard scrambled across the dirt to Gina.

Sparks shot from the webstone, wrenching Derrin from Gina's mind. A dome of light dropped in place over Balek. He straddled Gina's body and placed the crystal on her chest.

Ariek struggled to his feet, ignoring the stab of pain in his thigh. Balek gave a shout of triumph. Derrin threw himself at the wall of light, smashing his fists against the barrier and shouting obscenities.

* * * * *

Gina felt the loss of Derrin's embrace as a fierce, hopeless pain. She fought her despair, drawing on the strength of her sisters. Their love sustained her, allowed her time to focus once again on her task.

She must destroy the webstone.

The crystal had weakened, but its power still raged, drawing her toward the void. Balek's consciousness buffeted her, seeking entrance. It sucked her energy and sapped her resolve, promising rest if she only would accept it.

She spread her arms wide and resisted, opening herself to the will of the Goddess. Her body was a fragile construction, too frail to hold the Great Mother's full power. But she would offer it, nonetheless.

The suffocating weight of the webstone squeezed her chest. The glittering strands of the web constricted, imprisoning her. The spirits of her sisters, so far away on the edge of the Circle, wavered, then faded, until she stood alone.

The storm raged around her, stinging ice and unforgiving wind. Gina held the Center of the Circle, wondering how long she would last.

* * * * *

"Tarol's blood, Derrin! You won't break through it that way." Ariek wrenched Derrin away from the dome of sparks.

Derrin closed his eyes and concentrated on drawing one breath, then another. His fists were raw with pounding, but Balek's shield hadn't even shown a ripple, let alone a crack. Ariek was right. He would be of little use to Gina if he lost control.

Ariek paced the perimeter of the dome, peering through the wall of light. "The crystal has lost some of its power," he said. "There are sparks, but the strands of the web can't form. But how can we pierce it? Even if we link our minds together, it won't be enough."

Derrin swung around. "We have to find a way to enter it, even if it's only with our minds. We haven't much time. If Balek gets control of Gina's psyche…" A sudden thought struck him. "The rose crystal."

"What?"

He fished in his crystal pouch and extracted the stone he'd taken from the gown Gina had worn on her first passage through the web.

"What's that? I've never seen a crystal that color."

"It comes from Gina's world. She believed it aided her passage through the web."

"And you think it might help us to break through it now?"

"Yes."

"Then let's do it."

Derrin extended his consciousness to Ariek and formed the link they had shared many times, when building the twinned crystals. When they were joined, he added a link to Gina's crystal. Thus united, they approached the webstone's barrier.

The rose crystal glowed. Derrin sank his mind into the stone and channeled its power. He tested the strands forming the dome. They wavered at his touch. He drew a deep breath and signaled to Ariek. Together, they launched their combined will, augmented by Gina's crystal, at the web.

The strands cracked, and their minds slipped through.

The high wizard knelt beside Gina within the dome of light. The webstone fragment lay on her chest, in the center of the beaded rings. Sparks spewed outward and arched overhead.

Balek's hand moved to his breeches. He undid the laces, freeing his thick red cock. *You are too late, guttersnipe. Once I enter her, the web will never close.*

Derrin and Ariek circled and advanced, pressing in on his consciousness. Balek retaliated with a mental thrust.

Burning pain exploded in Derrin's skull. He shook it off and continued his advance, but the fire returned, licking at his mind until

Derrin feared his sanity would turn to ashes. Beside him, Ariek fell back.

Balek chuckled. *Your pitiful struggle is useless.* He parted Gina's knees and ran his hands up the inside of her thighs.

Derrin howled his rage. With one mighty effort, he wrenched his will from the flames and sent it diving toward Gina. Her eyelids fluttered and her head rolled to one side.

Derrin skimmed past Balek and entered Gina's mind.

Though Gina's body lay motionless under Balek, her spirit was still free. A dark storm enveloped her, obscuring the edge of the Circle. Derrin plunged into the maelstrom and fought his way to her side. Once there, he knelt before her, and offered his strength. Gina's fingers touched his head. He felt her acceptance.

Drawing on the deepest part of his courage, he surrendered his soul to the Circle.

A shaft of light pierced the darkness. The voices of the Na'lara rose in unison. Flames of pure gold surrounded Gina and Derrin, binding them together. Six arcs of light sprang from their combined aura and leaped to the outer edge of the Circle. The light shot round the ring, touching each of the six women standing on the rim, then returned to the Center. To Gina.

The web opened. Not the insanity of Balek's false construct, but the full force of the wilderness, the wisdom of each Sign, linked by "That which has no name". The webstone flashed and disintegrated into a heap of black ash. The dome of sparks vanished.

"No!" Balek's wail was a sound of fury and pain. He caught Gina's body and hauled her against his chest. The tip of his dagger pricked her stomach.

"You will pay, gutter wizard. Your whore will die."

Derrin launched himself out of the Circle and into his body. He lunged toward Balek.

He couldn't reach Gina in time. Balek's knife plunged. Gina's blood spurted.

The high wizard flung Gina's limp body away and laughed like a drunken maniac. With a shout of pure fury, Derrin sprang on him, driving him to the ground. His hands closed on the soft flesh of Balek's throat.

Balek clawed, gasping. Derrin tightened his grip.

A gurgling sound emerged from deep in Balek's throat. His eyes bulged and his face darkened to a color deeper than the finest wine. Derrin gave a swift twist.

The soft pop flooded him with satisfaction.

Balek's eyes went blank. Derrin stared at the contorted face of the madman he had killed, unable to look away.

"Derrin!" Ariek was bent over Gina, his bloody hands pressed to her ribs.

Derrin's triumph fled. He choked back a sob and met his friend's gaze, unable to voice his question.

Ariek shook his head. "She lives, my friend, but for how much longer, I cannot tell."

Chapter Twenty-Seven

"I am sorry, Derrin."

He started at Dahra's approach. "Is she…"

"Not yet, but I can do nothing more. Her mind drifts in the world of spirits."

Derrin massaged the sharp pain between his eyes. He'd fought to heal Gina's physical wounds, but her struggle with Balek had caused a mental trauma even his most powerful healing crystal could not touch. He and Ariek had carried her to the village of the Skyeagle Clan.

Derrin had dared to hope Dahra could save Gina's mind, but now, looking into the Na'lara's eyes, his courage faltered.

"She can't die."

Dahra was silent.

He paced a few steps away, toward the edge of the village. Incredibly, Gina had returned to the wilderness bearing the lost talisman of the Seventh Clan. She had stood in the center of the Circle. Had she found the stone in her own world? Yet even if she had, she didn't have the right to wear it. Something didn't fit.

He met Dahra's gaze "Gina wears the lost talisman. Why?"

"She is the Center of the Circle."

"That's impossible. The Na'lara of the Seventh Clan is the Center."

Dahra inclined her head. Derrin stared.

"Gina is of the Baha'Na," Dahra said. "She was conceived in the wilderness. She crossed the web in her mother's womb as her home burned. She returned bearing her grandmother's talisman. She is Na'lara."

Derrin's legs threatened to buckle. "It can't be true. The Blight worsened with her presence."

"No. The sickness of the land sprang from the spirit of the defiler, not from Gina's return to her home." Dahra advanced and laid one hand on Derrin's arm. "It is true, Derrin. No Outsider may wear the talisman."

His gut twisted, but his heart recognized the truth. The web had guided Balek to Gina not because of her knowledge of crystals, but because she had been born of the Baha'Na. Derrin had been blind not to realize it.

"May I see her?"

"Of course."

He ducked inside the Na'lara's dwelling, his eyes adjusting quickly to the dim light. The cloying scent of healing herbs hung low over the fire. Gina lay on her back on a spread of furs, the rise and fall of her breath coming in erratic spurts. Derrin lowered himself to the ground and touched her.

Her skin leached the warmth from his hand. Derrin gripped Gina's fingers and willed her eyes to open, but they did not. A gray pallor dulled her complexion. A shadow lurked behind him, death hovering just out of sight. His free hand brushed across his eyes and came away wet.

She drew a long, shuddering breath, then lay silent and still. Derrin tensed, every muscle in his body tightening in panic. His mind reached out, desperate to encounter a spark of Gina's life, something to hold for a brief moment before she was truly gone. He plunged into her soul, searching.

Her spirit did not stir. He forged ahead, into the farthest reaches of her mind, where memories lay buried in the soil of time. There, the ember of Gina's life force dwindled, surrounded by ashes.

Derrin cradled the spark, lifting it from the dust, leaning forward to caress the dying coal with his breath. It dimmed for the span of a heartbeat, and he feared his own heart would stop if the spark died. He blew another slow breath, fighting his despair, emptying his soul.

The spark leapt, then settled into a steady glow. Encouraged, Derrin cast his heart into the ember, offering it as tinder. The lick of a tiny flame emerged, and with it, his hope.

He fed the flame steadily, blending his life force with Gina's, giving her all his strength. If it meant he would travel beyond the veil in her place, so be it. The fire grew, then blazed. Derrin sensed Gina's mind awakening and knew the moment she recognized his presence. He poured his emotion into her and felt her response. The flames burned higher. Tears stung his eyes.

He wrapped her tight in his love and held her close, savoring the sweetness of her mind's embrace. Her spirit touched his, then dropped into a deep sleep—a sleep of healing, not death.

Derrin opened his eyes, almost surprised to find himself still within the walls of Dahra's dwelling. Gina hadn't moved on her pallet of furs, but her cheeks held a vibrant glow and her breath came deep and even. Her hand warmed his skin. He tilted his head upward and let out a long breath.

She would live. She would take her place with the Seventh Clan and wear the talisman as Na'lara.

The Circle and the People were complete.

He released her hand. He carried the blood of an Outsider. No matter that Zahta had named him a man after all his years of exile, he could never be part of the Baha'Na.

Leaning forward, he brushed the barest of kisses across her lips and whispered his farewell.

*****

The neat column of numbers refused to tally.

Beltha leaned back and rubbed her eyes. Ever since Ariek had loaned her the coin to start a life free of the slavers, she'd focused all her energy on providing a haven for girls who were worse off than she had once been. She selected her clientele with care and shared the profits.

Until a year ago, Ariek had been a frequent visitor, but he never bedded the younger girls, preferring to spend his nights in Beltha's chamber. She hadn't hoped for more—aristocrats didn't fall in love with women they had once paid for. Or so she had thought.

She picked up the quill, nearly crushing the shaft in her grip. The Bride of Lotark had stirred sympathy and jealousy in tandem, emotions Beltha wasn't used to mixing.

The door slammed against the wall. "Where is she?"

Beltha looked up from the ledger, quill poised above the parchment as if she'd been concentrating on her accounts.

"Ariek. So good to see you."

"Don't joke with me, Beltha. Where's Danat? I can't find her anywhere."

Beltha placed the pen in the inkwell and leaned back in her chair, her hands light on the armrests. She met Ariek's gaze. "Gone."

"Gone? What do you mean—gone?"

"She left you."

Ariek's blue eyes registered his disbelief. He gave a short laugh. "She couldn't have left me. Where would she go?"

"Loetahl."

He stared. Then he closed the door and advanced to the edge of her desk. Placing his palms on the polished wood, he leaned forward until she could smell the musk of his sweat. "What in Tarol's name is going on?"

She rose and crossed her arms. "Danat said she wanted to go home. Then she left."

"You let her?"

"I won't keep a girl in my house against her will."

He pushed off the desk and muttered an oath. "You should have kept her here until I got back."

"How was I to know when that would be?" She came around the desk and put a hand on his arm. "I asked her to wait, but she refused. She couldn't leave fast enough."

"She's afraid she'll be found."

"No. She wanted to get away from you. Damn it, Ariek, she wanted to kill your child!"

Ariek started, then caught Beltha's shoulders in a painful grasp. *"My what?"*

For the first time in her life, Beltha looked into Ariek's eyes and was afraid. "Let go of me," she said quietly.

His grip loosened. "Tell me everything. Now."

"I knew she was carrying. She denied it at first, then begged me for a draught to get rid of it. I refused."

Ariek paled. "Go on."

"She said the child could be Solk's, and she wouldn't have it—even though she admitted the father could just as easily be you." Beltha spread her hands. "She would have gone no matter what I did, Ariek. I gave her clothing and money. She left three days ago."

Love and anger warred in Ariek's eyes. Beltha tensed, wondering which emotion would claim victory.

"I'll find her."

She let out a long breath and watched the door slam.

* * * * *

Danat pulled the woolen cap low over the Mark of Lotark. One short, frizzy curl escaped. She poked it back in, hoping the black dye she had bought at the market would hold.

She shrank into the shadow of a large crate. So far she hadn't attracted too much notice in her rough boy's clothing, but she didn't want to force her luck until the ship set sail. Her hand touched a small pouch hanging from a cord around her neck. Beltha had given her gold and jewels, all the while grumbling about how Danat was the most stubborn woman she'd ever had the misfortune to meet. Danat almost smiled. It felt good to be stubborn again.

She closed her eyes and concentrated on the image of Loetahl she'd painstakingly assembled in her mind. Sunlight flooded the white sand. Green waters sparkled with tiny jewels of light. She ran along the shore under the palms, arms flung wide, her colorful silk *tara* whipping in the warm breeze.

Horses galloped alongside, unfettered. She splashed into the surf, watching tiny fish dart out of her way, the waves embracing her like a mother. She emerged from the water and dropped onto the beach. Warm sand dusted her skin…

"You there! Boy!"

Danat jumped. "Sir!"

A huge, unshaven man glowered down at her. "All hands on deck. She's putting out with the tide. Don't let me catch you in the hold again."

Danat nodded and rushed past him. She'd hoped to remain hidden until the ship was well out to sea, but it seemed now she had no choice but to join the rest of the crew topside. She swung herself up the ladder onto the deck. A shout came from above, where sailors ran the rigging.

Longshoremen were heaving cargo across the gangplank. In the harbor, a tugboat waited, its ropes taut. Danat fell in with a line of boys who were passing sacks of grain into the hold. She kept her head down and set to work, answering the greeting of her nearest companion with an unintelligible grunt.

The captain stood with his hands folded across his chest, watching his crew with one eye while he conversed with a man dressed in black.

Danat's gaze lingered on the stranger's broad shoulders and short, sandy hair. He shifted slightly.

Ariek.

A sack of grain fell with a thud at her feet.

"Clumsy oaf," the next boy in line muttered.

"Sorry." Danat grabbed the sack and heaved it, then turned in time to catch the next one. She stole another glance at Ariek.

He leaned toward the captain, speaking earnestly. The captain gestured to one of the mates, and the sailor joined the two men. She strained, but couldn't make out their words. A sack fell on her foot. She cried out and dropped to one knee.

Ariek turned and looked straight at her, his gaze narrow. The next instant he was beside her, hauling her to her feet. He dragged her from the cargo line and deposited her unceremoniously on the deck.

She sprawled on her rear, her arms thrown behind her to stop her fall. Ariek crouched over her, blue eyes glittering. He plucked the cap from her head and stared.

"Tarol's blood! What have you done to your hair?"

She swallowed. "What are you doing here?"

He leaned closer, his anger hitting her in waves of heat. "I'm asking myself the same thing."

Abruptly, he straightened and paced away, running one hand over his head. A gust of wind blew across the deck, sending a shiver up her spine.

He swung around and faced her. "I thought you loved me."

"I…I do, Ariek."

"What manner of idiot do you think I am? A woman in love doesn't risk her life running away from her lover."

"I am not running away."

"No? What do you call it?"

Danat scrambled to her feet. She'd never before been the focus of Ariek's anger. She barely recognized her gentle lover in the sarcastic stranger standing before her. Fear coiled in her stomach, but she raised her chin and resisted the urge to back away.

"I am not running away," she repeated. "I'm going home."

"Home." He spat out the word as if it were poison. "What about me, Danat? Do I mean so little to you?"

Danat looked away, toward the open sea. It wavered, dissolving in a sheen of tears. She blinked them back. "You mean so much, Ariek, but I've always known our love would end. I thought it would be when you got tired of sneaking past the priests."

He swore.

She swallowed past the lump in her throat. "Now, suddenly, I'm free. The Bride of Lotark is dead. You don't know the woman I am now."

"I know enough."

"How can you? I don't know myself. A few days ago, I had no choices. Now there are so many my head is spinning. I am sure of only one thing. I have to go home."

Ariek's eyes flashed with pain, then took on a more distant expression. "You could have asked me to take you there."

She looked away. "You are a wizard. You must stay in Katrinth. I cannot."

He moved closer, too close. "What of our child, Danat? Will you kill him?"

A rush of nausea surged. Hot tears spilled on her cheeks. "I don't know that it's yours."

"I don't care. I want him—or her—anyway."

"How can you, Ariek? How can you love him, knowing Solk could be his father?"

"How can you kill him, knowing he might be mine?"

Her knees buckled. A moment later, she found herself on the rough wood of the deck, with Ariek's arms around her.

"His father doesn't matter," he said. "Only his mother."

She shuddered. "I want him to be yours. More than anything, but when I think of Solk…"

He eased away and gripped her shoulders, searching her eyes. "Then don't think of him. Think of us. As a family."

She stiffened and tried to push him away. "No. I will not belong to any man again, Ariek, not even one I love. Forget me. I cannot stay in Galena, and you cannot leave the Hierarchy."

"I can do whatever I damn well please." He rose abruptly, leaving her suddenly cold on the deck. "Wait here."

She squinted up at him. "Where are you going?"

He strode across the deck and hailed the captain. After a few minutes of conversation the seaman nodded and shook Ariek's hand.

"It's all set," he said when he rejoined her. He grasped her hand and pulled her to her feet. "We'll have the captain's cabin for the voyage. There are several crates of clothing with the cargo, something should fit us." The deck lurched. Danat grabbed his arm.

"We're underway," he said. Her eyes widened when she looked to the dock and saw it was true. Ariek brushed her cheek with his thumb, then eyed her shorn head dubiously. "I've ordered hot water to be brought to our cabin."

"You're not going ashore?"

He drew a deep breath. "You'll not be rid of me so easily, Danat. You don't have to be my wife if you don't wish it. I just want to be by your side."

Danat's heart leapt into her throat. "You would go to Loetahl? For me?"

His eyes spit sparks. "Tarol's blood, Danat. I would go to the swiving Inferno for you! Surely Loetahl will be a more pleasant destination."

Her tears began anew. Though his countenance had darkened, she couldn't mistake the glint of desperation in his eyes. He loved her. She had been a fool to doubt it. And despite the storm of emotions her freedom had unleashed, her love for Ariek was a reality she did not doubt.

"I'd be honored to show you my homeland, Ariek," she said, then frowned. "But why would the captain offer us his cabin for the voyage?"

Ariek gifted her with a smile, the first she'd seen since he found her.

"Didn't you know? This ship belongs to my father."

Chapter Twenty-Eight

Water rippled over the red-gold rocks, carrying the first crimson leaves of autumn. Gina stared into the stream, dry-eyed, wondering if she would ever feel anything again. She had come to the Water Clan hoping to feel Derrin's spirit before letting it go forever, but the task eluded her.

Zahta touched her arm, offering strength. Gina met the old woman's gaze. She hadn't noticed before, but Zahta's eyes were so very much like Derrin's, not in color, but in shape and expression. A dull ache squeezed Gina's chest.

She shouldn't have come.

"I often found Derrin in this place as a boy," Zahta said, her voice soft. "When sorrow or anger weighed upon his spirit, he would skip pebbles over the water until his arm ached."

A painful lump in Gina's throat blocked her answer.

"Derrin's life has never been his own, Gina. The Goddess chose him to do her will even before he entered his mother's womb."

"What do you mean?"

"The Seventh talisman's disappearance set into motion the means for its discovery. My daughter encountered Derrin's father during the same moon that saw the destruction of the Seventh Clan and the loss of its talisman. After the Galenan was found dead, a clansman followed his backtrail to make certain he had traveled alone. He found the tracks of a man who had come from the village of the Seventh Clan."

"Are you saying the same man who killed my grandmother led Derrin's father to the Baha'Na so that Derrin could be born and bring the talisman back to the clan?"

The old woman nodded.

"That was just a coincidence."

"No. After the man who killed your grandmother and father took leave of the Galenan, he was taken by a direwolf on the hunt."

"But Derrin said the wolves don't hunt people."

Zahta nodded. "Even so." She placed her hand on Gina's shoulder. "The Goddess chose Derrin's path even before he entered his mother's womb. Do not judge him harshly, Gina. He followed his duty at every turn, even when he would have preferred to cut his own trail. Now his task is completed. Perhaps he does not know how to choose his own desire."

The old woman faded into the forest like a breeze. Gina picked up a rock and threw it into the stream. It landed with a satisfying plunk, so she picked up another one and threw it harder. She and Derrin had made love thinking they had no future. Did he regret their love now that she didn't have to leave his world?

She flung the third rock with all her strength. It hit a boulder and ricocheted back at her, missing her head by inches. She spun around and watched it land at the edge of the stream.

And froze, her heart leaping into her throat.

Derrin stood in the shadows. She blinked, sure she had imagined him, but he refused to disappear. How long had he been watching her?

He was leaner, hungrier than she remembered. Weariness haunted the angles of his face and settled in the hollows of his cheeks. He wore the uniform of the Hierarchy, with the addition of a scarlet sash at his waist. His eyes were gray ice, warning her to stay away.

Yet he was here. What did it mean?

She took a step toward him. His shoulders tensed, as if braced for a blow.

She took a second step, and a third. He watched her, holding himself so still he might have been a statue. She stopped an arm's length away, close enough to hear his sharp intake of breath, and wondered if he would leave without speaking if she didn't break the silence.

She eyed the red sash, a vivid stripe against his black tunic. Balek had worn one. She guessed at its significance. "Have you been admitted to the Upper House?"

"Yes."

The silence stretched between them. Gina waited for what seemed an eternity. She stole a glance at his face, but his gaze was fixed on something in the distance.

"Why are you here?" she asked at last.

"I'll not be coming again."

"Oh."

"You are of the Baha'Na. You are Na'lara of the Seventh Clan, the Center of the Circle." A tremor of awe tinged his voice, but pain of the lost boy he'd once been flickered in his eyes. Gina watched him master it with a skill born of long practice. "I'm an Outsider, Gina."

"That's not true, Gray Wolf."

He started, then looked away. "A name can't change the past."

"Forget your father. You don't have to take the blame for what he did."

He sighed. "I'm not speaking of my father, but of myself. I've lived too long among the Galenans to go back to a life with the Baha'Na. The People have an innocence I can never regain. You know that as well as anyone." His hand closed in a fist. "I murdered Balek rather than bring him before the High Council for trial, and I can't pretend I wasn't happy to do it. I would do it again in a heartbeat."

"Is Galena your home, then?"

"No. Not truly. But the Hierarchy has elected me to the Upper House, and I've accepted. There have been other changes as well. A more progressive leadership has come forward."

"I suppose you had nothing to do with that."

He met her gaze and she couldn't mistake the gleam of satisfaction in his eyes. The tension in his shoulders loosened imperceptibly.

"I may have made some suggestions to the right people," he said. "The restriction requiring wizards to dwell in Katrinth has been lifted and the apprentice fees have been substantially lowered. In the future, admittance to the Hierarchy will be based on talent, not family."

"Will you join the High Council, then?"

He shook his head. "There is another path I wish to pursue. The webstone is gone, but the ruin it spewed remains. There is much need of healing in Galena. I'm going to live near Sirth, where I can explore the power of natural stones like the ice crystal that sparked your vision. I suspect the true cure for the Blight lies within the wilderness. I've already accepted two apprentices."

"I'm sure you'll do well."

"Thank you."

Again, the silence lengthened and Derrin made no move to touch her. A hot rush of anger flooded Gina's veins, displacing her grief.

While she'd been grieving, Derrin had been picking up the threads of his life and planning a future that didn't include her.

"What of our joining, Derrin?" The words escaped before she could pull them back, unsaid.

His gray eyes hardened. "If I had known who you were, I would never have touched you."

"But you did touch me." The words sounded like an accusation.

"It was wrong. You must join with a man of the Baha'Na, not an Outsider."

"Don't tell me who I should join with!"

"You are Na'lara! You must choose a partner."

"I am *not* Na'lara! In case you haven't noticed, I'm not wearing the talisman."

He stilled. "Where is it?"

"I gave it to Pasha. She's my cousin and has as much right to it as I do." She crossed her arms over her chest and hugged herself tight. "How could I lead the Seventh Clan? I never ran in the forest as a girl. I didn't grow up learning the duties of a Na'lara." She tasted the salt of a tear she hadn't realized had fallen.

"I love the wilderness and the clans, but even after all that's happened, I can't imagine making a permanent life here. The world I grew up in is just too different. I've decided to go back."

Derrin caught her by the arm. "Go back? You can't!"

She pulled out of his grasp. "Why not? The Circle has agreed to call the web. If I can cross, it will be the will of the Goddess, so you don't have to worry that it will cause any harm."

"But you don't belong there. The web guided Balek to you because you belong here, at the Center of the Circle. How can you leave the Baha'Na? They are your people."

"*You're* leaving them."

"I have no choice!"

"Don't give me that—you're the one who told me there's always a choice." She glared at him. "You made yours and now I've made mine."

Derrin was silent, scrutinizing her, his gray eyes cloaked with an impenetrable fog.

"You would really return to the world beyond the web rather than stay with the clans?"

She shrugged, turning away from his intent regard. She attempted a light tone. "When you sent me across the web to escape Balek, I landed in a world I almost didn't recognize. It hadn't changed, but I had. My world needs healing as much as Galena does. I'm not going back to my old life, but a new one. If I can heal just one person who has lost hope, it will be worth it."

Derrin didn't answer. Gina squeezed her eyes shut and prayed she wouldn't embarrass herself by sobbing like a lovesick teenager. She counted her heartbeats, waiting for his polite words of farewell.

The warmth of his hands closed on her shoulders. She opened her eyes and what she saw in his made her breath go.

His palm smoothed over her braids, then cupped her cheek. "Your home beyond the web is a wondrous place, Gina. I don't have much to offer in its place."

His eyes were smoke, a banked fire. Her pulse skittered.

"Life in Galena wouldn't be easy for you," he continued, almost to himself. "The Temple of Lotark remains strong, despite Solk's death. Women are not honored as they are among the Baha'Na. The apprentices I've chosen won't be able to pay me the full fee, even with the Hierarchy's reduction in—"

"Derrin, what are you saying?"

He hesitated, then dipped his head and caught her mouth in a brief kiss. "I love you, Gina. I won't hold you here if you truly wish to return to your world, but will you stay?" He drew back. "Come with me to Sirth. There's a place for you there, if you choose to claim it."

A fierce joy exploded in Gina's heart. She stepped into the circle of Derrin's arms.

"I do choose it," she whispered.

His lips came down on hers to seal the promise.

Epilogue

The she-wolf raised its head. Derrin watched, amused, as the animal gave him a dismissive glance and returned to more pressing concerns—a midday nap under the shade of the porch roof.

The direwolf had joined Gina and Derrin the year before, appearing one night as they traveled from the village of the Seventh Clan to Sirth. Derrin had recognized the young female as a cub of the mating pair that had cared for him after his escape from Balek's pit. He'd expected it to turn back when they left the wilderness. It hadn't. The animal had watched Derrin and Gina build their new home, a snug cabin nestled in the foothills.

The sleek gray animal greeted each new apprentice with a tilt of its head and a flick of its tail. Five men and four women now pursued the discipline of wizardry under Derrin's tutelage. None of them had left luxurious homes to join him—a few had been almost destitute. Now they were thriving.

They'd brought their families with them—spouses, children, aging parents. Their homes encircled his own, transforming the sunny slope into a village. A wide common area anchored the center of the community, while an extensive garden meandered along the streambank. He could hear children there now, laughing and chasing the crows.

They had become an extended family, a clan united not by blood, but by purpose, living in the space Derrin once thought of as the void separating Galena from the wilderness. And Derrin found he no longer thought of himself as an outsider. He belonged to both worlds, as did Gina.

Research and experiments regarding the healing properties of natural crystals had proven fruitful, already mitigating the worst of the Blight's damage in the surrounding area. In the spring, he and Gina would travel to Katrinth and present their findings to the Wizard's Council. Derrin imagined Gina lecturing the assembly of old men and grinned. She'd be the first woman to do so.

He pushed open the door of the cabin and entered, setting the parcel he carried on a small table. Gina stood near the hearth, kneading bread on a long wooden table.

"You don't have to do that," he said. "Morak's mother said she'd be glad to take over the baking."

She looked up, a smile lighting her eyes. "I don't mind. I like it." She set the dough under a wooden bowl and wiped her hands on a cloth. "You're back early."

"Tarnik had a wealthy customer waiting, so he hadn't the time to haggle over our meager furs. I got a good price on the glassware we needed."

Gina came around the table to meet him, an enormous belly preceding her. Derrin was certain it had grown in the few hours he'd been gone, but how that could be possible, he didn't know. He thought of his child, curled under Gina's heartbeat, and waves of emotion rocked him. Love, pride, wonder, humility. In a few days, they would journey to the Seventh Clan, where Gina's kinswomen would assist the babe's birth.

He caught Gina's shoulders and kissed her, pulling her close until her heavy breasts pressed against his chest. His hand slid lower, settling on her round stomach.

The baby kicked. Derrin maneuvered Gina onto a bench by the table and knelt in front of her. He pushed her skirt up to what had once been her waist.

She slapped at his hands, but he ignored her protest and hiked the fabric up over her belly.

"What are you doing?" she asked, half-laughing.

"I want to watch the baby." He rubbed his fingers over her smooth skin, stretched so tight he could see the veins below its surface. The perfect globe moved, bulging comically to one side. He watched, fascinated, as a smaller kick rippled the skin above Gina's swollen navel.

Gina let out a groan.

He looked up. "What's wrong?"

"Oh, I don't know. Nothing, really. It's just that I feel so..." She grimaced. "Big."

His gaze dropped again to Gina's stomach, round and warm beneath his palms. He struggled to keep the laughter out of his voice. "You *are* big, Gina. You're huge."

He intercepted his wife's scowl with a grin, then scooped her into his arms. He carried her toward their tiny bedroom, staggering dramatically as he crossed the threshold.

"Heavy, too."

She landed a weak punch on his chest, but her eyes were laughing when he set her on the straw-filled mattress.

He nuzzled the curve of her neck. "And beautiful."

He slipped her dress up over her shoulders and let it fall to the floor, then tugged on the ribbon holding her hair. Gina scooted backward, to the center of the bed. The dark tips of her breasts puckered in the cool air and her round belly didn't quite hide the dark triangle between her thighs. Shining hair rippled like dark water over her shoulders.

She looked up at him through her lashes, then let her gaze travel the length of his body, lingering on the bulge below his waist. She caught her lower lip between her teeth and her breathing quickened.

A stab of desire fiercer than any he'd ever known shot through him. Before he knew what had happened, his tunic and boots were on the floor and Gina was untying the laces of his breeches. He urged her onto her hands and knees and entered her from behind. His hands roamed her buttocks and hips as she arched to take his thrusts. As her body opened to him, so did her mind. He plunged into it gladly as a wave of pure contentment broke over him. There was nowhere he would rather be than buried in Gina's body and mind.

Much later, he remembered the letter. He eased from her arms and retrieved the parchment from the pocket of his tunic. "I've been to Beltha's," he said. "She gave me this."

Gina looked at the seal. "It's from Ariek."

* * * * *

Derrin, I hope this letter finds you and Gina well and your apprentices flourishing. News of your success has reached Loetahl – every day I hear new tales of the rebirth of the Blighted forest. No doubt you know the Hierarchy has set up an adjunct Council here on the island, which I have joined.

My new home is an enchanting land. Horses run wild on the beaches and grasslands. The coastal regions are populated, but the interior is untamed jungles, teeming with bizarre creatures and plant life. A recent expedition into the interior uncovered a lost city. The archeologists are seeking a wizard to study the ruins of an ancient city and a cache of crystals found there. I hope to join them soon.

Keerak continues to grow strong. I think of him as my son, and hope, indeed, that he is, though his features belong solely to his mother. I haven't yet convinced Danat to wed me, but I am hoping in time she will accept me. Until then, I am content to wait.

Gina, your own time will be close when this letter arrives. Danat wishes you a speedy birth and a healthy babe. Derrin, I know you will be the best of fathers.

Your friend and brother, Ariek

* * * * *

Gina refolded the parchment. "He sounds happy."

"Loetahl is another adventure for Ariek." Derrin took the letter and let it drop to the floor. "Luckily, I don't have to travel so far for a challenge." He buried his face in Gina's hair and inhaled the fragrance of his home.

She turned and brushed her lips against his. "I'm a challenge?"

"You, our child, this whole life is a challenge." He fell back onto the bed, his hands urging her to turn until she straddled his torso. Their child rested on his chest, over his heart.

He spread his palms on Gina's stomach. New life grew beneath his fingers, waiting for his touch. A perfect blend of the worlds he and Gina shared.

"A challenge I'm more than ready for," he said.

About the author:

Joy Nash loves to write her dreams – and occasionally, her nightmares. She pens tales of love and adventure with a paranormal twist – stories filled with magic, mirth, and muscle. As a child, Joy loved books above all else. She harbored a secret desire to be a writer, but somehow became an architect instead. Years later, giving birth to three children in less than four years caused something in her brain to snap. Stories started pouring from her subconscious and she's been writing ever since.

Joy welcomes mail from readers. You can write to her c/o Ellora's Cave Publishing at 1337 Commerce Drive, Suite 13, Stow OH 44224.

Why an electronic book?

We live in the Information Age—an exciting time in the history of human civilization in which technology rules supreme and continues to progress in leaps and bounds every minute of every hour of every day. For a multitude of reasons, more and more avid literary fans are opting to purchase e-books instead of paperbacks. The question to those not yet initiated to the world of electronic reading is simply: *why?*

1. *Price.* An electronic title at Ellora's Cave Publishing runs anywhere from 40-75% less than the cover price of the exact same title in paperback format. Why? Cold mathematics. It is less expensive to publish an e-book than it is to publish a paperback, so the savings are passed along to the consumer.
2. *Space.* Running out of room to house your paperback books? That is one worry you will never have with electronic novels. For a low one-time cost, you can purchase a handheld computer designed specifically for e-reading purposes. Many e-readers are larger than the average handheld, giving you plenty of screen room. Better yet, hundreds of titles can be stored within your new library—a single microchip. (Please note that Ellora's Cave does not endorse any specific brands. You can check our website at www.ellorascave.com for customer recommendations we make available to new consumers.)

3. *Mobility.* Because your new library now consists of only a microchip, your entire cache of books can be taken with you wherever you go.
4. *Personal preferences are accounted for.* Are the words you are currently reading too small? Too large? Too...ANNOYING? Paperback books cannot be modified according to personal preferences, but e-books can.
5. *Innovation.* The way you read a book is not the only advancement the Information Age has gifted the literary community with. There is also the factor of what you can read. Ellora's Cave Publishing will be introducing a new line of interactive titles that are available in e-book format only.
6. *Instant gratification.* Is it the middle of the night and all the bookstores are closed? Are you tired of waiting days—sometimes weeks—for online and offline bookstores to ship the novels you bought? Ellora's Cave Publishing sells instantaneous downloads 24 hours a day, 7 days a week, 365 days a year. Our e-book delivery system is 100% automated, meaning your order is filled as soon as you pay for it.

Those are a few of the top reasons why electronic novels are displacing paperbacks for many an avid reader. As always, Ellora's Cave Publishing welcomes your questions and comments. We invite you to email us at service@ellorascave.com or write to us directly at: 1337 Commerce Drive, Suite 13, Stow OH 44224.

NEED A MORE EXCITING WAY TO PLAN YOUR DAY?

2006 CALENDAR

COMING THIS FALL

The Ellora's Cave Library

Stay up to date with Ellora's Cave Titles in Print with our Quarterly Catalog.

To recieve a catalog,
send an email with your name
and mailing address to:

catalog@ellorascave.com

or send a letter or postcard
with your mailing address to:

Catalog Request
c/o Ellora's Cave Publishing, Inc.
1337 Commerce Drive #13
Stow, OH 44224

Regular Features

Jaid's Tirade

Jaid Black's erotic romance novels sell throughout the world, and her publishing company Ellora's Cave is one of the largest and most successful e-book publishers in the world. What is less well known about Jaid Black, a.k.a. Tina Engler is her long record as a political activist. Whether she's discussing sex or politics (or both), expect to see her get up on her soapbox and do what she does best: offend the greedy, the holier-than-thous, and the apathetic! Don't miss out on her monthly column.

Devilish Dot's G-Spot

Married to the same man for 20 years, Dorothy Araiza still basks in a sex life to be envied. What Dot loves just as much as achieving the Big O is helping other women realize their full sexual potential. Dot gives talks and advice on everything from which sex toys to buy (or not to buy) to which positions give you the best climax.

On the Road with Lady K

Publisher, author, world traveler and Lady of Barrow, Kathryn Falk shares insider information on the most romantic places in the world.

Kandidly Kay

This Lois Lane cum Dave Barry is a domestic goddess by day and a hard-hitting sexual deviancy reporter by night. Adored for her stunning wit and knack for delivering one-liners, this Rodney Dangerfield of reporting will leave no stone unturned in her search for the bizarre truth.

A Model World

CJ Hollenbach returns to his roots. The blond heartthrob from Ohio has twice been seen in Playgirl magazine and countless other publications. He has appeared on several national TV shows including The Jerry Springer Show (God help him!) and has been interviewed for Entertainment Tonight, CNN and The Today Show. He has been involved in the romance industry for the past 12 years, appearing on dozens of romance novel covers and calendars. CJ's specialty is personal interviews, in which people have a tendency to tell him everything.

Hot Mama Cooks

Sex is her food, and food is her sex. Hot Mama gives aphrodisiac a whole new meaning. Join her every month for her latest sensual adventure -- with bonus recipe!

Empress on the Mount

Brash, outrageous, and undeniably irreverent, this advice columnist from down under will either leave you in stitches or recovering from hang-jaw as you gawk at her answers to reader questions on relationships and life.

Erotic Fiction from Ellora's Cave

The debut issue will feature part one of "Ferocious," a three-part erotic serial written especially for Lady Jaided by the popular Sherri L. King.

ELLORA'S CAVE
ROMANTICA PUBLISHING

Lightning Source UK Ltd.
Milton Keynes UK
UKOW051847200113

205125UK00001B/2/A